The Dubious Tale
of the
Winter Wizard

Nick McNeil

This book is a work of fiction. The characters, incidents, and dialogue are drawn from the author's imagination and are not to be construed as real. Any resemblance to actual events or persons, living or dead, is entirely coincidental.

You're so vain, you probably thought this book was about you.

"The worst thing I can be is the same as everybody else."

–Arnold Schwarzenegger

1

Shields collided with flesh as the crack of bone and wood echoed through the field. Bertly held steady as he absorbed the shock of a Rotter crashing into his wooden shield. The enemy fell as the impact of the blow sent a sharp pain through Bertly's shoulder. There was an opening to the right, and Bertly gripped the hilt of his sword. With the point of the sword, he stabbed and connected with the rib cage of the Rotter and the impact sprayed a mist of blood through the air. With his vision impaired, Bertly ripped the sword free, releasing a second gush of blood from the Rotter. The Rotter fell to the ground and dematerialized into dust. The wind washed away the powdered corpse.

It was the first time since the Eternal Cave that Bertly could feel the air move.

***

"Sir, don't you think readers will find this a bit confusing?" A young man sat at a wooden table, quill in hand. His face was freshly shaven, and his red eyes cast a blood-red glow upon the parchment atop the table. "Why not start at the beginning?"

Another young man, with a few more years to his life,

stood across the room, casually tossing crumpled pieces of parchment into a large recessed fireplace. The space was confined, with not much walking room between the two beds that had been laid out side by side. The man had long brown hair and was a head taller than the average fellow. He chuckled.

"Don't you see, Roderick? This is why *I* am the master and *you* are the apprentice!" The man's voice was appealing and exuded a depth of knowledge. Every sentence he uttered was spoken as though it were his manifesto. "Every great writer knows you begin at chapter seven!"

Roderick squinted, with his head tilted to the right. "Well, sir, what about chapters one through seven?"

"Blasphemy!" The man stuck his nose into the air and threw the rest of his papers into the fire. He squared his body with Roderick's, pointing the tip of his finger between his apprentice's eyes. "You throw those chapters out! They are rubbish. Useless words, nothing but a waste of ink." The man paraded over to the table and seated himself in a chair across from Roderick. The man placed the soles of his boots against the edge of the table, carefully pushing back, allowing himself to recline. "And where would *you* suppose I start, Roderick?" The man said Roderick's name as though he were trying to grab his attention across a crowded room.

"Why not the beginning, sir?" Roderick's voice cracked.

Roderick's master snickered, revealing the top layer of his ivory-colored teeth. "You make such a broad statement, my apprentice. *And where* exactly is the beginning?" The man took his boots off the table, allowing his chair to slam onto the floor. He shot out of his seat and wandered the room slowly. "Do we start just before the Blight, before the *truth*?" The man stopped pacing the room and looked back to Roderick. "Or do we kick off from where it all started, when Bertly was ten years of age? After all, this *is* the story of the greatest champion of all time."

"Second-greatest champion, sir." Roderick looked the man in the eyes and gave him a wink. His master strode to the table.

"That is subjective, Roderick!" the master said, hunched over, pounding his fists on the table.

"Well…don't most champions have significant achievements? Or are at least top of their class, or the top of the Mastery program, or soul-bonding, or, well—" Roderick hesitated. "The best at…um…anything?"

The man's fists lost their form. He bent back into an upright position.

"Bertly is the greatest champion of all time, Roderick, and that fact is as plain as the nose on your face. Now, can we please focus on the task at hand?"

"Yes, of course, sir. I am ready when you are." Roderick plopped his writing hand on the table, holding his quill tight.

The man sat back in the chair across from Roderick and once again placed his feet on the table, crossing his legs. "Now, let's start from the beginning."

***

Stonebank was a small village that boasted sunny, luminous weather year-round. The skies never shed a drop of rain. Despite the favorable climate of the village, the air often smelled as though a thunderstorm had passed by in the night. A dense fog rolled in each morning, its mist so thick a lamp could not project light from ten feet away. The fog kept the crops watered and the air crisp, allowing wildflowers to bloom. Before the crow of the roosters each morning, the fog departed.

Bertly's home in southern Noskar—which contained no more than fifty rooftops—lay nestled in a crevice of the Noskar Mountains. His cottage—like many of the cottages in the village—had a wooden door with stone walls stretching ten feet in each direction. Each home bore a tall chimney that rose high over a pointed roof.

Bertly's house lay at the entrance of the village. His father occupied the position of the village warden, and as a reward for having earned that position, the family had been granted the foremost cottage in Stonebank. Bertly's family had protected the inhabitants of Stonebank for ten generations. One day that duty would fall to Bertly.

***

"Why exactly are you talking in the third person, sir? Don't you think it'd be an easier tale if you said 'I' instead of 'Bertly' the whole time?" Roderick stopped writing. His eyes were focused on the papers before him, scanning them as if they could provide an answer to his query. He tilted his head upwards in a slow motion while Bertly leaned across the table with his arms stretched forward. Bertly's face was close enough that Roderick felt the wind of his breath. Roderick gazed into Bertly's lustrous red eyes, which themselves were filled with pointed annoyance.

"Two things, Roderick! First, this is not a *tale*. This is a documentation of nonfactitious historical events. And second, no authentic hero writes his own tale." Bertly sighed and pinched the bridge of his nose, just before his eyes. He shook his head and let his body fall back into his chair. "Sometimes I forget you are an apprentice, Roderick. You are lucky I have taken a liking to you."

Roderick dabbed the tip of the quill on his tongue and

waved it in the air. "But, sir, if no authentic hero writes his own story, wouldn't that make you a nonauthentic hero?" Roderick proceeded to sway his quill, staring at the point.

"It is unauthentic, Roderick. And no, it does not make *me* nonauthentic because *you* are writing it." Bertly inflated his chest, spread his fingers out, and placed his hand over his heart. "I am an authentic champion. I would never write my own tale."

"I thought this wasn't a tale?" Roderick lifted his eyebrows and displayed a half grin.

Bertly grunted. "Roderick! You are the scribe. The scribe does not chime in. The scribe records what they are being told."

"I thought I was the writer." Roderick's small grin turned into a wide smile.

"Will you allow me to continue, or are we to quarrel all night over the roles we play in recording the memoirs of the second-greatest champion of all time?"

Bertly took a breath as though he were preparing to dive underwater before he addressed his next grievance. "And *when* did we stop addressing me formally?"

Roderick pushed his chair in, pressing his upper body against the table. He clenched his quill in his white-knuckled fist and placed his writing hand on the table. "Sorry, sir, ready when you are."

"Thank you." Bertly placed his left foot against the table and nudged back, elevating the front legs of his chair off the ground. He rocked backwards in his chair like a disinterested schoolchild. The back legs of the chair teetered in a strained attempt to balance the weight upon them. "Now, where were we?"

***

Bertly peered out from the front door of his cottage, breathing in the air. He hoped this would not be the last time he caught a whiff of moon poppies, which dotted the landscape of his front yard and the many yards nearby.

Bertly was not eager to leave his village. Even so, he looked forward to the greater adventure that awaited him beyond Noskar, and his anticipation helped dull the ache of leaving home. The door opened behind Bertly. He loved the crackling noise the wooden door made every time his father pulled on the handle. Or perhaps he'd always hated the sound and had only now come to enjoy it because he was aware that, before long, he would hear it no more. Bertly would miss his father much more than the stone walls of their cottage, or the predawn fog, which rolled like smoke through the village.

"You ready, lad? The buggy should be here any minute." Bertly's father nudged past him—the man's wide frame barely fit through the door—and Bertly couldn't help but notice the bags beneath his father's eyes and the sad look within them. His father had always worn his beard long and he often took wonderful care of it, but this morning the beard was unkempt with wild stark-white hairs poking out here and there. Bertly had never seen his father in such a condition, and looking upon the man caused a lump to form in his throat. He had difficulty swallowing it down before uttering a response.

"Aye, Dadai." Bertly continued to look upon his village, and he couldn't help but wonder if the village would have memories of him. He was saddened to think that a place that had impacted him so might forget him the instant he was gone. Every moon poppy or drizzle bird he saw on his adventure would remind him of home.

Bertly's father stepped forward and lowered himself to one knee. Bertly took in a lungful of his village's clean air and turned to face his father, whose green eyes were misted and had taken on a glossy appearance. Bertly's father placed his hand on his son's shoulder. His hand was so large with his fingers splayed that this reassuring touch covered half of Bertly's back.

"Now, son, what did I tell you about speaking in that accent? You'll give away your origins if you go around like that. Best to have them guessing. Maybe they'll think you're a nobleman." His father smiled.

Bertly lowered his eyebrows and clenched his jaw. He took a modest step back, slipping from his father's grasp. Bertly squared his shoulders and positioned himself mere inches from his father and cleared his throat.

"Mind your place, peasant! I'll have my hounds on you quicker than you can say 'save me, Cordelia.' Are you not acquainted with who I am?" Bertly had changed his dialect on a whim so that he sounded nothing like the Stonebank resident he was.

His father's cheeks fell to rest, his eyes closed, and his eyebrows took the shape of a bird on the horizon. Bertly and his father peered intensely into each other's eyes, their breathing in sync. On their fifth breath, the men burst into laughter. Bertly snorted, trying to hold in his chortling, while his father wiped a small tear from the corner of his eye.

"I should never have questioned you, lad. You'll be fine. You're more intelligent and sharper than I ever could be. You certainly take after your mother." Bertly's father sighed. "If only she were here to send you off." He stood back and crossed his arms across his broad chest. "Now, do you remember what I've taught you?"

Bertly raised his fists and positioned them beneath his chin. "When in doubt, fight it out."

"That's right, son. If your mouth can't win the fight, let your fists do the talking." Bertly's father gave him a gentle nudge with a fist that nearly dwarfed Bertly's head. Bertly stumbled backward two steps, moving his arms away from his sides. Once he regained his balance, he stood idly before his father with his hands resting at his sides. He looked to the left of his father, in an attempt to avoid eye contact for fear that the lump would return to his throat, or that his father's eyes would appear watery once again.

"What if I don't make it into the Academy and all the training and studying we have been doing has been for nothing?" After receiving no reply, Bertly looked up and studied his father's face. He was nervous to hear the response, but it was a question to which he needed an answer. His father stared back at him and ran his fingers through his beard, smoothing a few wayward hairs.

"You are the first person in all of Noskar to be born with red eyes in over three thousand years. The Academy was created for folk like you." His father's voice gained depth and increased in volume as he finished his statement.

"Except for Polly. She was born a day before me and her eyes are redder." Bertly stared at his feet as he lightly kicked at the dirt.

His father's brow creased, and he shook his head. "Don't you worry about Polly. Her father is a fraud. She will never get into the Academy." Bertly's father closed his eyes and took a lungful of air, letting it out slowly. "Son, listen to me. You can't always be comparing yourself to others. You two are far from the same, trust me on that."

Bertly looked to his right as the sound of hoofbeats arose. Emerging from over the hill nearest his property came two horses pulling a wooden carriage. A woman dressed in brightly colored garments rode on top of the carriage. Bertly's father clapped him on the back. The force sent Bertly stumbling slightly forward.

"It looks like your ride is here, son."

Bertly stepped back and turned to face his father, who had already begun pulling Bertly into a rib-crushing embrace.

Bertly's father grinned. He placed a hand on each of Bertly's shoulders and knelt slightly to look his son in the eyes. "Okay there, lad, I will see you in two nights. Now go. The other students are waiting for you." He gave Bertly a gentle shove toward the carriage.

Bertly ran off, kicking up dust with his feet. The driver already had the carriage door open for him. He climbed into the carriage and chose the seat nearest the door. The driver closed the door before Bertly could settle in, nearly trapping Bertly's foot between it and the buggy. But Bertly paid the incident little mind. He was too excited and distracted to chastise the carriage driver, nor would he do so even if he were in a fouler mood. Today was the last day he would ever be an ordinary human again.

Bertly spent the remainder of the morning in the carriage, which was heading due east for Klovose. The carriage was quiet for a good portion of the ride, even though Bertly was accompanied by other passengers. But before long, the silence grew to be too much for them.

"I thought humans couldn't learn magic." Across from Bertly—and to the right of the girl next to him—sat two stocky dwarves, identical, with ruby-red eyes, and each only half the height of the average human. One sported a short braided beard, while the other wore his braid long enough that one could grab it with both hands. Bertly wasn't sure which dwarf had spoken. Or maybe it had been both at once.

He stared out the window as soon as the words reached his ears; he was in no mood for chatter. Without turning his head, he snapped, "I thought you had to be under eleven to test into the Academy."

The dwarf twins turned to each other, their eyes bigger than the moon, before turning their attention back to Bertly. "We're only ten," they shrieked. Every time they spoke, it seemed they shouted instead.

"But the…" Bertly stopped looking out the window and rubbed his cheeks with his fingers.

"Oh, the beards!" The boys smiled while rubbing their furry faces. "All dwarven men grow beards before their first birthday." The shouting was growing on Bertly; they sounded rather cheerful.

Bertly smiled. "No kidding." He paused for a moment. "To answer your question, humans *can* learn magic. Polly and I just happen to be the first ones to do it in a while."

"Three thousand years is more than a while," an elven girl with long blond hair interjected. She also had vibrant red eyes, and she sat to the right of Bertly. Her voice was so soft that he could hardly hear her over the crunching of the carriage wheels as they rolled across the rocky road.

"Cordelia was just waiting for the best. Isn't that right, Bertly?" Polly, the girl next to Bertly, smiled. She sat primly with her hands in her lap, immaculate posture, and her chin up. Her blond hair was rather wavy and flowed over her shoulders, and her red, doe-like eyes lay framed between two delicate ears. Her voice was elegant and frail, drawing the attention of all who could hear her speak.

"Yep." Bertly sighed; he would rather sit in complete silence than converse with Polly.

The carriage came to a stop and its occupants sat silently for a moment.

"I heard the tests are harder than ever this year," remarked an elven boy with sandy blond hair who sat in the far right corner of the cabin.

The twins chimed in, "Harder. But only five percent of

entrants make it into the Academy. Almost everyone attends the preparation program for at least one year."

"We're here." A muffled voice penetrated the cabin. The children scurried toward the windows, their little fingers parting the thin curtains to peek out. Bertly was forced against the glass by Polly and the two elves, who piled onto him.

"I can't believe we're already here." Polly's voice could hardly be heard over the giggling of the other children.

Bertly hesitated to respond, but decided that he would. This time. "All I see is a tent. It doesn't look how I expected. I imagined it to be much more—"

The side door of the carriage flung open, and the weight of the three children stacked atop him sent him flying out of the carriage and onto the dirt road. The three elves toppled after him to the ground.

Standing before them was the carriage driver. "Get up, now! Stop fooling around." The driver cast her shadow over the youngsters. "Head down this path here. You'll be at the testing grounds in just two minutes. Be sure to register before heading to the main hall."

"We thought we were going to the Academy," the twins contended.

"No. Only students and faculty are allowed on campus grounds. Now, I must be off." The driver bustled back to the carriage and was gone as quick as a drizzle bird.

***

Led by the twins, the group of red-eyed adolescents arrived at the Academy testing grounds. In front of them stood a leather pavilion that was at least half the size of Stonebank. The structure was onyx black with white scalloped edges.

"Friends, do you think registration is over near that long line?" Polly extended her arm, pointing to the left of the entrance.

"We'd reckon so." The two burly dwarves continued to lead the group towards the line. Bertly was stunned by their speed, for they were certainly not built for it.

A short while later, Bertly stood motionless in the line. His mind wandered from the conversation between Polly and the others. He soon found himself eavesdropping on another conversation nearby. He couldn't make out the faces of the two who were speaking, but he knew the conversation was most likely between a boy and a girl—elvish, according to the accents.

"Why do they even make us stand in this long line anyways?" the boy said.

"I heard it's because they need to register every red-eyed citizen in Pangea," the girl replied. Her temperament seemed much less dissatisfied than that of her companion.

"Why would they need everyone with red eyes registered?"

"Are you stupid?" the girl snapped, her even tone disappearing. "*Because* we can all do magic. Almost one in five elves is born with red eyes. Imagine if we all revolted, like the giants did in the Great War."

"Oh…right." The boy's voice grew somber. "I suppose that makes sense. Thank Cordelia for keeping us protected."

"Bertly? Bertly?" Bertly snapped his attention away. Polly was intently staring at him. She leaned her head forward so that her nose was only a breath's distance from his own. Bertly strained his back, arching it to be as far from her as possible given the circumstances. "Welcome back. I thought I lost you there for a second. Come on, the rest are already inside," Polly said. She reached out and grabbed Bertly's hand. Bertly whipped his arm up to his chest.

"I can get there just fine. Thank you," Bertly said in as polite a tone as he could manage. Polly's eyes appeared dazed for a brief moment before she turned around and resumed standing in the line that led to the registration desk. Bertly followed behind her until a tall elvish woman asked for his hand.

Bertly watched in horror as the woman placed a glass vial over his wrist, which immediately filled with his blood, apparently not even needing to touch his skin in order to accomplish this feat.

"You may progress inside," the woman said.

Bertly proceeded numbly through the entryway. Jarred by what he'd just witnessed, he clenched his hand and focused on it. There was neither a puncture wound nor any pain associated with the blood-drawing process. He hadn't felt a thing when the blood left his hand. His attention quickly shifted from his untouched blood draw to his new surroundings.

The inside of the pavilion was sectioned off into three areas, each with a number floating above the section. Bertly entered the pavilion and immediately noticed that Polly had settled to the right of the entrance. Bertly mistakenly made eye contact with her, which apparently Polly took to mean that she could rush over to him.

"Why is everyone staring at us, Bertly?" Polly asked him. He thought her question warranted a response, so he surveyed the room, and as his eyes scanned the individuals in the pavilion, theirs turned away from him, as if they were embarrassed to be caught staring. He begrudgingly admitted to himself that Polly was correct; the entire room was staring at them.

"Probably because we are the first humans with red eyes in over three thousand years. They've never seen people like us, Polly." Bertly snarled. "Now, where are we heading?"

"Right." Polly blushed. "They said to start with intelligence testing. If we score above an eighty, then we advance to combat testing." Polly inspected the space. "It should be just over there, room one." Bertly looked in the direction Polly indicated, and together, they walked toward room one.

***

Bertly and Polly sat parallel to one another with their hands folded, facing the head of the room. The space was square with white walls and desks in a grid pattern, and the students who occupied them sitting silently.

Polly leaned over to Bertly. "When do you think the test will begin?"

Bertly persisted in staring at the front of the room. "I am assuming once the instructor gets here."

Just as Polly opened her mouth to reply, a door near the front of the room flew open. Out of that door walked the largest dwarf Bertly had ever seen; the dwarf stood a foot taller than the standard of his kind. He was afflicted by a large scar that spanned from his eye to his cheek, though it might have extended even further than that— Bertly noted—if it weren't for the bushy, long, stark-white beard which grew past the dwarf's waist, obscuring what could have remained of the scar. The dwarf hobbled toward the front of the class, clasped his hands behind his back, and stood facing his students.

"Hello, I am Master Quinric. I have been the main overseer of the Academy entrance exam for over eighty years. I have seen many who have shown promise fail, and some who I thought belonged in Noskar rise up and become a master. Our judgment is not reliable, thus why you are here now, taking this examination. Cordelia has blessed only the fortunate with the gift of red eyes, and you are among those chosen. It is now your duty and responsibility to uphold the morals and wishes of our Cordelia." Master Quinric looked over the room. "Some of you will become doctors; others, craftsmen—and for the lucky—soldiers." Those in the classroom tried to hold back their laughter; however, a few students could not resist.

"Why is everyone laughing?" Polly whispered.

Bertly leaned in. "No soldier has fought in battle in over three thousand years. Not since Cordelia. Soldiers just train, relax, and get paid, without the worry of ever stepping foot on the battlefield. A soldier holds the most coveted position in all of Pangea."

Master Quinric cleared his throat, and the room fell silent. "This is the hardest year of testing we have ever had. This exam will require logic and reasoning beyond your years. Your mind will be placed in several different situations, and you must work your way out of them. Very few of you will be fast-tracked into the Academy this year." Master Quinric squinted while he analyzed the room. "It seems Cordelia has gifted us with more red-eyed blessings this generation. Now, best of luck." Quinric waved his hand across the classroom. As his hand swished, their tests and quills appeared on the desks. Bertly jumped as he watched such magic take place before him, but he settled down quickly and examined the supplies.

"Where is the ink?" Bertly asked Polly.

Polly observed the room. "I think we just write with them," she said, snatching the white-feathered quill in front of her. She jotted her name at the top of the exam sheet. Polly looked back at Bertly and shrugged. "Seems to work."

Bertly picked up his own quill and began to write. Shortly thereafter, he set his quill down. *Could it really be so easy?* he wondered as he glanced at the other students, who were still filling out their test booklets. Bertly, puzzled, flipped back to the first page of his finished exam and looked over his test again. There was no way it could have been so easy. He wondered if the questions on the test were trick questions; the scenarios were too easy to work out. Bertly examined the room again, completely stumped at how most of the students were sweating and flipping back and forth between the test pages. One student had even eaten half the feathers off his quill. Bertly flipped his exam packet closed, satisfied that he was, indeed, finished with the test. The booklet instantly vanished and reappeared in Master Quinric's hand. The dwarf yawned.

"Done so soon? I didn't realize we had made the test so challenging this year. A shame, I was hoping for more out of the first red-eyed human in three thousand years." Quinric rolled his eyes and looked over Bertly's exam, mumbling something about how lazy humans must be to not even finish their work, but as he advanced further through Bertly's exam, the dwarf's eyes widened. He flipped through the papers again—and then a third time—before he spoke.

Bertly's heart pounded as he awaited the decision of his instructor. He was terrified that he'd done poorly on his test. The silence seemed to last centuries before the instructor spoke.

"Impossible…how could you…this is the highest test score I have ever seen. I…I don't think a student has scored this high in a millennium," stammered the dwarf.

Bertly's anxiety melted into triumph. He could barely hide his burgeoning grin. He straightened his spine and sat in the perfect posture his father had taught—and often forced—him to sit in. "Young boy, you're an absolute—"

Another test materialized in Master Quinric's hand before he could finish telling the class exactly how wonderful Bertly was. This time the master audibly gasped as he brought his hairy hand to his chest.

"Another! And this one…it's a perfect score! Which of you just completed this examination? Speak!"

Polly slipped out of her seat. The screech that arose as her chair ground against the floor filled the room. Polly stood, her whole face flushed with the crimson of embarrassment. Bertly could tell. He felt it himself at that exact moment.

"You! Young miss, not even our holy Cordelia accomplished a perfect score. You must be a gift hand-selected by Cordelia herself!"

***

Bertly and Polly sipped on drizzle water as they waited in the main foyer for the rest of the students to finish their tests.

"You did so well on the test the instructor couldn't believe it. Isn't that amazing? I'm so happy for you. Can you believe the scores we got, Bertly? Aren't you happy for me?" Polly's blushed cheeks surrounded her contagious smile.

Bertly sat with his arms crossed, eyes forward, and answered in a monotone. "Yes, I am so happy."

"The next testing is in room three. Do you want to head there now? I think the other students will be finishing soon."

"Sure, whatever you want, Polly." Bertly continued to be short. He didn't intend to behave like a brat, but he couldn't help feeling upset that Polly had shown him up in front of so many people.

Bertly and Polly were on their way to the next room when Master Quinric intercepted them.

"Sprouts, where are you off to?"

"Room three, sir," Polly said with intent.

Master Quinric grunted. "Cordelia, no, you are going straight to the Grand Elder. The Academy does not care about your combat scores."

Bertly dropped his drizzle water on the floor. The combat testing was his only opportunity to upstage Polly, and he'd been confident that this was a challenge she would lose to him. His father had trained him in combat. The two had practiced every day since Bertly had been able to hold a sword.

"Sweet Cordelia, get ahold of yourself, boy!" Master Quinric grabbed his robe and whipped it away from Bertly's direction. A small amount of drizzle water splashed onto Quinric's robe.

Bertly shook his head. "Sorry, sir, I am shocked by…the whole situation."

"Why Cordelia chose two humans from Noskar, we will never know, but nonetheless, the Grand Elder has summoned you. Now, follow me." Quinric darted down a hallway much quicker than Bertly expected. Since leaving home, he had been repeatedly impressed by the swiftness of dwarves.

He and Polly followed Quinric beyond the three main rooms and through a well-lit corridor. At the end of the long hall was a single red door, where Quinric stopped. "Go along. He is expecting you." He gestured for them to enter the room.

Bertly reached for the door handle, but the door pushed open before he could grab it, and together he and Polly continued walking. The room they entered was very dark, with only one beam of light that appeared to float in the center of the room. Bertly searched the room in an attempt to find the light source, but there was none. Exposed within the beam was a giant, a man larger than a horse. Aside from his long white beard, his pale body was hairless. The giant rested with his eyes fastened shut.

"Bertly, son of Edfrid, please step into my light," the giant said, with a voice that sounded even larger than its source. Bertly was surprised that he could feel the bass of the man's thunderous voice booming beneath his feet. Bertly walked forward and immediately was surrounded by the warm light.

"Hmm...I haven't interpreted a soul quite like yours in many generations. You will achieve greatness in your lifetime, but will succumb to what you desire most." The giant's eyes remained sealed. "Your soul holds a tragic ending, young Bertly. But still, it is one worth possessing. I have not been curious about an entrant in many years, future master. Please make your time at the Academy well spent."

Bertly's chest pounded, and his knees were shaking. He stepped out of the light, unable to utter a response. He'd spent his entire life training for the Academy, and he'd been the first red-eyed human to be born inside the last three thousand years. And soon, he would be able to tell the residents of Stonebank that he would have the honor of attending school to become a master.

The master of Stonebank. It had a nice ring to it.

It was Polly's turn next, and Bertly eagerly watched as she stepped into the light.

The moment she did so, the Grand Elder opened his eyes. "It is you, Cordelia."

11

"Sir, you mean to tell me that Polly *is* Cordelia?" Roderick's eyebrows arched and his jaw dropped. "But I thought she—"

"Of course she isn't, you fool! The old giant was a bumbling idiot," Bertly interrupted. "Now stop intruding before you give something away."

"Sir!" Roderick shouted. "That is the Grand Elder you speak of."

"What kind of Grand Elder can't tell the difference between a reincarnation and a prophecy, Roderick? Plus, he *was* the Grand Elder." Bertly sighed. "Apparently, her soul almost resembled Cordelia's identically. It had always been rumored that Cordelia would one day be reincarnated. It just had to be her, of all people." The grudge was evident in his voice.

***

"So, Polly and Cordelia, aye?" Bertly's father, Edfrid, paced around the quaint room, grabbing items and clothing articles and placing them into a small knapsack. "I never would have put it together." Edfrid continued stuffing clothing articles into the knapsack. "These magic bags really are something else, son. Do they ever fill up?" Bertly's father chuckled.

Bertly lay on a mattress. "I don't understand. I work harder every day than she has her entire life, but she is the one being given everything." Bertly sat up. "I should be the chosen one." His face grew red.

Edfrid placed the bag on the floor. "I will be right back." Bertly's father strolled out of the room. Bertly heard a small crash followed by a slight thud before his father returned with a book in his hands, which he extended to his son. "Here, I want you to have this."

Bertly took the book from his father and ran his fingertips across the leather cover.

"It was your mother's. She wanted you to have it once you were thirteen, but I think now is a better time."

Bertly flipped open the cover, eager to find out what was inside, but his eyes didn't manage to scan a single word. Edfrid slammed the book shut. "Wait until you get to the Academy, son."

Bertly nodded. Though waiting to open the book would be more torturous than the carriage ride back from the entrance exam. It was pure hell sitting near Polly for so many hours, even more so than before, since he'd learned that she was a prophecy. Bertly was in the process of reaching for his knapsack when there was a knock at the cottage door.

"They're early," Edfrid said, his eyes a touch wider than usual.

Bertly dropped his book into the knapsack and opened the front door. He was confused to see that the knocker was a driver who had no carriage.

"Are you ready, boy? We are running late." The driver pointed his finger toward the sun.

"May I say goodbye to my father, sir?" Bertly asked.

The driver huffed and stamped a foot on the mat

outside. "You should have already said farewell." The tall and slender man peered at Bertly, who attempted to look as pathetic as possible. He did not want to leave without saying goodbye to his father. The driver sighed. "You have one minute. Hurry now."

Bertly looked to his father. Regret at leaving his father—his best friend—alone ate at him.

"Son, we don't have much time, but I'll give you a piece of advice before you go. It isn't always so bad being underestimated. Any other year, you would have been the greatest entrant since Cordelia herself." Edfrid twiddled his thumbs. "There is something I haven't been completely honest about." Bertly noticed sweat forming on his father's forehead, a sign of nervousness that was very rare for the warden of Stonebank.

"Yes?" Bertly asked hesitantly.

"You may find that some folk take notice of you once you leave Stonebank," Edfrid continued.

"What do you mean?"

"Well, as warden I have some pull around town." Edfrid shook his head. "Anyway, I have done my best to be sure word of you and Polly has never left Stonebank. If word got out…Bertly, you will learn in time just how important you may be. Because of that, I didn't want to take away what little childhood you'd have."

"Your minute is up." The driver appeared even more hurried, tapping his foot profusely. Bertly turned back to Edfrid and spoke quickly.

"I don't understand, Father. But I will make you proud, and I will be back in eight years, once I am a master. I will bring you and all of Noskar honor." Bertly made a fist and placed it over his heart. Before he had another chance to speak, the driver grabbed him by the arm.

The room stretched in various directions. Every

source of light vanished. The world's gravity gripped ahold of Bertly, and his body suddenly assumed the weight of a thousand pounds. The light came back almost as fast as it had been sucked away. His body mass and weight returned to normal.

Bertly's vision was blurred, and he saw the world as though he were looking at it through a water glass. His breakfast sat heavily in his stomach. He became overwhelmingly hot. Sweat dripped from his forehead, and beads of it dotted his hairline. Bertly was certain his morning meal was ready to exit his mouth. The driver handed Bertly a bag, and without hesitation, Bertly grabbed it and filled it immediately.

"It happens to everyone their first time, kid. Don't worry about it. You'll see the Academy once you regain your vision. I'm running late. I have to get going," the driver said, just a moment before disappearing.

Bertly wished he could have seen the sorcery the driver had used; however, his vision was still too impaired. A few minutes passed and Bertly's nausea remained, as did the poor quality of his eyesight. He heard a *swoosh* and felt a small gust of wind that he could only guess was produced by the same source.

"You're still here?"

Bertly blinked, but his eyes wouldn't clear. He did recognize the driver's voice, and he also could hear that the question was directed at him. The next words the driver spoke, however, were directed elsewhere. "Almar, can you please show young Bertly here to his quarters?"

"No problem, sir." Almar's voice was deep and raspy. By the sound of his speech, Bertly guessed he must have been in his seventh or eighth year. Bertly would have assumed Almar was old enough to be a master, but the driver did not address him as one.

"It happens to the best of us." Almar laughed. "Close your eyes; they'll adjust quicker."

"Thank you. I appreciate the help." Bertly stood and closed his eyes. His nausea was finally dissipating. After he'd gained his composure, he asked Almar, "What just happened to me?"

"You were shipped. Some wizards are born with the ability to send themselves anywhere in the world. The only catch is they must have already traveled there." Almar sighed. "It is a very rare gift. Sadly, most who are capable turn to crime or never aspire to be more than chauffeurs." He approached Bertly and placed his hands on Bertly's shoulders and physically turned him. "Now, open your eyes."

Before Bertly stood thirteen immense square-shaped towers that dominated the entire skyline. The structures were connected by colossal walls made from light red stone. There was not a single crack across the entire building. It looked as though it were newly constructed. Scattered randomly across the walls were a variety of windows and crenellations. A vast gate made of thick metal was the only entrance.

Luscious fields with compact structures and houses occupied the grounds outside the castle walls.

"Hard to believe she's over ten thousand years old, isn't it?" Almar acknowledged.

Bertly did not reply. He was captivated by the beautiful keep. Bertly had never seen a structure so large before. He calculated that it would take years to visit every room and to walk each corridor.

"Come, follow me. I will show you to your quarters." Almar walked ahead of Bertly and up to the castle gate. "Are you ready?" Almar winked and walked directly through the metal gate. He'd needed no key or code word. Bertly was astonished. One of the most famous places in all of Pangea left its front door wide open. An arm reached out from the metal door and pulled Bertly through. Bertly jumped.

"I knew I would get you with that one." Almar laughed. "Your room is just up these stairs. Lucky for you, you're close to the entrance. And the dining hall is just down that corridor." Bertly followed Almar as they strolled through the castle.

The inside was grand. The walls were decorated with large ornate paintings, and the stairs had elegantly patterned carpets covering them. The ceilings spanned nearly a dozen floors. Students rushed the halls in every direction. Everyone seemed as though they were already late to wherever they needed to be.

"I am quite excited to see your dormitory." Almar was walking at a quick pace. Bertly's vision had fully recovered, and he noticed pointed ears sticking out of Almar's black hair.

"Why is that?" Bertly questioned.

Almar happily answered, "Each race has designated dormitories. This is the first time the human wing will be open in thousands of years. I think everyone is a bit excited." Almar led Bertly up a small flight of stairs.

"Here it is." A group of students was already waiting near the entrance. Almar stood idly and stared at Bertly. "Well, aren't you going to open it?"

Bertly scanned the door. He looked all around the frame but was unable to find a handle. "I don't mean to ask the obvious, but how?" Bertly made a nervous laugh and waved his hand over the spot on the door where a handle would be.

"You mean, you don't know how to open it?" Almar gasped. The surrounding students let out a quiet giggle.

"Well, no. Do you?"

"Of course not. I'm an elf, not a human. Your people

should have taught you this."

Suddenly the door opened. Polly stood in the doorframe, wearing a radiant smile. Bertly dropped his belongings to the floor and stared at her. "Bertly, you're finally here. It looks like it'll be just us," Polly shouted. "I figured out how to open the door. I can show you later. Here, let me grab your things." Polly bustled over to Bertly and picked his bags up from the floor. "The room is just magnificent." She hurried back into the room. Bertly let out a big sigh and followed, with Almar not far behind.

Bertly never would have guessed his room would look like this. The room had grass rather than wood—or marble—flooring, and it smelled of fresh air, as though he actually were outside. Wind gently blew across his face, and he picked up the songs of drizzle birds. At the center of the space grew a large tree with a trunk wider than most cottages. Bertly looked up to see the same light red stone ceiling that spanned the main area of the castle. He turned his head to the side, and the walls, too, were made of the same stone. They were still inside, but the room did not smell, look, or feel as though it were indoors.

"This is impossible." Almar paced the room with his jaw wide open. "They said this wing had been blessed, but I could never have imagined to what extent."

"Isn't it splendid?" Polly added.

"I hate to ask, but where do we sleep?" Bertly questioned, glancing at Polly. Polly clapped her hands together and waved Bertly forward.

"This is my favorite part, follow me." Polly led Almar and Bertly to the tree. She placed her hand against the large trunk. After a moment, the bark on the tree split, creating an opening. Polly took her hand from the tree and the hole closed. "Now you try."

Bertly and Almar each placed their hands against the

smooth bark. Immediately the tree split around Bertly's hand.

"Ah, it isn't working for me. Must be a human-only thing." Almar removed his hand from the tree. "I will let you two get settled in. If you see me at the dining hall, feel free to sit at my table. I know it can be hard to make friends on your first day."

"Thank you for everything," Bertly said. He was genuinely grateful to the elf. If it had not been for Almar, Bertly would have likely suffered one embarrassment after another attempting to find his lodgings. Almar stopped just short of the door to the room and turned to face Bertly and Polly once again.

"I almost forgot; if you ever need your schedule, simply stick your arm in the air and say, 'Cordelia, reveal my schedule.' Get used to it. You will have to learn many reveal spells over the next eight years," Almar mocked and exited the dormitory.

The interior of the tree was lined with fluffy beds and several wardrobes. Bertly and Polly smiled at each other, dropped their belongings, and started jumping on the beds.

The two of them leaped from bed to bed. "What time is orientation?" Bertly shouted.

"Oh! I almost forgot." Polly hopped off the bed. "It actually starts in just a few minutes. We should probably head to the dining hall."

***

Bertly and Polly walked into the dining hall together, mesmerized by the lines of shimmering columns that lit up every inch of the room. The light was strong, but it was easy on the eyes. Floating lamps covered the walls in a warm orange glow, illuminating portraits of famous icons. A ruby-red rug split the room in half and was matched by banners that hung from the stone walls. On each side of the rug lay several wooden tables, which were occupied by young elves and dwarves.

Polly tapped Bertly on the shoulder. "Look, it's the twins."

Bertly peered in the direction she was pointing. The twins sat at a fully occupied table. Each was bantering back and forth while the entire group burst into laughter. Mixed within the group was Almar. He waved Bertly and Polly over once he caught a glimpse of them from across the hall.

As the two humans approached the table, Almar stood to greet and introduce them. "I am not sure if any of you have had the pleasure of meeting our human companions yet."

"We have. That's Polly and Bertly," the twins said.

"You two know Orin and Orîn?" Almar asked.

"Sure do! We rode in the same carriage to the entrance exam." Polly beamed.

"I'll be damned, anyone who is friends with the sons of the most famous dwarf in Academy history is friends with us." Almar gestured toward his schoolmates. The group unanimously squished themselves together, forming empty spaces for Polly and Bertly to sit in.

Bertly peered at the twins. "So, Orin—"

"Yes?" both twins interjected. Bertly considered specifying which twin he was speaking to; however, he found the situation too amusing and let the idea go.

"I hate to admit this, but I am not familiar with your father," Bertly said. The whole group turned their heads in his direction. Bertly did his best to conceal his slight embarrassment. "You see, no one from Noskar has ever been to the Academy. Polly and I have never really heard any stories about this place. Only that a bunch of wizards

with pointy hats and robes run around casting spells."
The table fell silent. Then an enormous laugh rumbled
from the students. Orin and Orîn almost fell out of their
seats.

With tears in his eyes, Almar chimed in, "Pointy hats.
That's really funny. Not many pointy hats around these
parts. I will say—some of the Elders do, however, wear
robes."

A deep voice echoed through the room, cutting off the
group's conversation. "Cordelia's blessing." The students
stopped speaking. At the front of the main hall stood an
elf with wrinkled skin and white hair. "Welcome, first-
year students, to your new home. As a reminder, this is a
closed-communication campus. There will be no letters
or voice bubbles until you have graduated. It will be hard
at first, but we find students who are not distracted by the
outside world make the best magicians. If there is an
emergency, your guardians will contact the Academy and
we will reach out to you."

The old elf took a deep breath. "There are more
students this year than any year prior. Soon, it will be
harder than ever to gain admittance to the Mastery
program." The elf took another breath. "Incoming
students, make these next eight years count. Only a
quarter of you will make it into the program, but for
those of you who *do*, you will have long and prosperous
careers in magic." The elf paused for a moment, taking
yet another breath. "This year, the apprenticeship
program has been altered. It no longer lasts three years; it
lasts five years."

The room filled with the chatter of students discussing
the change. But Bertly needed to start from the beginning
if he was to understand the elf's words.

"What is the apprenticeship program?" Bertly
questioned.

"You must serve under a master for three…um, five years before you can apply to the Mastery program. You must also complete your apprenticeship before you graduate," Almar answered, his face red with anger. Bertly noted that the new timeframe for apprenticeship was not being well received amongst the students.

The old elf continued. "If you are on your last two years, you will *not* have to serve five years under a master." The upperclassmen cheered. The remaining students booed. It did not take long before playful boos and cheers turned into arguments and whining.

"Silence." The lights in the room flickered, and the chatter and arguments came to an abrupt halt. The elf took one more breath. "One final thing: the curfew has been lifted this year. Please do not make us reinstate it." The entire hall roared, and students jumped to their feet.

"Curfew?" Polly questioned. She looked around the room, smiling at the excitement of her fellow schoolmates.

"No more curfew! No more rules!" the twins cried.

Almar laughed. "At the Academy, there is usually a curfew. It was only enforced because of the one-hundred-year curfew enforcement."

"There has been a curfew for the last one hundred years?" Bertly asked.

Almar leaned forward. "It has actually been much longer. There is almost always a curfew. They are forced to constantly reinstate one because some moron does something stupid. I can guarantee the curfew will be put back in place before the end of the year."

Bertly chuckled. "Ah, I see."

***

"Sir, weren't *you* the moron who got the curfew

reinstated?" Roderick blurted out, looking up from his parchment.

Bertly rolled his eyes and glared at Roderick. "Roderick, please." Bertly placed his knuckles against his forehead. "All I wanted to do was take it for a little ride."

III

"Bertly, rise and shine."

Bertly opened his eyes, and there was Polly's glowing smile hovering over him, filling his field of vision. Bertly grunted and rubbed the sleep from his eyes.

Polly was formally dressed, with her hair tied back. "Sorry to wake you, but I couldn't let you be late to your first day of class. Have you checked your schedule yet?"

Bertly yawned. He was in no mood to speak to anyone so early in the morning, but to see Polly's face first thing, to hear her voice before he even got out of bed—his agitation grew. He knew better than to display this irritation, however. "No, not yet. When does class start?"

Polly darted about the room, picking up her personal items and placing them back down again. "In less than twenty minutes, I think. Did you not hear the morning bells? They go off an hour before the first class."

Bertly bolted upright and pushed his blankets to the foot of the bed. "Why didn't you wake me up sooner, Polly?" Bertly practically spat her name as he hustled to his wardrobe.

Polly took a step back, giving Bertly room to gather his belongings and get dressed. She shook her head. "Well, I honestly assumed you were sleeping in on purpose." Polly raised her hand. "Cordelia, reveal Bertly's schedule." Polly stood still with her arm in the air, studying her empty hand, squinting as though that would bring the schedule to life on her pale skin. "Odd. It worked for me earlier."

Bertly raised his arm. "Cordelia, reveal my schedule." A piece of parchment appeared in Bertly's hand. "Fascinating. It must only work for your own schedule. I wonder if all reveal spells have this limitation." Bertly stood near his dresser and looked over his schedule.

"Bertly, we can look at your schedule while we are walking. You need to get dressed, or we'll both be late." Polly's words were slightly panicked and rushed.

"What do you mean both of us? You can head off without me," Bertly snapped.

"We can help each other get to class, of course. My first class is Magic for Humans. I am assuming we have first period together," Polly replied without an ounce of impatience in her voice. Bertly glanced at his schedule, saw the first course listed on it, and groaned.

***

Together—as demanded by Polly—the two scrambled through the corridors and wove through the masses of students in search of room 782. The halls were packed shoulder to shoulder with red-eyed classmates. They tried to keep their balance while fast-paced dwarves bumped the backs of their legs. Every set of eyes in the castle gazed upon them.

"Who do you think is teaching the class?" Bertly yelled as he upped his pace from a speed-walk to an outright run.

"Considering we are the only red-eyed humans, probably a human history teacher. Maybe someone who has specifically studied the history of human magic, or at least the theory of it." Polly shrugged as she ran alongside Bertly. He couldn't help but notice that her voice was even while running. He had the urge to groan yet again at this realization.

Bertly peered inside each classroom as they shuffled through the hallways. He was unable to see much, but he caught quick glimpses every so often. The classrooms had amphitheater-style seating, and the rooms looked large enough to fit at least two hundred students. The teachers ranged from young to old, male to female, dwarf to giant. As Bertly and Polly approached their classroom, the crowd thinned out. Polly scanned the room numbers, reading them aloud as she and Bertly passed them: another habit of hers that annoyed him.

"Seven hundred seventy-seven, seven hundred seventy-nine…seven hundred eighty-two! We're here," Polly announced.

Bertly opened the door to the classroom. As he was about to enter, Polly brushed by.

"Thanks, Bertly," Polly sang out.

The room was much smaller than the others Bertly had seen; it was flat and consisted of only eight workbenches.

"You're late." A giant with short frizzy hair and a chiseled jaw hovered over the classroom while he addressed Bertly and Polly. The giant stood with a graceful posture despite his enormous frame. "You know I have the right to drop you from this course, correct?"

The two humans stood in place, looking up at the giant, neither of them able to formulate a sentence in response to him. The giant stood silently, observing as Bertly and Polly stumbled over their words.

The giant sized them up and crossed his arms. He let out a monstrous laugh.

"I am only giving you a hard time. Lighten up." The

giant continued to giggle. "You should see the looks on your faces." The giant gestured toward the workbenches. "Please take a seat. I am Master Alestar. I will be your Human Magic teacher." As Alestar paced the front of the room, his heavy footfalls reverberated through the space. "I know I am neither a human, nor was I alive when the last red-eyed human walked this world. I know, I look stunning and youthful—" Alestar flexed his biceps. "But I am actually much older than I appear. I studied the theory of human magic in the city of Eskos for three hundred years."

"But, sir, how old does that make you?" Bertly asked. The words seemed to pop out of his lips before his mind could approve of them. He sank back in his chair and his cheeks began to heat. "Sorry, sir, I didn't mean to interrupt."

Alestar grinned. "Curiosity killed the koko, you know. Nonetheless, how does one ever obtain knowledge if not through curiosity? I will humor your question, small human." The elegant giant pulled up a tall barstool behind him. He rested his leg on the top bar, placing his elbow over his knee. "I am actually four hundred years old. I've spent most of my life fascinated by spells. If I was awake, I was studying. I graduated the Academy in just six years, mind you." Alestar smirked. "Once I had spent one hundred years orally learning every spell I could find, I had no choice but to move on to human magic. Human magic was much harder to study. No one actively teaches or practices it. It took me nearly centuries, but I believe I have learned all we have recorded on human magic." Alestar looked at Bertly and Polly. His red eyes were gentle. "Call me a fool, but I think our meeting was part of Cordelia's plan." A large bell filled the classroom. Each gong was spaced out and deep in tone.

"Well, if you two weren't so late, we may have been

able to get started on some spells," Alestar said with a gruff sigh. "I will see you both tomorrow."

***

Bertly and Polly pushed through the crowded hallways.

"Move. I will not be late again, *Bertly*," Polly said. He was startled at the harshness of her words. He had never heard Polly speak in an agitated tone and would have even thought it impossible for her to do so.

"What class do we have next?" Bertly questioned in an attempt to lighten the tone of the conversation.

"I am not sure what *your* next class is, Bertly. But *I* have racial history." Polly pressed forward through the crowd. Bertly searched each of his pant and jacket pockets. He pulled out a crumpled piece of paper.

"Polly, can I see your schedule, please?"

Polly avoided eye contact, but she shoved her schedule at his chest. Bertly held the schedules side by side. Once he'd read them in their entireties, he double-checked them due to disbelief. Bertly threw his head back. "Well, it appears we have every class together."

"That's wonderful, Bertly, but I am currently concerned with our *next* class," Polly said.

***

The duo arrived to a half-filled classroom. The desks were squished together and spanned twelve rows back.

"You got lucky this time, Bertly," Polly said. Her body language was more relaxed. Back to normal.

Bertly headed for the back row. But Polly cut him off. "Where are you going, Bertly? We can't see from back there." She grabbed his wrist and led him to the center of the front row. Students filled the room shortly after.

An elf with pale skin and blond hair, poised at the head of the classroom, stood gazing over the students. She tried to divide her attention but kept bringing her eyes back to Bertly and Polly. The bell rang.

"Good morning, class. I am Master Dova. This is Racial History Before the Blight. If you are not taking Racial History *Before* the Blight, then you are in the wrong classroom." A handful of students shuffled out of the room, and Master Dova waited until the last of them had exited before she continued. "Now, before we get into things, let's make sure we are all on the same page. Who can tell me the names of the five realms? Just shout them out, no need to raise your hand."

"Eplium," an elf shouted.

"Bablanca," a young dwarf said.

The room sat quiet. "Is that it, no other lands matter?" Dova asked.

Polly raised her hand.

"Just shout it out," Dova insisted.

"There is Noskar, the home of humans. Eskos, land of the giants. And of course…" Polly waited. "The Decomposite."

"Thank you, miss," Dova said cheerfully. "Now, please do not be shy. We have to break the ice in this class if we ever want an honest discussion. What are some things we know about each of the races?" Dova peered over the still, silent room. "This is a class of cowards, I see."

"Cordelia was the greatest elf," an elven boy answered.

"Cordelia was a dwarf. Everyone knows that." A young dwarf stood up and glared at the elven boy.

The elven boy rose. "You honestly think Cordelia was a halfling?" The whole classroom started to bicker as each race claimed Cordelia as one of their own.

"Settle down," Dova interjected. "I appreciate the

passion, but you should all know by now, Cordelia was believed to be a human. This is the accepted theory. Speaking of which, what do we know about humans?"

Comments flooded in from all over the room.

"They can't learn magic."

"No monsters in Noskar."

"They don't live very long."

"They're weak."

"They stopped the Blight and ended the Great War," Bertly howled. He couldn't help but take the negativity personally. He glanced at Polly to gauge her reaction, but she only displayed the same aloof smile as always.

"That they did," Dova added. She looked toward Bertly and Polly. Her body language was hard to read. Bertly could not tell if she was intrigued or annoyed by Bertly's comment. "Now, what do we know about elves?"

The students participated without hesitation.

"Pointy ears."

"Doctors."

"They're wise."

"Splendid," Dova responded. "And dwarves?"

"They like shiny rocks."

"They're strong."

"They remember everything they read and hear."

"Spectacular. Now, what about giants?" Dova looked over the classroom with wide eyes. She looked to every corner of the room, waiting for a student to speak up.

"They're big," Bertly said. The classroom broke into unified laughter.

"They live in a kingdom that has never fallen," Polly said. "Not even during the Blight. They say no traveler can ever stumble upon Eskos. It is a land that can only be found through instinct. It is said that giants even speak a forgotten language." She paused. "Well, a language that everyone else has forgotten."

Dova stood soundlessly and studied Polly. "Now then, maybe you should be the one teaching this class. Wonderful answer, female human." Dova gave Polly a wink. The bell rang. "Time flies when you're having fun, now doesn't it? Tomorrow please come ready to discuss a champion who is *not* from your realm."

***

"The rest of my day was filled with mathematics and writing courses. I will not bore you with the meager details," Bertly inserted.

Roderick bobbed his head in agreement. "Sounds good, sir. I never was a fan of math."

***

Bertly and Polly sat across from the twins and Almar in the packed dining hall. The tables that stretched the length of the prestigious hall were piled with food and so many dishes that the wooden tabletops were completely obscured.

"This is delicious." Bertly took a bite of a smoky, honey-sweetened turkey leg. He closed his eyes and smiled.

"They say the chefs use spells on the food," Orin shouted.

"Yep, ordinary food, extraordinary taste," Orîn added. They both took bites of their baked potatoes filled with melted butter and topped with cheese.

"I don't care how they do it, to be honest," Bertly grumbled, his mouth full of food, table manners disregarded. "As long as my taste buds keep dancing." Bertly moved on to a new dish before he finished chewing. "How late is this place open?"

"It's always open," the twins replied.

"Always?" Bertly repeated.

"Always." The twins filled their mouths with smoked turkey legs.

"I am quite curious. Did you two have a magic class today?" Almar asked, his eyes flicking between Bertly and Polly.

"Yes, but we didn't learn any magic." Bertly dipped his dinner roll into a creamy soup.

"That's because *someone* made us late." Polly nudged his shoulder.

"Oh, Bertly." Almar shook his head. "Why am I not surprised? Who was your professor?"

"Master Alestar," Bertly answered, once again with a full mouth. The twins and Almar stopped eating. The few students who were eavesdropping gasped.

"You're kidding," the twins challenged. They wiped their mouths with their shirts and gawked at the two humans.

"Seriously, Bertly, you are kidding, aren't you?" Almar repeated. Bertly and Polly glanced at each other. The half smile wiped off Almar's face. "You're serious?" He adjusted his posture. "You two *do know* who Master Alestar is?"

Bertly and Polly gave thin smiles in response. Almar and the twins looked at each other in disbelief. They looked at the surrounding students as well, whose eyes were wide with astonishment.

"He's a legend," the twins exclaimed.

"Master Alestar is the youngest graduate in Academy history. He has discovered nearly half the modern spells we use today." Almar's voice grew louder. "Not only that, rumor is, he soul-bonded with a gryphon." Almar stared at Bertly and Polly with his arms spread wide, awaiting their response.

"What's soul-bonding?" Bertly asked.

Almar let out a big sigh. "This was supposed to be a mind-blowing moment, Bertly, and you ruined it with your ignorance." The students who had been eavesdropping turned away to carry on with their previous conversations. Almar relaxed in his seat. "Soul-bonding is when you merge your soul with an animal's soul. It allows you to control an animal telepathically. The average wizard merges with their dog or koko. But some great wizards can bond with a sabretooth, bear, or even a mammoth. A gryphon is unheard of. It is the most intimidating creature since Cordelia's dragon."

Bertly and Polly's eyebrows rose a notch and their eyes widened.

"Are we going to learn how to soul-bond?" Polly asked.

Almar sat up straight and puffed his chest. "*This* is the response I was looking for. In short, yes. However, the Academy will not teach you until you are in the Mastery program."

"Did you hear that, Bertly?" Polly asked as she jabbed at Bertly with her index finger. "Even more reason to try really hard to make it into the Mastery program." Polly started to ask Almar another question, but Bertly jumped in, interrupting her.

"Does Master Alestar still have his gryphon? Is it *here*?"

"Of course he still has it. You are bonded with your animal until the day you're buried," Almar answered.

"Does he lodge it on campus?"

"I am not sure. No one has seen her in quite some time."

Bertly's racing mind drowned out the surrounding conversations. He didn't want to just be a famous wizard one day, he wanted to be the greatest wizard. Soul-bonding could be his chance to outclass Polly. He understood that a simple creature wouldn't do; Bertly would need to bond with the toughest creature in Pangea. He needed to cement his mark and follow in the footsteps of Cordelia; he needed to bond with a dragon.

IV

The morning bell rang and Bertly sprang out of bed. He needed to be on time for Master Alestar's class.

While Bertly changed his clothes and peered around the room, he spotted Polly's empty bed. "Polly, are you here?" he called out.

A muffled voice emerged from outside the tree cabin. Bertly rushed to finish changing, and once he was fully dressed, he flung open the front door. He came to an immediate halt, as he was still stunned by the fresh grass between his toes and the warm sun beating on his skin; such comforts made Bertly forget what had drawn him outside in the first place. The air smelled as though a thunderstorm had passed during the night.

"Good morning, Bertly. You're up early today. I brought you some breakfast." Polly sat underneath a small tree. The tree had grown to a short height, but it provided just enough shade to protect Polly's fair skin from the sun. She held a book in one hand and a fresh pastry in the other. "I hope you like cheese filling." Polly waved the pastry about for Bertly to see.

Who doesn't like cheese? Bertly thought indignantly as he sat next to Polly despite the fact that he didn't particularly wish to. His stomach growled, and though he wasn't Polly's biggest fan, he found her gesture to be kind.

"Thanks, Polly." Bertly tore off the plain bread edges of the croissant and only ate the cheese filling. "Did you bring that book with you?"

Bertly's stomach suddenly filled with butterflies as he remembered his mother's book. The commotion of his first day had jumbled his mind, and he was annoyed with himself for forgetting about it. His heart raced from excitement. Bertly had never heard the sound of his mother's voice. He didn't know the mannerisms or small quirks that made her unique. This was his first opportunity to connect with his mother.

"I mean, what good school wouldn't have a library, right?" Polly finished.

Bertly looked at Polly. "I'm sorry, I need to grab something from our room." He stood up.

She frowned at him. "Is it important, Bertly? We really should be off to class," Polly urged.

Bertly stood still for a moment. Polly had given him breakfast that morning and informed him of the school library, and she also knew how to navigate the castle better than he did. Bertly knew he wouldn't have time to delve into his mother's book right now, anyway. "It can wait. Maybe we can even arrive before Master Alestar today."

***

Bertly and Polly marched through the classroom doors of room 782. They headed straight for the workbench closest to the front of the class, eager to begin their lesson.

Reclined in a chair, with his feet propped up on a desk, sat Master Alestar. Bertly guessed that he had arrived quite early that morning, based on the chalkboard, which was already filled with notes.

"Look who decided to show up," Master Alestar said. "Maybe we can actually attempt some sorcery today." He leaped out of his chair and sailed toward the chalkboard. "As you can see, we have a lot to cover this morning. First—" Alestar cocked his head to the side. "Where are your notebooks and writing utensils?"

Bertly and Polly looked at each other. Their moon-shaped eyes locked, and both of their faces reddened. They looked back at Master Alestar, but did not answer his question. The answer was, after all, rather apparent.

Alestar smacked his palm against his forehead. "Polly, dearest, open the drawer on your left. There should be some extra notebooks and quills. Please grab one for you and one for Bertly as well." Polly reached into the drawer and pulled out two thin notebooks and a pair of quills, which were identical to the ones they'd used during their entrance exams.

"Sir, I worry we may need more than one each. These are rather...slim." Polly fanned her thumb across the notebook, emphasizing how few pages it contained.

"Then I suggest you write very, very small." Polly's cheeks deepened to an even redder hue at the instructor's comment. Alestar giggled. "Oh my. I've gotten you yet again. I am only kidding. Once you fill the last page, a new one will appear."

Polly sighed and offered a feeble giggle. Master Alestar looked her in the eye. "You need to keep your mind open. Magic's only limits are the ones we give it." Alestar's expression dulled. "There are more red-eyed students at the Academy this year than there ever have been before. I do not think this is a coincidence, magic returning to humans. I am glad the faculty has been able to downplay you two." Alestar turned back to the board.

On the top left-hand side of the chalkboard, the word *Age* was written in bold text. Alestar swiped his finger in the air, and an underline appeared beneath the word.

"Age," Alestar exclaimed. The enthusiasm returned to his voice. "What is the average age of a student who casts their first spell?"

Polly stretched her arm high above her head, wiggling her fingers.

"Yes, Polly?"

"The average age is thirteen, sir," Polly answered.

Alestar's voice grew. "And for hundreds and hundreds of years, that has been true." Alestar strolled in the direction of Bertly and Polly's workbench. "Until you two came along. When I was studying in Eskos, I spent an exceptional amount of time digging through the archives. I unfortunately found a lot of information I had already learned from our library here." Alestar pulled up a barstool and sat across from the two students. "Until one day, I stumbled across a journal. An old classmate of Cordelia, Reynolds." Bertly and Polly adjusted their posture and moved their heads in closer. "He did not mention Cordelia much, but one thing he did subtly imply caught my interest: A story about Cordelia conjuring her first spell at just five years old."

"Five!" Bertly shrieked. "Cordelia never ceases to amaze me." He shook his head.

Alestar leaned over the table. "That is not what I found most interesting. What I couldn't help but notice was that Reynolds was not impressed. He mentioned it quite casually."

Bertly's eyes lost focus. He stared down at the workbench. "Sir, I am not quite sure I understand."

"Don't you see?" Alestar hopped off his stool. "He was not impressed because she did nothing impressive. I believe it was normal for humans to conjure spells before thirteen. Cordelia may have even been average in her spell-casting abilities, for all we know."

"Do you think we can learn spells before we are thirteen, sir?" Polly screamed from excitement, almost falling out of her chair.

Alestar slammed his fists on the workbench. With his pearly-white teeth on full display, he unleashed a great smile. "Yes. I believe you can." He drifted back to the chalkboard. He waved his finger in a circle and chalk outlined nearly half the writing on the board. "Theory. Why do we admit students at ten instead of thirteen?"

Bertly raised his hand, his fingertips barely eye level.

"Male human." Alestar pointed his long finger at Bertly.

"So we can be prepared, sir."

"Precisely," Alestar cried out. "You must crawl before you can walk. We want all students to know the fundamentals of magic *before* they conjure their first spell. Why start learning at thirteen when you can already know hundreds of spells before then?"

Alestar extended his arm in the direction of a stool across the room and formed a fist. The chair slid across the floor faster than a rock across ice. He stopped it with his foot and took a seat.

"Conjuring a spell is no simple task. It takes the greatest level of mind over matter. In order to cast a spell, your mind must be completely clear. I cannot emphasize enough how empty your mind must be." Alestar's voice grew louder. "You cannot possess a single thought. You cannot even think about not thinking. Your mind must temporarily exit your body. Then, just in that moment, you think of the spell you wish to use. Are you with me?"

Polly interjected, "To be clear, we must completely empty our minds. That way the spell we wish to use is the only thing we are thinking about."

"Exactly," Alestar said. "For many students, saying the spell out loud is the easiest way to input the spell into their mind. However, once you have practiced enough, you won't have to say anything at all."

Alestar took a moment to ponder in silence. He glared at Bertly and Polly. "Why are you not writing this down?" His voice echoed throughout the room. Bertly and Polly jumped and followed Alestar's instructions. They started writing profusely.

Alestar returned to pacing at the head of the room. "Today we will start with a simple spell—conjuring a flower. It is called 'Tulipi Demori.'" A green stem grew from Alestar's fingertip, and a bud sprouted from the top end of the stem, shortly growing to the size of a grape before it burst open, blossoming into a cherry-colored tulip. Bertly and Polly watched in awe. Their writing hands lay still, as they could not take their focus off Alestar.

Alestar pranced to the workbench. He moved more gracefully than any giant Bertly had seen. He had always imagined giants as slow and clunky, considering they were half a body taller and a few times thicker than humans. Despite the professor's elegance, the floorboards creaked with each step he took. Alestar broke off the stem and placed the flower in Polly's hair. He glanced at Bertly and then back at Polly. "You try."

They sat with their eyes closed. For a moment, neither of them made a sound.

"Tulipi Demori," Bertly muttered. He peeked at his fingertips with one eye slightly open, but nothing was there. He took a deep breath.

Tulip petals started raining, seemingly from midair. The surfaces of the workbenches filled with crimson-toned flower petals. Bertly peered over at Polly, who held a bouquet of at least two dozen tulips in her hands.

"I knew it!" Alestar threw his hands in the air. "Being simpleminded may serve you wonders after all, little humans." Alestar turned his head in Bertly's direction. "Sweet Cordelia." Between Bertly's fingers rested one elegant, perfect tulip. Alestar grabbed Bertly and Polly by the wrists. "We must see the Elders. *Now.*"

***

Alestar escorted them through ten towers, eight bridges, and thirteen floors. Their destination was the top floor of the highest tower.

"Sit here, and don't touch anything." Alestar put his palm on an ornate blue door. The door was covered in dozens of intricate engravings. Bertly noticed his realm's symbol engraved at the center: a drizzle bird carrying Cordelia's warblade in its talons.

"What do you suppose they are talking about, Bertly?" Polly whispered.

Bertly took his time to answer. "I don't know. I'm guessing what class to put us in next."

Polly nodded.

Bertly and Polly waited with their thumbs twitching and their feet tapping. A creak echoed through the halls, and shortly after, Alestar emerged from the doorway, closing the door behind him.

"The council has come to a decision. We have decided to fast-track both of you. You will begin taking a new set of advanced courses first thing next week."

"That is wonderful news, sir," Polly yelped.

"Please let me finish." Alestar's voice was stern. "You are being fully fast-tracked. Your test scores were already far beyond any first-year students and possibly even some eighth-year students. You will be starting magic courses as though it were the start of your fourth year."

"Wait, sir, that doesn't mean—" Bertly's voice trembled.

"Yes, you will be graduating in eight years. This means you must find a master this year, or you will become ineligible for the Mastery program."

"Isn't the deadline in three days?" Bertly moaned.

Alestar sighed. "I am afraid so. I would not worry so much, little human. Each master chooses their apprentice. You two have become quite notorious. I am sure you will have to fight them off." Alestar winked.

Bertly's stomach sank. Alestar's intentions were appreciated, but Bertly knew he was only saying such things to calm his nerves. Bertly felt he should have let Polly take the glory. He remembered his father's words: *It isn't always so bad being underestimated.*

***

Almar slammed his book on the table, producing a distracting thud that quickly brought the group's attention to him. "Fast-tracked?" Bertly, Polly, Almar, and the twins were studying in the Academy library. From the outside, the library looked uninviting. Faded and cracked stone made up the outside entrance. When entering though, patrons were welcomed by the warm embrace of nostalgia and history. Rounded beams supported several stories, all filled with countless books. The students had heard about the faded brick and cracked stone entrance. It was famous for something; however, no one could remember precisely what.

"You'll move on to the Mastery program at sixteen!" Orin shouted. Orîn chimed in, "That's the youngest ever!"

"Shh." An upperclassman at a nearby table glared at the group. He held his pointer finger over his lips while mouthing the words, "Be quiet."

"Isn't the deadline in two days?" Almar muttered.

"Three," Bertly grumbled.

"I can relate to your suspense. I find out if I get into the Mastery program this week," Almar added. "Do you have any idea who your masters will be?" Almar said under his breath. His voice carried a hint of both jealousy and curiosity.

"I'm not sure. It happened so fast that we haven't had the time to connect with any professors yet." Bertly poked at his untouched food.

"Well…" Polly glanced up at the ceiling, as if considering whether or not she should say what she was about to say. Bertly immediately wished that she would shut her mouth. "I have actually already received a dozen proposals," Polly said. She looked down at her hands as her cheeks reddened. She didn't seem outwardly prideful. Bertly assumed she'd merely made the statement so the group would be aware that it was possible to find a master quickly, on such short notice. Still, he battled with accusing her outright of being a show-off. He held his tongue on that thought, but not his others.

"A dozen?" Bertly exclaimed.

A paper ball struck Bertly in the back of the head. Bertly turned. The same upperclassman as before placed his finger over his lips once again—this time his face was stiffened with rage. "Shh."

"A dozen," Bertly whispered. "Did you talk to anyone?"

"No. I checked the mail, and a stack of letters was waiting for me," Polly said.

"Mail. We get mail?" Bertly peered at Orin and Orîn. The twins were tinkering with a pocket watch. "Did you two know we got mail?"

"Absolutely," the twins said. They kept their heads down as they worked on their watch.

Bertly looked around the table in annoyance.

Polly placed her hand on Bertly's wrist. "Oh, Bertly, you simply raise your hand in the air and recite 'Cordelia, reveal my mail,' and poof, it'll be right there in your hand." Polly gave Bertly a once-over. "Bertly, have you not read the freshman handbook yet?"

Orin and Orîn giggled.

Bertly hadn't heard of any sort of handbook. He grabbed a dinner roll and stuffed it into the pocket of his robe. "Of course I have." He bumped the twins and Almar as he slipped out of his seat. Bertly walked as quickly as possible across the dining hall. He fled through the hall of the main entrance and to the door of the human wing. He plucked a hair from his head and placed it against the wooden door. It opened. Bertly bustled inside and raised his hand high into the air. "Cordelia, reveal my mail."

Nothing appeared. "Reveal my mail, Cordelia." Bertly's hand remained empty. He put his arm back down, then attempted to raise it with extra emphasis— practically punching it into the air. "Cordelia, reveal my mail, please." Still, nothing appeared.

Bertly's heart sank. He had received zero offers. His palms were coated in a film of sweat, and he fell to his knees. After moping for a moment, he sprinted inside and rummaged through his wardrobe until he grasped his knapsack. He reached inside, pulling out the leather-bound notebook his father had given him. He flipped it open and noticed immediately that there was an inscription on the inside.

Time is a virtue only few can enjoy.

Bertly didn't put much thought into the quotation. He turned to the next page.

Lightus: Conjures a floating light that follows the master.
Leveom Pristundis: Creates a magical barrier around caster.
Fleviinio: Creates a small flame.

Reptatis Exolus: Creates a stone covering around flesh of caster.
Clareatous: Heals minor wounds on applied area.

Bertly flipped through dozens of pages. Each of them was cluttered with spells. The names and descriptions were written horizontally, vertically, and diagonally, and there was scarcely a blank spot on any given page, as the author had crammed as much information as she possibly could into the book. Bertly opened the last page. There was nothing. He flipped back several pages until he found writing again.

There is so much to discover.

Bertly closed the book, gripped it tightly, and flopped onto his bed. He had a difficult time concentrating on any single thought. He heard the entrance door to the dormitory opening and slid his book under his pillow.

"Are you okay, Bertly? You seemed to leave in quite a rush." Polly gave him a lopsided grin.

"I'm fine, Polly. I just wanted to get some sleep." Bertly rolled over onto his side and pulled his thick comforter over his head. He heard Polly sit on her bed and rifle through her belongings.

Bertly reached under his pillow and pulled out his spell book once again. He opened it up to the second page, but had a tough time making out the words—it was too dark beneath the blanket for him to read the pages. He wished Polly would stop studying so he could dive into the spells his mother had left for him. *What did the first page say?* Bertly whispered, "Lightus." A dim light appeared and illuminated the small area under Bertly's comforter. His eyes widened in delight.

More thoughts rushed through the young wizard's mind than he could filter, but one kept recurring. *How did my mother obtain these spells? Did she learn them, or did she know them?* Accepting that humans couldn't learn magic, Bertly dropped the thought before he sent himself on a journey he couldn't complete. This wasn't hard because the boy's greed overtook him; this was his chance to surpass Polly. He recognized there was no way she had something at her disposal like his mother's journal. Bertly's mind flipped back to his mother. *But I am a human who knows magic,* he pondered. *Could she also have had red eyes?* The wizard shook his head side to side. *She would have been the most famous woman in all of the winter land if she had been red eyed,* he reasoned with himself. Bertly needed to find a way back home to speak with his father. He had more questions than ever.

Bertly's attention couldn't be pulled away as he devoured the journal, reading every spell and examining each page as carefully as possible. The sound of the morning bell made Bertly jump. A few minutes had turned into a dozen hours, and he hadn't even noticed them go by.

V

Polly and Bertly sat in room 782, quills in hand and eyes glued to the board. The school year had only started, but their notebooks were already thicker than any of their textbooks. Master Alestar had taught them more and poured more information down their throats than all of their other classes combined.

"Have you been able to socialize with any professors yet?" Polly whispered.

"No," Bertly dismissively replied.

"Aren't you worried about being matched up with a master this week?" she probed.

"No." Bertly turned his head toward Polly and glared. "Why would I be? I'm excited." Bertly, however, was nervous for his upcoming magic lesson with Master Alestar. The young human's hands were sweaty from how tight he was gripping his writing tool.

Alestar cleared his throat and puffed out his chest. "You know, they have magic for a reason, small humans," he said. "Try this spell. I made it up myself; it couldn't be simpler." The giant waved his hand, and the words *penmanship partnership* appeared on the chalkboard. He grabbed a quill and recited the words, then placed his quill on a piece of parchment. "Why write when the universe will do it for you?" As he spoke, the quill recorded each of his words.

Polly and Bertly grabbed their quills and repeated the words *penmanship partnership*. Neither of their quills stood on their own.

"You can't just say it," Master Alestar grunted. "You have to *say* it."

Bertly and Polly tried once more. This time Bertly did his best to add meaning to the words. He was unsure exactly what his teacher expected from him, but he tried his best to send his energy to the inked feather.

The quill stood on its own. "Wait, we could have been doing this the whole time?" Bertly whispered to Polly—the quill automatically recording every word he spoke inside his notebook. "I have permanent hand cramps already."

"Bertly," Master Alestar blurted, "is there something you would like to share with the class?"

Bertly looked around the empty classroom. He and Polly were the only students in human magic. "Sir, I believe I *have* shared it with the class." He gulped.

Alestar snapped his fingers and Bertly's quill caught fire and turned to ash within milliseconds. The young human looked at his dusty notebook with his jaw wide open. He did not know whether to be amazed by how easy magic was for Master Alestar or to be concerned with how he would take notes.

Bertly found his backup quill and tried the enchantment once more; it worked on his first try. Alestar snapped his fingers again, turning the human's second quill into ash.

Master Alestar continued as though nothing had happened. "The Academy doesn't want you to know this, but what the Academy wants its students to know and what students *should* know are two very different things," the giant said. "Are you with me so far?"

Polly raised her hand. "Do you mean something like forbidden magic, sir?"

"I wouldn't use the word *forbidden*." Alestar tapped his finger on his lips. "Maybe *discouraged* is a better word." The professor pulled out a glove, holding it inside his gargantuan palm, where it appeared tiny. "I am going to teach you about enchanted items."

"Yes." Bertly pumped his fist. "Yes, yes, yes."

"Ah, so you are familiar?" Alestar asked.

"Of course, sir," Bertly replied. "It's every wizard's dream to learn to enchant items, but I was always taught that only the select few the Academy chooses are allowed to actually do it."

"That is absolutely correct, little human." Alestar cleared the chalkboard and made space for more material. "The Academy, a long time ago, used to teach every wizard in the Mastery program how to enchant weapons; however, there were a lot of problems with the creation of illegal weapons and elixirs." The chiseled giant shook his head. "Their response was to ban the creation and teaching of enchanted items altogether. Now they only teach a few long-term masters how to do it. It is a shame. There used to be magic shops scattered all across Pangea. Now most of the enchanted items in the world are sold on the dark market. Aside from a few basic items."

Polly raised her hand. "Then why do they bother teaching any masters?"

"Wonderful question, young lady," Alestar responded. "Because the Academy still uses enchanted items themselves. Quite hypocritical, yes. But nonetheless, today I will be teaching you how."

Alestar strolled over to Polly and Bertly. "It is said that humans and dwarves were the first to ever discover enchanting. Who knows, it may come naturally to you." He placed the glove he was holding in the center of their worktable. Around the cuff, Bertly noticed there was a small leaf symbol stitched on. "This will also be great preparation for when you need to soul-bond. The magic is essentially the same; soul-bonding is simply on a much grander scale. The key difference is you must know the elements inside whatever it is you are enchanting. Mix the wrong compounds and the results can be...devastating."

Bertly shifted uneasily in his seat.

Alestar clapped. "But that is the worst-case scenario. We aren't bothered with that." He pointed his finger in the air. "You must take risks if you want to be the best."

Bertly reached into the drawer on the side of the workbench and pulled out an extra quill. At the top of his notes for the day he wrote, *You must take risks if you want to be the best.*

"I assume it goes without saying; however, I will recite it anyway." Alestar looked Polly dead in the eyes, then quickly focused his attention on Bertly. His eyebrows were narrowed, and his eyes moved up and down, as though he were looking for something. "Under no circumstances shall you tell anyone or anything what you learn here today. Is that understood?"

"Yes, sir," Bertly and Polly answered.

"Except for those two dwarves you always run around with," Alestar continued. "I went to school with their father. Excellent dwarf. You can tell them. Anyway—" the giant hollered, cutting himself off from his rambling. "You see this glove here? It appears to be a typical glove." He waved the leather glove around. "However, it is much more than the eye can see. When one wears this glove, it amplifies the user's magical ability. How did I do this, you wonder?" Alestar threw his hands in the air. "Great question. I combined it with drizzle bird blossom, one of the rarest plants in all of Pangea. It holds some of the greatest rejuvenation abilities known. By combining its power with that of a battle glove, you have yourself a glove that can repower the master or help him or her quickly recover. It allows you to put a lot more *oomph* into your spells." Alestar tossed the red glove to Polly. "Here, you take it, it is much too small for me, and Bertly will grow out of it in no time."

"Wow." Polly slipped on the glove. "Thank you so much, sir. I don't know what to say."

"'Thank you' is enough," the giant replied with a glowing smile.

Alestar bent over, reached under the workbench, and pulled out a handful of items. First, he placed a clay pot in the center of the table. "Right now, this is an ordinary pot; however, we can link it with an ordinary spell to make something extraordinary." Alestar placed his hands on the side of the jar and closed his eyes. "If I add a simple conjuring spell, such as water summoning." He turned the pot to show them the inside. "We now have a self-watering pot. You'll never have to worry about killing a pretty lily again." The inside of the pot had a few drops running down the side, not enough to drown a plant— just enough to keep it properly watered.

"Splendid, sir." Polly beamed. "I can only imagine all the wonderful items that could be made with such simple magic."

"Simple, yes. But not easy," Alestar warned. "For a powerful wizard it is easy, but a weak wizard cannot accomplish it." Alestar strolled toward his desk and lifted a light rock off the surface. "You see this stone? Picking it up is quite an easy concept, no? Everyone knows *how* to pick up a rock. However"—he placed the rock in between Bertly and Polly—"that does not mean everyone is strong enough." He gestured for them to try to lift it.

Bertly grabbed the stone and attempted to pick it up off the table. It didn't budge. The young wizard put both hands around the stone and tried to pull it toward himself—it hardly moved.

"Dwarven steel," Alestar called out. "The densest material in the world. If a dwarf is strong enough to wear the armor, there is no blade that can pierce it." Alestar picked the rock up with ease and placed it back on his desk. "Sometimes, things are more than they appear."

"Sir, I have just one question," Bertly said.

"Only one?" Alestar shook his head. "You should be more curious, young wizard."

"I am, sir," Bertly replied. "But like you said, this magic seems simple. It mostly requires practice by a strong wizard. My question is, why does Polly's glove have a symbol, but the pot does not?"

"You are asking the right questions, future master," Alestar shouted, clapping his hands in excitement. "Some items are much more powerful than others. In order for these items to harness such great powers, much more powerful magic must be used. We do this by etching in symbols that pertain to that element on the side."

Polly's quill moved on its own as Bertly frantically jotted down notes.

Alestar continued. "For example, if you choose to create a fire dagger, one would combine something with a fire element, along with etching a symbol of a flame on the side. When creating a corresponding symbol, it amplifies the magic that can be used. Keep in mind, you cannot doodle whatever you wish; each symbol must also be given its own enchantment." Alestar took a breath. "But we will get to that some other time. For now, baby steps."

The talkative giant grabbed a basic pot and placed it before Bertly. He reached for a bag sitting atop the table and untied the knot, keeping it closed. He flipped the bag over, and out poured fresh dirt into the empty pot.

"Okay, future botanist," Alestar cracked. "Show me how green your thumb really is."

Polly chuckled at Alestar's joke.

"Don't take too much amusement; you're next."

Polly's eyes widened, and she placed her hands over her mouth.

Bertly was ready to impress his teacher. The giant might not have guessed it, but Bertly's father was an avid gardener. Edfrid had crammed information into Bertly's head about plants and "proper soil for leafy friends" every harvest. The young wizard closed his eyes and recollected the lessons his father had attempted to teach him. Nitrogen, phosphorus, and potassium—key ingredients to healthy soil. The young wizard placed his hands into the soil and shut his eyes.

Bertly focused on each feeling in his body. The pressure of his heels on the ground. The softness of the shirt resting on his skin. He was unsure whether it was in his mind or actually happening, but the young wizard felt the blood coursing through his veins. He felt the energy inside his body and was able to pinpoint it as though it were physical and could be removed. He pushed the energy to his fingertips and released it into the dirt. He looked up at his professor.

Master Alestar scooted the pot away from Bertly. He ran his hand through the soil and rubbed the dirt between his fingertips. Alestar put his nose just over the filled jar and inhaled. "Hmm." He took a pinch of dirt and tossed it into his mouth. He swished it around as though he were rinsing his teeth. "Nitrogen enriched. Phosphorus. Potassium checks out. My small, tiny human apprentice, you may just be the worst mage in the world. This dirt tastes awful."

"Sir, are you serious?" Bertly looked at Alestar, cold and somber. "You're telling me you've eaten better dirt?"

"I haven't had worse." The giant spit the dirt back into the clay pot. "I am only kidding, Bertly." He ruffled the young human's long hair. "You may be the greatest wizard this time has ever seen…only time will tell."

"Seriously, sir?" Bertly blushed and he sat up in his seat. It took a lot to receive a genuine compliment from Master Alestar. "Do you really think I will become the greatest sorcerer of this time?"

"Oh, sweet Cordelia, no. Of course not." Alestar pulled out a new pot and filled it with dirt. "I said you would be the greatest *wizard*, not sorcerer. Polly will definitely be more powerful than you. I was only trying to make you feel better."

Bertly slouched back in his seat and crossed his arms. "Thanks, sir."

"Let's see what you can do, tiny blonde." Alestar positioned the clay pot in front of Polly.

The school bell rang.

"Shucks." Alestar slapped the side of his leg. "We will pick up where we left off tomorrow."

Bertly and Polly closed their notebooks, packed up their belongings, and headed for their next class—botany.

***

Bertly and Polly had their hands placed on top of glass jars with bunny beans hopping around inside. Each bean sprang around as if it were stepping on something hot. The young humans wore goggles covering more than half of their faces. They sat inside a lab, with gloves on and their hair tied back.

"I wish we could actually go outside for our gardening class," Bertly mumbled to Polly.

"Do not take your hands off the containers, please." A female elf with wrinkled skin and white hair spoke softly to the class. Bertly couldn't remember her name for the life of him. "The beans are strong enough to knock those glasses right over. Take turns one at a time observing the bunny beans as your partner holds the container down," the old elf carried on.

"What exactly am I looking for?" Bertly asked.

Polly waved a piece of paper in front of his face. "Why don't you ever check the worksheets, Bertly?"

"I thought those were just guidelines." He dismissed her.

"Yes, for passing the assignment." Polly grabbed Bertly's hand and placed it on top of the see-through container. "Hold this." She ran her finger down the paper. "It says we need to identify their age. We can tell by how many spots are on their stomachs."

"Don't you find it a little disturbing that elves and dwarves eat stew made out of beans that look like cute little bunnies?" Bertly questioned.

"I think we should worry about the assignment and not what other cultures eat." Polly pointed her finger around the glass, mouthing numbers to herself. She wrote down the age of one bean in her notebook. "I'm sure some other students think what we eat is weird."

"We eat mostly meat and potatoes. It's not very controversial." Bertly snickered.

Polly ignored his comment and continued to count the number of spots on each bean. Bertly cracked his knuckles and looked around the room at the other students. He wondered if another human would ever stroll through those doors or if it would always be just him and Polly.

"Bertly," Polly cried, "you took your hand off the jar."

Bertly jumped back and frantically looked around. The dozen or so beans were hopping in every direction. The beans were small, but they leapt higher than Bertly could

reach, and farther than he could stretch. The young
human cupped his hands and managed to trap one under
his domed fists. He looked for a place to lock it up. His
initial reaction was to place the fruit, vegetable, or
whatever family a bean belonged in, back into the original
glass jar; however, it was now bouncing uncontrollably. If
Bertly opened his hands, he presumed the bean would
slip right out. He couldn't help but wonder how the old
professor had managed to secure the bouncing bunnies in
the first place. She must have used a spell.

Bertly trapped the bean in his left fist then continued
to hunt down the remaining bouncing bunnies. The
young human looked over their workbench at the beans,
which were scattered everywhere. A few were on the
other side of the workbench, a few more on the floor,
and another handful were approaching the workbenches
of Bertly's fellow students.

Polly crawled around, smacking her cupped hands on
the floor. "I can't believe you, Bertly." Every time she
caught a bean, it slipped out of her fingers. "You couldn't
even make it five minutes into class this time before
inciting some incident because you don't want to read the
worksheets."

Screams sounded in a chain reaction, starting near
Bertly and slowly spreading to the other side of the
classroom. Unsuspecting students had tiny beans bounce
up their arms and into their hair, causing them to knock
over their jars—releasing more bunnies freely into the
room.

"Please calm down," the professor pleaded. "They are
completely harmless."

"I think one bit me," a student screamed amongst the
chaos.

"Oh, please," Bertly hollered back. His classmates
were only being dramatic. "They don't even have—

ouch." The young human whipped his hand back. He'd felt a small pinch inside his fist containing the beans. "Maybe they do have teeth," he mumbled to himself.

"They're in my clothes!"

"I think I saw one laying eggs!"

Vials crashed, and smashed test tubes sounded off like an orchestra of destruction. The professor screamed and pleaded for the students to calm down, but pandemonium had already struck. Students darted about, most of them out the doors, and a couple even fled through the first-floor windows. If Bertly didn't know any better, he would have assumed a famous witch or wizard was in town.

A light pink haze filled the room, and the beans dropped to whatever surface lay under them. Bertly was dizzy—not so dizzy he couldn't see straight, but enough to force him to sit. His bones felt light. He gazed over the classroom; the screams had stopped, and everyone was relaxed, either on the floor or the benches.

The old professor stood on top of her desk with her arms spread over the class—a pink haze discharging from her hands. She locked eyes with the young humans. "Bertly, Polly…the Elders' room. Now."

***

Bertly and Polly sat on the bench of an empty meeting room before a panel of nine seats. Most of the chairs were empty; however, Master Dova, Master Quinric, as well as Master Alestar occupied the few seats that were filled.

"What do you have to say for yourself?" Master Quinric snarled, spit flying from his mouth. "Most students would be suspended at the very least for such despicable behavior."

"We didn't mean any harm," Polly pleaded.

"And they speak out of turn." Quinric slammed his fists on the podium before him.

"Master Quinric, please show some restraint," Master Dova commented. "I am sure this was all a simple mistake."

"Are we going to ignore the fact that the old woman was being completely reckless, maybe even negligent?" Alestar interposed. "Every master knows it is strictly forbidden for lowerclassmen to study, tamper with, or experiment on any living creatures outside of a locked cage or habitat." The giant leaned back in his massive chair. "I am afraid the old bat may have broken more school rules than our helpless first years who are currently on trial."

"Are you mad?" Quinric snapped.

Master Dova took a long breath. "I am sorry, Quin, but I am afraid Master Alestar is correct. If we punish Bertly and Polly, then poor Miss Clover may suffer a worse fate."

That's her name. How could I have forgotten that one? Bertly's distracted mind reflected.

"You two get off easily this time," Master Dova continued. "But I would be wary if I were you. The Academy has close eyes on you both."

Bertly had to hold back a smile from the satisfaction he felt at Master Quinric's manic face—he really didn't understand why the old master despised him and Polly so much.

Bertly opened his mouth to speak, yet before a word could slip from between his lips, Polly spoke over him. "Thank you very much for your understanding," she said. "We won't be in here again, we promise."

"See you two tomorrow." Alestar winked.

Polly grabbed Bertly by the sleeve and dragged him

out of the interrogation room—or so it felt. Once the two reached an empty hallway, Polly stopped walking and turned Bertly toward her. "Don't you dare get me kicked out of this school, Bertly." Her already red eyes were blazing. "Or I swear—" Polly cleared her throat. She stepped back and brushed the lint off her clothing. "Just don't do anything stupid, okay?" Polly grinned, her eyes easily giving away her fake smile.

The young wizard wiped his sweaty palms against his pant leg. "Understood," he assured her. "Getting expelled is the last thing I want also."

"Good." Polly's eyes eased up. "Because I think we still have a lot to learn. Speaking of which." Polly tilted her head to the side. "Are you ready for our test tomorrow?"

"Test?" Bertly asked. "What test?"

Polly laughed and crossed her arms over her stomach. "Oh, Bertly, that's a good one."

VI

After three days of stress and no master, Bertly found himself sitting in racial history class, barely able to pay attention to his studies. He only had one hour left to find a master. Rather, a master had only an hour to find him.

Master Dova glanced at the hourglass in the back corner. "It seems we still have a little time. Now, let's get started on next week's lesson." Dova faced the crammed chalkboard and waved her hand to clear it. She flicked her finger and wrote across the board: "The Decomposite." She turned her attention to the class. "You know the drill."

A student from the back row shouted, "Dragons." The classroom cheered.

"Famous weapons," another voice projected.

"Forgotten spells."

"Hidden treasure."

"The Decomposite is a banned territory and is accompanied by nothing but death," Master Dova said in a chiding tone. The class fell silent.

Polly's voice trembled as she spoke up. "The Decomposite is glorified, but very few who travel there ever return."

"Pessimistic, but true. No realm permits traveling to the Decomposite." Dova nodded at Polly. "The

Decomposite is filled with wonder. However, very few who go there ever find what they seek." Dova flared her finger. "Death" was written across the chalkboard. "Every living creature in the Decomposite is the last of its kind. Every last beast by instinct travels to the Decomposite to protect its species. Once there, they become immortal by nature, but can choose mortality. When might a creature from the Decomposite choose a mortal life?"

There was no response from the class. Master Dova tried to make eye contact with some of the students, but they looked away or fiddled with their quills as soon as her eyes swept over them. She glanced at Bertly, who made eye contact with her by accident. "Bertly, what are your thoughts?"

Bertly rubbed his chin. "Um, possibly to soul-bond?" He gave a half shrug.

"Clever thinking, Bertly. That is not the most common reason for choosing mortality, but I could see it being a realistic one. Typically, creatures cannot handle the depressing life in the Decomposite, so they often try to return to Pangea. It is not long after returning to Pangea before most are hunted down. Either as a trophy or to sell to merchants for a high price. One dragon could make a family rich for at least three generations. Therefore, most rare monsters often don't make it past the Remnant Forest surrounding the Decomposite."

The tower bell echoed through the classroom. The students quickly packed their bags and shuffled toward the exit. "We will finish up the lesson on the Decomposite tomorrow," Dova added before everyone could leave.

Bertly was the first out the door. He only had thirty minutes left to find a master, so he hustled across the castle and stormed into his dormitory. *This is the end. After*

today my chances of becoming a master are over. Bertly smashed
his knapsack into the wall and fell face-first onto his bed.
He yelled as loud as he could into his pillow as his eyes
filled with tears. He rested for a moment and collected
himself before sitting back up and staring dead-eyed at
the ground. *Cordelia, please.* Bertly raised his hand in the
air. "Cordelia, reveal my mail."

Finally, a piece of parchment materialized between his
fingers. He sat still with his arm in the air, almost afraid to
look at it. He was terrified that it would not be an
invitation, but instead a notice that he'd missed the
deadline after all. With his eyes closed, he slowly moved
the piece of paper down through the air until it rested in
front of his face. After taking a few deep breaths and
exhaling them slowly, he opened his eyes to read the text.

Dear Bertly, son of Edfrid,

*Congratulations on receiving an offer from Master Alestar. If
you wish to accept Master Alestar as your master, please state
"Cordelia, I accept." If you wish to deny this motion, please state
"Cordelia, I do not accept." Please submit your answer before the
next cycle.*

Bertly jumped to his feet and shouted, "Cordelia, I
accept!"

***

"Sir, I had no idea this is how Master Alestar asked you to
be his apprentice." Roderick had a glowing smile across
his face. "This is exactly how you asked me. Why didn't
you tell me it was tradition?"

Bertly stared at Roderick with a blank look on his face.
"Oh, of course…that is *exactly* why I waited until the last
minute to ask you." Bertly faked a smile and signaled for
Roderick to continue writing.

***

Bertly, letter in hand, sprinted out of the human wing and headed straight for the library. He scanned the room for his friends, but quickly remembered that it was dinnertime as he took in the empty seats and unoccupied rows of books. Bertly bustled out of the library—bumping anyone who got in his way—and dashed through the dining hall toward his friends, knocking plates and cups out of his classmates' hands. "You aren't going to believe who just—"

"I don't know what I'm going to do. I can't go back home. All of my siblings have already gotten into the Mastery program." Tears rushed down Almar's face. Polly and the twins rubbed his back while they listened to him ramble. About what, Bertly was not certain. He understood, however, that he would not be getting accolades from his friends for landing a prestigious master, and he was irked by this knowledge. His curiosity got the better of him, however, and he pushed his own self-importance to the side.

Bertly walked up behind the group. "What's going on?"

"I didn't make it into the Mastery program, Bertly," Almar lashed out, his voice loud and his hands balled into fists. Almar looked at the ground after his outburst and shook his head.

Bertly's stomach dropped. Almar was one of the smartest elves he knew. "What?" Tears formed in the corners of Bertly's eyes.

"That's it, Bertly, I'm done." Almar wiped his eyes. "Tomorrow morning I receive my certification to perform legal magic, and that's it. I have to go and find a job somewhere." Almar blew his nose into a handkerchief. "I will never get to soul-bond or take my spirit quest."

Bertly flopped on top of Almar, giving him a big hug. Almar hesitated. Then he wrapped his arms so tightly around Bertly that Bertly could barely breathe.

***

Bertly turned away from Roderick and walked to the corner of the room, plopping onto the misshaped bed that took up a large portion of the room. It was fully covered by a blanket of long brown fur. "What was at stake became real for me that day. Acceptance into the Mastery program wasn't to be assumed." Bertly paused. "I had to say goodbye to my first friend in order to learn that."

"I am sorry, sir. I was the only one out of all my friends who got into the Mastery program. I know how you feel." Roderick gave Bertly an empathetic look.

Bertly pulled a piece of string from his pocket and used it to tie his hair into a sloppy bun. He laid the back of his head against the furry blanket. "My master taught me a great deal over the years that came to pass. Enough to prepare me for the carnage that would come during my time as a master." Bertly pointed at the parchment Roderick was writing on. Roderick nodded and continued to write while Bertly dictated the timeline.

***

It was a fortnight before Drizzle Day and Bertly sat with his apprentice overlooking Eplium. The sky was dark, and the city could hardly be seen—

***

"Wait, sir. Are you seriously skipping ahead nearly eight years?" Roderick sat back in his chair. "But what about your entire time at the Academy?"

"I am skipping the boring parts, Roderick. If we went through and added every small, minute detail, we would be here for the rest of eternity. This is a necessary time leap. Now, stop questioning my methods." Bertly sat up and gave his apprentice a dirty look. "Do you really want to hear about me studying spells every day for twelve hours? Every advanced course I ever enrolled in? All the useless spells Polly and I created?" Bertly's tone soothed. "Trust me, I am doing you a favor."

"Well, sir, yes, I sort of do," Roderick responded.

"Roderick, you know we do not have time for this. We must finish my novella before morning. You-know-who will be here before the crack of dawn," Bertly emphasized.

Roderick slouched in his chair and fidgeted with the parchment in front of him.

Bertly sighed. "Fine. Year one, Polly and I learned the fundamentals. We studied every spell the Academy had on file and practiced our pronunciation until we spoke everything with perfection. Year two, Polly and I started conjuring spells nearly every day. Year three, Polly and I wrapped up our racial history and culture classes. Year four, Polly and I started combat training. I was the top of our class, I might add. We also started to learn minor healing spells—the elves caught on the quickest, naturally. By year five, we were both able to conjure every spell we knew nonverbally. Polly and I also finished our training on how to be a good master." Bertly stopped for air. "There, now you know everything. Wasn't that exciting? Can we please move on?"

"Yes, sir, very detailed…can you at least tell me how you got the curfew reinstated?" Roderick begged.

The corner of Bertly's mouth quivered. "Fair enough, young apprentice. But first, tell me what you have heard." Bertly crossed his arms and shot Roderick a probing look.

"Well, sir, some people say you unleashed alligators into the elven dormitory."

"That was the twins," Bertly corrected.

"Others say you gave the Grand Elder a heart attack," Roderick said, with one of his eyebrows raised curiously.

Bertly scoffed. "That Elder died of entirely natural causes. He inspected Cordelia during her entrance exam, for goodness' sake. Next." He gave a dismissive hand wave.

"The most famous story is…" Roderick paused, but Bertly, growing impatient, urged him to continue. "That you stole your master's gryphon and started the second Blight." Roderick twisted the ring on his finger and avoided meeting Bertly's eyes.

Bertly sank into the fluffy bed. "Sadly, that one is the closest story to the truth." He gestured for Roderick to take note.

***

Bertly stood at a workbench with empty stools on both sides of him. He poured a green liquid into a vial of blue sand and snapped his fingers to light a fire beneath the sand. He stuck out his free hand, beckoning his stir stick, which floated effortlessly into his palm, and he used it to mix the solution, creating a giant pink cloud of smoke. He twirled his finger and the smoke cleared. Left inside the vial was a thick turquoise liquid. "I finished the stealth elixir, sir. What did you say we needed this for?"

"I didn't." Alestar was at the workbench next to Bertly, tinkering with an old sword. "How long have you been my apprentice, tiny human?"

"Just over five years now, sir," Bertly proudly replied.

"And you are moving on to the Mastery program next month." Alestar peered at Bertly and shook his head. "Astonishing. I can't say I don't credit myself mostly for the achievement." Alestar stared blankly at a point Bertly could not see. "A sixteen-year-old master." He snapped back. "You never would have made it this far if *I* weren't your mentor."

Bertly glared at Alestar and snapped his fingers. A gust of wind blew over Alestar's workbench, sending papers flying in every direction. "Weird, someone must have left the window open." Bertly tried to hold back his smile.

"Yes, most bizarre." Alestar waved his hand, sending his own gust of wind blowing throughout the room, knocking test tubes onto the floor, where they burst into many small pieces. Bertly stumbled back and fell over. "Weird, there it is again." Alestar winked.

Bertly picked himself up. "Well, sir, are you going to tell me what the elixir I've made is for? And why you have been polishing that sword all week?"

"I am disappointed in your lack of observation, little apprentice. I have been polishing *two* swords all week." Alestar reached behind his desk and revealed a second sword. "Tell me, how are you with a blade? I've searched the records but did not find your combat results from the entrance exam."

"How am I with a blade?" Bertly's stomach dropped. His hand craved the grip of a sword. "My whole life I dreamed of becoming the world's greatest soldier. I never wanted anything more than to bring prestige back to my race. My father is the warden of Stonebank. He trained me every single day in combat ever since I was old enough to stand."

Alestar strolled over to Bertly, sword in hand. "I asked if you were good with a blade, not for your life story. Not to mention, you still didn't answer my question." He presented the sword to Bertly.

Bertly grasped the sword and held it in the air, admiring the narrow, jagged blade. "Sir, I am more confident with a blade than a mermaid is in the ocean."

"Good. You may need to be. How fast can you pack your things?" Alestar's words were quiet and rushed.

"I have a travel-sized knapsack with me. I can leave now." Bertly started organizing his belongings, along with a few supplies from the classroom. "Sir, where are we going?"

"We are going to the Decomposite," Alestar stated bluntly.

Bertly dropped the items he was holding. "Sir, you're kidding. The Decomposite is strictly forbidden."

"Do you trust me?" Alestar looked deep into Bertly's eyes.

Bertly's hands started to sweat. "Yes," he replied. But only because he knew it was the answer his master expected of him. The Decomposite was dangerous. Alestar was rather old. Had he become demented at some point without Bertly having noticed? He had been sharpening swords and generally acting odd, but even that behavior wasn't out of line for his master.

"I will explain more on the way. But we must leave. Now. We, unfortunately, are running low on time." Alestar grabbed a prepacked bag and led Bertly out of the room. They headed toward the back gates of the castle.

"The stables, sir?" Bertly asked.

"Yes, did you plan to walk all the way to the Decomposite?" Alestar questioned. "I have a friend I would like you to meet." Alestar pulled open the heavy wooden gates. He walked to the back wall of the stables and traced a pattern along the stone bricks—which shuffled around, creating an entryway.

"You first." Alestar nudged Bertly through the entrance. The room led to an outdoor courtyard. Alestar whistled. The distant snap of large wings emerged, and a massive creature swept in. Its wingspan was at least thirty feet, from what Bertly could gauge. It had back claws like a lion, accompanied by razor-sharp talons on its front legs. It was covered in feathers and had a head shaped like an eagle. Bertly stumbled backward at the sight of the creature. He'd only heard tales of it, but there it stood before him. It was a gryphon.

It landed gracefully and rushed over to meet Alestar. The creature rubbed its face all over its owner. "Okay, okay, settle down now," Alestar said through small bursts of laughter. The gryphon jumped on top of him, sending Alestar crashing to the ground. "Clia, calm down, girl. You act as though I didn't see you yesterday. I have someone I want you to meet."

Clia hopped off Alestar and looked over at Bertly.

"This is Bertly, my apprentice. We like him." Alestar waved Bertly over.

"Stick out your hand and let her come to you," Alestar instructed. The gryphon stood even taller than Master Alestar. Bertly extended his shaking hand and flinched as Clia approached him and cautiously sniffed his fingers. After she'd had enough of sniffing, she pounced on top of him and rubbed her face on him just as she had done to Alestar. Bertly's nervousness turned into excitement as he let out a monstrous laugh.

"Would you look at that? She likes you." Alestar chuckled. "I hate to break up the party, but we are in a hurry."

Alestar whistled. Clia popped up onto her feet and bowed down for Alestar to climb onto her back. "Come on over, Bertly, and hold on tight."

Bertly mounted Clia, gripping her feathers as tight as

he could. Clia flapped her wings, stirring up a great dust cloud underneath them.

***

"Sir, you got to ride a gryphon?" Roderick shrieked.

"Roderick, do you or do you not want to know how I got the curfew reinstated?" Bertly demanded.

"Sorry, sir. Please continue. I was merely excited. The gryphon is the rarest creature in all of Pangea. Even more so than a dragon." The elf squealed.

***

The wind blew through Bertly's hair as the gryphon soared into the sky. Even during the toughest storm, he had never felt a wind so strong against his skin. After only a minute of flight, the massive castle faded into a small pinpoint on the horizon.

"Something else, isn't it?" Alestar was sitting behind Bertly, keeping him secure on the large beast.

"I don't know how to describe it, sir." Bertly looked over all of Pangea. If he'd climbed the highest mountain in the world, he would still not have had such a view.

"Luckily with Clia here, we can turn a two-week hike into a few-hour flight." Alestar patted her gently on the side. "I know you must be confused, Bertly, so I am going to be completely honest with you. You may not be ready to hear this, but I am not sure we have much of a choice." Alestar eased up on the reins, and Clia stopped generously flapping her wings and turned to gliding. "I do not think that the phenomenon of us having more red-eyed citizens than ever is a good thing."

"It could be from population growth, sir," Bertly chimed in.

"Not this quickly, Bertly. The Academy student body has nearly quintupled in just a few years. Cordelia is creating as many red-eyed inhabitants as possible. She is building an army."

"An army?" Bertly shouted. "What the heavens for? The world is at peace for the most part, aside from standard, petty criminals. And even the crime rate hasn't risen much in the past few years. What could she possibly need an army for?"

"That is what we are going to find out. For the last few decades, on the same date each year, I receive a letter from an old friend in the Decomposite. It has been two months and I have not heard from him. He is protecting something that *cannot* fall into the wrong hands." Alestar's body tensed. "Shortly before you and Polly arrived, the Grand Elder revealed a prophecy: 'When it is Cordelia's time, a pureblood shall rise from mankind. An army shall render, for all life will hinder.'" Alestar took a deep breath. "Mankind hasn't had a red-eyed host since Cordelia herself. Then you and Polly come along."

"Sir, you think Polly and I are the purebloods?" Bertly gasped.

"Yes, I do. And I think the rise in red-eyed bodies is the army." Alestar made a chirping sound and Clia started her descent. Bertly felt the air grow thicker, and a chill worked up somewhere beneath the wind. "If it is truly Cordelia's time, then we have dark days ahead of us. The last time Cordelia came to us, she was here to end the Blight. If she is returning, then so is the Blight."

Bertly's eyebrows squished together. "The Blight, sir?" His palms began to sweat, he felt nauseous. "Like when the undead roamed the planet?"

"Precisely," the giant responded. Bertly was concerned by the lack of concern in Alestar's voice.

"Why are you so calm about this, sir?" the young

human couldn't help but ask.

Alestar smirked. "That is a fair question." He looked back at Bertly. "Because, even if the Blight has returned, it will take decades before any sizable army could be constructed. We have time. Plus, you and Polly are here now." He looked back ahead. "The last human who possessed magic, as we all know, was Cordelia. Therefore, I find it hard to believe that you two won't surpass even the most experienced wizarding families."

Constructed? Bertly pondered. *Why would Alestar choose this word?*

Clia descended until she hovered just above the tree line. "Look just ahead. You can see the Remnant Forest." A dense forest compiled of dead trees filled the horizon. The leaves were black and dehydrated. "Thank Cordelia for Clia here; we can soar right over it." Alestar scratched her behind the ear, and the beast's sides rumbled as she purred. "Listen to me very closely, Bertly." Alestar's voice went dull. "Under no circumstance should you ever pass through there. Not even I would subject myself to the evils that lurk in that forest."

"Understood, sir. May I ask what there is to fear?"

"Hunters. They will track you down and slaughter you for sport...or worse, they'll sell you to the Zoo."

"The Zoo?" Bertly asked.

Alestar took a deep breath. "It's a massive colosseum where they force rare species to fight to the death. The Zoo is the hub of the Decomposite."

Bertly was astounded. He'd not heard of such horrors before and had certainly not been taught of them in any of his classes. "But we have nothing to worry about, right, sir? We aren't a rare species." Bertly's question was more of a reassurance to himself than a plea for an actual response. To his dismay, Alestar replied anyway.

"That does not matter, small human. They will think

you're a chameleon, only disguising yourself as human. Not to mention, I do believe that a red-eyed human classifies as a rare species." Alestar nudged Bertly and gave him a half smile.

Clia let out a soft caw. Bertly looked to the horizon, where he could see that they were approaching the edge of the forest.

"My old friend Therron lives north of here in a small village. We will land just beyond the forest and walk into town. We don't want to draw too much attention with Clia here." Alestar gave her another friendly pat.

Bertly spotted movement on the horizon. "Sir, what is that? Just northeast." He pointed to indicate the movement.

Alestar peered into the distance. He let go of Clia's reins and made a diamond shape with his fingers. He closed one eye and looked through the diamond. Bertly had seen this behavior before and had once attempted to convince Alestar to get fitted for spectacles for his myopia, but the old man claimed he could see just fine, so Bertly dropped the issue. He wished now that he hadn't. "It's smoke." Alestar grabbed the reins and snapped for Clia to fly faster.

They landed just beyond the forest. "Clia, you stay here and listen for my call. You know where the village is." Alestar grabbed the two swords from his travel sack and handed one to Bertly. "Do you have that stealth elixir?"

"Yes, sir." Bertly patted the inner pocket of his cloak.

"Keep it close. The village is just half a league ahead." Alestar led Bertly at a steady pace. The air gradually became heavy and thick with the scent of smoke. A vile scent traveled through the wind.

The quaint village was littered with devastation and gore. Red was the new color of what was once a peaceful community. Heads and limbs were left scattered throughout the dirt roads; not a single body was fully intact. Blood dripped through the cracks of floorboards inside cottages. The smell was unbearable. Bertly looked around the village and observed that every structure was left undamaged by whoever had committed the slaughter and started the fire. Alestar and Bertly navigated through the town, seeking the source of the smoke—and doing their best to avoid the human organs that were spread almost meticulously across the ground.

"I see flames. Just beyond that small tower," Alestar said. Bertly couldn't see more than a few paces through the smoke and wondered if his eyes truly were in better shape than those of the old man.

Despite the thick fumes, the raging fire peeked through the haze in the distance. The smell grew worse. Bertly could feel the heat from the flames. Alestar clenched his sword with both hands as he rounded the tower, with Bertly only a few steps behind. Alestar came to a sudden halt. He loosened his grip and let the tip of his blade hit the ground. Bertly was overcome with a wave of nausea.

Dismantled and mangled, random limbs filled the cracks between torsos. The townspeople were being used as kindling.

VII

Bertly sat on the steps of a nearby stoop as he watched Alestar extinguish the fire. Bertly had heard horror stories of the Decomposite, but never thought he'd live one of them. Alestar stood with his arms extended and his eyes closed, his body completely still while he concentrated on his task. Bertly could not tell how he was doing it, but the fire began receding. There was no visible lake, river, or even a pond—so he couldn't be using water to put the fire out. Bertly had learned many of his spells from observing his master, so he assumed that Alestar must be pulling the oxygen from the surrounding air to smother the fire. Bertly stood up and extended his arm. He slowly curled his fingers into the shape of a claw, feeling the connection he had with the fire. The flames shrank with it.

"Your intuition surprises me no more, little human." Alestar put his arms down. "I will let you take it from here." He plopped on the steps next to Bertly. "It won't be long before you surpass me, my apprentice. Knowledge is the only advantage I have on you these days."

"How sure of that are you, sir?" Bertly snickered.

Alestar gave Bertly a small nudge. "Last I heard, you need your master's signature to get into the Mastery program, is that still true?" Alestar tried not to laugh as Bertly shot him a menacing stare.

A crackling could be heard to the left of Bertly, and he peered in the direction of the noise. A slightly decayed elf, who wore tattered clothing, was wandering about the area surrounding them. Its motor skills were stiff, but it still managed to cover ground efficiently. It had patches of skin missing over its entire body, along with broken-off fingers. The creature's mostly detached jaw was hanging from its face by only a few tendons.

Alestar placed his hand on Bertly's shoulder and put his finger over his lips as he drew his sword. Bertly followed, pulling his sword out from his travel sack.

"Should we take the stealth elixir, sir?" Bertly whispered.

"Not yet. If there is one foul creature, there are two. And those elixirs only work for a short time," Alestar replied.

"Sir, have you seen one before?"

"No, but I know what it is."

"What exactly is it, sir?"

The rotting elf jerked its head and looked straight at Bertly, as if it knew he had been there the entire time—as if it were almost sentient and could detect the intentions of humans. The elf let out a series of painful screeches before it burst into a sprint, heading straight for Alestar and Bertly. Its arms flailed and its jaw flapped side to side as it charged them head-on. Bertly grasped his sword with both hands and dug his feet into the ground, his face burning. Before it was in range, Alestar stepped in front of Bertly and drove his sword between its eyes. He ripped his sword out and delivered a powerful kick to the elf's chest, sending its body summersaulting across the ground.

"That was a Rotter." Alestar removed a rag from his

pocket and used it to wipe the leftover blood from his blade. "And more are coming. That screech was a rally cry."

"Sir, this doesn't mean..." Bertly's voice trembled.

"No, Bertly, your instinct is correct. The second Blight has commenced." Alestar turned and faced Bertly. "I came here because I feared someone sought what this village was meant to protect—Cordelia's warblade."

"Cordelia's warblade still exists?" Bertly asked in astonishment.

"Yes, and by the looks of it, they haven't found it yet." Alestar pointed to a small well next to the burnt pile of corpses.

Alestar walked up to the well and clasped his hands. A soft yellow light emerged, its glow intensifying around him. Small pieces of rubble and ash levitated off the ground, hovering just a hair above the surface. A spiral staircase emerged. "I hope you are ready, tiny human. Only the dead know what evils Cordelia left to guard this place."

At the bottom of a long stairway rested a dark cave. Beyond the entrance to that cave lay a narrow room that was completely covered in bat droppings and bones—it appeared to have been abandoned for centuries, but that was not the case. An eerie howl came from inside the cave.

"How welcoming," Alestar cracked.

Farther ahead lay two paths, both too dark to see down.

"Well, I suppose this is where we split up. I will take the left, and you can take the right." Alestar indicated for Bertly to press forward.

"Sir, are you serious?" Bertly shouted, his voice echoing in the cave. He didn't like how shrill those echoes were.

"Okay, settle down. You can take the left, and I will take the right."

Bertly rolled his eyes. Alestar laughed and gave Bertly a pat on the back. "A fork in the road, which direction does your intuition tell you, my apprentice?"

Bertly looked as far down both pathways as he could. "Why do I have to choose?"

"Because…Cordelia was a tiny human, and you are a tiny human. What other connection do you need?" Alestar put his hands out, mocking Bertly's confusion.

"Good logic, sir." Bertly shook his head. "And just so you know, I am actually pretty tall for my species."

"Huh, is that so? Nonetheless, you still seem quite miniature to me. When you are at least *this* tall, I will stop referring to you as 'tiny.'" Alestar held his hand up to the top of his rib cage.

Bertly snapped his fingers, and the ground beneath his feet rose, bringing him up to eye level with Alestar. "There, now I am at least *this* tall."

Alestar kicked the dirt step out from beneath Bertly's feet. "You are a clever one. Once you pick yourself up, please choose a direction."

Bertly guided Alestar down a twisted trail that led through several lost rooms, and the two came to a stop when they entered a particularly ghastly room.

"It smells awful in here. More Rotters, sir?" Bertly asked.

Alestar's nostrils flared. "No. This time we have ghouls." Alestar drew his sword. "Press forward."

Bertly pulled out his blade and treaded onward, traveling deeper into the dungeon's depths. Unfamiliar footsteps echoed from within the dungeon. Step by step the footfalls grew louder. The sound was deep and rhythmic, like that of an army marching forward.

Alestar grabbed Bertly. "Stay close."

Bertly could hear the rustling of cloth and the jingling of armor. The sounds came to an abrupt stop.

"Lightus," Bertly whispered, and instantly the room was illuminated by the dim light he had called forth. Loud screams came from every direction. The ground rumbled from the small army of ghouls circling them.

Two sunken eyeballs sitting within large sockets stared directly at Bertly, and the wide smile of the ghoul revealed several fangs as long as fingers. Bertly stepped forward and dug his sword through the chin and out the back of the ghoul's head. He stepped back, pulling his sword free from the creature's skull, and the ghoul dropped lifelessly to the floor.

Bertly expected to feel more from his first kill— sympathy, remorse. Anything. Instead, there was an odd numbness to the act.

He stepped back and swung his blade, slitting the throats of numerous ghouls in a single swipe, after which a red mist of blood filled the air. Bertly swung his torso in a semicircle, gutting another handful of ghouls. Blood dripped from his face like the sweat from a hard day's labor. Slicing his blade right through the ghouls' rotten flesh satisfied Bertly. He jammed the butt of his sword into the skull of another before piercing the jugular of a ghoul who struggled, writhing about on the ground. Bertly quickly glanced back to check on Alestar. He had already exterminated the majority of the ghouls. Before Bertly could press on, the half-dozen ghouls still standing scurried off into the shadows.

"I'm not sure what to be more afraid of, you or the ghouls." Alestar had a smile plastered on his face.

"Believe it or not, sir, I am actually a bit rusty." Bertly massaged the back of his shoulder. "It's been a few years."

"Regardless, remind me not to get on your bad side."
Alestar chuckled.

"I don't mean to nag, but we should press on." Alestar
gestured for Bertly to lead the way. Bertly did as his
master suggested and had started to walk ahead when
Alestar placed his hand on Bertly's shoulder. "On second
thought, maybe I should lead us this time. You ran us
into a pack of ghouls."

They proceeded with caution deeper into the dungeon,
passing through every ominous room. Alestar assumed
that Cordelia must have hidden her warblade somewhere
that was nearly impossible to find.

"What exactly makes Cordelia's warblade so special,
sir?" Bertly asked.

"Fair question, human. Her blade itself possesses
magical abilities, though to what extent, no one knows.
But what we do know is that her blade was essential for
her success on the battlefield," Alestar said.

"Do we know any of the magical attributes, sir? I
heard her blade can grow?" Bertly gave a half shrug.

"You are partly right, tiny human. Her blade has the
ability to extend and retract of its own will. And no
matter how long it grows, it does not become any heavier
for the wielder." Alestar looked at Bertly and arched his
eyebrows. Bertly could tell he was supposed to be
impressed, so that was exactly the way he responded.

"Impressive, sir. But how does one work it? Seems a
bit dangerous if it randomly extends and withdraws."
Bertly tied his blood-drenched hair into a ponytail.

"We don't know for certain. Some say that the blade
has a mind of its own, while others suggest that Cordelia
somehow soul-bonded with it in order to control it,"
Alestar responded.

Bertly took a moment to think. "I feel like it must
have a mind of its own, sir. I doubt even Cordelia could

soul-bond with two things. Not to mention, if she did soul-bond with it, doesn't that imply it has a soul? Meaning it most likely has a mind of its own?"

Alestar stopped walking. "You are sharp, my young apprentice. It took me years before I came to that conclusion." Alestar picked up his pace once again. "I really have taught you well."

Bertly spotted a dull glow toward the end of the path. When he looked closely, he could see a small flickering light.

"Do you see that, sir? In the distance?" Bertly asked.

Alestar gave an agreeing nod and drew his sword. They continued down the dark tunnel until they arrived at a large golden door, which bore countless symbols written across its surface. The door was clean and shiny, like it had been untouched by time. Alestar put his sword away and straightened his posture. He cracked his knuckles and studied the door. "This is it. It is identical to the one in my readings."

"Sir, you mean to say you've never been down here?" Bertly asked.

"Sweet Cordelia, no! Why would I ever come down here alone? Do you know what they say lurks in these shadows?" Alestar squealed.

Bertly gulped. "No, sir. What lurks in these shadows?" Whatever courage he had was lost.

"Oh, it's…nothing…" Alestar's skin went pale. "Just ghouls. Lots of ghouls."

Bertly failed to understand how his master could possibly be so terrified of ghouls. After all, Alestar had recently slaughtered a small army of them. It made little sense at all. Alestar stepped up to the door and shouted commands in a language Bertly did not recognize. The door emitted a flash of bright light, but it did not open. Alestar repeated the spell in a different tone. The door again shined brightly but still did not open. He shouted the words louder and slower. Another flash, but the door remained closed.

"Huh. According to my studies, that was supposed to work." Alestar placed his hands on his hips and glared at the door. He tapped his foot against the floor.

"What language was that, sir?" Bertly's curiosity got the better of him.

"It is the language of my people." Alestar crossed his arms and plopped on the ground. He continued to analyze the door.

Bertly was impressed that Alestar spoke the forgotten language. He wondered what else he knew simply by virtue of being a giant. They seemed so wise—especially the elder ones. "Sir, is it true that only giants know how to find Eskos?" Bertly inquired.

"No. All species native to Eskos know how to find the motherland. Bertly, is now really the time for this?" Alestar rubbed his chin.

"Sorry, sir. You're right. It can wait." Bertly sat on the soft dirt and directed his attention toward the door.

Alestar rose back to his feet and let out a frightening yell. He said the command over and over. "Stand back, tiny human." Alestar dug his foot into the ground and bent his knees. His arms were postured as though he were about to take off from the starting line of a footrace.

The stone around the door started to crack. Bats scurried as debris fell from the roof. Alestar extended his arms. "If the door won't open…then I will rip it out." Alestar pulled his arms back in toward his chest. Bertly could feel the energy radiating from his master. The golden door started to slide forward.

Out of nowhere, a bolt of red light shot out from the door and through Alestar's chest. The impact sent him soaring over Bertly's head.

"The door cannot be ripped out...noted," Alestar said through hefty breaths as he lay motionless on his back.

Bertly could not contain himself. He let out a monstrous laugh. "I will get camp set up, sir. Even if we do open this door, I'm not sure you'll be ready to fight. You've won against the ghouls, sir, but you've lost your battle with that door." Bertly continued to chuckle as he shuffled away.

"Are you going to laugh, or are you going to be kind and help your master up?" Alestar groaned.

***

Bertly and Alestar sat across from each other, warming their hands over a fire. Two thin blankets were laid out side by side not far from them.

"So, after we get the warblade tomorrow, how are we getting out of this place?" Bertly washed the blood out of his hair with the little water he had left.

"Supposedly, Cordelia will show the way. But my studies haven't been proving to be completely accurate." Alestar scowled at the golden door. "We should get some rest. We have a long day tomorrow."

"Shouldn't one of us stay up and keep watch?" Bertly asked, stressed over the whole situation.

"No need to worry. Giants are very light sleepers. We can hear a spider crawl across its web a quarter league away." Alestar snapped his fingers and the flames from the fire darkened.

***

Bertly opened his eyes, an idea having occurred to him. He snapped his fingers, reigniting the fire.

"Give a warning next time," Alestar hissed.

Bertly stepped in front of the golden entrance. He plucked a hair from the back of his head and placed it against the door. A vibrant red light blasted through the center crack of the door. Bertly took a step forward, and suddenly the door slowly creaked open on its own.

Alestar sprang to his feet. "How did you know to do that?"

"It's the same way Polly and I open the door to our dormitory." Bertly shrugged and his mouth curved into a smile.

Inside the room, there sat a pedestal on which rested a rather large straight blade made of mammoth ice. It was held by a grip plated with dragon scales. The sword had a jagged, curved cross guard. A carefully engraved pommel was forged into the shape of a dragon's head. Bertly took a step into the room.

Alestar grabbed Bertly by the collar. "Wait, it's too easy."

"Sir, I hardly think cracking the riddle to the door was *too easy*. After all, you certainly struggled with it," Bertly responded.

"Plucking a measly hair is *too easy*." Alestar scoffed and tucked a lock of hair behind his ear.

"True, sir, but you needed a hair from me or Polly. Someone could spend a lifetime down here and never open the door if they didn't have one of the chosen ones, like me." Bertly gave a half smile. Alestar let go of Bertly's collar, and the two slowly approached the sword. Alestar jerked his head in the direction of any noise he heard.

"Do I just grab it?" Bertly asked.

Alestar shrugged, clearly unsure. Bertly was surprised that his master didn't know. Bertly inspected the sword. He clutched the dragon-scale grip and lifted the sword off the pedestal.

The moment Bertly grabbed the sword, he and Alestar

crouched and studied the large hallowed room.

Bertly held the sword above his head and smiled triumphantly. "See? Nothing to worry about, sir." He sliced the sword through the air. "It's as light as a feather." It had just enough weight on each side that it balanced perfectly in Bertly's hand.

Bertly heard feet trampling across the ground. The sound was loud enough that it echoed across the entire dungeon. Bertly looked to the golden entryway, where a horde of ghouls was stampeding through.

"Bertly, the sword!" Alestar shouted.

The sword that grows. Bertly gripped the sword tight with both hands and lunged back. As the sword rounded his body, the tip of the blade burst out, extending the length of the room. In one fell swoop, the protracted mammoth ice carved through the bodies of hundreds of ghouls. They dropped like canaries in a coal mine.

"Sweet Cordelia," Alestar blurted. "Let me see that thing."

Bertly handed Alestar the warblade, which suddenly retracted, completely disappearing.

"Interesting. It only obeys your commands. This helps confirm my theories. We need to get back to the Academy." Alestar tossed the blade back to Bertly. "Cordelia is supposed to show us the way out, but how?"

"Cordelia, reveal the way back." Bertly held the sword out in front of him. A bright light shot out from the grip.

"Well then, Mr. Cordelia, please lead the way." Alestar bowed and extended his arm in the direction of the golden gates. Bertly kicked dirt in Alestar's direction as he walked past.

***

Bertly led Alestar through unknown rooms and twisted,

dark pathways. It was only an hour before they stumbled upon the spiral staircase in the well.

"It seems Cordelia's way is much quicker than ours," Alestar commented. "Shall we?" He gestured toward the stairs.

Bertly putted his way up the steps, with Alestar just a few feet behind him. When they reached the top, an army of thousands of Rotters awaited, swords and shields in hand. When they caught a glimpse of Bertly emerging from the staircase, the Rotters banged their swords against their shields in unison, drowning out all other sounds. The rhythm of their march caused the ground to shake.

"Too easy," Alestar said.

VIII

Bertly, with his knees shaking, stood at the top of the staircase overlooking the largest group of individuals he had ever seen. Rotters filled every open space in the village streets. The humid air coupled with Bertly's anxiety made it hard for him to breathe.

"Maybe we should go back into the dungeon, sir." Bertly lifted his eyebrows. Alestar turned back and after one step came to a halt. The bottom of the well was quickly filling with sand.

"It seems the dungeon's only entrance is no longer an option." Alestar turned back to Bertly. "Let me go ahead of you."

"Sir, it's a death trap out there." Bertly placed his hand across the railing, blocking Alestar's path.

"I think I can reason with the beasts. Something is controlling them. Rotters are not this orderly. If they were thinking on their own, they would have already swarmed us." Alestar squeezed past Bertly and stepped onto the ash-filled street.

Alestar approached the Rotters with his arms up to show the creatures that he carried no weapons and was not a threat to them. "We know where the warblade is. Kill us now and you will never find it!" Alestar shouted louder than Bertly had ever heard him shout. The army rested their weapons and lowered their shields. "I wish to speak with your leader." The undead army stood so still they appeared to be frozen in time. "Your master? Ruler? Commander?" Alestar listed many synonyms for *leader*, Bertly assumed in hopes that one of the words would prove recognizable to the Rotters. There still came no response from the army.

"I don't think they have a master, sir," Bertly shouted.

"Nonsense. Who gave them all the weapons and armor?" Alestar replied.

An unfathomable scream tore through the air as the undead army parted down the middle.

"I hope that isn't their leader, sir," Bertly exclaimed, gravely concerned with the source of the noise.

Another scream echoed through the air, and Bertly was acutely aware of the pain of the crying beast; its scream had infiltrated Bertly's mind and lodged itself deep within his heart. The creature's agony spread through his body.

From the parted sea of soldiers emerged a horselike creature, which was fused with a humanoid. The skinless creature pulsated with black blood that coursed through its translucent veins. Bertly could clearly discern every muscle fiber and tendon that held the sickening abomination together. The humanoid rider had no visible legs, and it pulled harshly on the gray mane of the horse to control its movements. The rider grasped the horse tightly with its sharp claws, which were attached to long arms. The horns atop the rider's head curled in so tightly that the points of each nearly touched.

Alestar let out a forceful whistle. The creature, standing only a tad shorter than Alestar, screamed. Blood shot in a projectile from its mouth as it thrashed its head. The monster stretched out its slender arm and extended its claw, suggesting that Alestar immediately hand over the warblade.

"I don't have the warblade on me, you see." Alestar took a step toward the beast. "But I know where it is."

The monster let out another scream. The entirety of the undead army focused sharply on Alestar. The soldiers postured their bodies like they were ready to strike at a moment's notice.

Alestar grabbed the hilt of his sword. "No one needs to act rashly. I can give you what you want."

The creature's soulless eyes peered at Alestar as it let out another horrid shriek. The decayed soldiers marched toward Alestar.

He drew his sword, and with his open hand, he made a fist and pounded the ground. Upon impact of the giant's fist, a massive dense dirt wall sprang from the soil, blocking the path of the rotting army.

Sand poured over the tops of Bertly's feet. He climbed out of the well and stood next to Alestar. Sword in hand.

"Is there a plan B, sir?" Bertly asked. Dirt started to drop from the wall.

"Unfortunately, we did not have much of a plan A." Alestar placed his hand on Bertly's shoulder. "You need to tell the Elders what we have seen here today. When they do not believe you, show them Cordelia's warblade."

"Why can't you tell them, sir? And how do you plan on getting us out of here, anyway?" Bertly pressed.

"If Clia had stayed put as I instructed her, she should have been here by now," Alestar replied. A decomposed arm punctured the dirt wall, causing a massive crack to run up the side. "You have to make a run for it, Bertly. I will hold them off."

"I'm not leaving until Clia arrives," Bertly cried out. A parade of arms and heads burst through the barrier, causing it to collapse.

"The air may be thick enough." Alestar took a deep

breath. "Get ready, Bertly." Alestar gripped his sword with both hands and aligned it vertically with his nose. The air turned cold and dry. Rotters funneled in from all directions. At that moment, a layer of ice formed over the Rotters. "I used the water in the air to freeze the Rotters momentarily. Hurry, take them out, Bertly!"

Bertly gripped the warblade tight. In one fell swoop, he decapitated over half a dozen rows of Rotters. Their frozen skulls cracked as they crashed onto the ground. Blood poured out of the veins that had been disconnected from their heads. Their lifeless bodies slumped over, leaving in their wake an echo of cracking bone that rattled through Bertly's ears.

Alestar whistled again. Bertly looked to the sky for Clia, but she was nowhere in sight. The back rows of Rotters crawled over the pile of headless elves. Alestar postured up as the air grew colder once more. The Rotters could barely move their legs, but this time, they were not frozen.

"I must have sucked too much water out of the air last time," Alestar hollered.

Before Bertly started swinging, the blade on his sword extended on its own to accommodate the task at hand. He cocked the sword back and swung the blade faster than the wind. Every Rotter standing between Bertly and the nearby homesteads dropped to the ground.

A pool of blood formed under Bertly's feet as the slaughtered bodies bled out. He took a moment to catch his breath. Bertly heard another painful screech, and he turned toward the noise. As quick as lightning, the skinless horseman carved through the pile of corpses and got within one stride of Alestar.

Alestar wound his sword to strike, but before he could lunge forward, the beast pierced its claw through his chest. The creature's arm completely punctured the giant's body. The abomination wiggled the claws that stuck out of Alestar's back as it screamed in his face.

"Alestar!" Bertly cried. He stuck the tip of his sword in the direction of the beast. The mammoth ice extended far enough to pierce the creature's rib cage. Smoke and black blood poured from its shredded side.

Alestar gripped his sword and drove it through the head of the horse. The skinless monster let out a revolting cry and collapsed to the ground. Its arm tore out of Alestar's chest, bringing a river of blood along with it. Alestar fell to his knees. Bertly tried to take off running toward the giant, but a Rotter grabbed him by the ankle, bringing him to the ground. Bertly smashed the heel of his boot repeatedly into the monster's nasal cavity, causing its face to collapse. He scurried to his feet. Rotters were climbing up Alestar's back.

"Alestar!" Bertly shouted. Alestar threw the Rotters from his back, but there were too many, and they quickly overcame him. They poured in from all sides. Alestar swung his blade to keep the Rotters as far back as possible.

Bertly gripped his sword and drew his arm back. He lunged forward to strike, but was unable to move his arm. Rotters had him restrained. Bertly jerked his arms and body, but even with great effort, he could not break their grip. Bertly peered back at Alestar, who was looking straight at Bertly, his eyes filled with affection. Rotters had ahold of every inch of Alestar's body. His arms were stretched until they were spitefully ripped from his body. Fingernails burrowed into his skin like bugs.

"Alestar!" Bertly cried again, his voice cracking as he felt the cold teeth of the Rotters pierce the skin of his back. He gripped Cordelia's warblade until his nails dug into his skin. His arm would be torn off before he turned his sword over. Sweat poured down his face; he could practically feel his arm detaching from his body already.

A loud squawk tore through the air, causing a momentary pause in the ongoing battle. Bertly looked toward the source of the squawk, but before he could identify the creature, a set of talons gripped each of his shoulders and lifted him into the air. Clia had come for him. She flew low to the ground toward Alestar, but the Rotters pried at her face and wings. Clia called toward him. The pitch of her shriek made Bertly's head throb. A couple of Rotters climbed up Bertly's chest. Clia shook her wings, breaking free of the Rotters. As she flew into the air, a few gripped onto Bertly's limbs, but they did not manage to hold on for long.

Bertly stared helplessly at the quaint town of horrors as it drifted into the background. Thoughts raced through Bertly's head, and he tried to slow them down so he could breathe, but was unsuccessful. His heart pounded through his chest and he felt horribly sick. Every time he closed his eyes, his head spun faster. His vision blurred, and then all went black.

***

Bertly opened his eyes to a blurred gryphon standing over him. Clia's beak was nearly touching his nose. His vision returned gradually, and once he could see well enough, he looked around and recognized the light red stone surrounding them—they were in the courtyard where Bertly had first met Clia. His memory rushed back.

Alestar.

Bertly went cold. He felt as though he were submerged underwater and he couldn't swim back to the surface for air. Bertly heard Alestar's words echo through his head. *You need to tell the Elders what we have seen here today.*

Bertly picked himself up with strength he didn't know

he had. He patted his pockets, which were empty. In a panic, he repeatedly searched them all again. Clia let out a soft caw, and within the cavern of her mouth, Bertly could just make out the glint of Cordelia's warblade. "Thanks, girl." Bertly scratched Clia behind the ear and sprinted for the top floor of the highest tower.

Out of breath, Bertly stood, bent over with his hands on his knees. The lavish blue door stood between him and the Elders. Bertly gazed at the door. "Damn." He tried his best to recall how Alestar had managed to open the door when he'd brought Bertly and Polly there. He stepped up to the door and took a deep breath, but was in no mood to sort out the puzzle of prying it open. He viciously pounded on the door. "Open up!" He struck its wooden frame with both hands. "Please open the door!" His hands turned red from his efforts, but he continued thrashing.

The door creaked open, and out hobbled an old dwarf, Master Quinric. Quinric looked Bertly over from head to toe. "You're an absolute mess. Where have you been?" Master Quinric grabbed his nose. "And what is that pungent smell?"

"Sir, it's Master Alestar. We went to the Decomposite," Bertly exclaimed.

Quinric's expression hardened. He looked around the corridor, to ensure no one was eavesdropping, Bertly assumed. Satisfied that they were the only two in the corridor, Quinric grabbed Bertly by the collar and pulled him past the blue doors and into the room. "Where have you been? Where is Master Alestar?" A vein popped from Quinric's neck.

Loud footsteps echoed through the hallway—their pace was slow. Quinric let go of Bertly's collar and turned in the direction of the footsteps. Rounding the corner was a giant with short red hair. He moved much slower and firmer when compared to the elegance of Alestar's gait. This giant dragged his feet when he walked, and he stood slightly crouched over. "How may we help you today, Bertly?"

Bertly was taken aback for a moment. He had never met this giant.

"Sir, I think the Blight has returned," Bertly shouted.

The giant straightened. "Do you know what these statements mean, human apprentice?"

Bertly wished he could lie. "Yes, sir. And I can prove it."

***

Bertly stood front and center before the Council of Elders, in an empty courtroom that was large enough to hold a thousand observers. He felt like he was on trial. Bertly studied the Elders and noticed there was not a single human among them. He did, however, recognize Master Quinric, Master Dova, and the old elf from orientation.

Master Dova leaned forward. "You have caused quite a stir here today, Bertly. What do you have to tell us?" The Elders sat quietly, waiting for Bertly's reply.

Bertly filled the council in on every detail. From riding Clia, to the ghouls in the dungeon. He mentioned he was close enough to smell the breath of the Rotters. He wasn't sure which was worse, Rotter breath or the smell of burning corpses, since the two carried a similar putrid aroma.

"Are we supposed to take the word of a child?" a dwarf—whose hair was closer to white in color than it was blond—shouted.

The council broke into a debate. "This child could never have overpowered Master Alestar," a young elf rebutted. His head was directed downward, but Bertly could still see the point of his ears.

"Why would he lie?" Master Dova interjected.

"The Blight has been over for three thousand years. Why would it return now?" the giant stated.

"He should be expelled," the graying dwarf replied.

Bertly reached into his pocket and removed Cordelia's warblade. Every beam of light in the room was drawn to the mammoth ice, causing it to reflect and illuminate every corner of the grand courtroom.

Quinric stood. "That cannot be."

Bertly held the handle of the sword above his head. "Cordelia's warblade." It felt natural in his hand, as though it was meant for him. The blade emerged from the grip. "Master Alestar gave his life to ensure this did not fall into the wrong hands." Despite his stress, the power of Cordelia's spirit coursed through him; with the warblade in hand, he felt unstoppable.

"That is a fake. The warblade only answers to Cordelia," barked an elf with long gray and black hair.

Master Dova expectantly extended her hand. "Please let us examine the blade." When Dova grasped the sword, the blade retracted back into its grip. She handed it down the line of Elders. The blade did not reveal itself to any of them. Master Dova offered the warblade back to Bertly. "The blade calls to you. This is your warblade now."

"You are going to leave the warblade with a child?" The elf with gray and black hair fumed.

"Cordelia and her warblade have chosen Bertly." Dova clenched her fists and peered into the eyes of the elf. "Who are we to question?" She loosened her grip.

"While it may take some time before an army big enough to cause concern may be constructed, safety is no longer guaranteed." Dova glanced at the council members. "The curfew must be reinstated immediately.

Double up the castle security."

Constructed. Why did both Master Alestar and Master Dova use this word? Bertly questioned.

"What will we tell the students and faculty?" Quinric asked.

"That young Bertly here took Alestar's gryphon for a joyride. The punishment for stealing and jeopardizing an endangered species is that the curfew will be reinstated. For twenty years." Dova peered into Bertly's eyes. "Consider this our condolences for losing your master, a giant we all cared for deeply. In any realm-ordered trial, you would be facing half your life in prison for entering the Decomposite."

Bertly's heart broke in half, he'd lost the closest friend he had, and he was to lie about it. The young wizard had seen his master nearly everyday for seven years and now he was expected to move on as though nothing had ever happened. Alestar was more than a master or friend, he felt like part of who Bertly was as a human. Alestar was Bertly's role model, and Bertly wanted nothing more than to carry out his legacy. The young wizard would need to end the Blight himself; unfortunately he needed to become a master first.

"How many were there?" Quinric shouted. "How many Rotters did you see?" The council mumbled to themselves, but focused their attention on Bertly.

"It was hard to say, sir. I was operating on adrenaline alone," Bertly replied. "But to be honest, they didn't seem all that powerful; we were mostly caught off guard." The more it settled in, the more Bertly realized one on one, the Rotters were nothing in comparison to him. In fact, he told himself, given the opportunity, he would fight them again. The young wizard squeezed the grip of Cordelia's warblade.

"Best guess," Quinric urged.

"Fifteen thousand. Twenty at the most." Bertly shrugged.

"We have time. Eplium's army has nearly one hundred thousand elves ready for battle. The Rotters will not cross the forest and challenge them until they know they can win," Quinric added.

"How long until they have enough?" the old elf from orientation asked.

"Assuming they have another twenty thousand somewhere else, well, it is possible they could grow to one hundred thousand in about ten years' time."

"But what if they have more?" Bertly rebutted. The frustration of having to keep Alestar's death a secret was beginning to settle in.

"That is highly unlikely," an Elder interjected immediately.

Bertly snarled, "As unlikely as the return of the Blight?"

Quinric rose to his feet. "Know your place, human."

Bertly wanted to banter back and forth with the old master; however, he could not risk his status at the Academy. He knew he had to become a master as soon as possible if he wanted an opportunity to avenge his master's death, for only masters could use magic freely across Pangea. The young wizard also knew he would need to learn how to soul-bond before he could ever become powerful enough to do anything. No famous wizard was ever unaccompanied; they all bonded with a legendary creature. Bertly knew that had to be his first task, soul-bond, and then he could become a master, and once he was a master, then everyone would have to listen to him.

"We have time to answer, but not enough time to grow enough soldiers," Dova said. "Reach out to the realms. Let them know what is happening. We must come together once more." The council members stood and shuffled out of the room. Dova remained seated, with her eyes locked onto Bertly.

"This is going to be hard, but we must ask you to remain at the Academy and to carry on with your studies. We must keep you close. I am sure you understand why," Dova murmured.

"Yes, ma'am." Bertly had never wanted to go home more than he did at that moment. "Will I still get to go on my spirit quest?"

"Of course. You will be allowed to do all regular Academy activities. We just want to be sure you're close by, for when we need you. Assuming you are accepted into the Mastery program, of course." Dova gave him a half grin.

***

"Wait, sir, you didn't get the curfew reinstated at all?" Roderick asked.

"No, my young apprentice. It was merely a protocol to protect the students from the same fate as my master." Bertly turned away from Roderick and faced the fireplace.

"I'm...I'm sorry, sir. I had no idea...I always wondered why you didn't mention your old master much." Roderick leaned back in his chair and peeked out a small window. "I reckon the sun will be up in less than a handful of hours. We should probably get back to writing, sir. Where did you want to pick up?"

Bertly took a breath and adjusted his posture. "Naturally, Polly was worried sick about me the following morning. It was the first time in years we hadn't slept in the same room together." Bertly smiled and laughed to himself.

"What did you tell her, sir?" Roderick asked.

"I told her I fell asleep in the workshop." Bertly's smile dulled. "I couldn't bring myself to tell her the truth. I let her believe the lies the Academy told and kept the warblade to myself." Bertly sank back into his enormous bed.

"We spent the next month loafing around, waiting for our acceptance letters into the Mastery program. Polly and I knew we would get our certificates to perform magic legally off campus grounds; however, the Academy turned the brightest and best students away for random reasons every year." Bertly sighed. "To be honest, I was more worried for Polly and, after a couple of years, the twins. I knew the Academy would accept me. They weren't going to let me out of their sight."

***

"Bertly, what class are you looking forward to most in the Mastery program?" Polly asked. She was lying on her bed, studying a book of spells.

"Soul-bonding, obviously." Bertly lay on his own bed, twirling the stealth elixir he had never used.

"I can't wait for the spirit quest. I hear every sorcerer who is able to complete it unlocks a new ability." Polly stopped reading her book and stared off into space. The school bell rang, and Polly leapt out of bed. "It's time, Bertly!" she shouted.

The two humans raised their arms into the air and made identical commandments—"Cordelia, reveal my mail." A piece of parchment appeared in each of their hands.

"You first," Bertly said.

"We will do it at the same time." Polly winked at Bertly. They tore into their letters.

Dear Bertly, apprentice of Alestar,

Congratulations on completing the requirements for your Legal Magic Certification. You are now permitted to perform minor healing, intermediate summoning, and advanced conjuring spells off campus. Upon further evaluation, we have reviewed your request for the Mastery program. On behalf of the Nine Elders and the Academy, we would like to congratulate you, Master Bertly, on your acceptance into the Mastery program. Classes begin next cycle.

Bertly was taken aback for a moment; this was the first time he had ever been called "Master."

"Bertly, I got in!" Polly sprang up and jumped on the bed. "Cordelia, reveal my schedule. What classes did you get, Bertly?"

Bertly summoned his schedule and handed it over to Polly.

"We have the same classes again. I can't believe this happens every year." Polly's cheeks turned pink.

Bertly's face went blank and he fell back onto his bed. "Wonderful."

IX

Bertly and Polly sat in the front row of a rather empty classroom. There were less than a dozen students occupying the desks. At sixteen, Bertly and Polly were the youngest students in the room by at least three years. They itched in their seats, tapping their feet and twiddling their thumbs.

"I can't believe we are about to learn soul-bonding, Bertly," Polly gushed.

Bertly was not in the mood for small talk; however, he shared equal excitement about soul-bonding. "I hear the master for this course is new this year. A young elf."

"I heard he is a foul professor." An elf with short brown hair and glasses leaned next to Polly. "A student got on his bad side, so the professor tricked him into bonding with a fly."

Polly shot back in her seat. "That's awful," she said. She looked over at Bertly with a concerned expression on her face. "You'd best behave in this class."

Bertly gave Polly a dirty look. "Why do you assume I won't behave?"

"You did recently get caught trying to take your master's gryphon out for a ride...or did you forget?" Polly giggled.

"A troublemaker, eh?" the young elf added.

Bertly's cheeks turned red. "Where is that dumb teacher, anyway?"

The young elf rose from his seat and shuffled to the head of the classroom. "My name is Master Theleärdehil." The color drained from Bertly's face. "You can call me Thel for short." The young elf smirked at Bertly. "This will be the hardest, but most rewarding class you will ever take." Thel pulled up a chair and took a seat. "What has drawn you to this class?"

No one raised their hand to answer the question, and several seconds of uncomfortable silence followed before Thel spoke again. "This is not rhetorical. You can all perform certified magic. Why not go work? You do not have to continue your studies. You are choosing to be here…are you not?" He crossed his arms over his chest.

A dwarf with long blond hair raised her hand. Thel nodded for her to speak. "I want to learn how to bond with an amazing creature. A dragon, hopefully." A handful of students chattered in agreement.

"So, you wish to bond with a creature to make it your trophy?" Thel questioned.

"Not a trophy, sir. But…something to show off. Well, no, it is more of an accomplishment of my hard work and studies." The dwarf's voice trembled.

"A trophy." Thel gripped the arm of his chair. "Any other reasons?"

A petite elvish girl in the back row chimed in, "I want a companion. A friend to go along with me anywhere I go."

Thel eased his grip from the chair. "A much better answer." He stood up and began handwriting on the board. "A creature is not your slave. If you want it to bond with you, it must comply." He turned to the classroom. "Sure, you can take control of a chicken or an elf mouse. But if you want to bond with something beautiful or magnificent." Thel placed his hands over his heart. "A mammoth or a dragon." His smile grew. "Then it must also want to bond with you. You can only telepathically control the minds of weak animals. A dog or koko, sure. But you will never control the mind of a dragon."

Polly raised her hand.

Thel pointed to her. "Yes?"

"So a dragon must *choose* to bond with you, since we cannot control it. Because a dragon is too strong-minded?" Polly asked.

"That is correct. Some people control kokos because they want to use their healing abilities; however, no doctor has ever been able to bond with a phoenix for its healing abilities. Why is this?"

Bertly raised his hand. "Because the doctors don't want to bond with the phoenix; they want to bond with its healing powers."

"Exactly!" Thel shouted enthusiastically. He turned back to the board. "It is not hard to soul-bond. It may be one of the easiest theories you learn. What makes it so challenging to most sorcerers is that you need a heart that is pure enough to form such a connection." Thel stopped writing. "Most of you will bond with a creature you love dearly; however, it will not be the animal of your dreams. But…if you listen to me and take my teachings seriously, then maybe, possibly, you will have a chance at a creature greater than you deserve." Thel clapped twice. A girl screamed in the back row. Bertly noticed desks shuffling and chairs tipping over.

Slithering across the ground was a serpent with a body that extended farther than the length of the room and a frame that was the width of a horse. "This is Slithers." The snake coiled at Thel's feet, piling up into a ball nearly as tall as Thel himself. "This is proof that I am not blowing smoke. I know what it takes to bond with a legendary creature…and it is not easy."

***

Bertly lay with his limbs sprawled across his dormitory grass. Polly was resting against a small tree nearby, with several vials and test tubes spread out before her. She grabbed a small blue tube and mixed it into a large tube that contained a red liquid.

"What do you plan on doing first, Bertly? Soul-bonding, your spirit quest, or are you going to take on an apprentice?" Polly asked.

"I want to get my master's certificate as soon as possible. I plan to take my apprentice along with me on my spirit quest, and I will bond with an animal along the way." Bertly snapped his fingers and extended his arm. A branch from the large tree in the center of the dormitory stretched out and wrapped around his arm. It pulled him to his feet.

"You are a very lazy human, Bertly, son of Edfrid." Polly added a green powder to the mixture.

Bertly shrugged. "I plan on finishing up in three years."

Polly tilted her head and squinted her eyes. "Three years? But you must have an apprentice for at least five."

"Five years?" Bertly shouted.

"Yes, when they changed the apprentice requirements from three years to five, the same rules applied for masters." Polly shook her head. "Do you ever read the pamphlets I leave on your bed for you?"

"I always wondered how those got there." Bertly flopped next to Polly. "What are you making?"

Polly put a cork in the vial and shook it. The mixture turned bright orange, momentarily straining Bertly's eyes until the light dimmed. "Smash this on the floor and it'll create a flash big enough to briefly blind a giant."

Bertly sat up. "Wow, Polly, I'm impressed."

"I'm not naïve, Bertly. I understand the dangers of a spirit quest." Polly gave Bertly a small smile. "We should head to bed. It's late."

"I wish the sun would go down when it's dark out. This room always makes me lose track of time." Bertly popped up and headed toward the living quarters inside the tree.

"Bertly, aren't you going to help a lady up?" Polly sat on the ground with a smile on her face and her hand reaching out.

***

The air was cold, and the scent of necrotic flesh filled the air. Bertly was surrounded on all sides by Rotters. The Decomposite hadn't changed much since he'd been there last. The Rotters' faces were blurred, and they crawled upon the ground, inching toward him. Bertly couldn't move. He called for his master, but received no answer. The claws of the Rotters scraped against the ground. The noise was intolerable.

He was frozen, still calling for Alestar. But the only noise that returned to him was that abominable scratching. He accepted his fate as the Rotters crept forward. When they reached his feet, they craned their necks to peer at him. That was when he saw their faces. They all had the same face: the face of his master. Alestar.

The scratching continued.

Bertly jolted upright from his nightmare. His heart pounded, but he was able to convince himself to return to sleep. He was still groggy, after all, but there a remnant from his nightmare left over—he heard a muffled scratch and opened his eyes again. His vision hadn't adjusted to the dark room yet, and the scratching noise continued to irritate him.

"Lightus." A small ball of white light materialized at Bertly's command, floating directly behind him. He wanted the scratching sound to go away on its own. He had been comfortable in his bed, and rather than be frightened, the sound merely annoyed him. He looked over at Polly, who was fast asleep—obviously unaffected by the obnoxious sound. The scratching noise grew louder. Bertly wanted the issue resolved so he could go back to sleep, but if he woke up too much, he would be unable to return to his dreams. He glared at Polly, so blissfully unaware of the noise. She'd probably want to know what it was. If he could get her to investigate it, he could cozily return to sleep.

"Polly," Bertly whispered as loud as he could without speaking full volume. "Polly, go see what that noise is." Polly remained motionless in her bed. Bertly groaned as he slipped into his boots. He was too sluggish to put on a full set of clothes, so he left the living quarters in just his flannels.

He tiptoed across the outdoor room with his hand firmly wrapped around the hilt of the warblade. The scratching grew significantly louder, and the scratches picked up their pace, coming in a quicker frequency. Bertly plucked a hair from the back of his head and slowly extended it toward the door, behind which came a growl, and Bertly flinched at the sound of it. He lightly tapped his hair against the door to open it, and he instinctively jumped back and assumed a defensive stance. A larger shadow tackled him to the floor. Two talons pinned Bertly to the ground as he was smothered by an abundance of feathers. Bertly dropped his sword.

"Clia!" Bertly shouted. "What have I told you about

sneaking around the castle?"

Clia touched her beak to Bertly's nose and refused to break eye contact.

"How did you find my dormitory?"

Clia stepped back and hunched forward, as she had before their first flight.

"You want to go for a ride...now?" Bertly asked.

Clia let out a screeching caw that echoed through the room loud enough to startle him.

Bertly lunged forward and grabbed her beak. "Shh, okay. Okay. I guess right now is fine." Bertly latched onto Clia's feathers, being careful not to tug too hard on them, and climbed aboard.

Clia attempted to tiptoe through the castle corridors; however, her talons made a clicking noise every time they connected with the stone flooring.

"I can't believe I'm riding a gryphon, who is supposed to be in Eskos, through the Academy halls right now." Bertly nudged Clia in the side with his leg. "You do know the main hall is just around this corner?" Clia picked up her pace, but halted and squared up with the castle entrance. "You've got to be kidding me."

Bertly hugged Clia around the neck and closed his eyes. She erupted into a full sprint across the main hallway, sending the rugs under her feet flying out behind her. Just as they flew through the exit, Clia lifted off into the air. She soared straight into the sky, spinning in circles.

"You know, you *can* go flying on your own," Bertly shouted. His arms and legs were wrapped around Clia as tightly as possible. He wasn't accustomed to riding her yet, and he felt much better if he had a firmer grip. Clia stopped elevating and leveled off. In the middle of her flight, she let out an echoing squawk, tucked her wings in, and dove forward like an arrow.

"Where are you taking me?" Bertly cried. Clia zoomed past a small nest of trees beyond the castle entrance and through a large crack in the mountain—on its west side behind the Academy. The crack was slim at the entrance but quickly grew into a sizable canal. Clia landed gracefully at the base of the mountain.

"Lead the way. You seem to know where you want to go." Bertly gestured for Clia to walk through the canal, to which she responded by tucking her wings in tightly, crouching her head, and crawling through with more caution than she'd exhibited in the halls of the Academy.

Not long after entering the canal, they exited the other side and emerged into city that was buried in shrubs, leaves, and other greenery. All that could be made out through the plants were the vague shapes of what were once cottages or shops. Climbing plants grew from gardens and clung onto homes and street signs. Most homes seemed to have found a new purpose, housing animals and providing shade for growing mushrooms. Weeds filled each crack, and fallen trees blocked the roads. The town was surrounded with grass fields, which accompanied a calm lake. The stars shined brighter there than above campus. The town was silent, all the memories and lives of the village long forgotten.

Clia bent her front legs, allowing Bertly to easily slide off her neck. The moment Bertly's feet touched the ground, Clia took off running. Bertly stood with his legs touching and his arms wrapped around himself.

"Clia, it's freezing," he shouted. Clia poked her head from around the corner of a crumbled building and cawed. While still hugging himself, Bertly jogged over to her, trying his best not to lose his balance. When Bertly rounded the corner, Clia was sitting there, waiting for him. She gestured with her beak toward the ground. Buried halfway in and halfway out of the ground was a hefty brick engraved with elaborate writing.

I have no legs to walk, no lungs to breathe, I have no life to live or die. Yet I do them all. What am I?

"Yet I do them all." Bertly's teeth chattered. "It's too late and cold for this, girl."

Clia puffed her feathers and flared out her wings.

Bertly stepped back. "I was only kidding…lighten up." Bertly knew better than to anger a gryphon. "Wait, this is easy. Master Alestar tried to stump Polly and me with this one our second year." Bertly cleared his throat. "Fire."

The engraved words lit up in a bright, glowing red that certainly resembled fire. The stone safe parted down the middle and revealed its innards to Bertly. Resting at the bottom was a small green whistle attached to a brown piece of string. Bertly examined the stone case for any more items. He found a piece of folded parchment and nothing more. Bertly unfolded the wrinkled paper.

Whistle at own risk.

"Another riddle," Bertly grumbled.

Clia started to dance around Bertly, gently poking him with her beak.

"Is this what you brought me all this way for?" Bertly's face lost all expression. "A whistle and riddles?" He felt what he'd dubbed his "angry vein" as it popped out on his forehead.

Clia sat on the ground and stared at him, obviously trying to sit still, but unable to do so because she was jittery with excitement. He could see that excitement reflected in her gleaming eyes. Bertly groaned and blew the whistle, but not a single noise came out. Clia did a backflip and sprang into the air, twirling in circles so quickly she became a blur. She gradually stopped spinning and floated in the air while looking expectantly at Bertly. He blew the whistle, and it was silent once again.

Clia did a corkscrew in the air and flew toward him.

She crash-landed on top of him and rested her chin on his chest. Her head was nearly the size of Bertly's torso. He scratched Clia behind the ear to reward her for what she'd shown him. The whistle was why she'd flown him out there—Clia was the only one who could hear the noise it made.

"This means I will call you if I need you now, okay?" Bertly looked Clia straight in the eyes. "That means no more sneaking around the castle...got it?"

Clia broke eye contact with him and pretended to be distracted by a bird that had been chirping in the background.

"Got it?" Bertly emphasized.

Clia grunted.

"Okay, good. I will use this whistle to call you every now and again." Bertly used the brown string to tie the whistle around his neck like a necklace. He then tucked it under his shirt. "Can you please take me back to the castle now? I'm freezing."

It only took two cycles before "every now and again" turned into a nightly routine. Nearly every night Bertly snuck outside to the castle entrance. He had figured out that it was safer going out the entrance than trying to sneak across the castle and to the back stables. Every night Bertly blew the silent whistle and braced for Clia's greeting. He knew by how quickly she arrived that she was always just around the corner, waiting to hear the whistle of her friend calling her.

***

Bertly and the twins were in room 782, tinkering away on a workbench. They were working on a wooden crossbow. The crossbow had no string, and there were several cracks running down the side of it, as well as a faded black leather grip with a blue snowflake sewn onto the side.

"It's done!" the twins shouted.

Bertly held the crossbow high above his head. "This may be our greatest one yet." Bertly's nostrils flared and the corners of his mouth turned up.

"Hand it over." Orîn jumped on the table and snatched the crossbow from Bertly's hands.

"I'm the oldest, I should go first." From the ground, Orin tugged on the crossbow, which sent Orîn tumbling off the table.

"Sweet Cordelia, don't break it again," Bertly cried. He leaped over the workbench and ripped the crossbow from the twins. "I will do the honors."

The twins jumped back to their feet. "Yes, sir," they shouted. Orîn sprinted to the classroom door and pulled the latch, locking them all inside. Orin ran to the corner of the room and pulled out a birdcage with a sheet over it. Orin pulled the sheet from the cage, revealing a blue drizzle bird. Its feathers were dark blue and its beak light blue. It was round like a melon and was no bigger than Bertly's fist.

Bertly climbed on top of the workbench. "Unleash the beast," Bertly roared.

Orin opened the cage. The drizzle bird sat on its perch, dead asleep, making its grand reveal less entertaining than anyone was expecting. Orin shook the cage. The bird's eyes popped open and he flapped his wings profusely. He flew out of the cage, all the while bobbing up and down in the air; he was hardly strong enough to hold up his own weight.

Bertly closed one eye and took aim. The crossbow didn't have a single arrow loaded into it. He pulled the trigger. A white light formed in the center of the crossbow where an arrow would've normally been placed.

The light quickly formed into an arrow made of ice. The arrow shot out of the crossbow quicker than a bolt of lightning and flew straight into the gut of the drizzle bird, sending it plopping onto the ground. The bird made a small squeak when its body hit the floor.

"Got him!" Bertly was standing on the workbench with the crossbow thrown over his shoulder. Orin retrieved the bird and brought it back to the workbench for the three of them to examine. The bird was frozen solid.

Bertly examined the bird and then rolled it over onto its other side. "No puncture wound."

"Check," the twins shouted.

Bertly tapped the bird. "Frozen solid."

"Check."

"And now, we wait…" Bertly stared at the bird, blinking as little as he could. The twins tried their best to match his concentration. The squishy bird lay motionless on the workbench. The ice around the bird eventually cracked. The drizzle bird puffed its feathers and flapped its wings, shaking off all the ice on its body. Orin held up the birdcage, without any hesitation, and the drizzle bird darted right back inside the cage.

Bertly put an arm around each twin. "We did it, boys. A nonlethal freezing crossbow. What should we call her?"

"Snowflake," the twins hollered.

Bertly's face went dull. "Very original."

Bertly strolled across the room and flopped into the chair behind Master Alestar's old desk. He reached into his knapsack, which was placed behind the desk, and pulled out an apple. He threw his feet onto the desk and reclined in his chair.

"I hope your new apprentice is fun," Orin shouted.

"Yeah, they'd better be good with building weapons," Orin added.

"And making potions, too."

"And setting gators into the elf's dormitory."

The twins burst into laughter.

"Settle down now. We will have plenty of time to corrupt the poor victim." Bertly took a massive bite out of the apple. "To be honest, I haven't even met an undergraduate yet." Bertly continued to take large crunching bites of the apple and proceeded to chew them with his mouth open.

"Are you serious?" Orin cried.

Orîn chimed in, "Isn't the deadline tomorrow?"

Bertly spit out the pieces of apple he was chewing on. "What are you talking about?"

"How do we know this and you don't?" the twins shouted.

"I was never assigned an apprentice," Bertly fumed.

Orin hopped onto a barstool next to the workbench. "A master chooses their apprentice." Orîn jumped onto a stool next to Orin. "How do you not remember this? You had a huge ordeal over it your first year." Orin and Orîn started to tinker with the crossbow.

Bertly's eyes widened. He flew out of his chair. "Oh, sweet Cordelia. What time does the registrar close?"

"At five," the twins replied. "It's at least seven now."

Bertly fell back into his chair. "Blast. I will have to go first thing tomorrow."

"They're probably out of students," Orin replied.

Orîn jumped in. "Every master has most certainly chosen an apprentice by now."

Bertly took a bite of his apple. "I'm not waiting a year for the next class. I'll take whoever they have to offer."

X

Bertly held a book in his hand while he sat on the floor next to the registrar's office, waiting for the grumpy old dwarf who worked the front desk to open it. Bertly had, unfortunately, had several encounters with her before. The previous encounter of theirs had involved bread pudding and a turkey leg at the dining hall. He somehow doubted he'd be able to persuade her to work in his favor. His nerves hit him harder when he heard footsteps echoing down the nearby corridor.

Rounding the corner was a stubby old woman, who could've easily been considered short—even for a dwarf. Her hair was half gray and she wore a chain around her neck with her reading glasses attached. She had a bag in one hand and what looked like tea in the other. "What are you doing here, Bertly?" the old woman grumbled, not bothering to make eye contact with him.

Bertly sprang to his feet the moment she addressed him and hustled over to her, reaching for her bag. "Good morning, Miss Dots. Here, let me grab that for you. Oh, and I don't know if you've heard, but it's actually *Master* Bertly now, ma'am." Bertly bit his tongue, albeit a bit late. He hadn't intended to lord his status over her. "Not important. I came to see if you had any apprentices left?" Bertly gave her a half smile, attempting charm.

"No," Miss Dots said simply as she shuffled past Bertly and reached to open the door to the registrar's office.

Bertly rushed ahead and opened the door for her. "Miss Dots, it would mean the world if you could *just maybe* take a tiny little peek at the list. See if anything is there." Bertly gave a slow shrug accompanied by what he hoped was another charming smile.

Miss Dots groaned and hobbled over to her cluttered desk, pushing aside a few books to make a place for her tea. She looked directly at Bertly for the first time. "The deadline is today, *Master* Bertly. Every student has already chosen their master."

Bertly put his hands together and gave Miss Dots his best puppy-dog eyes. "Please."

"You're lucky I'm a morning person." Miss Dots blew on her cup of tea and rummaged through a stack of papers. She perched her glasses at the tip of her nose and held the stack of pages out before her, slowly scanning them. Once every few moments she would lick her thumb and flip a page. After what felt to Bertly like an hour, the woman spoke.

"It seems as though we have one apprentice left."

Bertly scratched the back of his head as he wondered precisely why only one would be left. Why had no one chosen this lonely apprentice? Miss Dots held out a wrinkled transcript and waved the paper in the air, which Bertly immediately snatched from her. "Thank you," Bertly shouted.

"You should know this apprentice has been turned down the last two years in a row." Miss Dots calmly took a sip of her tea. Bertly was nearly out the door of her office, but he paused at her last statement.

"Why is that?" Bertly asked.

"He went through six masters in his first year. Bad

luck or something," Miss Dots replied.

"Sweet Cordelia." Bertly's eyes widened. "That is awful luck. Maybe I don't need an apprentice this year."

"Is that all, Master Bertly?" Miss Dots stared at him while rifling through more papers and continuing to drink her tea. She was already pretending he'd left. Bertly did not care that her patience with him was running thin.

He held his finger in the air. "One more thing—where will I meet my new apprentice?"

"Here. Same time tomorrow. Is that all, Master Bertly?" Miss Dots continued to dig through her piles of paper.

"Yes, Miss Dots. Thank you again." Bertly folded his future apprentice's transcript and put it in his pocket. As Bertly strolled out the door, he could not help but feel a tremendous weight lifted from his shoulders. He was still on track to finish the Mastery program on time.

***

"His test scores are excellent. He scored in the top ten percentiles for nearly every category. The top three in logic and reasoning." Bertly was scanning his apprentice's transcript while sharing dinner with the twins and Polly. "He even finished in the top eight at the Clash Tournament. On paper, this apprentice seems excellent."

"Please forgive me, but what exactly is the Clash Tournament?" Polly asked. Her cheeks reddened a little.

"It's the Academy's annual dueling tournament," Orin replied.

"One on one. First to submit—or get knocked out—loses," Orin added. The twins popped up and pretended to sword fight.

Polly stopped eating. "You're kidding. How barbaric." From the look on her face, Bertly could tell Polly would not be participating in the annual Clash Tournament.

"It's tradition," the twins shouted.

"That doesn't mean we have to act like animals." Polly grimaced. The twins plopped back into their seats.

"Polly, this is your sixth year. How do you not know about this?" Bertly continued to examine the transcript, turning it over, trying to find information he had not already read.

"You just pulled a Bertly," the twins interjected. Polly attempted to cover her smile, but Bertly could still hear her giggling.

"So why is this apprentice still available?" Polly asked. "It seems odd that another master hasn't tried to request him yet."

"Good point," the twins concurred.

"Well, that's the curious part." Bertly stopped eyeing the transcript and instead picked at his fingernail. "No one wants him because they think he is bad luck."

"Bad luck?" the twins questioned.

Bertly gave a nervous laugh. "He may or may not have gone through six masters in his first year."

Polly almost choked on her food. "Six masters? Oh my. Cordelia bless his soul."

"Who would agree to be his sixth master?" Orin shouted.

"What an idiot," Orîn finished.

"You have really chosen an apprentice with great potential, Bertly." Small tears formed in the corners of Polly's eyes from laughter.

"And I am sure *your* apprentice is so much better— aren't they, Polly?" Bertly crossed his arms and gave Polly a dirty look.

Polly's laugh halted. She cleared her throat and looked down at the table. "Well, his master actually did pass recently."

Bertly rolled his eyes.

Polly continued. "He served four years with his old master, so he will actually only be doing one year with me before moving on to the Mastery program." Polly perked up. "It's quite funny. He is actually a year older than me. But I am *his* master."

"That *is* funny." The twins giggled.

"When do you meet this older gentleman, Polly?" Bertly teased.

"He is actually supposed to meet us here for dinner. He should be here any minute." Polly peered into the dining hall. "Look out for a blond elf with a black streak in his hair."

Bertly did not have any intention of actively looking for Polly's new apprentice; however, he could not help but gaze over the crowd. Without much searching, Bertly spotted the lofty blond elf entering the dining hall. The man was the tallest head in the room, with biceps and pectorals that were clear even through his clothing. Bertly could see his defined jawline from across the room. *Please do not have a black streak in your hair,* Bertly silently begged of the elf, but of course, the elf turned his head, and running down his luscious blond hair like a skinny waterfall was a midnight-black strip of shiny hair.

Bertly's tongue slipped. "You have got to be kidding me."

"What was that, Bertly?" Polly asked.

Bertly cleared his throat. "Oh, I was saying I think I see him." Bertly pointed.

"That must be him." Polly stood on top of her seat. "Devdan!" Polly shouted, waving her hand at the elf.

The crowd parted for the elf as he walked over to meet Polly. Nearly the whole dining room—men and women alike—appeared to watch him as he marched by with his air of magnificence. Bertly barely repressed an annoyed grunt.

"You must be Polly. Please call me Dev." Devdan extended his hand toward Polly and slightly bent his knees to be more eye level with her. "It is a pleasure to meet you. I look forward to being your apprentice this year." Devdan kissed her hand. "I hope to serve you well."

Polly's cheeks grew red. "The pleasure is all mine." Polly slipped her hand away and giggled.

"I hope to serve you well," Bertly mocked under his breath.

"These are my friends." Polly gestured toward the twins and Bertly. "This is Bertly."

Bertly waved with what he was sure was a blank look on his face. He could tell he already did not like Polly's new apprentice.

Dev smiled and placed his hand on Bertly's shoulder. "I cannot wait to spend more time together this year, Bertly." His resting hand felt like the best massage Bertly had ever received. "You have built quite the reputation around campus." Devdan turned his head toward the twins.

"Twin dwarves," Dev shouted. "You must be Orin and Orîn. Your father is a legend."

"None other." Orin and Orîn sprang up and bowed.

"You really have made the right friends, Polly," Dev said with a radiant smile. "Please forgive me, but I must be off. I have a meeting with Master Grukkas soon."

"The combat teacher?" the twins asked.

"That is correct. I meet with her every night for personal training. I have to defend my title at the Clash Tournament this year," Dev replied.

"You won the Clash Tournament?" Bertly shouted.

"Two years running. I plan to make it a third." Dev winked. "Do you plan to enter this year, Bertly?"

"I plan to win this year," Bertly said.

"I love the enthusiasm, Bertly." Dev rubbed Bertly's back. "I will see you all very soon." Dev strolled off, causing the dining hall to once again come to a stop to simply watch him walk away.

"You really found a winner, Polly," the twins shouted.

"I am so excited. He seems like a joy." Polly turned to Bertly. "I cannot wait to meet your apprentice. When did you say you'll meet him?"

"Tomorrow morning." Bertly groaned.

***

The next morning, Bertly was less than enthusiastic about waiting for Miss Dots outside the registrar's office. He was inclined to show up late after Dev had crushed his confidence; however, he did not want to disrespect Miss Dots after she had done the favor of finding him an apprentice at the very last minute.

"You showed up," Miss Dots said as she lumbered around the corner. "The last three masters have gotten cold feet."

"I want to get my certificate as soon as possible." Bertly opened the door for Miss Dots. "My new apprentice will just be a small barrier."

"It may be worth waiting another year. Better than this being your last year." Miss Dots flopped behind her desk. Bertly briefly pondered what Miss Dots said, but brushed it off because he was the first red-eyed human who had existed since Cordelia herself. If anything, it was he, Bertly, who was the exception.

"You can take a seat right over there until your apprentice arrives," Miss Dots said.

Bertly headed for the comfy-looking chair in the corner.

"Are you Master Bertly?"

Bertly heard a weak and annoying voice. He turned. Standing in front of him was a chunky elf who looked five years too young to be in the Academy. He had dry and disorganized black hair that was cut so terribly, Bertly was sure the elf had done it himself. His arms were too small for his body—they dangled worthlessly at his sides. His legs were short and shaking, with his feet pointing in different directions.

***

"Sir!" Roderick shouted. "That is not at all how your apprentice looked." Roderick's face had turned red.

"That is *exactly* how I remember him." Bertly stuck his nose in the air and reclined onto his massive bed.

"I am sorry, sir, but you are delusional." Roderick threw his quill onto the table and crossed his arms. "That is not how that striking elf looked...sir."

Bertly looked over at Roderick. "So tell me, Roderick, how would *you* describe my apprentice?"

"Well, sir, I am glad you asked." Roderick snatched his quill and started writing.

***

Bertly heard a deep and intimidating voice. He turned. Standing in front of him was a mature elf who looked old enough to already be a master. He had gorgeous black hair that resembled the midnight sky itself. His arms were toned, and he had legs so firm, they appeared to be planted into the ground—

***

Bertly shot up. "Roderick, this is absolute blasphemy. Have you no memory at all?"

"I am an elf, sir, my memory is actually quite superb," Roderick shouted.

A loud growl filled the room. The tone was deep enough to feel the vibrations in one's chest. Roderick's eyes widened as he shot back in his chair.

"Look, you have gone and upset the furry bed." Bertly pet the brown fur he was lying on. "Can we *please* get back on topic?" Bertly reclined onto the bed.

Roderick glared at Bertly. "Yes, sir."

***

Bertly heard a slightly annoying but tolerable voice utter his name. He turned. Standing before him was an average elf, with average-looking black hair, and who was, in general, very average.

"That is I. Who is asking?" Bertly replied.

The elf stood up straight and splashed a giant smile across his face. "Hello, sir, I am your new apprentice, Roderick."

XI

Bertly shoved his way through the crowded hallways with his apprentice following close behind. He was anxious to take Roderick to room 782. It was Bertly's main dwelling place, and Roderick had no clue just how much that room meant to him, nor how much time they would be spending there.

"Where exactly are we going, sir? I have never been to this part of the castle," Roderick shouted, trying his best to talk over the sound of all the students bustling through the corridors.

"To your new sanctuary, apprentice." Bertly turned and started walking backwards so he could face Roderick. A sly smile was forming in the corners of his mouth. "A place where we can experiment with magic freely." Bertly knocked over two elves as he carelessly walked backwards through the hallways, not stopping to help them up or even apologize for his offenses. "An abode to build and create our own masterpieces."

Roderick's eyes lit up. "Unbelievable, sir. I can't believe the Academy gave you special approval to enchant items."

Bertly came to a sudden halt, causing Roderick to bump into his chest. Bertly slapped his hand over Roderick's mouth. "Quiet. Are you trying to get us expelled?" Bertly leaned in. "Obviously, we are not *allowed* to enchant items. But rules are meant for the weak. Ones who need protecting." Bertly let go of Roderick. "First lesson, Roderick, do not question what is or is not against the rules. Only question what will or will not make you a better sorcerer." Bertly turned back around and passed through the hallways facing forward. Master and apprentice continued through the corridors until they reached an area where students no longer visited. "And here we are, 782," Bertly announced.

"Seven hundred eighty-two?" Roderick scratched his head. "But, sir, I thought all the rooms were odd-numbered in the Academy."

Bertly smiled and tapped his nose. "Ah, all but one." Bertly opened the door to a small room stocked with gadgets and gizmos—a room where weapons and shields lined the walls, and miscellaneous items cluttered the desks and surfaces. On a workbench near the front of the room, the twins were fiddling with a mug. "This is our workshop. The twins and I have been coming here nearly every day for the past three years. This is the classroom of my master." Bertly lost his smile. He wished Alestar could've met Roderick. Alestar would've been proud to see his apprentice as a master.

"Hello, Bertly," Orin shouted.

"And other Bertly," Orîn cracked. Orin was tightening screws on a mug while Orîn held his hands around it. Bertly could tell Orîn was trying to enchant the mug.

Bertly gestured toward Roderick. "Orins, this is my apprentice, Roderick."

"Greetings, Rod," the twins replied.

Roderick stepped into the room. "Hello, it's a pleasure to meet you. It's quite a—"

"He has a baby face, Bertly," Orîn interrupted.

"Are you sure he is over ten?" Orin added.

Bertly glanced at Roderick and tried his best not to laugh. His stomach started to hurt from restricting himself.

"I am actually fourteen," Roderick snapped.

"Now, now, baby-faced apprentice, do not take what they say seriously." Bertly bent in close enough for only Roderick to hear. "Their brains match their size." Bertly winked.

Roderick grinned. "Did you build all these items yourself, sir?"

"With the help of the dwarves and Polly, we created most of what you see here." Bertly twirled in a circle with his arms sprawled out. He was excited to finally share his workplace with another student. Until now he had always kept his workshop just between himself, the twins, and Polly.

"Bertly, come check this out," the twins interjected.

Bertly strolled over to the workbench at which the twins were sitting. Orin held the mug in the air. It was made of smooth wood and had three small switches on the side of it.

"Push here and it'll keep your drink warm," Orin explained.

"Great for tea," Orîn said.

Orîn snatched the mug out of Orin's hand. "Push here and it'll make it cold."

"Fascinating," Bertly said. His hands were clasped behind his back, and he turned his head to view the various working parts of the mug. "What about the third switch?"

"We don't know yet. It's just in case," the twins replied.

Bertly chuckled, then snatched the mug and examined it more carefully. The sound of a test tube breaking came from the back of the classroom.

Bertly jerked his head. He was unable to catch everything—however, he saw the last moments of Roderick's fall to the floor. When Roderick hit the ground, his back foot knocked a broom that was propped against a nearby worktable, and the handle of the broom—on its way to the floor—collided with a bottle filled with blue liquid, which was resting on top of the workbench. As Roderick began pushing himself up, the vial crashed onto his head, dousing him in the blue liquid. Roderick's entire body froze. Small ice crystals covered the surface of his figure.

"Well, that didn't take long," Bertly said.

The twins let out an outrageous laugh. "He really *is* bad luck."

A small muffled noise came out of Roderick's iced-over body. "I an ill er ing oo aye." The twins and Bertly stiffened. They fixated their attention on Roderick, who was failing at an attempt to articulate something to the group. "I an till her thing you aye."

"Sweet Cordelia, he is fully conscious." Bertly snapped his fingers, and the ice around Roderick's body turned to liquid.

"I can still hear everything you say," Roderick pushed out as he gasped for air.

"Outstanding, some of your senses stayed fully intact," Bertly said as he examined Roderick.

"Interesting indeed," the twins yelled.

Roderick stood up and wrung out the bottom of his shirt. "What was that, sir?"

Bertly snapped his fingers again. A gust of wind shot across the classroom, causing papers to flutter through the air. Roderick fell back onto his rear. His clothes were completely dried. "It's a freeze potion. Nothing you won't be able to construct by the end of the year," Bertly replied.

Bertly walked over to Roderick and extended his hand to help him to his feet. "I sure hope this bad-luck gossip is nothing more than a rumor. We have a spirit quest in just a handful of cycles."

Roderick gasped. "Sir! You are kidding, right?" He looked Bertly in the eyes intensely; it seemed as though he were waiting for him to crack a smile. "Most masters and apprentices are together for at least two or three years before going on any sort of intensive quest, let alone a spirit quest."

Bertly rolled his eyes. "Lesson two—do not worry about what others typically do or do not do. If someone has never done something before, then be the first to do it."

"I see." Roderick glanced over the room, looking at all the various knickknacks. "So, where are we going, sir?"

"I like the attitude adjustment, apprentice. Come, follow me." Bertly strolled across the room and over to a map that was pinned on the wall. The map was a fully detailed depiction of Pangea, with every mountain and lake drawn on it. All the major cities and realms were labeled in fine detail. "We are going to the mountains just behind Noskar. The Academy is here, at the most northern part of Pangea." Bertly poked his finger on the symbol of the castle and dragged it across the map. "We will travel *all the way* here, to the most western reach of the world."

Roderick gasped. "Sir, that is quite the journey. I thought most don't travel more than a couple of nights beyond the Academy. Won't going to Noskar take at least…" Roderick started counting on his fingers.

Bertly held out his hand, offering it to Roderick. Roderick looked at him with confusion. "I thought you might need a few more fingers." Bertly busted up laughing. "I will do the math for you; the trip will take about forty nights."

"Forty!" Roderick shouted.

"Most of that will be traveling. It should only take two days to get through the mountains. My father has taken me through those mountains more times than I can count. Plus, we will have help carrying all the equipment. Polly and...her *apprentice* will be tagging along." Bertly remembered how much he disliked Dev. He was not dreading the trip with Polly so much—he had learned to almost tolerate her. But Dev, he was an entirely new type of annoyance.

"Sir, if you don't mind, why are we going all the way to the Noskar Mountains? Don't most students retrieve their spirit quest item from somewhere more...local?" Roderick stuttered.

"That is a fair question, little elf. I am sure that traveling to the human realm was not on your list of things to do." Bertly walked over to a nearby bookshelf. He ran his finger across the book bindings as he browsed the titles. He stopped at the book titled *Famous Creatures and Beasts and Monsters* and slipped it off the shelf. He began to swipe swiftly through the pages. "Aha." Bertly walked back over to Roderick and slammed the book on a worktable next to the world map. "Take a look here, Roderick. This, this is the most famous creature in all of Noskar."

"Incredible, sir, the sheer size seems unfathomable," Roderick said.

"Growing up, Polly and I heard countless tales and stories about this beast. We have both been mesmerized by him since we were children."

"Are you talking about Cordelia's dragon?" the twins interrupted. Bertly had almost forgotten they were in the room. The twins had a knack for falling quieter than an elf mouse when they were focused.

"Yes, boys, I am," Bertly replied. "Sweet Cordelia's dragon. Polly and I are going to each retrieve a scale and bring it back. Many have brought back dragon scales over the centuries, but none have brought back a scale from the King of all Dragons."

"Sir, don't you think there may be a reason no one has ever returned with one of his scales?" Roderick asked.

"No guts, no glory," the twins said.

Bertly rolled his eyes. "Don't worry so much, Roderick. I obviously have a plan."

Bertly did have a plan—however, it was not to steal a scale from Cordelia's dragon. He did not intend to irritate his future dragon. Bertly was going to soul-bond with the King of all Dragons, and Polly was going to have a front-row seat to that monumental event.

***

Bertly and Polly sat front and center for Thel's Mastery seminar on soul-bonding and spirit quests. Polly was trying to write her notes down just as quickly as Thel was writing them on the chalkboard. Bertly found it quite odd that Master Thel handwrote everything—all his other professors used magic to write on the board. Regardless, Bertly could not concentrate on the lecture. He was too wrapped up in thinking about the details of his spirit quest. Polly nudged Bertly and gestured for him to pay attention to the board.

"There is no one-size-fits-all method to soul-bonding," Thel said. "What works for one person will not always work for another." Slithers wiggled across the floor and stopped next to Thel, where he rested. His body nearly came up to Thel's waist. "Soul-bonding requires you to split a piece of your soul and transfer it over to another living soul. The greater the creature, the more of your soul you must give up. This is why one person can only bond with one mammoth, but another can bond with a dozen kokos." Slithers raised his head, and Thel gently pet him on the top of his head. "Slithers here is the only partner I will ever bond with." Thel couldn't hold back his smile. "And I am okay with that. Not to mention, even if I were to pull off another soul-bond, there is no telling what it could do to me. I gave up a lot to bond with him. The soul is not meant to be ripped apart; it is quite dangerous. This is why some even believe soul-bonding is unnatural…mostly in human cultures." Thel kept looking over the classroom; however, Bertly could tell his eyes glanced over at him and Polly after making his last remark.

"After you know the dozen spells required to perform the soul-bond, the rest is up to you. You have to be truly willing to give up part of yourself, or it will not work. Many masters fail several times before ever finding success, and most of the time, they settle."

The classroom bell rang and the students started to pack their belongings.

"One last thing before you go," Thel said. "This year we are instituting a timeframe on spirit quests."

The students stopped packing their belongings. Bertly adjusted his posture and started giving his full attention for the first time that period.

"The spirit quests this year are limited to seven days. This should not affect most of you, since most students do not travel more than a night beyond the castle."

Conversations sparked all across the room.

Bertly's stomach dropped. He considered biting his tongue, but he couldn't hold back. "Sir, that is outrageous. Most students take at least a fortnight to complete their spirit quest."

"I was also a student once, Master Bertly. I am quite

aware of the wasted time that comes along with a spirit quest. Most finish in just a few days and then take time to...hmmm, how to say it...blow off steam." The classroom chuckled. "That is all for today. I will see you all tomorrow."

Bertly sat in his seat, fuming, as the other students shuffled out of the classroom. Polly placed her hand on Bertly's shoulder. "Let's go talk about this back at the dormitory." Bertly could tell she was trying to stop him from doing or saying something regrettable, and he knew she was typically right, so he stood up and left the room with her.

Just as Bertly was walking out the door, he heard Thel yelling behind him, "I am sure you will figure something out, Master Bertly. You are a resourceful young man."

***

Polly was sitting on her bed while Bertly paced around the room, anxiously trying to figure out how the two would accomplish their quest, given the restriction they'd just learned.

"We can always take a leaf from the tree in Eplium," Polly suggested.

"That's what every elf and their mother before them did. I will not be doing something so predictable and overdone, but thank you for the wise suggestion, Polly," Bertly asserted. Polly sighed but did not respond to his little outburst, which irritated him even more for some reason.

"Bertly, I'm sorry, but I'm not sure we have much of a choice. Getting back home to Noskar will take at least fifteen nights...if we are productive. And that is not including the time it takes to get through the mountains," Polly said.

Bertly quit pacing the room. Polly looked at the floor and let out a long sigh before getting up off her bed and putting her arm around him. Standing next to Bertly, Polly looked short—her head barely reached to his chest. "It's okay, Bertly. We will figure out something else."

"It's not that, Polly," Bertly said. His shoulders slouched.

Polly leaned backward and examined him with her eyebrows drawn together and her lips slightly parted. "What do you mean?"

"We can still do our quest. We can still go to Noskar." Bertly continued to stare at the floor. He felt bad that he had been lying to Polly the past few months. While Polly annoyed Bertly up to his ears, she was most likely the only reason he'd ever managed to make any of his deadlines, and she was always so irritatingly pleasant and helpful—he knew her intentions were good, and she *had* managed to help whip him into shape.

"You are going to have to explain yourself." Polly tried to look up from under Bertly's chin so she could make eye contact with him.

"I know a way we can get to Noskar in one day," Bertly replied.

"Bertly, are you about to tell me you're a shipper? Teleportation would be quite convenient right now." Polly nudged Bertly softly in the side with her elbow.

Polly's joke helped Bertly lighten up; he could not help but let half a grin show. "I can't teleport, but I have the next best thing. How does a creature faster than a dragon sound?"

She stared at him for a moment. "You don't," Polly blurted, eyes wide with a hand over her mouth.

Bertly looked her in the eyes. "I do."

***

Bertly was strutting through the main entrance with Polly right behind him, who was crouched and tiptoeing as quiet as a thief in the night.

"You really don't have to sneak around like that. I walk through here every night and have never been caught. Each night the hall monitor sneaks away to the midnight buffet, so he won't be back for at least fifteen minutes," Bertly said as they exited the castle.

Polly straightened her posture and started strolling, but even with the air of confidence she projected, Bertly could tell she was slightly embarrassed. As they rounded the side of the castle, Bertly pulled out his whistle and gave it a blow.

"Thank Cordelia your whistle is broken, Bertly," Polly yelped. "You shouldn't be trying to draw attention to us when we are out past curfew."

Bertly laughed. "Oh, it works, trust me." In a full sprint, Clia came bursting around the corner, running as though she were being chased by a horde of Rotters. When she spotted Polly, Clia came to a screeching halt and cocked her head back so far Bertly couldn't see her neck. She looked at Bertly, then at Polly, and again at Bertly.

"Don't worry, girl." Bertly put his hand out and walked toward Clia. The gryphon kept her eyes locked on Polly. When Bertly reached his hand closer to Clia, she rubbed her face against it while keeping eye contact with Polly. "This is Polly, my friend. We sort of like her." Clia broke eye contact with Polly and nuzzled into Bertly, nearly knocking him over. "Come say hello, Polly."

Polly approached Clia with patience, and Bertly was impressed by the straight look on her face—that she didn't seem the least bit intimidated by the massive gryphon. Polly reached out to pet Clia. To Bertly's surprise, Clia did not react at all. He could tell she did not mind Polly's attention.

"So, what is your master plan, Bertly?" Polly asked.

"With Clia here, we can get to the Noskar Mountains in a single day. I would ask her to take us somewhere in the mountains, but gryphons don't do well in the snow. I will have her drop us off in Noskar, and we can do the mountain trails by foot. It shouldn't take longer than three nights in total to navigate to the Dragon's Crypt," Bertly replied.

Polly was calculating the trip out in her head. Bertly could always tell by the way she twirled her hair when she was thinking, and how her expression changed—her eyes revealed easily that she was preoccupied. "So Clia will fly to Noskar, drop us off, and fly back to the castle. She will then fly back to Noskar to pick us up, and then travel all the way back to the castle. Bertly, doesn't that seem a bit much, even for a gryphon?"

Bertly nodded in agreement. "It is a bit much, even for a gryphon. Not to mention, I would never make her fly through the mountains. A gryphon can deal with moderately cold temperatures, but in the snow, things can go wrong fast." Bertly climbed aboard Clia and extended his hand to Polly. Without hesitation, she grabbed ahold and hopped onto Clia, where she sat just behind Bertly. "On the way to the mountains, we are going to make a stop at my father's house. I know he will be more than thrilled to watch over a gryphon for a few days. It will give Clia enough time to rest, and then we can all head back to the Academy."

Clia started to flap her wings, rustling up the leaves and nearby branches so that they flew in all directions. Polly began to lose her balance, but as she was falling, she grabbed Bertly around the stomach and pulled herself in. Bertly looked down at her arms wrapped around him and blushed. Immediately he was annoyed with his reaction.

He was even more annoyed that his immediate instinct was not to forcefully remove her hands from him. He simply let her hold onto him. It was necessary, after all. Otherwise, he surely would have shoved her away from him.

"I just hope our apprentices can keep their lips sealed about this," Polly shouted over the noise of Clia's wings.

"Me too," Bertly replied. "Now don't let go. Her speed is overwhelming at first." Bertly whistled and Clia rocketed into the sky. She flew through the air so rapidly Bertly and Polly could barely manage to keep their eyes open. Bertly gave Clia two taps with his foot, and she leveled off into a graceful glide through the sky.

"The view is magnificent, Bertly," Polly said as the two of them gazed over Pangea's rolling green mountains and various forests.

"I still haven't gotten used to it. Is this your first time flying, Polly?" Bertly asked.

"Yes...and I am absolutely terrified." She squeezed Bertly a little tighter.

"Well, you're doing a good job of hiding it."

Polly loosened her grip and burst out laughing. Bertly gave Clia two taps with his other foot, and she turned back toward the castle.

Clia dropped them off at the castle entrance. Bertly gave Clia a big hug, wrapping his arms around her head, since she was too big to hug anywhere else. Clia looked at Polly, blinked, turned her head quickly away, and then raced off back behind the castle.

"She really is magnificent, Bertly." Polly's eyes were sparkling. She peered toward Bertly. "Just to be clear, what exactly is the plan?"

Bertly cleared his throat. "We will meet up outside the castle with our apprentices in a few days. We cannot reveal Clia until nightfall. So we will head into town and grab some supplies first. I will grab Clia some food; she will need to be well energized for this trip."

Polly nodded in agreement.

"Once the sun has set, we will all meet back up and leave for Stonebank. We should arrive just after dawn."

"Sounds like a plan, Bertly. I will follow your lead." Polly nudged him. "So is this where you have been sneaking off to every night?"

Bertly chuckled. "I didn't think you noticed. I tried to be quiet."

"Oh, Bertly, just like you assume I haven't noticed that notebook you are always trying to sneakily read." Polly winked at Bertly.

Bertly's eyes widened and he gulped. He quickly gave a half turn and started walking toward the castle entrance. "We are done here. I do *not* want to find out what else you know."

"What's wrong, Bertly. What do you have to hide?" Polly chuckled and ran after him.

XII

The sun was close to setting and not a cloud was in sight, and drizzle birds could still be heard singing from almost any tree. Bertly and Roderick were standing just outside the castle entrance. Roderick was shuffling through a travel sack, pulling out various items. Bertly stood in front of him, watching his apprentice with his hands on his hips.

"Do you have the elixirs?" Bertly asked.

"Check," Roderick replied.

"Our money purse?" Bertly rubbed his thumb and pointer finger together, making a gesture of two coins rubbing together.

"I am still not sure why we have a money purse, sir. We only have a couple of coins," Roderick said.

"Roderick, do you not understand how a checklist works?" Bertly snapped with his nostrils flaring.

Roderick's eyes widened. "Check."

Bertly's anger washed off his face. "Do you have the flask?" He grinned and rubbed his hands together.

"Yes, sir. The water is packed," Roderick answered.

Bertly smacked his palm against his forehead. "Not *that* flask, you dope."

Roderick stared blankly at Bertly for a moment. He

shook his head and rifled through the travel sack. "Right, sir, of course. I can't believe I forgot." Roderick waved around a plain gray flask.

"How could you forget such a sacred tradition?" Bertly shook his head. "Every sorcerer has their first drink after they complete a spirit quest."

"Incredible, sir. I had no idea it was a tradition," Roderick replied.

Bertly stuttered. "W-well, it is more of an…unwritten tradition."

"Did you boys pack any nourishment?" Polly emerged from the castle gate with Dev just behind her, who was carrying a large travel sack on his back. The size of his frame disguised how big the bag really was, even for a magic satchel. Dev was one of the few students at the Academy who was as tall as Bertly, aside from the giants, who towered over all races.

"An elf never forgets to pack food," Roderick said.

"It is true. You should never question an elf's diet, ma'am," Dev interjected.

Bertly stood with his jaw slightly open, watching as the elves corrected Polly—a rare phenomenon, but one that brought him immense satisfaction. His open mouth seamlessly turned into a smile. "Yes, Polly. How could you be so ignorant?" Bertly winked.

Polly's cheeks turned a little red. "They must have skipped over it in our elven history class," she replied. Bertly could tell she was slightly embarrassed. Not from her blushing—Polly blushed at nearly everything. He could tell by the way she held her hands behind her back. Polly almost always talked with her hands; it was only when she was embarrassed or sleepy that she didn't use body language to communicate.

Once the group settled down from laughing, Dev chimed in, "I do not mean to sound pessimistic just before getting started, but how do we plan on getting to Noskar and back in just seven nights?"

"Yes, Master Bertly, why don't you inform us?" Polly glanced at Bertly with a fake smile and batted her eyelashes.

Bertly cracked his knuckles and peered at Roderick and Dev. He lowered his eyebrows. "Have you two ever heard of master and apprentice confidentiality?"

Roderick and Dev turned to each other, neither seeming to have any clue what Bertly was referring to.

"It is a rule that states that whatever a master tells an apprentice must be kept between that master and apprentice."

"Interesting, sir." Dev rubbed his chin. "My old master never mentioned that."

Bertly puffed his chest and crossed his arms. "It's right in the rule book. Check for yourself if you don't believe me."

Dev pulled out a small book from his back pocket. "Do you know which section it is in, sir?" Dev flipped through the pages of his paperback. "I never leave my dormitory without the Academy's official guidebook."

Bertly whipped his head back and his eyes went around. "We do not have time for this, Devdan. We need to be back here in seven days," Bertly snapped.

"Of course, sir. My sincerest apologies." Dev placed the book in his back pocket and diverted his attention back to Bertly.

"Are we all on the same page here? Whatever I am about to say, you must swear on Cordelia you will not tell a living soul."

"Yes, sir," Roderick—always eager to please—blurted instantly.

Before answering, Dev looked over toward Polly. She gave him a small nod. "Of course, sir. My lips are sealed."

The tone of Dev's speech was slightly off. Bertly could not tell exactly what it was that was different, but the familiar charm that rang with Dev's voice was gone.

Bertly clapped his hands. "Wonderful. Unfortunately, I must leave you two in suspense for a couple more hours, just until nightfall. We cannot risk having any students or faculty spotting us."

Just as Roderick opened his mouth to speak, Bertly interrupted. "One last thing, no asking any questions until we get to Noskar, understand?" He glared straight into Roderick's eyes.

Roderick, with his mouth open, quickly shut it. Bertly could tell by the way Roderick was biting his bottom lip that he was itching to ask him a question about asking questions.

"Understood, sir," Dev replied.

Bertly cocked his head to the side. "Roderick?"

Roderick took a deep breath and let it out slowly. "Understood...sir."

Bertly clapped his hands. "Wonderful. Now that we are all on the same page, let's get a move on." Bertly turned and took the group down the same dirt road that led to the castle entrance. "We are going to make a quick stop at the village up ahead, and then we will be on our way."

"Sir, what do we need to grab? I thought we packed everything?" Roderick asked.

"Roderick!" Bertly shouted. "Can you not last one minute? I thought we agreed, no questions until Noskar." Bertly noticed that both Polly and Dev bit their fingers as they attempted to hold back smiles.

Roderick's eyes widened. "Sorry, sir." He instantly broke eye contact with Bertly and looked forward down the pathway.

The group continued down the dirt road and toward a

thick forest. On each side of the path was luscious green grass, which stood higher than Bertly's waist. Random lavender plants spread across the entire field, adding a fresh smell to the air. A few leagues past the Academy was a dense forest that stood in between the school and the village. It was clustered with trees ten times taller than a giant.

"I am personally excited to visit the college town. In my seven years, I have never been." Bertly could tell Dev was trying to ease the tension with his little announcement.

"The town is modest in size, but it has the necessities. Most of the occupants are storeowners. I think most of the business comes from Academy students trying to get supplies in order to create their own potions," Bertly replied.

"I am curious, what are we picking up, Bertly?" Polly asked as she walked with an enormous map of Pangea spread wide open.

Bertly hesitated. "Food…for our fifth companion." Bertly started to kick a rock down the dirt path.

"Oh…right." Polly gave a half grin and continued to survey the map. "Bertly, do you think we could make one quick stop on our way to Noskar? There's a place along the way that has intrigued me for quite some time." She looked up from her map. "It really is no detour. I am sure Cl—" Polly stuttered. Bertly shot her a wide-eyed look, alerting her to the fact that she'd nearly spoiled the surprise. "I am sure *they* could use the break anyway."

Bertly kicked the rock down the dirt path once more. "Hmm, what kind of detour?"

"The Eternal Cave. It's between the White Lake and Stonebank." Polly smiled as wide as seemed possible. "*Please*, Bertly."

Bertly burst out laughing. "You don't seriously believe

that old myth, do you?" He wound his leg back and kicked the rock as hard as he could. It flew off to the side and was lost in the tall grass.

"What myth, sir?" Roderick asked.

Bertly stopped walking and turned. "Roderick." A vein was bulging from Bertly's forehead. He could feel it protruding. "If you ask one more question, I swear on my own good looks, I will seal your lips shut until we get to Noskar. Do I make myself clear?"

Roderick gulped. "Yes, sir."

Bertly turned back around and started kicking another pebble down the dirt path. "Sorry, Polly, but I don't think we will have the time."

"Oh, come on, Bertly, it will take less than an hour—the cave is tiny. I know you love magical treasure." Polly folded her map up. "Plus, this is my spirit quest, too. Shouldn't I have some say in where we go?"

"Magical treasure? Count me in," Dev said.

Bertly grunted and kicked another rock into the tall pasture. "I suppose we can make a brief stop, Polly." Bertly stopped walking and glanced up. The pathway was blocked by a wall of redwood trees.

"It sure is dark, sir. I hope the forest isn't too thick." Roderick's voice trembled. Bertly could hear his footsteps creeping closer to him, and when he looked back, he saw that Roderick was gripping his travel sack tight and was following Bertly so close he was only a hair behind him. Bertly sighed. His instinct was to taunt his apprentice, but he also understood that a good master knew when to provide comfort. Bertly figured this was one of those times.

"I would not worry, Roderick, this forest is quite new. It hasn't had time to grow much yet. That's why it still has no name." Bertly marched forward. "Let's not waste any time, then."

After the first dense row of trees, the plants thinned and the air grew humid and warm. Bertly felt small beads of water drip onto his face from the water built up on the tree leaves. The ground was soft from the constant water falling onto it. Plants and flowers emerged from every inch of the forest floor, making the forestry appear beautiful and alive. When Bertly took his attention from his immediate surroundings and looked closely into the distance, he could see small flickering lights.

"It looks like you lucked out today, Roderick." Bertly slapped him on the back, causing him to nearly fall forward. "It seems the forest *is* quite small."

Roderick exhaled. "Thank Cordelia." He adjusted his posture and started marching forward alongside Bertly.

"What are you going to do when we get to the mountains, little apprentice?" Bertly asked, emitting a small chuckle.

"What do you mean, sir? Are the mountains dangerous?" Roderick shook his head. "No, wait, I mean..." Roderick's eyes were shifting about to look in all directions as he was stuttering. Bertly could tell he was trying to rephrase what he had said so it wouldn't be a question. "I meant, I had no clue the mountains were dangerous."

Bertly frowned and gave a slow nod.

Where the group emerged from the forest, the dirt road returned, and just down the pathway was a charming village filled with several shops and homes. The town was lit by lanterns hanging from street posts and store porches. There were antique stores, potion shops, a tailor, as well as a blacksmith. Despite the sun having set, townsfolk were walking in and out of stores and wandering along the streets. In between the retail shops, there were saloons inviting potential customers inside with live music playing.

"I present to you…" Bertly spread his arms out like wings. "The village that never sleeps."

"Polly, maybe we should ditch Master Bertly and Roderick and do our spirit quest here," Devdan cracked. He gazed around the lively town, and Bertly watched as Devdan became visibly distracted by every young woman who walked in or out of the nearby saloons.

Polly had her eyes locked on the live band inside a bar across the road. "You don't need to convince me." Polly chuckled. She pointed toward a store sign. "Maybe the Drunkin' Dragon has a scale we can steal." The entire group burst out laughing.

Bertly interrupted the joyous laughter to bring them back to earth, "We can come back to celebrate *after* our spirit quest. For now, we must get a move on. The sun is nearly set. Everyone grab any last-minute supplies and meet back here in fifteen minutes."

The group nodded in agreement and parted ways.

As Roderick began to split from the group, Bertly grabbed him by the collar. "I don't think so. You're staying where I can see you." Bertly let go of Roderick's collar and led the way.

Roderick followed closely behind him. "Can I ask just one question, sir?" he muttered.

"No," Bertly stated. "Even if I said yes, you've just wasted your one question asking me if you could ask a question." Bertly glanced over toward Roderick.

Roderick let out a big sigh, his shoulders slumped, his gaze fell to the ground, and he kicked up dirt.

"Okay, fine, one question," Bertly said.

Roderick straightened his back and cleared his throat. "I don't mean to question you, sir, but something has been worrying me."

"Roderick, spit it out," Bertly groaned.

Roderick exhaled. "Do you think it is a wise decision

to go on such a dangerous mission with *me* as your apprentice, sir?" His voice quivered.

"Roderick, I will emphasize this again." Bertly placed his hand on Roderick's shoulder as they continued to walk. He had to speak louder than usual in order for Roderick to hear him over the music that filled the streets. "I am the first red-eyed human since Cordelia. I do not worry myself with odds, chances, or luck. I already know I am lucky, there is no denying it." Bertly took his hand off Roderick's shoulder and pointed toward a storefront named Wiggly Willie's. He gently nudged Roderick in the direction of the store. "To be honest, it's that blond elf that I worry about." Bertly snarled his upper lip.

"Really, sir?" Roderick sprinted ahead a few steps in order to open the door for Bertly. "Most people seem to like him. He has been voted 'Most Liked' every year that I've been here."

"Most liked?" Bertly shouted as he walked past Roderick. "Who does this voting?"

"The student body, sir. We vote on all sorts of candidates each year for the yearbook," Roderick replied.

"Yearbook? What yearbook?" Bertly bellowed.

"Hello there, travelers. Welcome to Wiggly Willie's. The one-stop shop for anything wiggly. I am Willie. How can I help ya?" An old man with short gray hair and a long beard stood behind a counter. He had wrinkles in the corners of his eyes and lines around his joyful smile. "Oh my, a fellow human." Willie squinted. "A red-eyed human," he exclaimed, his face filled with excitement. Willie emerged from behind the counter and extended his arm to greet Bertly. "It is a pleasure to finally meet you. I haven't seen another human since my hair was black. I've heard rumors about you attending the Academy, but after a few years went by, I didn't think you'd ever stop into town."

"Did you really hear about me?" Bertly tried to hold back a smile. Notoriety was the first step to becoming a great master.

Willie's eyes widened and he craned his head back. "Well, of course." He threw his hands into the air. "Every human in and outside Noskar knows who Bertly and Polly are." He started rubbing his hands together in a giddy manner. "Sweet Cordelia, you are the first red-eyed humans since the goddess herself."

Roderick and Bertly slowly turned their heads toward each other. They locked eyes and their jaws dropped. Bertly snapped his head back toward Willie. "You mean to tell me"—Bertly placed his finger on his chest—"that every human in Noskar knows who I am?"

"Absolutely, Master Bertly." Willie's smile grew even bigger—it engulfed his entire face. He ran behind the counter. "Anything you want is on the house. Anything for Cordelia's children."

Bertly found himself practically choking on the air. "Pardon?" He cleared his throat. "Could you repeat that last part?"

"Everything in this shop is free for one of Cordelia's children. Now, can I get you something wiggly?"

***

Bertly and Roderick walked out of Wiggly Willie's, each with a huge bucket of worms in his arms. Though they were only shopping briefly, the number of people in the streets seemed to double. They tried to keep straight faces as they navigated through the crowd, but they both looked as though they had just seen a ghost.

"Sir, I really want to ask a question right now."

Roderick was leaning back, trying to keep his body from falling forward. The bucket of worms he carried was larger than his torso.

Bertly continued to trek forward and stared into the village. His eyes were not fixated on any one thing, but his mind was. "He called me one of Cordelia's children," he said, still in a state of disbelief.

"I have never heard that phrase before, sir," Roderick replied.

"Me neither, but it sounds like a very good thing." Bertly came to a halt and placed his arm across Roderick, halting his stride. When Roderick came to an abrupt stop, his bucket jolted, and the contents flew upward—a few worms slapped the bottom of his chin. "Do not mention any of this to Polly."

Small beads of sweat formed on Roderick's forehead. "Sir, you are starting to ask me to keep a lot of secrets. I maybe should have mentioned this before. I am not the best secret keeper, sir."

Bertly's face grew hot. He spoke slowly and in as stern a manner as he was able to, "Roderick, I swear, if you crack…Especially with what I am going to show you later. Not even sweet Cordelia—"

A deep voice called for Bertly. He looked over the swarm of drunken villagers, and—several inches taller than the rest of the crowd—Bertly spotted Dev's sunny blond hair.

"Is everything okay, Roderick? You look awfully pale," Polly asked.

Bertly wrapped his arm around Roderick, placing his hand on Roderick's far shoulder. "He's sick…from the worms," Bertly interjected.

"I hate worms," Roderick added.

"Oh my." Polly placed her hands over her mouth. "Well, let's meet up with our next companion so we can get those worms off your hands." She looked at Bertly. "It is plenty dark now."

Bertly nodded. "If we leave now, we can be at the Eternal Cave before dawn." He led the group through the bustling town and back onto the dirt road they had originally embarked upon. The road ran straight through the village; however, it couldn't be seen at night due to all the bar hoppers. Shortly after leaving the village, the dirt road faded back into tall grass. Bertly knew rolling hills covered the lands beyond, though he wasn't able to see very far out due to the lack of light.

"This should be far enough." Bertly stopped walking and placed his bucket of worms onto the ground. He pulled out his whistle from under his shirt, and before turning around, he blew his silent whistle as hard as he could. Bertly tucked it back into his shirt and then spun to face the others. He looked to Polly and the two shared a knowing glance; then he turned his attention back to Roderick and Dev. "I am sure you two have been curious as to how we will pull this adventure off in such a short time."

Both of the elves nodded in agreement.

"Well, your questions are about to be answered." Bertly smiled at Roderick. "I suggest you place that bucket down now."

Roderick dropped the bucket onto the ground and groaned. He instantly massaged his newly freed arms.

Bertly listened for the sound of Clia's wings and was relieved to hear the familiar flapping in the distance. The others didn't react, which Bertly assumed was due to the music from the village being too loud for them to recognize a far-off noise they'd never before heard. "Do you remember what I said about no questions?" Bertly smiled.

As Roderick and Dev were nodding, a dark shadow accompanied by a gust of wind flew over them. Dev ducked and covered his head as his blond hair fluttered in all directions. Roderick screamed and flew headfirst onto the ground. Clia landed on the ground in front of Bertly and came to a screeching halt. Her talons dug into the ground and created long, deep lines across the grass-covered dirt. There was not enough space for her to slow down, so she knocked into Bertly, sending him summersaulting backward. Without hesitation, Clia pounced on top of Bertly and nuzzled her face into his neck.

"Down, girl," Bertly said as he gasped for air. "Let me catch my breath."

"Sweet Cordelia!" Devdan shrieked, gripping his hair at the roots with his jaw wide open. "Is that what I think it is?"

"He asked a question," Roderick cried out from the ground. He was still attempting to stand up after Clia had knocked him over. "See, sir, it isn't just me." Roderick was breathing heavily in and out with his hands on his knees.

Clia grabbed Bertly by his belt and gently lifted him into the air. Bertly was able to prop back onto his feet with the assistance of his trusted pet. He brushed himself off and petted Clia behind the ear. "I will let this one slide. He at least had causation for his slipup."

Polly strolled over to Clia and scratched her under the chin. Clia lifted her beak high into the air, extending her neck as far as it could stretch. "This, boys, is how we are getting to Noskar. However far we can walk in three nights, she can fly in an hour. We will be in Noskar by midday tomorrow."

"Wait, sir, do we have to ride that thing?" Roderick shouted, his face a pale mask of pure terror. Clia whipped her head and glared at him.

"Her name is Clia, and she is the only reason we have any shot at finishing this quest," Bertly snapped.

Devdan interjected, "Ma'am, you seem to be comfortable with Clia, and I haven't made any promises to *you* about not asking questions." He peeked at Bertly and then looked back at Polly. Bertly could tell that Devdan didn't want to make eye contact with him. "If she can fly as quick as you say she can, then how are we going to hold on tight enough to stay aboard, especially for half a day?"

Bertly scowled at Dev.

"Good question, my apprentice," Polly replied. "Gryphons have special feathers, which possess a gripping-like power. While you could easily break out of their grip when desired, they still provide enough support to keep you latched on." Polly rubbed her hand against the natural pattern of Clia's feathers to better reveal them. "Anyone who mounts a gryphon is latched on tightly." Polly smoothed Clia's feathers back into place. "That is if the gryphon gives you permission, of course. If Gryphons so choose, they can make their feathers as slippery as oil."

"Astonishing," Dev exclaimed. He picked up the bucket of worms Roderick had been carrying and walked toward Clia. Clia cocked her head to the side and brushed past Polly and Bertly. She looked Dev in the eyes and then buried her face into the bucket of worms. Her large head knocked the bucket out of his hands, spreading the worms all over the ground, which she then proceeded to pick at. "Remember me as the elf who brought you worms." Dev chuckled as he petted Clia's head.

"Worms are the key to a gryphon's heart," Polly said.

"She's nice to everyone. Don't feel special," Bertly cracked with his lips puckered and arms crossed.

Roderick approached Clia slowly from the back with

his arm extended. "Hello, girl." He got closer and lunged forward to pet her on the back leg. Clia jolted her back leg out and flung Roderick away from her, sending him back toward Bertly and Polly.

"I thought you said she was nice to everyone, sir?" Roderick squealed. One of his hands was over his stomach while the other rubbed his head.

Bertly grunted and lifted Roderick to his feet. He grabbed the bucket of worms and pushed it into Roderick's arms. Clia twirled her head toward Roderick and licked her beak. She did a short prance and chowed down.

"Enough fooling around. It's time to go." Bertly tied back his hair and climbed onto Clia. He reached out his hand and helped Polly hop on. Bertly jerked his head when he heard a loud thump. He peered over his shoulder and saw Roderick lying on his back with his head between Dev's ankles.

"Sweet Cordelia, Roderick." Bertly shook his head. "Devdan, would you please assist my incompetent apprentice?"

"Of course, sir." Dev grabbed Roderick under his armpits and lifted him onto Clia. As soon as he climbed aboard, Roderick wrapped his arms around Polly's stomach and fastened his eyes shut. With his long legs, Dev climbed on with ease.

"Hold on tight," Bertly shouted. Clia extended her wings and began flapping. She kicked her back leg and burst into a sprint. Bertly had butterflies in his stomach from the quick takeoff, and when he looked back toward the dirt road, he saw that they were hovering above the ground. Bertly felt Clia's feather's grip around his body. She bolted into the sky; Roderick screamed at the top of his lungs.

"To the Eternal Cave, Clia," Bertly hollered. The entire group was linked together like a chain.

Clia let out one massive caw and flew to the west.

XIII

Bertly sat straight with his fingers wedged between Clia's feathers, glad that those feathers provided a natural grip so that his fingers wouldn't be curled long after he'd let go, as they had been the first few times he'd ridden her. Polly lay asleep with her face resting against Bertly's back. Roderick was still clinched around Polly's waist, shivering, and Dev was leaning back with his head and neck propped against Clia's tail.

Clia screeched, causing Polly to jolt awake and let out a small yelp, which encouraged Roderick to scream. Clia stopped flapping her wings completely and began her descent.

"We're here," Bertly announced.

Roderick squinted and looked out, his eyes roving over their new surroundings. "How can you tell, sir? It's pitch black."

"What did I say about asking questions?" Bertly snapped.

"Well, Bertly, if we truly are at the Eternal Cave, then technically we are in Noskar," Polly said. Bertly snapped his head back and glared at her.

Bertly pressed his lips together and tightened his grip. "A gryphon can see in the dark just as well as they can in the daylight."

"How well can they see in the day?" Roderick asked.

Bertly took in a deeply exaggerated, loud breath. "Well, Roderick." He let out a long sigh. "They can see well."

Roderick was silent for a moment, but the silence was weighted, and Bertly anticipated yet more questions. Roderick never disappointed in that regard.

"How does she know where the Eternal cave is?" Roderick probed.

Bertly grunted. "Well, most likely because she is nearly a thousand years old, and she can fly far and fast, so it wouldn't be a stretch of the imagination to assume that she has likely been to—or at least, over—every inch of Pangea." Bertly took a deep breath in and admired the crisp air in an attempt to ease his frustration. Noskar was the only place he had ever experienced with such thin air that was so easy to breathe.

Roderick opened his mouth to ask another question, but Dev quickly slapped his hand over the lower half of Roderick's face. Bertly looked back at Devdan, who was shaking his head side to side.

Bertly felt a small jerk. The feeling of floating had disappeared. Clia squawked and then shook her feathers vigorously, which sent the entire group flying in various directions.

"Clia, you couldn't have waited another minute?" Bertly shouted.

Roderick groaned. "Sir, you can't honestly be complaining. I have spent more time on my hind than my feet since I met this bird." Clia kicked her back leg, causing a mist of dirt to spray Roderick. Polly and Devdan burst into laughter.

"Serves you right," Bertly hissed.

Bertly looked out to the horizon, where a small soft orange glow was breaking above the trees. The sun coming through provided enough light to reveal the surrounding areas. The group had been dropped in the middle of a misty yet, sun filled forest. Its canopy was covered by thick sequoia trees that let through just enough light to allow mushrooms and wildflowers to grow. Random vines stretched between most of the trees, giving the forest a sense of disorder. Mixed into the rich landscape were noises of small creatures scurrying across the ground and drizzle birds singing songs. When Bertly listened closely, he could hear water crashing against rocks.

"Polly, I presume you know where we are going?" Bertly asked.

"I think so." Polly shrugged and laughed nervously. "The tale is, life lives just beyond love's teeth. The ring bestows, to the one who does not seek."

"What exactly does that mean?" Dev asked.

Bertly crossed his arms and sighed. "It means there is a ring behind a waterfall. Love is forever, waterfalls are forever," he explained. "It's all a dumb cliché."

Polly rolled her eyes. "Luckily for us, the ring of youth is quite a popular legend. Many have sought to find it. Therefore, the riddle has already been solved. There is a famous waterfall around these parts, and just behind it is the room that is supposed to bear the ring." Polly began marching toward the sound of the water crashing on rocks.

"Stay here, Clia. We will be right back," Bertly instructed the gryphon, who simply cooed in response.

"If everyone knows where it is, then why hasn't anyone found it yet?" Roderick inquired.

"That is a good question, Roderick." Polly was pulling down vines and plowing through plants as she led the way to the waterfall. "They say the ring only presents itself to the one who seeks it the least. It isn't something you look for and find." Polly climbed over a fallen tree covered in moss.

Bertly hiked just behind Roderick, heaving him over any log or large boulder they had to climb over. A handful of paces ahead, Bertly watched as Polly and Dev came to a halt.

"You guys need to come and see this," Polly shouted. Bertly could barely hear her over the sound of the water crashing—even her outside voice was rather prim and quiet, he noted.

When Bertly and Roderick caught up, they found themselves overlooking an enormous waterfall. The water poured between large rounded boulders and crashed into a vast lake. Jagged rocks poked through to the surface at the base of the waterfall.

"It really does look like a mouth with teeth," Roderick observed.

"Remarkable." Bertly rubbed his chin. "How do we get in?" The group took a minute to analyze the mouth of the cave. The water was crashing so hard against the rocks it created a mist large and high enough to be mistaken for a rolling fog.

"I suppose we could try to walk through it," Polly suggested.

"How does everyone else get in?" Devdan asked.

"I'm not quite sure." Polly puckered her lips and tapped her finger against her chin. The group stood silently, observing the waterfall.

"That's it, I've lost my patience," Bertly announced. He shoved past Polly and Devdan and stood on a boulder just in front of them. Bertly rolled up his sleeves and bent his legs. He dug his feet into the rock as far as he could, pushing the moss and dirt to the edges of his boots. He closed his eyes and extended his arms. The air grew colder. The mist coming from the crashing water turned into snowflakes.

Roderick was holding his tongue out, attempting to catch snowflakes. "Look, I caught one," he mumbled, barely intelligibly, with his tongue sticking out. Devdan glared at Roderick with his index finger over his lips, and Roderick slipped his tongue right back into his mouth as he diverted his attention back to Bertly.

Bertly clenched his jaw as his face slowly turned red. A loud crackling noise filled the air. The waterfall stopped running because the source was frozen solid. The remaining water that was suspended in midair fell into the lake at the bottom of the waterfall. Just behind where the waterfall stream once fell rested a small cave.

"There it is," Polly shouted. She yelped and hopped onto the rock next to Bertly. "Thank you, Bertly." Polly hugged Bertly tight around the stomach; her head barely came up to his chest. Bertly scowled and held his hands straight in the air, fighting the urge to wipe his hands on his clothing after she'd let go.

Polly ran to the bottom of the lake and then halted. She turned back and looked at Bertly. "Bertly," she shouted, "I have one more request."

"No. That was exhausting," Bertly yelled back. "Didn't Master Dova teach you molecular conjuring?"

"She mentioned it once. Come on, Bertly, no one's master teaches them as much as Alestar constantly taught you."

Bertly's heart started pounding at the mention of his master, and his breath caught in his throat. The odor of burning corpses and the decaying flesh of the Rotters overwhelmed the misted scent of the waterfall. He became light-headed as images of Alestar shuffled through his head at a rapid pace. He couldn't pinpoint any of the images long enough to remember them, but he did see the Rotters, and, just like in his nightmare—they all had Alestar's face. Bertly had done his best to repress his feelings from the traumatic experience, but he couldn't help but feel angry all over again. He needed to avenge Alestar. Part of the young wizard wanted the Rotters to breach the forest just so he could kill them. If the Elders weren't going to act, then he knew he had to— his only wish was that he could at least tell his friends.

Bertly's knees gave out, sending him sliding off the rock. Just before he crashed to the ground, something grabbed his arm and pulled. Bertly looked up and saw Devdan.

"That was a close one." Devdan pulled Bertly to his feet. "I had a feeling you might have overdone it." Devdan started to brush the dirt off Bertly's back.

Bertly grunted and squirmed away. "I am just fine," he snapped. "I simply lost my footing. I could cast that spell ten times over." Bertly brushed off his pant legs and stomped to the bottom of the hill near Polly. He dropped to one knee and submerged his arm under the water. Bertly glanced up at Polly. "I've always found it easier when I can touch the object."

"I'm not judging you." Polly gave a dismissive head nod. "I want to get to the cave."

Bertly looked back down at his arm and closed his eyes. Soon after, the top surface of the water started to freeze over. The fish that were swimming in the lake moved slower and slower. Before long, the entire lake was one giant ice block filled with whole fish.

"Splendid," Polly gushed. Without hesitation, she sprinted across the frozen ice and toward the cave.

Bertly opened his eyes and saw that Polly was already halfway to the cave. He sprang to his feet and dashed across the ice. "Wait for me," he hollered. Bertly looked back at Devdan and Roderick, who were slipping around on the ice—both of their arms were flailing as they struggled against the ice to stand on their feet.

"What sorcery are you using to walk on this, sir?" Roderick shouted as his feet slipped again, causing him to fall onto his back.

Bertly hollered, "No sorcery, my apprentice." He sprinted across the frozen water, leaped into the air, and then slid across the ice. "It is called 'being from the west.'"

"It rains and snows almost every day during the winter in Noskar, just not in Stonebank. Walking on ice is second nature to us," Polly said as she reached the entrance of the cave. The ledge was about as high as her chest and—without struggle—Polly pulled herself up and over. Bertly was just behind her.

The cave was small and damp. No more than ten occupants could fit inside. Pointed rocks hung from the ceiling and occasionally released small water droplets. A smooth, rounded boulder lay in the center of the cave. The melon-sized rock was pearly white and propped on top of a gray stone pedestal. Rooted on the pedestal was a small placard with golden writing.

"What does the placard say?" Bertly asked.

Polly approached the stone pedestal. "Place your hand on the stone and yours will appear," she recited.

"Well, that is oddly straightforward." Bertly looked at Polly and gestured toward the smooth stone. "Ladies first."

"Since when are you a gentleman, Bertly?" Polly rolled her eyes and placed her hand on the stone. The stone illuminated a radiant white the moment she touched it. Bertly squinted and looked at Polly—her eyes were wide, and an enormous smile covered her face. The rock went dim. Polly examined her hands. "Shucks, I thought it was working."

Bertly heard rocks cracking and crumbling behind

them. He looked back toward the cave entrance and watched as Devdan climbed into the cavern. Devdan waved toward Polly and Bertly then turned back around. Bertly heard a loud grunt and then saw Devdan haul a huffing and puffing Roderick up and over the ledge. Roderick flopped onto the ground like a fish out of water.

"Roderick, you do realize you have to walk back, correct?" Bertly said.

Roderick lay across the floor with his limbs spread out like a starfish. "Sir, what is so special about the ring of youth that I am torturing myself so?" He grunted.

"It extends your life," Polly explained. "The legend goes, there was once a very powerful wizard. At the time, no one's gift in sorcery compared to his. Through his incredible talents, he became rich and famous. He eventually became so overcome with greed that he desired to keep his life of success forever. He spent the rest of his life trying to discover the secret to immortality. He was never successful, but they say he was on the right track just before he died. As his last contribution, he hid a ring in this cave to one day be given to a lucky traveler. No one knows exactly who the ring is waiting for, but it is supposed to add years of life to whomever it chooses."

"Unbelievable," Roderick said. "Let me try." He leaped from the floor and rushed toward the white stone. "What do I do?"

Bertly smacked his forehead. "You touch it," he rebuked.

Roderick reached out his hand and placed it on the smooth boulder. For a short-lived moment, the boulder illuminated, filling the entire cave with a bright white light. But the light left as quickly as it came, fading back to ordinary.

Roderick surveyed the stone, checking under and around it. Roderick scratched his head. "How do I know if it worked?"

"Well…do you have the ring of youth?" Bertly questioned.

Roderick peered at the hand he had placed on the stone, holding it two inches from his face as he studied it. "No."

"Then it didn't work!" Bertly shouted.

"Let me give it a go," Devdan said. He strolled over to the stone. Polly stared at Devdan with intensity, and Bertly could not tell if she was excited or nervous. Devdan placed his hand on top of the smooth boulder. The stone started to glow; however it faded almost instantly, never giving off a strong light. "Well, that is disappointing," Devdan mumbled.

"It's a trick," Bertly declared. "Even if a ring did present itself, how would any of us know if we lived a few years longer or not?" Bertly looked over the group and awaited a response. "Exactly. No one knows the day they are going to die. Therefore, there is no way of proving whether or not it adds anything at all."

"Fine," Polly said, exasperated, with her hands on her hips. "If you are so sure, then why don't you touch the rock and prove us all wrong?" Polly pointed toward the stone. "Once nothing happens, then we can head straight to Noskar."

Bertly glared at Polly. He puckered his lips, contemplating whether or not to humor her.

"Come on, sir. Give it a try," Roderick urged.

"What have you got to lose, sir?" Devdan said.

Bertly grunted and dragged his feet toward the stone. He reached his hand out and placed it on the boulder. The rest of the pack leaned in and locked their eyes on the rock.

The rock showed zero reaction to Bertly's touch.

Bertly smirked and nodded to himself. "I told all of

you this was a hoax." Bertly attempted to remove his hand from the stone, but it was stuck as though it had been glued there. He shook his arm a few times to try to strip his hand from the stone, but the stone and pedestal stood motionless. "I can't get my hand off!" Bertly shouted.

A blinding light burst from the stone. A yellow light that surged with energy and swirled around the stone and Bertly's hand.

"What's happening?" Roderick screamed.

"I think it's working!" Polly exclaimed.

The stone started to wrap around Bertly's hand. Bertly shook his arm viciously, desperately attempting to remove his hand. His efforts were so strenuous that droplets of sweat dripped from his forehead onto the stone.

Polly ran over to Bertly and placed her hands on his shoulders. "Try to relax. I don't think you are in danger of being harmed," she insisted.

Bertly eased the muscles in his arm and took a deep breath. The stone continued to shrink until it formed into the shape of a circle around Bertly's pointer finger. The stone stopped glowing. Left around Bertly's finger was a smooth white ring.

"You have got to be kidding me," Bertly groaned.

Polly screamed and jumped into the air. "I knew it was real."

Roderick sprinted toward Bertly and examined the ring. "I can't believe it," he said. "You actually get to live longer, sir." Roderick looked up at Bertly with an enthusiastic smile.

"Congratulations, sir," Devdan added.

"In all honesty, I don't want it."

Polly and Roderick jerked their heads back.

"I have been dealt a good deck of cards," Bertly continued. "I don't want to cause disorder to my fate."

"Well, Bertly, if you do not want it, then I would be glad to relieve you of your burden." Polly's eyes narrowed, and she expectantly reached out her hand.

"It's all yours," he replied. Bertly grabbed the ring and tried to slide it off his finger, but it wouldn't budge. "It doesn't seem to be coming off." Bertly continued to tug on the ring.

"Don't rip your finger off, sir," Roderick shrieked.

The ring started to heat until it reached a burning temperature, and Bertly could practically feel the ring melding into his flesh—branding him for life for a second time. He yelped and ran toward the cave entrance. He hopped onto the ice floor and stuck his hand against the ground.

"Bertly, what's going on?" Polly asked. There was a slight hint of urgency to her voice as she and the group quickly followed Bertly out of the cave and gathered around him. A puddle formed around Bertly's hand. The ring was burning through and melting the ice.

"It's getting tighter," Bertly yelled. He clenched his teeth as tight as he could. He did his best to keep a dull face—he did not want the others to know how much pain he was in. Bertly exhaled and fell onto his side. "It stopped." He sighed. Bertly held his hand up to examine his burnt finger, and his eyes grew wide and round at what he saw—the white band was gone. Left behind was a burn mark on his finger in the shape of a ring.

Devdan crouched next to Bertly. "Let me take a look, sir. Us elves are quite good with healing magic."

"It's gone," Bertly said.

"What do you mean gone, sir?"

Bertly raised his hand toward Roderick. "I mean it's no longer on my finger, Roderick," he fumed.

"Bertly!" Polly ferociously screamed. Bertly flinched at the sudden loudness of her voice.

Roderick slapped his hands onto his face. "Sweet Cordelia," he cried.

"What?" Bertly shouted. "Are you two trying to give me a heart attack?"

Devdan looked Bertly in the eyes and stood up cautiously.

"What is it?" Bertly asked.

Devdan took a step back. Bertly's heart started racing.

Dev pointed to the ground. "Take a look in the ice, sir."

Bertly peered into the reflection of the ice. His heart pounded through his chest; his stomach filled with butterflies. Bertly ran his hand across his hair-covered cheeks, noticing his defined jaw. He felt his protruding Adam's apple along his neck where the scruff stopped growing. He looked down—his body was thicker. He had not gained any fat, but he had another layer of mass surrounding him. Bertly stood up, and he felt even taller, not by much, but he now stood comfortably taller than Devdan.

"Sir, you look at least twenty, not sixteen," Roderick cried.

Bertly clenched his jaw. "Great work, investigator." His heart was racing and his body shook.

"I didn't mean it like that, sir. You look…stronger, uh, wiser." Roderick's mouth snapped shut.

"It suits you, sir," Devdan added.

Bertly looked at his reflection in the ice and ran his hand down along his jaw. He stood and examined his physique. His cloth top and bottoms still fit; however, he would not have minded a size larger—it would probably be more comfortable, he thought.

Polly walked up to Bertly, her eyes round and her mouth open. She placed her hands on Bertly's arms and ran them up to his shoulders. She ran her fingers across his beard. "I…I don't know what…" Polly looked Bertly intensely in the eyes, almost as though she were looking for something.

Bertly gave a half grin. "I guess when the legend said the ring adds a few years, it meant quite literally."

XIV

The group sat aboard Clia, ready for departure. Roderick's back was soaked from slipping on the ice on their way back from the Eternal Cave. Bertly tried to sit comfortably aboard Clia, but he could not find a comfortable position. His pants were too tight, and when he sat, they became wedged in areas he preferred to remain untouched. He also felt a tightness from his top across his back whenever he leaned forward. His boots were the only clothing article that still fit the same.

"Is everyone ready?" Bertly asked.

Roderick's arms were gripped around Polly's waist, with his eyes glued shut. "Ready, sir." He quivered as he spoke.

"Likewise," Devdan announced.

Bertly whistled and Clia launched into the sky like a firework. In moments, she broke above the barrier of the misty forest and was en route to Stonebank. Straight ahead were jagged, ghost-white mountains. The sky-piercing highlands stretched across the entire horizon. The sun broke above the peaks, where the pine trees breached the powdery snow that covered the entire landscape, bringing life to all of Noskar.

"It's beautiful," Devdan said. "I was always taught in school that Noskar was empty and barren. But…it's absolutely stunning."

Roderick studied the horizon and looked down toward the landscape. "Me too," he said. "We were always told it had no life." Roderick sniffled. "But snow…snow is the most heavenly thing I have ever seen. It looks like Cordelia herself wrapped a soft blanket around the land."

"Just wait until we get to Stonebank," Polly said, her voice gratingly cheerful as always.

Devdan and Roderick sat in silence until Clia neared the mountains. Roderick had finally loosened his grip around Polly. Bertly had never seen him so fixated.

Clia extended her wings, slowing her pace and gently gliding through the air. "Sir, I have a question," Roderick jabbered.

"I am in a good mood," Bertly rejoiced. "I will humor your question."

"Why hasn't Clia batted an eye toward your new…look?" Roderick questioned.

"That is *actually* a good question, my apprentice." Bertly smiled. "I asked Alestar the same thing after he burned off his hair and eyebrows in the lab by accident once. He told me a gryphon doesn't recognize someone by their appearance. They detect their humans based off smell and body language."

"Intriguing, sir. So, if I lost my head, Clia would still recognize me?"

"Yes, that is correct." Bertly glanced back at Roderick and gave him a cynical smile. "But maybe we should test it just to be sure."

Roderick's eyes went wide.

"Oh, stop it, Bertly." Polly nudged Bertly in the back. Roderick tightened his grip back around Polly.

Bertly pointed. "Straight for that split in the mountains, Clia," he shouted. As the group approached the mountains, a cascade of snow came tumbling down the mountainside. As the snow fell, it slid over a triangular-shaped edge in the side of the mountain, sending more snow flying in opposite directions.

Polly closed her eyes and pointed her nose in the air. "Ah, the sound of an avalanche." Clia flew through the triangular opening and exited into a valley surrounded by 360 degrees of mountain. At the bottom of the valley was wide-open land with beautiful green grass. The sun shined brighter and the air smelled clean, as though a thunderstorm had just passed through.

Bertly heard the melody of drizzle birds dancing through the air. "We're home," he sang. Bertly felt the Stonebank air flowing through his hair, and peered down. "Sweet Cordelia," he blurted.

Polly leaned over the side of Clia in order to look at the same spot on the ground that had Bertly so unwound. "Heavenly day," she cried. "What has happened here?"

Devdan's eyebrows rose nearly to the top of his forehead. "It's magnificent."

"Is this the capital city?" Roderick asked as he gazed over the valley. "I've never seen a city this large before."

"I don't think so. If I am not mistaken, Noskar doesn't have a capital," Devdan clarified.

"What's happened to our home?" Bertly whistled for Clia to descend. "Who are all these people?"

"I'm not sure, but I am quite curious to find out." Polly's shocked face quickly turned into a smile. "This is almost exciting." She giggled. "Why didn't Stonebank look like this when we were growing up?"

"Ma'am, I am a bit confused. You seem not to recognize your own home," Roderick chimed in.

"The last time we were home, Roderick, there were no more than two hundred residents," Polly replied.

"You're kidding," Roderick said.

Devdan shook his head. "I find that hard to

believe…incredible."

What used to be a quaint village of no more than fifty rooftops now housed more cottages than Bertly could attempt to count. Around the entire border of the city, new homes were being constructed. Bertly's old house, which used to be at the edge of town, was now in the middle due to all the homes that had been newly built around it. The expansion of the city spread out in every direction. Luxurious homes lined the sides of the mountains, and in the center of town were several multistoried buildings that appeared to be extravagant shops and saloons. Thousands of humans lined the streets in such a way that it reminded Bertly of the hallways at the Academy.

Clia landed gracefully on the soft as silk Noskar grass. The group hopped off the gryphon and gathered around Bertly.

"Where do you suppose we should hide Clia?" Polly asked.

Bertly undid his bun and let his hair down. "There's no need," he said. "We didn't anticipate this many folks to be here, so I am assuming Clia has caught the eye of many. We may as well head into town and find my father."

Shortly after heading toward the city, in the background Bertly heard playful screams of children. "Right on cue."

Two barefoot children darted out of the crowded city and across the soft grass toward Bertly and the group. "Mommy, look! It's a gryphon, it's a gryphon!" A few dozen paces behind the children was a middle-aged woman, whom Bertly presumed to be their mother. Not far behind her were countless other curious citizens.

When the children approached, Clia scurried to hide behind Bertly, who wasn't even wide enough to cover half her face. "You will have to forgive my little ones," the mature woman yelped. "During their bedtime stories, I always told them gryphons left Noskar centuries ago." She spoke of her children, but her eyes never left Clia. "But here one is, more beautiful and glorious than I could have imagined." For the first time in several minutes, the woman glanced toward the group and away from Clia. "How did you come across such a creature? I couldn't imagine the lengths—"

The woman stopped talking and looked intensely at Bertly. "Red…" She peered at Polly. "Eyes." The woman's skin turned white. "Red eyes," she screamed. "Red eyes!" Over and over she cried as loud as she could. Other people started shouting along with her. The whole town came to a screeching halt in order to give their full attention to Bertly and Polly. The town was absolutely motionless.

"Are we about to be mobbed, sir?" Roderick whimpered.

Bertly put his arm out, pushing the group behind him. "I wouldn't rule that out, my apprentice. Something odd is happening here." The mob was so silent a needle drop could be heard from across town. Bertly put down his arm and puffed out his chest while a smile radiated across his face. "Roderick, do you remember the conversation we had with Willie?"

Roderick cocked his head. "Of course, sir. But what does—" Roderick's jaw dropped. "Sweet Cordelia."

Bertly stepped forward. He reached inside his cloak and pulled out Cordelia's warblade. He squeezed the dragon-carved grip and held it above his head. "I have returned!" he cried. The mammoth-ice blade shot out of the handle. The crowd erupted into an enormous celebration. Applause and cheering filled the entire city.

"What in Cordelia's name is that?" Polly shouted.

Bertly winked. "Her warblade." Roderick and Devdan stood with their eyes wide open, Roderick was biting down on his bottom lip, and all were admiring the majesty of the warblade.

"When did you get that!" Polly questioned.

Bertly choked on his own spit. "Oh, um, from Alestar." Polly didn't appear convinced for a second.

The noise of the crowd saved Bertly as their cries became too loud to ignore. They started to recite something, but Bertly couldn't make out the words. He listened closely; the human's voices began to synchronize. The town's roars became clear as day. "Winter Wizard!" they chanted.

"The Winter Wizard?" Roderick rubbed his chin. "I have never heard of this wizard before."

"Neither have I," Polly said.

Bertly looked back at them, popped his collar, and winked. "Me neither." He had an enormous smile plastered across his face.

Bertly noticed movement at the back of the crowd, and the roaring of the people soon faded. The people of Noskar parted quickly to yield to a visitor who was fast approaching Bertly and the others. At least two dozen fully armed soldiers marched out. The soldiers came to a halt, then formed into two orderly lines and faced each other. Both lines of soldiers stepped back, creating a pathway.

Emerging from between the soldiers was a wide-framed man, a head taller than the average man. Despite his beer belly, he had defined biceps that were bigger than a normal man's thigh. The sides of his head were shaved, but the top ran long. Gray hairs were sprinkled throughout his mane and beard. His tattoo-sleeved right arm held a large war hammer.

The man walked out past the guards and stood

between them and Bertly. He tossed the war hammer over his shoulder. "So, the Winter Wizard has returned home."

Bertly crossed his arms and curled his lip. "You've grown old…and fat."

Both men locked eyes and stared intently. The whole town had gathered to observe the occasion, and they all stood silently with their attention fixated on the confrontation. Neither man blinked as they walked toward each other until their noses were less than a foot apart. Bertly stood slightly taller; however, he was completely overshadowed in size. Simultaneously, Bertly and the man broke eye contact and burst into laughter. They dropped their weapons and wrapped their arms around each other.

"I've missed you, son," Edfrid whispered. "Stonebank hasn't been the same without you." The men picked their weapons back up off the ground.

Bertly shook his head and gave a lopsided smile. "Stonebank doesn't seem the same at all."

Edfrid chuckled. "Aye, that is true. I have a lot to catch you up on." Edfrid's attention suddenly turned to the whole of his son and he examined Bertly very closely. "Son, you look like you've aged over ten years. What have they been feedin' you over there?"

Bertly laughed. "It seems I have a lot to catch you up on, as well."

"Hello, Edfrid," Polly interrupted.

Edfrid peered his head around Bertly to look at where Polly stood waving her hand with a luminous smile across her face. "Polly," Edfrid exclaimed. "I almost didn't recognize you, you've matured so much. Your hair has gotten even lighter."

Bertly turned and faced his friends. As he turned, Clia quickly scurried—likely fearing she'd been exposed—and attempted next to hide behind Polly. Bertly pointed. "This is my apprentice, Roderick."

Roderick stood with his neck tilted back, giving an awkward wave.

"And this is Polly's apprentice, Devdan," Bertly announced, nearly mumbling Devdan's name.

Devdan stepped forward. "You can call me Dev, sir. It is a pleasure to meet you."

"It is great to meet all of you." Edfrid flung his hammer from his side and dangled it in the air. A guard rushed over and grabbed the hammer from Edfrid. "And who is your feathery friend?"

"This big baby is Clia. She gets a little shy around new people." Bertly surveyed the city. "We didn't anticipate such a crowd."

Edfrid nodded. "Well, then, let's get her somewhere a little more private." He clapped his hands. "You must all be tired from your long journey. Come, follow me. I will try to get you up to pace on our way to the castle."

"The castle?" Bertly shouted.

Edfrid laughed. "I know, quite the change." The guards parted the busy streets and kept the walkways clear for Edfrid, Bertly, and the others. Clia followed them from above. Bertly looked around the city and noticed pairs of guards scattered throughout.

"Do all cities in Noskar have royal guards?" Roderick asked. "Despite our large army, we don't have any in Eplium."

Polly rolled her eyes—a gesture Bertly had, until that moment, thought was reserved specifically for him, but now it seemed that Roderick, too, could cause Polly to lose her perfect composure, and that thought made Bertly feel rather content. "It's because humans don't behave themselves as well as elves," Polly said.

"The young lady is right," Edfrid said. "With

Stonebank as the unofficial capital of Noskar, we now have too many people to watch over. We need the extra help to keep things in order."

Together, Bertly and Polly squealed, "The capital?"

"Aye, once you and Polly were accepted into the Academy, word spread like wildfire across Noskar of our two red-eyed humans. Before we knew it, people were flooding into Stonebank by the dozens, eventually the hundreds."

"Why, sir?" Polly asked. "I love Stonebank, but we don't have much to offer."

Edfrid nodded. "Aye, but everyone wanted to live in the same city as the children of Cordelia. The folk of Noskar don't just believe you were random chance; they all believe you were given to us by Cordelia herself."

Bertly's stomach churned as he noticed Devdan wink at Polly. That elf was so ridiculously charming that it repulsed him. What was even worse was that the charm wasn't an act or a ploy—no, Devdan *was* charming.

"I always knew you were special, ma'am," Devdan said.

Bertly fought the urge to childishly feign vomiting while Polly did her best to hold back a smile, but her rosy cheeks gave away that she was rather swayed by the suave elf.

As Bertly paced through the streets, every set of eyes examined him. He had somehow gone from being unnoticeable to being a spectacle for them to behold—all within a few years. It was also possible that the ring had something to do with it. He almost felt like a stranger in his hometown.

"But why would everyone want to live here?" Bertly asked. "What quality of life were they seeking? I understand why people are drawn in now." Bertly looked around at the countless storefronts, saloons, and homes.

"But at the time—when Polly and I left—we were just a small village."

"Humans haven't had a sense of community in hundreds of years. We have been cast out by the elves, dwarves, and giants since Cordelia left. You've given people a reason to come together again. You've given them hope."

"Hope for what?" Bertly prodded.

"To be acknowledged again by the rest of the world. Our people felt like nothing," Edfrid explained.

"Why, because you don't have magic?" Devdan interrupted. "That seems petty."

Bertly glared at Devdan. "That's easy to say when you're an elf. Your people have commanded this world with magic since before Cordelia."

"Settle down, now. I don't think he meant to offend." Edfrid placed his hand on Bertly's shoulder. "We are almost at my favorite part of the city." The group wandered farther until their pathway was obstructed by a large stone statue.

Towering higher than any building in town was a sculpture of Bertly holding Cordelia's warblade and shield. Statue Bertly wore a crown and a dragon-scale cape. "We didn't know you had her warblade when we built this. You don't also happen to have her shield and cape on hand, do ya?" Edfrid slapped Bertly on the back and laughed.

Clia circled above while Bertly stood captivated by the statue. Every inch of the delicately carved sculpture brought goose bumps to his body. Around the figure was a circular pathway that allowed people to view it from all angles. On the outskirts of the pathway were taverns and saloons. The people inside seemed to be fancier dressed than the average commoner Bertly had passed on his walk over.

Edfrid wrapped his arm around Bertly. "I know you always said when you were younger, 'One day, Dadai, they will build statues of me, and all of Pangea will know who we are.'"

A tear formed in the corner of Bertly's eye.

"Where is my statue?" Polly shouted. "I have red eyes, too."

Edfrid faced Polly. "While human, you weren't born in Stonebank, Polly." He shrugged. "Since you moved here when you were young, some folk don't consider you a true native of Stonebank."

Polly's face went dull and she broke eye contact with Edfrid.

"Cheer up. Not many people get referred to as a child of Cordelia."

"That's true, sir." Polly gave him a half smile. "It is a title I will wear with pride."

Edfrid turned toward Bertly, who was still captivated by the statue. "Tell me, son, what brings you to Stonebank?" He rubbed his beard. "Don't get me wrong, I couldn't be happier to see you, but I wasn't expecting you for another two years, when you embarked on your spirit quest."

"Well, that is actually why we are here." Bertly's mouth curved into a smile and he puffed out his cloak. "Polly and I were fast-tracked our first year at the Academy."

"Sweet Cordelia, why am I not surprised?" Edfrid smiled and shook his head. "Come, the castle is just up these steps."

Edfrid and the guards led them through the multistoried city. There were balconies on every floor, where people could easily weave in and out of each establishment. The conversations rang with positive tones, and Bertly had yet to see even one upset or grumpy citizen. As the group rounded the corner toward the steps, people were waiting for them with lavender flowers in their hands. When they noticed Bertly turn the corner, they cheered and placed their lavender on the road and steps.

"Winter Wizard!" the city chanted. Bertly pulled his cloak to the side so people could see Cordelia's warblade mounted on his hip. He walked with his chin up and chest out.

"You seem to have adjusted to your newfound fame quite fast," Edfrid said with a chuckle. He gestured for Bertly to look up.

At the top of the wide staircase was a palace built into the side of the mountain. A large indentation had been carved out of the mountain, and a box-shaped white castle nestled inside. Four flat towers filled the missing space of mountain. Each tower was connected by massive walls that were more than half the height of the citadel. In between the four towers, at the center of the castle, was an archway large enough for a mammoth to walk through.

"No gate or door?" Bertly questioned. "Seems a bit risky."

"Aye, but no one can enter Stonebank if we don't let them in." Edfrid crossed his arms across his chest. "Unless they fly in on an ancient, mystical creature, of course." Edfrid led Bertly and company up the stairs toward the castle entrance. "The mountains are too steep to climb, and not many folk have means of flying. On top of that, we are in the center of the city. If an enemy ever gets this far, the city is already lost." Edfrid lifted his shoulders in a half shrug and gave a petty smile. The group reached the top of the steps and stood in the entrance of Bertly's father's castle. Edfrid extended his arm toward the interior of the castle. "Here we are. They just finished her a couple of months ago."

Clia descended and landed on the steps just behind the group. Bertly turned. "Clia, you stay here unless you hear me call for you." He looked directly into her eyes. "*Only* if I call for you. Understand?"

Clia grunted and flopped across the steps, her head drooping slightly downward.

"Good girl."

Bertly walked through the archway and marveled at the interior of the castle. A light blue rug divided the snow-colored room. Long banners with pictures of every warden of Stonebank were stitched with elegancy and fine detail. In between each banner hung ice-crafted lanterns that illuminated the entire throne hall. The way the light reflected off the lamps caused the room to sparkle. Following just behind Bertly were his companions, as well as the city guards.

Roderick tapped Bertly on the shoulder. "Excuse me, sir."

Bertly didn't turn toward Roderick—he continued to examine the intricacy of the ceiling. "Yes, Roderick?" He couldn't look away from the fine craftsmanship of the ice-carved crown molding around the perimeter of the hall.

"Why doesn't the ice melt around the lanterns?" Roderick asked.

"Mammoth ice," Edfrid offered. "It took me over ninety nights in the mountains to find a pack of those horned fur balls."

"It's never cold, yet it can hardly be melted. They say even a dragon bellowing fire can barely melt mammoth ice," Polly added.

"Incredible," Roderick said.

Devdan nodded. "Indeed."

Bertly strolled to the throne displayed at the back of the main hall. "That is made of mammoth ice, too!" his father yelled across the hall. Bertly reached out and ran his hand across the transparent throne. The chair was covered in divine engravings. Fixed on the backrest was Noskar's emblem, a drizzle bird carrying Cordelia's warblade in its talons.

"Check the back side. It has Noskar's new unofficial animal on it," Edfrid directed.

Bertly rounded the chair, only to see that carved on the entire back of the throne was a spectacular mammoth. Bertly felt something brush against him. He peered down, and at his feet was a small furry creature with a fluffy tail and whiskers nuzzling against his leg. Bertly yelped. The fuzzy animal looked up at him with its oversized eyes and big pupils and meowed.

Bertly rounded the chair with the little animal in his arms. "So the official animal of Noskar is a koko." Bertly's friends tried their best to hold back smiles.

"Oh, don't mind Oats. That little koko comes and goes as he pleases," Edfrid replied.

"You've given it a name?" Bertly's nose crinkled as he gave a half smile. "And you chose 'Oats'?"

Edfrid's jaw dropped and his eyebrows snapped together. "I found him in the kitchen playing with the oats and brown bread. He likes oats." Edfrid stomped to the throne and snagged Oats. The koko was able to rest its whole body inside Edfrid's enormous hand. "Leave me and Oats alone." Edfrid nuzzled the koko against his face and then placed him on the ground. Oats scurried off and ran down a hallway toward another wing of the castle. Edfrid plopped onto his mammoth-ice throne and threw one leg over the armrest. "So, what do we have planned for this spirit quest?"

"We?"

"Yes, *we*. Why else would you come and see your old man? You need my help."

Bertly broke eye contact with his father and inspected his fingernails. "Well, we were sort of hoping you could watch the gryphon for us."

Edfrid took his leg off the armrest and sat up straight. "You want me to babysit?"

"You will love it. You like your koko." Bertly shrugged and laughed nervously. "Clia is basically the same…just slightly bigger." As soon as Clia heard her name, she came sliding through the castle hall, tearing up the finely woven, light blue rug. She galloped across the hall and did a jump stop right in front of Bertly. Bertly turned to his father, scratched the back of his head, and gave a nervous laugh.

"I assume you don't have the gold to replace that."

The color drained from Bertly's face.

Edfrid surveyed the rest of the group, but no one responded. "Great, that settles it. I'm coming with you, and in exchange, I will look past the rug." Edfrid leaped out of his chair. "Besides, you will need me to navigate through the mountains. Where are you trying to get to, anyhow?"

Bertly put his hand over his mouth and cleared his throat while puffing out his chest. "The Dragon's Crypt." He smirked.

Edfrid's eyes widened, but he quickly snapped back to focus and regained his composure. He gave a dismissive wave. "I can get all of you to the Dragon's Crypt in less than two nights."

Roderick shrieked. "Dragon's Crypt." His breaths started to quicken. "I thought you said it was just a cave, sir?"

"Oh, Roderick." Bertly strode toward Roderick and placed his hand on his shoulder. Bertly's eyes were sparkling. "It *is* a cave…a cave to which many dragons and humans have famously laid waste."

Roderick's eyes rolled to the back of his head and he collapsed onto the floor.

"Oh heavens," Polly shouted. She rushed over to Roderick and placed his head in her lap while shooting Bertly an annoyed glare. Bertly stood over them with his arms crossed.

"Are you sure you don't want to leave him behind with the gryphon?" Edfrid cracked.

Bertly shook his head. "I wish it were an option."

Edfrid walked over toward Roderick and Polly. He grabbed Roderick by the jaw and turned his head side to side, inspecting him. Edfrid bent over and picked him up as though he were a rag doll. He threw Roderick over his shoulder and walked toward the castle entrance. "Follow me. I will take you to the stables so you can board your gryphon. There is still plenty of daylight left." Edfrid turned his head back toward the group. "We can leave at midday."

***

The students followed Edfrid out the entrance of the castle and to the courtyard at the bottom of the steps. Clia followed close behind, walking on her tiptoes and slowing her pace every time she walked past something breakable. Once she reached the courtyard, she lifted into the air and tailed them from above. Bertly followed his father through the crowded streets, watching Roderick bounce up and down on Edfrid's shoulder with each step he took. Masses of people gathered around to admire Bertly and Polly. Bertly found the entire situation rather bizarre: if it were not for the royal guards clearing the pathway, they would've never been able to navigate the streets.

To the east side of Stonebank was a massive open

field. The southern and eastern areas were the only undeveloped land in Stonebank. In the middle of the field was a colossal steel barn. It was large enough to be mistaken for a small castle.

Edfrid led the pack toward the gigantic steel structure. "The people agreed to raise taxes to build this stable," Edfrid said. "The belief is that one day, Bertly, you will come riding home on Cordelia's dragon, and when you do, they want him to be able to live here, in Stonebank."

"That explains why there is no fence around these stables," Devdan said.

"Aye," Edfrid replied. "Given that it was meant for a dragon, I suppose it should suffice for your gryphon." Edfrid looked back and gave Clia a once-over. "Not that she seems much smaller." With Roderick hunched over his shoulder, Edfrid kicked open the barn doors. "Welcome to your humble abode, feather dragon." Troughs of fresh water lined the side of the barn, and several haystacks were sprawled throughout. A huge tank filled with live fish covered the opposing wall. In the back was an enormous pit of boiling water. Clia walked slowly into the center of the room, gazing at her temporary home. "We even built it on top of a natural hot spring. Maybe gryphons like the hot water as much as dragons." Edfrid shrugged. Clia started skipping around the room, running through every stack of hay.

Roderick started to shift around on Edfrid's shoulder. "You're up," Edfrid bellowed as he dropped Roderick from his shoulder onto the floor. Roderick let out a big grunt and rolled onto his back.

Bertly blew his whistle and Clia came to a screeching halt. She glared directly at him. "We have to go now, girl. I won't be back for a few days," Bertly explained. "Will you be okay without me?" Clia tilted her head; she studied Bertly for a moment and then dashed off and jumped into the hot spring.

Edfrid slapped Bertly on the back. "I think the gryphon has left the nest."

Bertly shook his head and threw his arms in the air. "No kidding."

Edfrid adjusted his coat and cleared his throat. "Well, no reason to stand around." Edfrid marched toward the exit of the barn.

Bertly overheard Roderick talking to Devdan. "Why is he in such a rush? He doesn't even know we are on a deadline."

"He probably misses his son," Devdan whispered back. "It's been years since they've seen each other."

Outside the barn, several royal guards were lined up, double the amount that had escorted them there. The guards approached Bertly and the rest of the group and extended to them daggers, swords, shields and light armor. Edfrid clapped his hands. "Suit up, everyone."

"Sir, why do we need so many weapons?" Roderick screamed.

Bertly, Edfrid, and Polly burst into laughter. Bertly wiped a tear from the corner of his eye. "Are you serious?"

Roderick had a blank look on his face.

"My young apprentice. Only a madman would go into the mountains unarmed."

"I'm pretty sure even a madman would know better." Polly chuckled.

The group suited up and chose their favorite weapons among their diverse options. Polly put on every layer of armor available; however, she chose no weapon. Roderick took a small sword, and Devdan chose two daggers, one for each hand. The elf did a double take at the display of weapons and snatched a long sword as well. Edfrid put on a metal chest plate and grabbed his war hammer.

Bertly took a shield but did not equip any armor because he was not going to risk losing any of his speed or mobility.

"Are you ready, son?" Edfrid asked.

Bertly looked back toward his group; they all nodded. "Yes, sir."

Edfrid marched forward toward Stonebank's southern and only entrance. The royal soldiers began following behind. Edfrid turned to face them. "Stop!" he shouted. "No guards. I will be back in three nights."

A soldier with a uniquely marked shield stepped forward. "Sir, we can't leave you unprotected."

Edfrid threw his hammer over his shoulder and glared at his group of soldiers. "I don't mean to be blunt…but I could squash every last one of you."

The guards looked at each other, each one's face filled with indecision.

"I need you to clear traffic, not to keep me protected. You will stay here, and that's an order. I will be back in three nights." Edfrid turned back around and headed for the entrance. "I forgot to ask you, Bertly." Edfrid adjusted the strap on his chest plate. "What bolt went loose in your head that is driving you to the Dragon's Crypt?"

"Well…" Bertly nibbled on his bottom lip. "We want to steal a scale from Cordelia's dragon."

The mumbling amongst the soldiers stopped.

Edfrid scoffed and crossed his arms. "What makes you think her dragon is still alive?"

"Cordelia wasn't with her dragon when she left. Therefore, we don't know for certain that he is gone." Bertly threw his shield over his back and cracked his knuckles. "Cordelia's dragon has always lived there. If he was residing anywhere, it would be there."

"Why has no one explored Dragon's Crypt if such a

legendary creature lives there?" Devdan questioned.

"Oh, many have. The issue is none have returned to tell the tale." Bertly grabbed a few strands of his hair and began braiding it. "None except for the Stonebank wardens."

Edfrid gave a loud battle cry and banged his hammer against his metal chest plate.

Devdan smiled. "I presume you're a warden, Edfrid?"

"Our family have been wardens since before we settled in Stonebank," Edfrid replied.

Roderick glanced at Bertly. "Does that make you a warden, sir?"

Bertly scratched the back of his head and opened his mouth to answer; however, no words came out. He glanced toward his father.

Edfrid gave a half smile and nodded his head.

Bertly looked back at Roderick. "Technically...no." Bertly rubbed his chin.

"Why not, sir?" Roderick probed.

"It takes a special ceremony...the type that can make a man a bit anxious." Bertly laughed nervously.

"Just spit it out, son," Edfrid exclaimed.

"You see, not just anyone can become a warden. Our family line possesses something special that allows us to become wardens." Bertly stood up fully and checked his hair, which Polly had finished braiding. He nodded toward Polly as a sign of thanks. "For most creatures, mammoth blood is highly poisonous. It can make a horse drop in a flash." Bertly snapped his fingers. "It's a great defense mechanism—a predator takes a big bite out of your leg, gets a little blood in its mouth, rolls over."

Polly nudged Bertly softly in the side.

"Sorry, I'm getting sidetracked." Bertly cleared his throat. "For most creatures, mammoth blood is highly poisonous; however, for a lot of the men in my family...when we drink it...the blood works as a...how do you put it?" Bertly tapped his finger on his chin as he stared off into space. He couldn't compare it to anything else.

"It's better than the greatest potion in the world," Edfrid interjected. "No elixir is like it."

"You drink mammoth blood?" Roderick screamed.

Bertly glanced back at him and shrugged.

"That's right," Edfrid said.

Devdan picked up his pace from the back of the group until he came within close range of Bertly and his father. "I am still not sure I understand how it works, sir."

"The truth is, if you can survive drinking the mammoth blood, the blood will cooperate with your body," Bertly replied.

"I used to look like Bertly. After I survived the ceremony, I was left with the body I have now," Edfrid added.

Bertly pulled a long piece of hair off the cuff of his shirt and dropped it on the grass. "We are all naturally tall in this family, but the reason my father looks like he is half giant is because...well, he drank mammoth blood and survived."

Polly slapped a hand over her mouth and shook her head.

Devdan pressed his finger over his lips. "Extraordinary."

"Incredible, sir," Roderick said. "Terrifying and disgusting, but absolutely incredible." Roderick started flexing his arms. "Why don't you drink the mammoth blood, sir?"

The color drained from Bertly's face. "You see, Roderick." He took a deep breath. "Every so often, a man in our family doesn't survive the ceremony. While we are the only ones we know of who do survive, there is still a risk of it going wrong."

Roderick looked down and started kicking the dirt road the group was walking along. "I see, sir."

"Only someone who truly desires to be a warden and the ruler of Stonebank follows through with the ceremony," Bertly said.

Edfrid walked closer to Bertly and put him in a headlock. "I can't wait for you to perform the ceremony, Bertly. Governing Stonebank isn't meant for me." Edfrid released Bertly and ruffled his hair, making his braids come half undone. "You will make a much better leader. Only a handful of years until you're done with the Academy."

Bertly undid his messed-up hair and retied it. He looked away from his father and gulped. "Right, sir. It's every man's honor." Bertly closed his eyes and took a deep breath as he marched ahead, toward the exit of Stonebank.

The group came upon the triangular opening they had flown through when they arrived. At the edge of the opening was a steep drop-off—the side was so flat it could not be climbed. Just to the right of the entrance was a large wooden basket with an intricate pulley system. "Everyone climb aboard." Edfrid gestured toward the crate. The group shuffled into the wooden container except for Roderick, who froze at the entrance.

"Wait, sir," Roderick exclaimed, his eyes shifting about as if he were calculating the exact dimensions of the crate. "We have to go in that thing?"

Edfrid cocked his head. "Of course. How else will we get down?" He chuckled and shook his head. "We haven't lost anyone in years." Edfrid reached out and pulled Roderick into the wooden elevator. He locked the door behind him and then began to crank a giant wheel placed in the middle of the basket, which made the wooden elevator descend the mountain.

XV

Edfrid turned the wheel at a slow pace, carrying the wooden elevator farther down the mountain with every turn. Bertly's vast view of Noskar was gradually obstructed by the treetops rooted at the base of the foothills. He looked down toward Roderick, who stood motionless, pale faced, with his arms glued to his sides. Bertly considered soothing him; however, truth be told, he preferred Roderick's silence over his comfort. Edfrid continued to crank the massive wooden wheel, and it wasn't long before the group arrived at the bottom of the mountain.

When the crate made contact with the soil, Roderick scuffled past everyone and burst through the gate of the wooden basket. As his feet touched the ground, he let out a huge sigh, as though he had been holding his breath the entire way. Roderick's hands rested on his knees while he panted, standing along a dirt pathway, which weaved through a small forest and ended just at the feet of the Eastern Noskar Mountains.

"Boy, if being taken down one mountain has you winded, how do you plan on climbing up several?" Edfrid beckoned.

Roderick turned and looked toward Edfrid as the rest of the group shuffled out of the wooden elevator. "How many mountains do we have to climb?" Small beads of sweat formed at the top of his forehead. "I thought we were just navigating through them."

Bertly rolled his eyes. "Roderick, you must have assumed that when I mentioned navigating through the mountains; I had also implied we would have to climb some."

"Um…no, sir. I did not assume that." Roderick's eyes grew round and his cheeks turned quite red. "Don't most people take hiking trails when they go through the mountains?"

Edfrid and Bertly roared with laughter. "Hiking trails?" Edfrid cried. "In the mountains?"

"We do not have hiking trails in the Noskar Mountains. Everything grows much too quick in these parts." Bertly placed his hand on Roderick's shoulder and crouched down to eye level.

"Plus, it wouldn't make much sense for a hidden cave to have a pathway leading directly too it, now would it?" Bertly raised his eyebrows. "Wouldn't make for much of a secret." Bertly stood back up and began walking along the dirt road toward the small forest.

Roderick nodded his head and followed close behind. "If this cave is such a secret, then how come you two were able to find it?"

"Well, I don't actually know where it is specifically. It's been many years since I've been." Bertly adjusted the lapels on his cloak. "My father is the one who discovered it. He took me to the entrance many times when I was younger." Bertly shook his head. "But we never went inside." He peered toward Edfrid. "How did you ever find that cave, Father?"

Edfrid coughed and choked on his own spit. "Oh, um." He seemed startled. Bertly had never seen him stumble over his words before. "It was so long ago. I hardly remember." Edfrid cleared his throat. "You are the only folk I am showing other than Bertly."

"If you do not mind me asking, sir," Devdan interjected, "how do you know for certain that the cave is the Dragon's Crypt?"

Edfrid looked at Devdan blankly.

"Trust me, Devdan." Bertly chuckled. "You will know once you see it."

"Have you ever heard the human phrase, 'stepping into the dragon's mouth'?" Polly asked.

Devdan's eyes lit up. "Yes, actually I have."

"Well, that is where the phrase comes from. But I will leave it at that." Polly held up her hands. "I have never been there myself. I've only heard stories from Bertly about what the entrance looks like."

Devdan pushed his finger against his lips and squinted his eyes. He appeared to be thinking, perhaps considering what had just been said.

The group arrived at the entrance of the small woodlands. The ground was covered in mushrooms, and the trees were spread thinly about. When Bertly peered straight back, he could see the mountains through the trees. Drizzle birds sang in the trees as small mice with fuzzy tails and pointed ears scurried across the ground.

"Is that an elf mouse?" Roderick asked. "I didn't know you had those in Noskar."

"Oh, yes." Edfrid crinkled his nose and snarled. "Those vile creatures have made their way across all of Pangea."

Polly clapped her hands. "I think they're rather cute."

"I used to have two of them as pets," Roderick added. "Until they mated and had two dozen babies." He looked down at the ground. "Then my parents made me get rid of them."

Polly rubbed Roderick on the back. "I am so sorry for

your loss." Bertly gave a half smile, as he couldn't tell if Polly was humoring or mocking Roderick.

As the group navigated the forestry, small continuous popping noises came from the snapping of stems and crushing of mushroom caps. A wide variety of different-colored mushrooms covered the sides of the trees. There were more shapes and sizes than the mind could think up, and Bertly felt as though he were walking inside a rainbow.

A loud scream echoed through the forest. Roderick and Devdan came to a screeching halt, and Bertly and Polly watched as the two looked in every direction, trying to determine the source of the scream. Bertly, Polly, and Edfrid continued through the forest as another eerie scream filled the air.

Devdan drew his sword. "Ma'am," he yelled, "are you not worried about that screaming?" Another scream reverberated through the forest. Roderick jumped behind Devdan.

Polly stopped walking and turned around. "My apprentice, I appreciate your concern." She placed her hand on her hip. "But you *really* are not from around here. That noise you hear? That comes from screaming peppers." Polly gestured with her head for him to continue walking. "They are the official plant of Noskar."

Roderick's palms were pressed against his head, and his fingers were wrapped around his ears. "That seems like an awful choice."

Bertly and Edfrid stopped abruptly and jerked their heads toward Roderick.

"I mean…what a unique choice." A flush crept up his face.

Bertly and Edfrid grunted and focused their attention back on the trail.

"They may be quite loud," Polly explained, "but you

should really try eating a few of them." She held her
finger in the air. "Your whole body will be warm for
hours. They are quite coveted during the wintertime. A
pepper farmer is one of the highest-paying jobs in
Noskar."

Roderick flinched as another scream riffled through
the air. "I can see why."

"You know," Edfrid bellowed, "maybe a stop at
Lemon's Pepper Farm isn't the worst idea."

"Hmm." Bertly tilted his head and pressed his lips
together. "I like your thinking. The temperature of the
mountains at night goes well below freezing. We could
use the extra warmth."

"Aye." Edfrid nodded.

"How cold, sir?" Roderick squealed.

Bertly gave Roderick a dismissive wave. "After a few
screaming peppers, you will be fine, my apprentice."

They emerged through the last few trees in the forest,
which revealed a large stone cottage resting in a grass
field. The home had tall and wide front windows, and a
tall wooden fence that extended out from the sides. The
fence formed a box shape behind the house and stretched
for what appeared to be several acres. Bertly walked on
his tiptoes to try to peer over the fence; however, he was
still not tall enough. He presumed that if he jumped, he
would be able to see over, but it was not worth the effort.

Bertly glanced at Edfrid. "I hope you brought your
coin purse. We spent our last coin on worms."

Edfrid patted his sides and searched his coat and pant
compartments. He stopped walking and started searching
through his pockets frantically. He peered at Bertly. "It
seems I have forgotten my pouch."

Bertly slapped his hand against his forehead. "Aren't
you the king?" He started to massage his temples.
"Couldn't you just *command* him to give you the peppers?"

Edfrid stropped in his tracks, grabbed Bertly by the shoulder, and looked him in the eye. "I am *not* that kind of ruler. I do not knock on my people's doors and demand their belongings. This is a land of free people."

Bertly stepped back and gave his father a small smile. "Let me get this straight." Bertly pressed his fingertips together. "You won't demand he give you the peppers because *that* is morally wrong, but...you're okay with tricking and stealing from him?"

Edfrid stroked his beard and nodded. "I suppose you have a point."

"We could just ask him for some," Polly interjected.

"Not a chance," Bertly and Edfrid said together as they shook their heads. "Would never work."

Edfrid tapped his chin. "Aha," he shouted. "I have an idea."

***

Bertly, Roderick, Polly, and Devdan stood at the back fence of the farm. For the moment, the peppers' screaming had stopped, and the farm was silent. Bertly curved his body around the corner of the fence and craned his neck to better watch the front of Lemon's house. Edfrid stood on the porch and knocked on the front door.

"This is a terrible plan," Devdan mumbled.

"Oh, it is absolutely awful. But I have learned over the years to always go along with my father's plans." Bertly turned his head. "Somehow—no matter the situation—he always finds a way out of it." He looked back toward Lemon's house.

Stepping out of the cottage was a short man with blond hair. From the back, he could've been mistaken for a child, but from the front his wrinkles gave him away.

Even across the entire farm, Bertly could see the old man's crinkled skin.

"What's he saying?" Roderick asked. Bertly remained silent, keeping his attention on his father and Lemon. "What's he saying, sir?" Roderick repeated.

"I am not answering your stupid question, Roderick," Bertly snapped. "You're the elf, why are you asking me?"

Roderick gasped. "I'm sorry, sir. But that is just a stereotype. We elves—"

Bertly held his hand up to silence Roderick as Edfrid stretched and put his hands behind his head.

"That's the signal," Bertly said. Polly and Devdan faced each other and interlocked their hands while Bertly placed each of his feet into their palms.

"Be careful, Bertly. If you startle the peppers, Lemon will know. It isn't common for more than one or two of them to be screaming at a time," Polly said as she and Devdan boosted Bertly over the fence.

Bertly scaled the fence and landed firmly on the other side, and Bertly could make out Roderick's mumbles as soon as he landed. "Wait, if it took two of you to get him over the fence, how is he getting back?"

Bertly shook the comment off, deciding he would be better off worrying about that in a few minutes rather than right that moment.

He pulled a bag from his travel sack and walked to the nearest pepper plant. With their tiny eyes shut and small mouths closed, the red screaming peppers slept like babies. Bertly gently plucked each pepper with as much delicacy as he could, being careful not to wake the sleeping peppers. He was sure to grab enough for everyone to stay warm for over a week. As he turned to head back toward the fence, something caught his eye. Bertly jerked his head.

Resting on the other side of the pepper farm—near

Lemon's back door—was one giant golden pepper. This pepper was the size of a banana, and it hung solo from a single vine, taunting Bertly to come and pick it. Bertly looked at the pepper, then at the fence. The opportunity to enchant something with the golden pepper was an urge the Winter Wizard couldn't fight off. He knew the others would start wondering what was taking him so long, but he also understood that his father couldn't carry on a conversation with Lemon for the whole night; no one could.

Bertly's heart pounded, and he took a deep breath. He looked back and tiptoed toward the golden pepper. He focused on the floor, being sure to step over every twig to avoid making a sound. A small buzzing noise filled the air from the sounds of the sleeping peppers, and Bertly found it almost soothing. He stepped up to the golden pepper and gulped. He opened his travel sack, ready to shove the golden pepper into it and make a break for it if he needed to. He reached out slowly and grabbed the pepper where its stem met the trunk of the plant. He started to break the stem of the pepper, but this one was a light sleeper; its eyelids wiggled, and its lips started to move as Bertly attempted to break it from its vine. Bertly froze as small beads of sweat formed along his hairline, and he remained still until he was sure that the pepper had gone back to sleep. Bertly let out a small sigh and continued to peel the pepper from the plant trunk.

A small drop of sweat ran down Bertly's forehead, and from the tip of his nose, the droplet fell and splashed between the eyes of the golden plant. The pepper's eyelids shot open and it stared through Bertly's eyes as it would through a window. The pepper let out a debilitating screech, awakening every pepper on the farm. In an instant thousands of peppers were screaming simultaneously.

"Sweet Cordelia," Bertly shouted. "They can probably hear you back at the Academy." Bertly shoved the golden pepper into his travel sack and sealed it shut, bringing its noise to an end. However, there was still the issue of the entire farm of peppers screaming.

Bertly dashed for the fence. Several options ran through his mind. He considered creating dirt stairs from the ground, similar to the wall his master had created at the Decomposite, but he had no clue how Alestar had done that. Bertly was nearing the wooden fence. His next best idea was to burn a hole straight through, but again, he had to dismiss the idea. It would take him far too long to create enough fire to burn a hole large enough to squeeze through—if he already had a source, then he would stand a chance.

Bertly was only two steps from the fence, and there was not enough time to think up a plan. On instinct, he tucked his head into his chest and smashed into the fence shoulder first. The wooden pickets cracked in half, splintering in every direction. Bertly summersaulted across the ground and crashed into Devdan's legs.

"What happened?" Polly screamed.

"The peppers have gone mad!" Roderick cried.

Devdan grabbed Bertly by the shoulder straps and helped him to his feet. "I don't know what happened," Bertly replied as he dusted himself off. "I was delicately picking them, and out of nowhere they went ballistic."

"Never mind, Bertly." Polly frowned. "Let's get out of here."

Bertly poked his head around the fence to get an update on his father's situation. As he turned the corner, he saw Edfrid several paces away, sprinting straight at him. His father's lips were moving, but no one was able to hear him over the screaming peppers. Edfrid waved his arm forward and back. This time Bertly heard his father's roaring voice.

"Run!" Edfrid hollered. The group turned instantly and took off, running for the mountains. Bertly saw Polly and Devdan running ahead, but he couldn't see Roderick in front of him or in his peripheral vision. Roderick had just been right next to him. Bertly whipped his head back and saw Roderick slowly taking off with his head thrown back and his arms pumping; however, he could not keep up with the rest of them. Just behind Roderick, Edfrid came swooping in, throwing the elf over his shoulder. Bertly stumbled, as his eyes had been off the road for too long. He wobbled for a few steps but managed to keep his footing. He focused back on the road and continued to run until the sound of the screaming peppers started to fade.

The group came to a stop and threw their hands over their knees. Everyone was breathing in and out at a quick pace. Roderick lay hunched over Edfrid's shoulder, panting quicker than anyone.

"What are you so tired for? I carried you the whole way." Edfrid slouched his shoulder, letting Roderick fall. Roderick let out a squeal when he hit the ground. Bertly expected him to pick himself up, but instead he simply lay on the ground moaning.

Polly drew in a long breath. "We've been running for so long, I had almost forgotten why we started running in the first place."

"I didn't, ma'am." Roderick sat up. "That screeching was awful."

"I regret choosing so much armor," Devdan added.

Bertly caught his breath. "That is why I chose not to wear any armor." He puffed his chest out. "I never sacrifice speed."

"Do you think I should take off my armor, sir?"

Roderick pulled himself to his feet, slipping on occasion due to his clunky armor. "For more speed?"

Bertly looked Roderick up and down. "I think it is best you keep your armor."

"Something must have upset the queen pepper." Edfrid exhaled. "That's the only thing that would set them all off like that."

Bertly's stomach sank. "Queen pepper?" His voice cracked.

"Oh, yes." Edfrid stood slouched against a tree, breathing heavier than normal. Bertly was the only one in the group who was fully recovered from their run. All the high-altitude flights with Clia must have helped. Edfrid continued, "There is one queen that soothes all the peppers. She gives off a low buzz that keeps them calm."

Bertly held his breath.

"Every now and then one gets disturbed and cries out, but, for the most part, the calming hum of the giant queen pepper keeps the farm composed."

"Theoretically speaking." Bertly started to play with his braided hair. "What happens if the queen pepper, say, dies or...wanders off?"

"I'm not sure how much wandering a pepper does." Edfrid snickered. "But if one were to be stolen—which is a serious problem pepper farmers face—it could be sold for a high price. A lot of wizards use them in powerful elixirs or for enchanting." Edfrid pulled the hood of his fur cloak over his head. "But to answer your first question, if the queen goes missing, then the peppers scream until they exhaust themselves."

"And fall asleep?" Bertly asked.

"No. Until they die," Edfrid replied bluntly. "It is a travesty every time a queen pepper dies or is stolen. The farmer loses their entire harvest for the season." He looked down at the ground and sighed. "Anyhow."

Edfrid clapped his hands. "We should be off. The sun is beginning to set. I would like to set up camp before sundown." Edfrid pointed. "On the bright side, at least we made some great time. The mountains are no more than an hour away."

Bertly's heart was pounding and his hands were shaking. He wanted to speak up so they could go back and return the golden pepper, but there was a slight stubbornness stopping him from telling the group the truth. The idea of looking ignorant and careless ate at him. He knew it was the wrong decision; nonetheless, he'd rather let Lemon's harvest go to ruin than embarrass himself. Bertly shook off his ill expression and followed his father toward the hills.

The group marched in single file, silently, behind Edfrid. "Bertly, do you have any of those screaming peppers?" Polly was hugging herself. "It is getting quite bitter."

"Yes," Bertly replied.

Polly glanced toward Bertly and stared at him for a moment. "May I have some, please?"

Bertly reached into his travel sack and pulled out two screaming peppers and handed them to Polly. Both crops lay with their eyes shut, resting helplessly.

Polly snatched the peppers out of Bertly's hand and popped them into her mouth. Tiny screams started, but quickly faded as Polly chomped down on them. "Thank you, Bertly." Polly swallowed the last bit of food she had. "It is quite interesting the peppers were so calm." She turned to Bertly's father. "Edfrid, didn't you mention that they scream until they die?"

"Hmm…that is peculiar. I was always told that is how it went." Edfrid looked at Bertly in the corner of his eye. "I suppose it is just an old wives' tale." He enunciated and drew each word out slowly.

Bertly cleared his throat to try to hide the tremble in his voice. "It's hard to find reliable information these days."

"Sir, what exactly makes the mountains so dangerous?" Roderick interrupted.

"Great question, my apprentice." For possibly the first time, Bertly was more than eager to answer Roderick's impulsive questions. Anything to change the topic. "Many folks outside Noskar don't think that we humans have many monsters in our lands. But that couldn't be further from the truth. The fact is, they all live in the mountains. Always have."

Roderick's jaw chattered. "What kind of monsters, sir?"

"Oh, nothing out of the ordinary," Bertly replied. "Wolves, bears, mountain bats, sabretooth tigers, lions, mammoths, and of course"—Bertly held his fist in the air—"the King of all Dragons." He peered over and saw Roderick's pale face and dilated pupils. "You puzzle me, Roderick, why are you so afraid of combat and confrontation? Didn't you place rather high in the Clash Tournament?"

Devdan burst out laughing. Bertly jerked his head toward Devdan and then back toward his apprentice. "Roderick, why is he laughing?" Bertly snapped.

Roderick pinned his mouth shut.

"Roderick," Bertly yelled, "I demand you tell me."

"He cheated." Devdan snorted, wiping a tear from the corner of his eye.

"Roderick." Bertly placed his hand over his mouth and shook his head. "I don't know if I should be disappointed or proud."

Roderick jolted his head back. "Excuse me, sir?"

"Yes, Bertly." Polly glanced sideways. "Please explain."

"It takes a lot of courage to cheat," Bertly replied.

"Some may say it takes a coward to cheat, but I say, if you ask a coward to cheat, they won't be able to do it." Bertly walked to the side of Roderick and placed a hand on his shoulder. "It isn't something I would do, but it actually takes a lot of bravery to attempt cheating."

Roderick cleared his throat and looked away from Bertly. "Aren't you going to ask how I cheated, sir?"

"It's not important." Bertly shrugged. "You did something I didn't know you were capable of, and you have surprised me." Bertly put him in a headlock. "There is hope for you yet."

Edfrid stopped in his tracks and spread his arms like wings. "Welcome to the Noskar Mountains."

Bertly had been so wrapped up in his conversation with Roderick he didn't notice their destination fast approaching. Bertly continued along the dirt path that had led them there, and all the while he tracked the upcoming route with his eyes, noticing that it blended into the mountainside. He knew from then on, they would be relying on his father's navigation.

The sun was setting just over the mountaintops, casting a pink and orange tint over the sky. The sun finally stopped reflecting off the snow, giving Bertly's eyes a much-needed rest. The constant squinting had started to give him a headache. The mountains all looked the same, steep and jagged, but the sizes varied greatly, from mounts Bertly could've scaled in a matter of minutes, to highlands that stretched to so extreme a height it hurt his neck to look up at their peaks.

"Please tell me we don't have to climb to the top of that," Roderick cried.

"Today is your lucky day, little elf." Edfrid chuckled. "The entrance is not very high. It is just deep within the mountains."

Roderick nodded. "I suppose that is better."

Edfrid pointed. "That crevasse over there. It looks perfect for camp tonight. I am assuming you all shoved plenty of supplies into those magic bags of yours."

"Absolutely, sir." Devdan patted his travel sack. "We have everything you could need."

"Grand," Edfrid replied. "I will gather firewood while the rest of you set up camp."

The group moseyed over to a small indentation in the side of the mountain and set up bed pads and their cooking pot.

"Sir?" a quiet voice mumbled.

"Yes, Roderick," Bertly replied.

Roderick twisted the ring on his finger. "What exactly is a mountain bat?"

"They are bats the size of geese." Bertly spread his arms wide to show the size of their wingspan.

"Th-that is terrifying," Roderick stuttered.

"I have to say, sir," Devdan said. "I am not fond of the sound of these bats, either."

Bertly leaned in. "What makes them so disturbing is they can also walk."

Roderick's eyes widened.

Bertly heard the loud snap of a tree branch close by. Roderick screamed. Bertly whipped his head in the direction of the noise. It was his father returning with firewood.

"What's gotten into him?" Edfrid asked.

Polly giggled. "He thought you were a mountain bat."

Edfrid dropped the branches he had gathered in the middle of the campsite and stared at Roderick. "What are you going to do when you see a dragon?"

"I'm trying not to think about it." Roderick walked over and started to set up the wood for a campfire.

"Do you think we will see a dragon tomorrow?" Devdan exclaimed.

"If my memory serves me well, and I can still get around the mountains...yes. The passage isn't far; it is merely impossible to find." Edfrid tapped his nose. "For anyone who doesn't know where it is."

"Like the land of the giants," Roderick added as he stood and wiped his hands on his chest. "Done, sir." Bertly, Polly and Devdan walked over to the pyramid-shaped, stacked wood. Each of them, including Roderick, closed their eyes and extended their hands over the firewood. Black smoke soon emerged from the tree branches, and not long after there was a full blaze.

Edfrid clapped loudly enough to cause an echo in an open field. "Bravo, bravo." He plopped next to the fire and extended his arms toward it. "Now, who has a tale to tell?"

XVI

The sun had fully set, and a new chill had settled over Noskar. The footsteps left behind by Bertly and the others were already covered by a fresh layer of snow. The group huddled around the campfire, shivering and rubbing their hands to keep warm.

"I think we should give everyone their gifts now, Bertly," Polly forced out as her teeth chattered.

Bertly raised his eyebrows. "I had almost forgotten." Bertly shot to his feet. "Why didn't you speak up sooner?" He placed his hand in front of Roderick. "Apprentice, travel sack."

Roderick's shaking hands could barely grasp the straps well enough to slip the sack off his shoulders. "I'm not sure how much those thin blankets will help, sir."

Bertly snatched the bag out of Roderick's hands and pulled out several bedsheets.

"I will take anything at this point," Devdan said.

"These are enchanted blankets. The twins, Polly, and I worked very hard on these." Bertly walked around the circle and handed each person a cover. "We had to catch and kill at least two hundred fire geckos in order to make these strong enough."

Devdan wrapped himself in the blanket immediately. "It feels like the sun is inside this blanket," he observed.

A relieved grin spread across his face as he closed his eyes.

"It's incredible, sir." Roderick's eyes were closed as well. He, too, had a smile plastered across his face. "Warmer than the ones back at the Academy."

"This really is something, son." Edfrid ran the sheet between his fingers. "You could sell these for a high price at the Stonebank market."

"As much as I would love to, I don't think that's an option," Bertly replied.

"We could get expelled for selling enchanted items before we graduate the Mastery program," Polly explained. Edfrid wasn't as familiar with the procedures and punishments of the Academy as the students were, and Polly was always willing to jump in with any information she could provide.

"Isn't it also against school rules to practice enchanting outside of class?" Devdan asked.

"Rules are meant to protect the weak, Devdan," Bertly grumbled. "We do not worry about things that do not pertain to us."

Devdan glanced at Polly in what seemed like disbelief. She raised her eyebrows and gave a half grin. Bertly knew Polly wasn't much of a rule breaker, but he knew she also felt restricted by the Academy's guidelines.

Not a single drizzle bird sang as a light snow dusted the campsite. Bertly heard a loud snoring; he peeked over only to see Roderick plopped over on his side and fast asleep.

Polly put her hand over her mouth and giggled. "I think I am going to get some shut-eye as well." She leaned back and rested her head across her arm. "Goodnight, everyone. I can't wait to steal a dragon scale tomorrow."

Devdan fell back and flopped his head onto his travel

sack. "I am going to try to get some rest as well."

Bertly turned toward Edfrid. "It looks like it is just us."

Edfrid smiled. "Good, we have a lot to catch up on." He tapped his chin. "For starters, how did you grow so old so quickly?"

Bertly wiped his hand across his face and let out a slow sigh. "Long story short, it turns out the Eternal Cave is real. However, contrary to popular belief, it does not ensure that one will live longer, it just makes you older."

"Well." Edfrid choked on his own spit. "That is quite the false victory."

"Tell me about it." Bertly looked at the ground and played with the snow next to him, slowly building a pile of it by his feet. "Not only do I not live longer, I assume, if anything, I have jumped ahead a few years, shortening my life."

"Aye." Edfrid opened his mouth to speak further but no words came out. He placed his hand on Bertly's shoulder and gave him a small squeeze. Bertly's father had always struggled with providing comfort, but Bertly understood his intentions.

"So how many people are now in Stonebank, do you reckon?" Bertly asked after a moment of intense silence. He needed to talk about anything else.

"Right." Edfrid adjusted his posture so that he sat up straight. "If I was forced to guess..." Edfrid looked up at the stars and mouthed words to himself. "Almost a million, I would say."

Bertly cocked his head to the side and rubbed his temples. "There were no more than three hundred when I left."

"After the Academy class roster was announced, and people saw two humans from Stonebank on the list—" Edfrid paused and shook his head "—we had hundreds a day showing up for the first few years alone. People believe Stonebank is blessed."

"Well, of course it is—it has me." Bertly's smile was wide enough to show all of his teeth. Edfrid shoved Bertly and laughed. Bertly cleared his throat and sat up straight.

"There is something I have been meaning to ask you about." Bertly glanced at Edfrid, who nodded for Bertly to continue. "Before I left for the Academy, you gave me a notebook. You said it was Mother's. But it was filled with all kinds of spells and—"

Edfrid held out his hand for Bertly to stop. "I had a feeling you would ask about this, and you have a right to know." Edfrid closed his eyes. "When I met your mother, we were both young and careless." A trace of a smile formed in the corners of his mouth. "We did whatever we wanted, and without a care in the world. We traveled all over Noskar, explored every new place we could find. Collected more artifacts than one could imagine, and amongst many of those came old spells and even some riddles. But once you were born, our traveling and exploring stopped." Edfrid took a long breath. "I knew that your mother, in her heart, felt that she could never be tied down. The duties of motherhood became too great for her, and one morning she was gone, along with almost every treasure we discovered." Edfrid opened his eyes. His smile had dwindled. "She didn't say goodbye or leave a letter. She just left two things. A journal and a map. She knew you were special, Bertly, we both did. She left them both behind because she wanted you to be a famous wizard, and she left us because I wanted you to have a normal childhood."

Bertly clenched his notebook from the outside of his pocket. "So she may still be alive?"

Edfrid held back tears. "I don't know, son. When she

left, she went looking for that." He pointed to Cordelia's warblade.

The thought of his mother visiting the Decomposite made the young wizard shiver in fear. For some reason Bertly did not fear for himself against the Rotters, but worried greatly for someone without magic. But maybe she checked elsewhere and not the Decomposite; the Winter Wizard didn't wish to think on it anymore. As he typically did, Bertly attempted to bury the thought away deep inside. "A map?" he asked.

Edfrid reached into his side pocket, removed a folded-up piece of parchment, and handed it to Bertly. Bertly unfolded the paper and examined its contents. The parchment was a detailed map of Pangea with every mountain, lake, river, and city labeled. Scattered across the map were several trunk icons with X's through them.

Bertly pointed to the map. "What are these chest symbols?"

"Ahh." Edfrid folded his hands and rested them on his stomach. "You see, all that traveling we did, it wasn't for nothing…we were searching for lost treasure."

Bertly's eyes sparkled and he leaned in closer to his father.

"We traveled all over. It started in Noskar, and it wasn't before long we found ourselves in Eplium."

"How long did you travel for?" Bertly asked.

"Hmm…at least ten years." Edfrid rubbed away the small snowflakes that had built up in his beard. Bertly felt an excitement emerging within him. This was one of the very few times his father had opened up to Bertly about his mother.

Bertly looked back down at his mother's map. "Remarkable. You must have seen everything."

Edfrid slouched over and held Bertly's shoulder. "You could explore this world for a hundred lifetimes, and I don't think you'd discover half of what Pangea has to offer."

"What's this location in the Decomposite?" Bertly pressed his finger against the map. "It's the only chest that isn't crossed off."

"It's the only place I never allowed her to go." Edfrid let go of Bertly's shoulder and took a deep breath. "We agreed we would travel to every spot on that map before we had children. When the time came, and that place was the last on our map, I couldn't do it." Edfrid sat up straight. "I didn't want to throw away our lives in the Decomposite on our last trip. I wanted to have you."

Bertly wanted to respond to his father, but he didn't know how. He knew his father loved him, but he'd never understood how much Edfrid had truly wanted to be a father.

"If I had gone on that trip…" Edfrid closed his eyes. "I don't think she would have left us."

"You can't blame yourself for this," Bertly said, knowing old emotions were resurfacing for his father, but he couldn't restrain his curiosity. "Do you think that is where she went?"

Edfrid nodded.

Bertly became flooded with emotion; he was confused, frustrated, and excited all at the same time. "I always thought she had passed away."

"No…I don't know where she is now." Edfrid's bottom lip quivered. "I always thought she'd come back. You know, after she went to the Decomposite and found what she was looking for."

Bertly's head ached. He rubbed his temples so he could attempt to think clearly. "Why are you telling me this now? Why are you giving me this map now?"

Edfrid looked at Bertly and shook his head. "What was a ten-year-old going to do with a map leading to the

THE DUBIOUS TALE OF THE WINTER WIZARD   219

Decomposite?" He sighed. "There is never a good time with this stuff."

Bertly pressed his lips and lifted his head. "Thank you." He bent the map back into its already creased folds and tucked it into the cover of his journal. "I'm glad you told me."

Edfrid smiled without showing his teeth and closed his eyes. "I think it's time to get some rest." He slouched onto his side. "Goodnight, Bertly. I'll see you in the morning."

Bertly leaned back and rested his head against Roderick's travel sack. "Goodnight, Father." Bertly snapped his fingers, adding oxygen to the campfire. The flames grew and left a warm glow over the sleeping group.

Bertly couldn't tell the difference between his frustration and excitement. He rested his head against Roderick's bag and stared at the stars. He knew, logically, he should be mad at his mother; however, he couldn't help but empathize with why she might have left. Bertly could never imagine settling down forever; he also felt the pull to travel all of Noskar. He wondered how much of his mother was a part of him. Did she also share his desire for glory? Maybe traits and emotions he never understood about himself could be explained if he met her.

One question he could not get off his mind was, were the map and journal related? *The notebook!* He'd completely forgotten to ask his father about the spells written inside. He propped himself up and peered at his father. Edfrid was snoring softly with his mouth half open. Bertly would have to wait for another time to ask him.

He rested his head once more. The stars had faded, and what had been a black, midnight sky was now a blue blanket over the earth. The morning sun hadn't yet peeked over the hilltops, but Bertly could feel it warming his skin. The first drizzle bird rang out its lovely morning song. Bertly had lost track of his thoughts and let the entire night slip away from him.

Polly stretched her arms and legs as far as seemed possible. She let out a big sigh and rubbed her eyes. "Morning, Bertly," she said mid yawn. "How did you sleep?"

"I slept great." Bertly thought about mentioning the fact that he hadn't fallen asleep, but he didn't want to explain what had kept him up all night. "Our blankets worked perfectly."

Bertly sat up and quickly scanned the campsite. The fire was out, but the coals were still red and smoking. Devdan and Edfrid were both shuffling around in their beds, so Bertly assumed they would be up soon. He glanced at Roderick, whose face was pressed flat into the ground, with a stream of drool running down the side of his mouth. Bertly leaned over and scooped up a ball of snow that hadn't been melted by the fire. He hovered the snowball over Roderick's head. He looked at Polly and pressed his pointer finger against his lips. Bertly dropped the ball of ice.

Roderick jolted out of his bed and smacked the snow off his face. "Sweet Cordelia!" he screamed.

Bertly and Polly burst into laughter. "Rise and shine, little apprentice."

***

Bertly stood at the base of the mountains, distributing peppers to his traveling companions. He took a prolonged breath of the crisp Noskar air. The sun was peeking just over the hilltops—it was that fleeting moment where the entire landscape was perfectly balanced between night and day. A soft blanket of snow covered the sharp, gray mountain peaks. Bertly could tell by how low the snow fell on the hills that winter was in full season.

The group hiked through the trails that had developed naturally through the dips and inclines. Though the mountain slopes were not very steep, they were covered in snow, which made them much more difficult to traverse.

Bertly marched to the front of the group, ahead of his father. He reached his hand out and clenched his fist. "Why did I not think of this before?" The snow slowing their path had turned into water. "Now we will have a clear path."

"Wait a minute, Bertly." Polly spoke out. "That water could turn into ice. It may be better to turn it into steam instead."

Bertly rolled his eyes and then turned toward Polly. "If that will make you happy." He knew Polly's presumption was correct. The colder it got, the faster the water would freeze, if it did not freeze instantly. "Just so you know, it takes a lot more energy to turn snow into steam than to turn it into water." Bertly whipped back around and then clapped his hands. Several hundred paces of snow turned into a thick mist, leaving behind a clear path wide enough for two people to walk side by side. Bertly gasped—out of breath. He had to inhale quick gulps of air in rapid succession to regain his composure. He was not overwhelmed, but the spell had taken some stamina from him.

"Don't worry, Bertly." Polly placed her hand on his shoulder. "I can trade off with you."

Bertly turned to her and bobbed his head. His pride wanted to clear the path by himself, but he needed to save some energy for when they arrived at the Dragon's Crypt.

The group followed Edfrid through canals and crevices as Bertly and Polly traded the responsibility of transforming the snow into steam.

"This isn't so bad." Roderick beamed. "There are hardly any hills at all."

The group was traveling through channels in between the mountains. The walls beside them were a few times taller than Bertly. Above them, on top of the walls, was flat land. The tops of the stone walls rotated between flat trails and steep mountain slopes. The channel's width was inconsistent, ranging from single-file accommodation to wide enough for the whole group to walk side by side. There were several twists and turns, enough to disorient even the best navigator.

"In all honesty, the hike to Dragon's Crypt is not physically demanding," Bertly replied. "The only thing preventing most from finding it—" he stuck his nose in the air "—is they don't know where it is."

Roderick rubbed his chin. "Interesting…" He glanced up. "And what about the monsters, sir?"

Bertly and Polly chuckled. "I may have been exaggerating a bit about the…*quantity* of monsters." Bertly shrugged. "Mind you." He raised his voice and stuck his finger high in the air. "All the creatures I've mentioned *do* exist here in the mountains." Bertly lowered his hand and shook his head. "And run-ins are by no means a rare occurrence."

"How often do humans really get attacked in these parts?" Devdan asked.

Polly gave an unconcerned wave. "Oh, when we were younger, we heard a few stories that *may* have been true."

"Such as?" Devdan prodded.

Polly rolled her head back and grinned. "Some people

may or may not have been...eaten."

"Eaten?" Roderick shrieked.

Bertly glanced toward his father, who had a habit of always chiming in when there was mention of missing mountain people. He noticed his father had his war hammer drawn from the satchel on his back. Bertly slipped away from the group and walked ahead a couple of steps next to Edfrid. "You're too quiet," he noted.

"Aye," Edfrid replied. "We're being followed." He clenched his hammer tighter.

Bertly kept his voice low. "How can you tell?"

Edfrid motioned his head to the right. "On the cliff above us, about three dozen paces behind us, snow keeps falling off the ledge. It hasn't happened on the right side; neither is it happening in front of us."

The feeling of being stalked left an unsettled, nervous churning in Bertly's stomach. "Any clue what it is?" He did his best to keep his composure.

Edfrid shook his head. "I haven't been able to get a look at it. Whatever it is—" he glanced back "—it's confident jumping down from a high vantage point." He looked at Bertly. "That rules out bears and wolves, and it's too bright out for a mountain bat. Only other thing that would hunt us down would be a large koko."

"A lion or sabretooth tiger, then," Bertly added.

"Pray to Cordelia for a sabretooth. At least they hunt solo sometimes." Edfrid gestured for Bertly to drop back. "Go talk with your friends, and let them know what's going on. It's getting closer."

Bertly acknowledged his father and slowed his pace, blending back into the group behind him. Bertly crept to Roderick and wrapped his hand around Roderick's mouth. Roderick grabbed Bertly's wrist, pulling on it and trying to break free. Despite Roderick's efforts, Bertly's hand stayed firmly clasped over his mouth. "Listen very closely," Bertly said. "We are being followed." Roderick's scream was muffled by Bertly's hand. "We aren't sure what it is yet, most likely a lion or sabretooth."

Roderick let out another muffled screech.

Devdan drew his sword.

"It's a good thing we have the Clash Tournament champion with us," Polly whispered as she slipped on a red glove.

Bertly clenched his jaw and drew his warblade. He wasn't sure what was worse: being hunted by a deadly predator, or the possibility of Devdan being the one to slay it.

"What is that glove for, ma'am?" Devdan asked.

Polly wiggled her fingers. "Bertly's master gave it to me. It allows me to cast spells at several times their normal strength." Polly sighed. "The only issue is it is only strong enough for a couple of spells before needing to be recharged."

Devdan's eyes widened.

"Roderick, I don't know when it'll be, but when I say run, you run." Bertly let go of Roderick's mouth. "Do not look back—just run. Let me know you understand."

"I understand, sirrrabretooth!" Roderick's body shook as he let out an unbearable scream.

Peeking its head just over the cliff was a beefy white sabretooth tiger. Its fangs were as long as Bertly's forearms, and its body would be big enough for several people to ride on. It discharged an echoing roar just before it leaped off the edge and toward the group of travelers.

Polly faced the fanged tiger and clapped her hands, ensuring that a wall of ice formed just where the tiger was about to step, causing it to ram face-first into the ice barrier.

"Hurry!" Edfrid shouted.

Devdan grabbed Roderick and threw him over his shoulder as the group raced behind Edfrid. They sprinted through tight canals, scraping their arms and shoulders against areas that were too narrow, but they had no time to worry about injuries. The group trailed close behind Bertly's father. Every hundred paces there was a new fork in the road, and like a salmon swimming upriver, Edfrid knew exactly where to go. The snow and ice made Bertly slip nearly every other step, and each time he rounded a corner, he feared they would hit a dead end.

"Why does it want to kill us?" Roderick's voice fluctuated in tone and depth as he bounced on Devdan's shoulder.

"It doesn't want to just kill us." Edfrid plowed through the snow, leaving a trail behind for the students to follow. "It wants to eat us."

"Hibernation is soon," Polly cried.

The cold air dried Bertly's throat as he inhaled faster and faster. Each bump and scrape made every step harder. Bertly's pants and cloak were tattered. He feared the group would make a turn and hit a long straightaway. The twists and turns were the only thing keeping the white tiger from catching them. The long-furred beast relentlessly chased them, thrashing its body into the walls and corners of every narrow turn.

"We need to figure something out," Bertly said, panting. "It can run for much longer in the snow than we can."

"There isn't anywhere to take cover," Devdan puffed. Bertly was impressed with Devdan's physical ability. He knew he was the school champion, but still, outrunning a sabretooth tiger with another person over your shoulder was no small task.

"Aye," Edfrid replied. "Then we make a stand." Edfrid came to a screeching halt, planted one foot into the ground, and pivoted his body swiftly around. He shoved the still-running teenagers behind him and drew his war hammer. "Stay behind me." Edfrid stood with his hammer in hand and his knees slightly bent. Bertly could hear the stretch in the leather from his father tightening his grip.

The sabretooth stopped chasing them and came to a standoff with Edfrid, looking hunger-mad in the eyes. The tiger licked its chops as drool fell from its mouth. It paced the pathway side to side; its shoulder blades stuck out past the top of its head with each step it took. The tiger roared and Edfrid returned with his loudest battle cry.

The two charged each other full force. The tiger leaped toward Edfrid with its claws protracted and mouth wide open. Edfrid braced his body and shoved the shaft of his war hammer horizontally into the tiger's mouth. The sabretooth whipped its head around, trying to rip the hammer from Edfrid's hands, but the warden of Stonebank didn't give. Edfrid pushed forward, swinging his hammer to the side, slamming the tiger into the wall. He pressed its skull against the stone and grinded its face down the side of the canal. The tiger snarled and fell onto its side. Edfrid leaped toward the beast, but before he could make contact, the animal rolled fully onto its back and kicked him with both of its hind legs, sending Edfrid flying through the air and slamming onto the ground.

Bertly took off without hesitation. Devdan dropped Roderick to the ground and bolted toward the tiger, only half a step behind him.

"Wait!" Polly reached out and grabbed Devdan's shoulder, but he broke free on his first stride. The tiger sprang to its feet, glared at Bertly, then raced to Edfrid.

While Devdan sprinted, Polly stuck out her arm and grunted. She formed a fist and tucked it into her chest. A spear made from stone shot from the side of the mountain, knocking the tiger onto its side. The beast did a barrel roll, getting snow all over its face and in its fur. The sabretooth turned its attention to Devdan, who was sprinting at it full force. He leaped in the air and stabbed his sword into the shoulder of the beast. The tiger wobbled back and stared Devdan in the eyes, blood dripping from its side. Bertly stood, waiting for his moment to strike with the warblade, but he didn't want Devdan to become collateral damage.

"You're lucky I missed." Devdan pulled a dagger from his boot. "I was aiming for your neck." He shuffled to the side and lunged forward, with the tip of his knife heading straight for the side of the sabretooth's head. Just before the moment of contact, the tiger threw its body into Devdan, knocking him to the ground. Devdan's dagger stuck into the side of the beast, yet it reacted as though it had only a splinter in its side, not a blade. The tiger pressed its paws down on Devdan's chest, crushing him into the ground, causing him to groan.

Bertly saw his opening: he throttled the grip of Cordelia's warblade and struck his arms forward. The tiger looked up and glared at Bertly as the mammoth-ice blade protracted from the handle. The white beast hurled Devdan's body to the side as it attempted to evade the extending warblade. The sabretooth's reflexes lived up to Bertly's expectations—a blade that had plowed through an army of Rotters left no more than a flesh wound on the white-furred brute. The tiger regained balance without hesitation and stomped on the ice blade, smashing it against the ground. The force of the creature's pounce ripped the warblade from Bertly's hands and pinned it against the snowy ground. As the sword left Bertly's hands and hit the ground, the ice blade retreated into the grip.

"Bertly, melt the snow and splash him!" Polly screamed.

Bertly didn't understand why she was asking this of him. If she thought the snow being melted would cause the tiger to slip, she was mistaken.

"*Now*," she emphasized.

Bertly glanced up at the white monster, and he saw his father getting to his feet behind the tiger.

"Bertly, kokos hate being wet!" Polly exclaimed.

Bertly, already bent over from trying to pick up his sword, dropped to his knees and punched his fists into the ground. The blanket of snow covering the ground turned into water. The tiger picked up its pace and charged in Bertly's direction. The Winter Wizard turned his palms face up and lifted them above his head, sending the water full force at the tiger. The splash drenched the creature, but it kept charging. Roderick stepped out in front of Polly and clapped his hands. The body of water covering the tiger turned to ice.

Bertly jerked his head back and saw Roderick with his hands clasped together. Bertly looked back at the white tiger. Its body was covered in ice, and the beast looked as though it were frozen in time.

"Roderick, was that you?" Bertly experienced an alien sensation; his anxiety had turned into pride. He felt triumphant, even though he was not the one to slay the beast.

"Ever since we left the Eternal Cave, I have been trying to figure out how you made that waterfall freeze." The way Roderick puckered his lips together as he spoke indicated to Bertly that he was trying to hold back a smile. "Sir."

"I truly am a great master." The corners of Bertly's mouth turned up. "Just being around me can teach one how to slay a sabretooth."

Devdan shuffled on the ground and attempted to help himself up.

"Come on, guys! Now is our chance to get away," Polly yelled.

Bertly grabbed the warblade from the ground. He clenched the grip and bent his knees, readying himself to strike; however, his blade didn't extend from the hilt. Bertly glared at the grip. He shook it in an attempt to extract the blade. "It's not working."

"That's fine. Help your father and let's go," Polly stressed.

Edfrid emerged from around the back of the sabretooth tiger and walked along the side of it. His shoulders were slouched, and a menacing glare was glued to his face as he dragged his war hammer across the ground. The weight of the heavy head left behind a trail as it was lugged across the dirt. Edfrid stopped to examine the head of the white tiger and turned his attention to its eyes. Edfrid stuck his hand into the open mouth of the sabretooth and gripped its upper jaw. Bertly heard the ice around the creature's face start to crack as his father yanked and ripped the upper jaw from the beast's skull cavity. Polly jumped back and yelped.

Edfrid turned and walked away without saying a word. After a couple of steps, he stopped and tossed the sabretooth's teeth to Bertly. Edfrid clutched his hammer with both fists and let out a monstrous roar. He heaved the hammer above his head, turned, and plowed it straight into the tiger's cranium, knocking its head clean off. "Let's go." Blood poured from the opening where the animal's neck had been attached to its head. "The entrance isn't far from here." Edfrid snatched the tiger's teeth as he walked past Bertly.

***

The group was silent from that moment on—most were injured, and all were exhausted. The sun was starting to set, and the well-lit mountains were casting their long shadows over Noskar. The temperature was quickly dropping, or perhaps the peppers were wearing off. Bertly assumed it was a bit of both. Edfrid led the group through the labyrinth of crevices with his war hammer slung over his shoulder. Devdan followed just behind Polly, who was the only one thus far unscathed by their journey, yet she seemed the most distraught. Bertly knew she was mad about the sabretooth being killed, but he couldn't wrap his mind around it. He didn't understand why she was upset; if the creature had gotten its way, they would've all been supper.

"I am freezing, sir." Roderick's teeth were chattering. "Can I have some of those peppers?"

Bertly shook his head. "Sorry, little apprentice, we need the rest for the trip back."

Edfrid led the group through a narrow passage. Bertly had to shuffle his body horizontally just to fit. Above, the mountains were closed off, and the group squeezed into a tiny mountain hole. On the other side, the pathway opened back up; however, very little light came through the top. They were not in a cave, but they weren't on an open road, either.

"Can I have a blanket, then?" Roderick asked.

"They have limited use, Roderick," Bertly replied. "They will hardly last us through tonight."

"Do not worry, boy," Edfrid added. "We will be there any—" He paused as he turned the corner. "Second." They came to a dead end.

Nestled between the foothills rested a statue that someone had carved into the shape of a dragon's head. The stone figure was delicately crafted, with each scale finely detailed. The eyes were larger than dinner plates, and the top of its head was higher than a cottage roof. The mouth of the dragon was carved wide open, revealing an entrance to the inside of the mountains. A thick layer of steam bellowed from the mouth of the cave. Bertly could feel the heat on his face.

Bertly walked toward the entryway. "Elves," he exclaimed as he walked toward the mouth of the dragon. As he turned back around, he caught a glimpse of Polly. "And, Polly... I present to you—" Bertly stood in the entrance of the cave and held his hands in the air "—the Dragon's Crypt."

Roderick's body trembled. "S-sir, can I w-wait outside?" he stuttered.

"You always have that great attitude, Roderick." Bertly clapped his hands. "I love it." He whipped around and stared down the throat of the stone dragon. The steam rolled out in abundance, making a blanket so thick Bertly couldn't see the tips of his fingers when he stuck his arm out. He closed his eyes and took a deep breath, letting the warm mist fill his lungs. Bertly took a moment to gather his thoughts as he adjusted to the humid air.

Edfrid walked up to Bertly and placed a hand on his shoulder. "You're as ready as you'll ever be."

Bertly looked to his father and nodded. Without unsheathing it, Bertly clenched the grip of his warblade and marched into the mouth of the dragon—his body vanishing as the intense steam consumed him.

XVII

Bertly stood just beyond the dragon's mouth and examined the crypt as he waited for the others to catch up. The air was humid, but the steam was much less cumbersome than it was at the entrance. Bat droppings covered the ground, adding a heavy odor that carried through the haze. When he closed his eyes, he could hear water droplets splashing in the puddles scattered across the floor.

"Cozy," Polly teased.

"What's that smell?" Roderick squinted as he used his shirt to cover his nose and mouth.

"Dragon scales, my apprentice." Bertly took a deep breath. "Breathe it in. He is so close I can almost taste it."

"I think it's the bat dung, sir." Roderick gagged. He tilted his chin upward and met Bertly's eyes with a pathetic look on his face. "I don't think it's dragon scales."

"I was speaking metaphorically, Roderick." Bertly grunted and clenched his jaw. "We do not have time for your nonsense." He pointed down the pathway. "Onward!" he yelled.

Bertly led his companions through the steamy passageways of the Dragon's Crypt. Torches along the walls were already lit, exposing remnants of old camps.

The broken pottery and cobwebs were signs the dungeon had been long abandoned. There were pieces of broken armor and miscellaneous weapons dispersed throughout the cave.

"I wonder how the torches manage to stay lit considering the air is so damp?" Polly questioned.

"Dragon's flame, obviously." Bertly kicked a metal helmet across the ground as he walked. "A small mist isn't going to put that out."

Polly walked up to Bertly and clutched his cloak. Water squeezed out from the cloth and dripped onto the floor. "Pretty wet for a small mist."

Bertly rolled his eyes and continued to lead his father and friends deeper into the crypt. Farther ahead was a single pathway that coiled like a snake, and its twists and turns led directly down into the darkness. Bertly came to a stop and peered into the cave's depths. The torches' intensity had dissipated, but there was still enough light to illuminate the empty metal cages that hung from the walls.

Devdan cleared his throat. "So, are we also going to find a mound of hidden treasure when we stumble upon this dragon?"

"Dragons do not have a means by which they can hide treasure, *Devdan.*" Bertly pressed his lips together and narrowed his eyes. "Everyone knows that is just a myth." He let out a long breath. "He is down there. If you don't want to come, you can wait here." He snapped his fingers. "Lightus." A small glowing orb appeared and lit the path ahead. Bertly adjusted his scabbard and marched headfirst along the trail. "Roderick, you'd better be following me," he snapped.

The group climbed deeper into the dungeon's passages, and the farther they went, the more they noticed that many pathways had either collapsed or led to dead ends. The explorers' pace slowed, and Bertly could tell the others were growing tired. They would need to set up camp somewhere in the caves—and soon.

Bertly's mind wandered until he caught a glimpse of a green light in the distance. He gripped Devdan's shoulder and shook him, all the while pointing at the bright green spot. "Check that out."

"What do you suppose it is?" Devdan asked.

Edfrid took the lead. "Let's find out."

They stumbled upon a small indentation that appeared to have once served as a room. An altar was placed in the center and was covered in green, glowing runes. The area was packed with empty sacks and crates, which Bertly kicked to the side as he walked toward the glowing altar.

Devdan pried open a wooden crate. "It's empty."

"So is this one," Edfrid added.

"What do you suppose these are?" Bertly asked. His first instinct was to swipe the runes right off the altar; however, the last time he'd snatched something, it didn't go over so well for him, so he naturally had second thoughts.

"They're glowing crystals, sir," Roderick replied.

"They're *runes*, Roderick," Bertly snapped.

Roderick scratched his head. "What's the difference?"

"It means they're enchanted," Polly responded. "Humans used to use them to bring life to cities and towns." Polly's eyes glowed and a smile stretched across her face. "These are beyond rare. Only the old capital has these now." She stood next to Bertly, who was trying to touch them as gently as possible.

"I'm sorry, ma'am." Roderick shook his head. "I don't understand. How will that add life to a city? Does it make plants grow or something?"

"No, no." Polly chuckled. "How do I explain this?" She tapped her finger on her chin. "Here is an example.

Old mill owners used to use runes to make their water mills turn without having any running water."

"Outstanding," Roderick replied.

"That is almost hard to believe," Devdan added.

Bertly turned around. "Oh, believe it, Roderick." He stepped down and held the runes out in his hand. "When Cordelia was alive, old Noskar was a place like you have never imagined." Bertly continued toward Roderick and Devdan. "We used runes to make carriages run on their own."

The elf's eyes grew.

"People used these to start campfires, to make ladles turn on their own, to keep their cottages warm during the winter." Their jaws dropped and Bertly stepped closer. "We will use these to bring that prestige *back* to Noskar." Bertly looked to his father. "And we will start with Stonebank."

"Warm a cottage during winter," Edfrid mumbled. "Bertly, the vapor is thinning."

"So it is." Bertly put his hand out and looked around. "These runes must have been creating the steam." Bertly opened his travel sack and placed the runes inside. "A great way to ward off intruders."

Roderick gulped. "Sir, does this mean there isn't a dragon?"

"Of course not." Bertly ruffled Roderick's hair. "It just means we have to travel a bit farther."

***

The travelers voyaged onward. They dragged their feet and carried on without conversation. Bertly's feet were sore and throbbing; he wanted to somehow stick them in a bucket of ice and hot water at the same time. His neck and lower backed ached from all the hiking. The voyagers navigated farther in the crypt's shadows until they arrived at a wide and hollow room. Small holes and burrowed paths were etched into the walls.

Roderick's knees started to shake. "What do you suppose lives in those?"

"Do you really want to know?" Bertly countered.

Roderick looked to the ceiling and peered at the adjacent walls. "On second thought, I think I will pass."

"Do you see the way out, Bertly?" Edfrid asked. "I don't want to be in here for very long."

There was a rustling noise in the distance, and when Bertly was able to concentrate on the noise, it appeared to be getting louder. He knew what was coming and it was getting closer. His breath quickened and his heart raced. Bertly surveyed the nearby walls, but he couldn't find any openings.

"What's that?" Devdan pointed. "In the distance?"

Diagonally from the group, on the other side of the immense room, was a single trail.

"What's that sound?" Roderick asked. The rustling echoed throughout the chamber and was now loud enough that everyone was able to detect it.

"Let's go." Edfrid sprinted toward the pathway. Loud screeches filled the room.

"Sweet Cordelia." Devdan drew his sword. "What is that?"

"Mountain bats!" Bertly shouted. "Now, let's get out of here." The students took off and ran to catch up to Edfrid.

Pouring in from the holes were bats the size of small children. Some crept along the walls while others flew straight at various members of the group, seemingly without distraction. Shark-tooth-like fangs lined the entirety of their faces. The bats' gray, furless wings spanned nearly the full width of the passageway.

Neither Devdan nor Bertly's father were carrying Roderick. Bertly looked back out of pure instinct, and trailing several dozen paces behind the group was Roderick—panting and moving his feet as though bricks were attached. Closing in on Roderick from all angles were a half-dozen mountain bats.

Bertly slipped as he attempted to turn around faster than his body was able to handle, but he regained his footing and hurried to catch up with his apprentice. He was only a few steps from Roderick, but a hungry bat also hovered mere feet from the elf, with its enormous mouth wide and ready to ensnare its prey. The bald and eyeless creature swooped to grasp Roderick with its sharp talons. As Bertly drew his warblade and leaped into the air, he could see strands of drool running between the bat's teeth, the manic look in its eyes, and time felt as though it had slowed dramatically.

While airborne, Bertly managed to puncture the bat with his sword, driving it through the side of the creature's head—the point of the blade emerged through its opposing ear. The bat dropped Roderick to the ground, and Bertly landed beside his apprentice.

Bertly grabbed Roderick by the collar and threw him over his shoulder. As he sprinted, he truly felt the muscle mass he'd gained from the Eternal Cave; it felt as though his feet and legs moved without any effort or even input from him.

Bertly's father and the others stood at the passage's exit, gesturing for him to run quicker. Bertly hollered and took off even faster, kicking up rubble and dust behind him—pelting Roderick right in the face, Bertly hoped. Without putting on the brakes, he rushed through the exit, almost knocking over both Devdan and his father.

Bertly looked back to ensure he'd escaped the mountain bats, but even the quickest of glances revealed that he hadn't come close. A dense cloud of leathery, flapping wings rushed toward him and the others. Polly slipped on her glove as she stepped back into the cave. With a single snap of her thin fingers, an eruption of fire filled the room. The on-and-off screeches of the cave bats turned into a constant howl as the fire scathed the beasts. The dark cloud was set ablaze, and scores of bats dropped to the floor. As the bats fell in rapid succession, Polly threw her head back and her knees buckled, straining under the weight of her magic—Edfrid snatched her before she hit the ground.

"Come, boy, take her from me." Edfrid held Polly out. "That stopped them, but only for now." Devdan rushed over and took Polly from Bertly's father. With his hammer, Edfrid slammed the side of the entryway, causing the frame to collapse. "It'll be a little rough, but we should be able to open it back up on our way out." Edfrid holstered his war hammer. "But for now, it should keep those things off our tails."

Bertly and Edfrid glanced over at their group. Devdan held an unconscious Polly, and next to Bertly was a traumatized Roderick.

"Let's set up a small camp and let everyone rest for a little while," Edfrid said. "I think we could all use some rest."

***

Bertly sat propped against a cave wall near the group's modest-sized campfire. His clothes were almost dry now that the steam had died down. Polly, Devdan, and Roderick were fast asleep, which left Edfrid and Bertly as the only travelers alert, once again. Edfrid sat across from Bertly on top of a stone. He was tinkering with something, but through the dim light of the campfire,

Bertly couldn't see very well what it was.

"What are you working on?" Bertly asked.

"I am making something for your little apprentice. He did well today," Edfrid replied.

Bertly chuckled and raised his eyebrows. "You're making something?"

Edfrid muttered to himself, fumbled with the item in his hands, and held up something that resembled a necklace. "I used the sabre's teeth." He poked the fangs, which were attached to a string. He'd bored holes in the incisors of the beast and had strung them through with a bit of leather. "I shaved the big ones down a little. Didn't want to break the little man's neck." He smirked. "Not to mention, they would have hung to his belt loops." Edfrid and Bertly shared a chuckle.

"What's so funny?" Polly rubbed her eyes as she gauged her surroundings. "What happened?"

"She's awake." Edfrid stood and walked over to Polly. "How are you feeling?" He put the back of his hand against her forehead. "You did quite a number on those bats back there."

Polly cocked her head. "I did what?"

"You set some thousand bats on fire, Polly," he explained. "To tell the truth, you saved us all."

"Oh." Polly looked down and slumped her shoulders. "I see."

"Don't dwell on it, Polly." Edfrid placed his hand on Polly's shoulder. "I know you didn't want to do it, but you were saving your friends."

"I know, but those bats didn't know any better." Polly appeared pale and saddened. Her eyes were moist with tears that threatened to spill. "They were only acting on instinct. That doesn't mean they deserved to die."

"Oh, Polly, don't you worry about that." Edfrid chuckled and patted her on the back. "A little fire isn't going to stop a horde of mountain bats."

"Really?" Polly asked. She managed a weak smile.

"You may have gotten a few." Edfrid shrugged. "But there are still plenty left to ruin our trip out of here, trust me on that."

Bertly cleared his throat. "I don't mean to interrupt." He looked to Edfrid and gave a forced smiled. "But I have something I want to ask you, and I don't know when else I will have the time."

Edfrid peeked at Polly, then looked back at his son. "Do you want to go for a walk?"

"It's okay." Bertly shook his head. "I think Polly already knows anyway; she's just been too nice to come out and fully say it."

Polly looked confused.

"Aye." Edfrid gestured for Bertly to continue.

"Before I went to the Academy"—Bertly tugged on his earlobe—"you left me a notebook."

Edfrid's face paled. "Aye."

"I don't understand." Bertly undid his bun and wove his fingers through his hair, attempting to pull out the knots. "It's filled with a hundred times more human spells than the Academy archives contain." Bertly saw by the relaxed look on Polly's face that she understood exactly what he was referring to. "Who is she? Am I actually fully human?"

Edfrid gasped and choked on his own spit. "Sweet Cordelia, yes, you are a human." He cleared his throat. "Look, your mother was obsessed with spells, magic, and treasure. The issue was, treasure was the only thing she could achieve. She believed if she practiced magic hard enough and long enough, she could learn it." Edfrid stopped fidgeting with the sabretooth necklace. "She believed all humans had magic, and it was just tucked away somewhere." He glanced at the ceiling. "We

traveled everywhere, and we came across many journals
and spells. Over the years, it all added up." Edfrid peered
back at Bertly. "I think it's good that you have it now.
That journal and map will serve you much better than
they have me." He looked down. "They've brought me
nothing but old memories."

"What map?" Roderick asked.

Bertly jerked his head and frowned at Roderick. His
apprentice's eyes were shut and his hands were under his
head, serving as a pillow. "You're supposed to be asleep."
In Bertly's peripheral vision he saw a puddle not too far
from Roderick. He snapped his fingers and splashed the
water across his apprentice's face.

Roderick leaped to his feet. "It's not my fault, sir." He
used his sleeve to wipe the water from his face. "You
should have taken that walk your father suggested if you
truly wanted privacy."

"It's true, sir," Devdan added. "I was only resting my
eyes."

Bertly's face turned red. "And you two didn't think to
speak up?"

Bertly's apprentice and Devdan turned to each other.
"Well, no. It sounded too interesting, sir," Roderick
replied.

Bertly looked to Devdan for his explanation—he only
nodded in agreement with Roderick. Bertly snarled and
shook his head. "Unbelievable."

"Don't put too much stress on it, Bertly," Polly
chimed in. "I don't think Roderick or Dev will say
anything."

Bertly glared at the elves.

They both shook their heads, and Roderick waved his
hands about, signaling that they wouldn't say a word.

"Good." Bertly adjusted his shirtsleeves and stuck his
nose in the air. "Let's be on our way, then. I'm sure

you've all had enough time to rest." Bertly grabbed his travel sack and marched deeper into the crypt and the mysteries it contained. His companions followed close behind. The alternate paths and dead ends ceased to spring up. What was once a maze had turned into one long route.

Edfrid cleared his throat. "Roderick," he grumbled.

Bertly's apprentice perked up. "Yes, sir?" Roderick asked.

"Hold out your hand. I have something for you." Roderick reached out as he was asked and Edfrid placed the necklace he'd crafted into Roderick's palms. "It's a gift."

Roderick blushed. "A gift?" He ran his fingers down the tusks of the sabretooth. "Is this from the tiger?"

"Aye." Edfrid squeezed the back of Roderick's neck. "This trophy is yours. Not many folk can say they've stopped a sabretooth tiger dead in its tracks."

"I get it, sir. Dead in its tracks." The little elf chuckled. "That's a good one, sir."

"The joke isn't funny when you point out the punch line, Roderick," Bertly said.

Roderick didn't respond to Bertly, but instead continued to inspect his necklace. He ran his fingers across each tooth. "The fangs looked much larger when it was chasing us."

Edfrid placed his hands in his pockets. "Aye, they were," he replied. "But they were much too large to go around your neck."

Roderick smiled, untied the knot that held the piece together, and tied the necklace around his neck. He tucked his chin into his chest, in what seemed like an attempt to examine it on himself.

"It looks great, Roderick," Polly said, with a kind smile stamped across her face.

Bertly's apprentice puffed his chest and stuck his nose in the air. He walked with a new strut, which looked familiar to Bertly, but he brushed the familiarity off for that moment. Bertly was proud of his apprentice's accomplishment, and even though he struggled to take him seriously considering his rosy cheeks, Bertly knew his apprentice was attempting to hold back his excitement at the gift he'd been given as well as the pride he surely had in himself.

Bertly and company persisted with their search through the Dragon's Crypt. The hallways seemed to stretch far over the horizon, and every time Bertly thought he saw a turn coming up, he found it was only his eyes playing tricks. The damp and cramped passageways were lined with triggered traps. Scattered around the traps were yet more pieces of abandoned armor and skeletal remains.

"Sir, I think this is probably a great sign that we should turn back," Roderick said.

Bertly sighed as he watched the apprentice in whom, moments ago, he'd had all the confidence in the world as he bit his nails like a forest rat. Bertly had no clue how he managed to do so considering they'd already been bitten to the quick.

"Wrong, Roderick. It is important to always learn from the mistakes of others." Bertly, fighting the urge to smack at it, pulled Roderick's hand out of his mouth. It had, after all, been abused enough for one day. "These kind fellows have taken the time to show us where not to step." Bertly winked.

"But, sir, what if we are the ones showing the next explorers where *not to step*?" Roderick drew quotation marks in the air with his mutilated hands.

"Think about it, Roderick." Bertly squeezed the back of his apprentice's neck and gave him a shake. "Why would someone go through all the effort to set up dozens of traps if not to protect something very important?" Bertly raised his eyebrow and peered into Roderick's eyes. "Hmm?"

"Maybe..." Roderick fiddled with the cuff on his cloak. "It's a diversion, sir?"

Bertly straightened his posture and peered ahead. His eyebrows narrowed, and his lips pressed together and made a slight *pop* when he opened them to speak. "Fair point, my apprentice." Bertly pointed his finger in the air. "Nonetheless, carry onward," he bellowed.

As Bertly walked, he noticed a glowing halo ahead. It did not have the same illuminating effect as the altar had—its light was not as concentrated. He had seen many unique light sources; however, every time the light had eventually revealed itself to be a torch. Bertly squinted, and this time, he saw something different. He did not see a single light, but a rectangular-shaped light.

The group reached the end of the tunnel, where an ominous wooden door blocked their path. Shining through the cracks of the door was a bright light—the first they had seen that wasn't from a spell or torch. Bertly pulled the lever and pushed the squeaky door open.

In the center of the room, a pile of skeletons and miscellaneous bones was stacked two heads taller than Bertly. The walls were painted in dried, crusted blood, and the floors were stained in more places than not.

"I think this is the wrong room." Roderick whipped his body around and dashed back out the door.

Edfrid snagged Roderick by the collar and lifted him into the air. He held the small elf apprentice up to his eyes and shook his head at him.

Bertly and Devdan drew their weapons. "No, my apprentice, I believe this is the right room," Bertly replied. Clearly reassured that he'd gotten the message, Edfrid placed Roderick back on his feet, and when his hands were free of the whiny elf, he used them to remove his hammer from its holster.

Filling the wall behind the pile of skeletal remains was a golden sculpture that towered several stories high. The statue was carved into the shape of a magnificent dragon. Every feature from the missing scales to the battle scars was etched into the piece, and pouring out of the eyes were two streams of water that fell into a large pond, then settled at the feet of the statue. The golden dragon shined bright, illuminating the entire underground hall.

Bertly felt a sense of wonder—happiness consumed him. "The King of all Dragons."

"You did it, Bertly!" Polly rejoiced. "You led us to the King of Dragons."

"Aye, but where is the dragon?" Edfrid asked. The group bobbed their heads about, surveying the room. They did not venture far from each other, nor did they travel much beyond the cave entrance. Bertly looked around as well, but it appeared to be a barren, empty room with no recent signs of life. The bones of the dead had no meat left, and the dried blood was dark and flaking. He walked over to the pile of stacked bones to examine their size and shape. Mixed with human bones, to his surprise, were dwarf and elf bones. Most nonhumans did not know of the Dragon Crypt's existence, let alone where it was.

"S-sir?" Roderick stuttered.

Bertly glanced toward his apprentice, who was pointing to something across the room.

"What's that?" Roderick's hand shook as though he were meeting someone for the first time.

Bertly concentrated on what the young elf was trying to show him. Across the room was a massive object with long brown fur covering it.

Bertly placed his finger over his mouth and gestured for Roderick to join him. Together they tiptoed and gathered the rest of the group. "Across the hall is the largest land creature I have ever seen. It would have that sabretooth for supper." Bertly surveyed his friends' faces—all had gone pale.

"I'm unsure of what it is. I know of nothing that grows to that size...unless it's the first furry dragon." Devdan snickered, which Polly quickly responded to with an elbow in his side.

"Stay here. I am going to try to get a better look at it," Bertly declared.

Edfrid grabbed Bertly's wrist as he stepped away. "Devdan and I will wrap around the far side so we can come in from behind if things go south."

Bertly nodded and tiptoed past the pile of bones, toward the furred beast.

As Bertly crept closer, the improved proximity did not help him identify the creature; its head was turned away from him. Bertly needed to get closer, but he couldn't conjure up a plan on how to do it. If the creature awoke while Bertly was within striking distance, it could be a quick ending for him.

Bertly slipped off his heavy boots and snuck on the soles of his feet—he needed to be as stealthy as possible. Bertly's brain froze; everything about him seemed to move at light speed while his body was stuck, motionless. Visualizations of turquoise liquid consumed his sight. Memories of Alestar and the stealth elixir they'd created rushed into his mind. He rifled through his travel sack and pulled out a filled vial. Everything snapped back into place and Bertly regained his focus. He shook his head to rid himself of the intrusive thoughts. He hated how they emerged from nowhere and afforded him no answer as to why they came.

Bertly popped the cork out of the vial and looked back at his friends. Bertly tipped his glass, drank the liquid, and then he vanished. He looked down and could not see his own hands or feet.

Although being invisible did give him a confidence boost, Bertly took slow, cautious steps toward the beast. For all he knew, the creature could smell him better than it could see him; it did dwell in a dimly lit cave, after all. Without his shoes, his footsteps were silent. He rounded the front of the creature and examined its massive head. The animal's skull was far larger than Bertly's torso, and its snout could've fit half of his arm. The features of the furred beast were familiar; it looked no different than a standard bear, apart from its size.

A crash came from the center of the room and echoed throughout the area. The screeches of bats traveled through the crypt. Bertly lashed his head toward the racket and couldn't help but notice Roderick as he stood immobile behind a collapsing pile of bones. The skeleton pieces slid out and spread across the floor in a macabre avalanche.

The furry beast grumbled and stretched out its hind legs. It rolled onto its four legs and stood up. The bear's face was an arm's length above Bertly, and its shoulder blades were as tall as a giant. It lifted its front paws off the ground, straightening its spine. The brown bear rubbed its back against the cave walls, highlighting the top of its head, which spanned well over two stories. Bertly had planned on encountering a grizzly bear at worst. However, this beast was nearly three times the size of any grizzly he had ever laid his eyes on.

"Over here." The bear glanced at Edfrid, and so did Bertly. Bertly's heart sank as he watched his father taunt the animal. "I'm right here. Come and get me."

The furry beast plopped back onto all fours and turned its attention toward Polly and Bertly's apprentice.

Edfrid smacked the head of his war hammer into the palm of his hand. "My throne hall needs a new rug."

The bear whipped its head around, saliva foaming from its mouth.

"I see that got your attention." Edfrid went into his battle stance, and Devdan was a step behind him with his sword drawn and ready to fight.

Tension spread through Bertly's body, clenching all of his muscles while his mind replayed the previous brushes with death they'd faced on their trip. It had taken two miracles to save them from near death—one from Roderick and the other from Polly. The group was pressing their luck, and it was probable they would not be so fortunate a third time.

This beast was far more dangerous than either the mountain bats or the sabretooth. Bertly guessed this bear could've had a tiger for a snack if it so wished. Thoughts accelerated through Bertly's head, and he wanted them to slow down so he could focus, but they wouldn't. He had to make a quick decision. The bear was creeping in Roderick's direction. Bertly couldn't help but remember why he'd chosen this specific spirit quest. It wasn't just so he could collect a scale from the King of Dragons—it meant much more to him. Bertly's ultimate goal, since he had first learned of soul-bonding, was to bond with a dragon, and he knew there was no better choice than the greatest dragon of all time. To become the greatest champion of all time, Bertly was certain, he needed the greatest spirit animal of all time.

Bertly darted toward the gargantuan beast and placed his hand against its back leg. His finger sank deep into the animal's long brown fur. Bertly grew dizzy as everything around him spun, and his world appeared as though he were looking out through the eye of a storm. He could feel the energy escape his body. He tried to pull his arm from the bear, but he couldn't break the connection.

Thel's teachings rang through his memory: *"The greater the creature, the more of your soul you must give up."* Bertly tried to remember what came next, but his mind was drawing only blank space and shades of white, black and gray; he couldn't put together a complete thought. He was exhausted. Bertly knew it was illogical, but he wanted nothing more than to sleep. His body was pulling him to the ground, and he allowed it. He couldn't move. Bertly's vision blurred and light slowly faded to black. Sounds muted, and the racing of his heart echoed through his head. It was all he could hear. His body was paralyzed, and he was completely invisible.

For some reason or another—he felt oddly comfortable.

XVIII

"Roderick, are you asleep?" Bertly slammed his fists on the table. His apprentice yelped and flailed his arms, scattering the parchment laid out in front of him.

"No, sir, of course not." Roderick rubbed his eyes and scampered around the table, gathering the displaced materials and flipping through them in search of his quill. "I was only resting my eyes."

"That is the definition of sleeping, Roderick," Bertly snapped.

"Well, sir, I was conscious. My eyes were just closed." Roderick stacked all the papers, placing them in one orderly pile. "That isn't quite sleeping."

Bertly closed his eyes and rubbed his temples. "Roderick...what is the last thing you have written down?"

"Let me check." Roderick flipped through the stacked pile, plucked a handful of pages from it, and dragged his finger along the bottom sentence of the last page. "It's seems we have just arrived at Stonebank, sir." Roderick looked up with a grin.

"What?" Bertly lashed out. "You have nothing about the peppers?" He leaned forward and nearly touched noses with Roderick. "Or the sabretooth, or the gross cave, or the mountain bats, oh, for the love of Cordelia—"

Bertly threw his head back and pointed to the furry bed that consumed more than half the room. "My spirit animal." He took a deep breath. "You didn't even jot down my soul-bonding with *the bear*?" Bertly's furry companion gave a deep grumble that vibrated through the room and made the flames on the candles flicker. "Now even she is upset."

Roderick looked Bertly in the eye and gulped. He waited several breaths, during which he stared at his master with a straight face, and then lost his composure, crumpling into a fit of laughter. "Sir, I am only kidding." Roderick wiped a tear from the corner of his eye. "The last thing I have is you passing out." The young elf yawned. "Speaking of which—we've been at this all night, and I am starting to wear out, sir."

Bertly glanced outside and saw the sun peeking over the Noskar Mountains. "It is almost morning. We will hear her dragon's wings flap at any moment." Bertly strolled to the corner of the room and flopped back onto his bed. "We are nearing the end, my young apprentice. We will be done writing soon, and then you can sleep the entire flight."

Roderick gasped. "You expect me to sleep while riding on the back of a dragon?"

"I don't see why not," Bertly replied, a smile spanning his face. "It can't be much different than a gryphon."

Roderick's jaw dropped to his chest, where he'd also brought his hands to hover over his heart. "I am not sure if you recall, sir, but I didn't do so well riding the gryphon." The young apprentice's hands started to shake as they clenched at his chest.

"Never mind that." Bertly crossed his arms. "We do not have time to ponder your unreasonable fear of flying, Roderick." Bertly pointed to the papers on the table before Roderick. "Back to your job, scribe."

***

It felt nothing like waking up. The blackness in Bertly's eyes slowly faded, and the images of his world became clearer. His hearing was dull, as if something were covering his ears, except nothing was there. Bertly's body was numb, and there was a pressure on his back from lying on the ground; however, he couldn't feel the wind across his face. He knew it was there because he heard it in the trees, though his skin felt untouched by it, as if he were sitting indoors. He could still feel and move his limbs, but they were uncoordinated. His hearing started to come back before his vision fully recovered. He heard the campfire crackling, and his stomach growled. He took a deep breath to smell the smoke, but nothing was cooking.

"You're awake."

Bertly turned his head. Resting next to him, wrapped in a blanket, was his young apprentice.

"You've been out for quite some time, sir."

"How long is 'quite some time'?" Bertly asked.

Roderick exhaled into his hands and rubbed them together. "Nearly an entire night and a day, sir. We have traveled quite far."

Bertly's posture stiffened.

"We are no more than a few hours from Stonebank. The only reason we stopped and set up camp was because the sun went down."

Bertly looked around. The sun was rising over the hilltops, and the drizzle birds were starting to sing. "What happened? Why did I pass out?" Bertly surveyed the campsite. "Where is everyone?"

"They are out collecting breakfast, sir." Roderick poked a log in the campfire with a stick, sending fluttering embers into the air. "Do you really not remember anything?"

Bertly closed his eyes and tried desperately to uncover the last thing he could recall. Bertly sat up—a sheet of snow rested across his body. His motor skills returned, but the feeling in his skin was still dull. He could hear Roderick's teeth chattering, yet he couldn't feel the cold from the ice lying across him. Suddenly, an influx of memories rushed through Bertly's head. "Where is that bear?" he shouted.

Roderick perked up. "She's out with the others, helping them gather breakfast, sir."

"What?" Bertly sprang to his feet while a touch of vertigo overcame him, but he managed to fight it.

Roderick stood and met his master's eyes. "What's the matter, sir?"

"Explain to me what is going on, Roderick." Bertly grabbed his apprentice by the collar and yanked him. "Now."

"I d-don't know, sir," Roderick stuttered, as he had a hard time pushing a sentence out of his mouth. "You turned invisible and then the bear growled really loud and then you reappeared, but you were asleep on the ground."

Bertly let go of Roderick. "And then what happened?"

"And then the bear walked over to Polly and me and started rolling around in the pile of bones," Roderick replied. "I think she thought I was trying to play with her."

Bertly lowered his chin. "She was…trying to…*play?*"

"Yes, sir." Roderick nodded. "Not only that, she has escorted us the entire way back." Roderick's eyes glowed. "She even fought off an entire pride of lions."

"It worked." Bertly's knees buckled and he fell back into the snow, his behind cushioning his fall.

"What worked, sir?" Roderick asked.

"The soul-bonding." Bertly's face relaxed, as did the

rest of his body. "It actually worked." He looked at Roderick. "I did it. I soul-bonded with the largest land animal Pangea has ever seen." Bertly sprang to his feet and leaped onto Roderick. "I will be even more famous, my apprentice! People will sing songs of the Winter Wizard and his dragon-sized bear."

Roderick's face was squished into the snow. "About that, sir."

Bertly continued to sit atop his apprentice. "But why would she be with the others right now?"

"About that, sir," Roderick insisted.

"Shouldn't *my* bear be with *me* right now?" Bertly looked at Roderick. "Why would they only leave *you* to look out for me?"

"Sir, I need to tell you something," Roderick yelled.

"Well, why didn't you speak up, then?" Bertly hopped off Roderick and helped his apprentice to his feet. "Yes, my dashing apprentice?" Bertly brushed the extra snow from his apprentice's shoulders.

Roderick avoided eye contact. "There is something I should probably tell you."

"I believe you just said that. Lay it on me." Bertly felt as though his smile was permanently imbedded in his face.

Roderick lightly kicked at the slushed snow near his feet. "Something sort of happened after you passed out, sir."

Bertly's face lost all expression. "Go on."

"Well, you see." The young apprentice paused to pick the dirt from under his fingernail. "After you passed out, sir. You see, Polly. Well…"

Bertly grabbed Roderick by the shoulders and shook him. "For the love of Cordelia, spit it out, Roderick."

Roderick cleared his throat. "After you passed out, sir, Polly also soul-bonded with an animal."

Bertly let go of the young elf and took a step back. "What kind of animal?" He sighed and looked down.

"Well, it turns out the bear was guarding something." Roderick twisted his neck about to look his master in the eyes. "On top of the waterfall, there was a nest."

"And what lived inside the nest?" Bertly asked, unable to suppress a slight eye roll, the urge of which had been pressuring his orbits for a few moments.

"There was a dragon, sir." Roderick took a few steps back. "Polly soul-bonded with...uh...with that dragon."

Bertly grabbed his hair and screamed as he pulled it. "Polly soul-bonded with the King of all Dragons?"

"Well, sir." Roderick lifted his chin. "It actually wasn't."

Bertly let go of his hair and dropped his arms. "It wasn't?"

"No, sir." Roderick shook his head. "It was actually a baby dragon."

"A baby dragon?" Bertly cocked his head. "How big was it?"

Roderick spread his arms. "No bigger than a dog, sir."

"Ha. Doesn't sound like much of a dragon." Bertly's frown curled into a smile. "So it's like a big lizard, then?"

"Well, I assume it'll grow, sir. Fairly large, at that." Roderick peeked at Bertly and coughed, cutting off his own sentence. "But for now, yes. It's very much as you've said, like a really big lizard."

Bertly placed his hands on his hips. "I bond with a bear bigger than a carriage, and Polly bonds with something meant for a reptile tank. Almost pitiful." Bertly forced a cheerful laugh that even he wasn't convinced by. "How is Polly holding up?"

"Pardon, sir?" Roderick's voice cracked.

"Is she taking it well?" Bertly puffed out his chest and placed his hands behind his head. "You know...the fact that she chose her one and only bond to be a mere lizard. How's that sitting with her?"

Roderick's face went blank. "You know, sir, she was upset earlier, but she has started to feel better. I suggest you don't make mention of it though; I think she's still sensitive about it."

"I'm not surprised. She probably knows I'll be the talk of the school when I arrive, riding on the back of my bear." Bertly whipped his head from Roderick and peered into the trees of the forest nearby. "What's that?"

"What is what, sir?" Roderick replied.

Bertly gripped his chest. "I sense something." He focused on the trees, and emerging from the shadows of the forest were Edfrid and Devdan. Bertly glanced behind them at the trees, which shook as though an earthquake were imminent. The snapping of branches echoed through the quiet morning wind. Stepping out of the woods was Bertly's mammoth-sized bear. The furry creature didn't look as ferocious as he remembered. In fact, it almost seemed gentle in the way it moved. The giant bear made eye contact with Bertly and trotted over. It stopped just in front of Bertly and flopped onto its rear end.

Polly peeked out from behind the trees. "Well, aren't you going to greet your new companion?" Buzzing around her head like an annoying housefly was a sleek and beautiful red baby dragon. Its tail was slender, and its scales shined as though they had been polished.

Bertly reached out and patted the bear twice on the head. "Hello," he said to it. The fuzzy beast responded with a small satisfied growl.

"What are you going to name her, Bertly?" Roderick asked.

"I am not giving *it* a *name*." Bertly shooed Roderick. "And *why* does everyone keep saying 'her'?"

Polly crossed her arms and grunted. "You're not going to give her a name?" she blurted.

Bertly shot a disgusted look at his friend. "No, Polly. I am not *giving her a name.*"

"But why not, sir?" Roderick probed.

Bertly threw his hands in the air. "Because, Roderick, she is a bear. If bears wanted names, then they would give themselves names."

"Um. Well." Roderick scratched his head. "I suppose you have a point there."

"She is a bear, so that is what I will call her." Bertly crossed his arms and flared his nostrils.

"Bear?" Roderick asked.

Bertly nodded. "Yes, her name is Bear."

"Bear." Polly clapped. "What a cute name."

"No, Polly." Bertly stomped his foot. "She does not have—" Bear rolled onto her back and started to wiggle around.

Roderick ran over to Bear and rubbed her belly. "I think she likes her name, sir."

Bertly sighed. "I can see that." Bear was sprawled out with her stomach exposed and her limbs dangling to the side. Her belly was large enough for multiple people to use as a mattress. Bertly snapped his fingers. "That is enough shenanigans." Bear rolled over onto all fours. "It is time to get going."

"Quite the rush from the boy who has been carried the whole way back," Edfrid interjected.

"I want to impress Master Thel," Bertly explained. "We have a chance to return two days early...*from Noskar.*"

"Wow, Bertly." Polly placed her fingertips together. "I am so proud of you. Since when did you become so mature?"

Bertly's cheeks grew hot and he turned his head so

that he wasn't looking directly at Polly.

"Maybe it was the Eternal Cave," Roderick suggested.

The Winter Wizard snapped his fingers, which sent a cold gust of wind zipping past his apprentice, blowing him onto his back. "I do not need your sarcasm, Roderick."

"Sir, if you do not mind," Devdan said, "I have a question for you."

Bertly looked toward the tall elf. "Yes, Devdan?"

"Please call me Dev." Polly's apprentice placed his hand on his chest. "But I was wondering, what will Master Thel say when you two return to Stonebank?"

Bertly looked to Polly for clarification; however, by the look on her face she was just as confused. "What do you mean?" Bertly asked.

"Well, your mission was to return with the scales of the King of Dragons." Devdan shrugged. "We never obtained the scales from the King of Dragons."

Bertly pointed to Polly's spirit animal. "We have more than enough scales right there." The small red dragon was wrapped around Polly's shoulders. "There have been a few students before who have returned with dragon scales, but none have returned with them still attached to the dragon." Bertly pumped his fist in the air.

"That's good enough for me, sir," Devdan replied.

"Yes, yes." Bertly gave a dismissive wave. "We must be off now; we have wasted enough time." At that moment, Bear walked next to Bertly and crouched over, offering him a ride.

"Astonishing, sir!" Roderick yelled. "You didn't even have to signal her."

Bertly was amazed. Bear knew exactly what he wanted, as though she'd read his mind. "Obviously, Roderick, that is the entire point of soul-bonding. Everyone knows that."

***

Bear stomped through the snow with Bertly upon her back. The wizard had his chest puffed out and his head level. Polly's dragon lay curled into a ball on Bear's head. Riding just behind Bertly was his father, along with Polly and her apprentice.

"Sir?" Roderick asked.

"Yes, my apprentice?" Bertly had a smug look on his face as he surveyed the white landscape.

"Why do I have to walk while everyone else gets to ride Bear?" Roderick panted as he schlepped his feet across the ground. "I've never sweat so much in the snow before."

"Because, Roderick, it builds character," Bertly snapped.

"Well, sir." Roderick glared at Bertly and snarled his upper lip. "I sure hope I can walk from here to Stonebank in two days."

"Stop talking madness," Bertly groaned.

"How do you plan on getting Bear back to the Academy, sir?" Roderick shouted. "Does she know where it is? Or did you plan on her riding on Clia's back, too?"

Bear came to a halt. Bertly stared deep into his apprentice's eyes and extended his hand. "Get on."

Roderick locked arms with his master and climbed aboard Bear.

"Do not ever raise your voice like that to me, little elf." Bertly glanced back. "Are we clear on that?"

"Understood," Roderick replied.

"Nonetheless, you have made a good point, my apprentice." Bertly focused his attention back on the road. In the distance, on the side of the mountain, the wooden elevator that led to Stonebank could just be seen. "I have not fully thought out my plans just yet. This could become quite the predicament."

"Don't worry, son," Edfrid said. "I can have a few of my guards show her the way to the Academy. You'll just have to wait a few weeks for her to arrive. Maybe less if she gives the soldiers a ride there. Just from riding her back home, our trip has been nearly cut in half."

"Is that okay with you, Bear?" Bertly patted her on the side of the head.

The fuzzy beast let out a gentle growl and plowed through the high snow. She didn't mind.

"Wonderful. That settles it, then. Roderick, Polly, Devdan and I will leave for campus today, and in roughly two weeks' time, Bear will arrive at the Academy."

A small chill came over Bertly as the temperature dropped. He was gaining feeling back in his body; however, he still couldn't feel the breeze across his skin. The group trekked through the long shadow cast over Noskar from the high Stonebank hills until they arrived at the wooden lift.

"I suppose this is where we shall part ways," Edfrid said. "No point in straining myself lugging you all up to Stonebank when you will be leaving right when you get to the top." The warden of Stonebank slid off the massive bear and walked toward her head, near Bertly.

"Fair enough." Bertly hopped off Bear and landed next to his father.

"When will I see you again?" Edfrid asked.

"I suppose a lot more often," Bertly replied. "Now that I am a master, I am allowed to come and go as I please. Not even the Elders can tell me where I can and cannot go anymore. And I have reliable transportation," he said as he patted Bear's haunches. "Well, the Elders *can*, but it is pretty tough to take away a master's ranking, for it is mostly a sign of knowledge, not just entitlement."

"Aye." Edfrid's cheeks turned rosy and a smile

covered his face. "You can come home for Drizzle Day, then," he insisted.

"What's Drizzle Day?" Roderick inquired.

Bertly, Edfrid, and Polly gasped. "It's only the greatest holiday in the world!" Polly shouted.

"I want to come back for Drizzle Day," Bertly's apprentice begged.

"Aye, and you will," Edfrid told Roderick.

Bertly looked at his father and gave him the tightest hug he could muster. "We will see each other sooner rather than later." Bertly stepped back and reached into his shirt, pulling out Clia's whistle. He blew the whistle and waited a moment.

"Sometimes it takes a minute." Bertly blew the whistle again, but still there was no sign of Clia. "Peculiar."

"Maybe we can go and grab her," Edfrid added. "Everyone else can stay down here with Bear. After this adventure, I'm not sure I have it in me to crank her all the way up the mountain."

Bertly chuckled and looked back to his acquaintances. "I will be right back. Stay here while my father and I retrieve Clia."

The Winter Wizard and his father arrived at the top of the mountain and stood in the entrance of Stonebank. The smell of the air was the only thing Bertly recognized of his hometown.

"It's quieter than usual." As Edfrid approached the city, he seemed in a rush. "The streets are half full."

Bertly looked all over the city, and nowhere did it seem as busy as it had when he'd first returned. He observed the city's castle. "Look, near my statue, there is a huge crowd of people." Bertly and his father took off. They turned every head that was still walking the streets, and it was not long before the masses flocked to them. People shouted, "The Winter Wizard!" and, "The warden!" Bertly and Edfrid, being the two largest folks in town, were able to shove their way through the crowd.

Bertly's priority was looking for Clia. Still, he couldn't help his excitement over all the people herding around him. "Pardon me, my magnificent people," the Winter Wizard sang. "Oh, for me?" He grabbed a blue rose from a woman in the crowd and held it up to his face. People gathered just to lay out flowers and offer food.

"Oh, thank you, thank you," Bertly said as people gifted him all sorts of small items. His ego had grown so large he could physically feel it developing inside him. "You are all far too kind."

"I see I raised a very humble young man." Edfrid shook his head.

"I am a man of the people, Father." Bertly waved and shook hands with every human he could as they bustled through the crammed roads. "What can I say?"

As Edfrid pushed through the crowd, the citizens' hands were all over him; however, he seemed not to notice. "Aye, then act like one."

"I do," Bertly shouted.

"Ah, is that why you stole the golden pepper from Lemon's farm?" Edfrid countered.

Bertly's chest tightened and his skin crawled. He looked at his father with a blank face as he stopped shaking the hands and greeting the residents of Stonebank.

"When you were knocked out, before the trip back, I had to go through your sack to get peppers for everyone."

Bertly's mouth dried up, and he couldn't muster a defense or an explanation.

"Are you going to at least attempt to make up some horrible excuse?"

Bertly shook his head. "I don't have one." The tugging

and prodding from Bertly's fellow humans was now closer to bothersome than it was encouraging.

"What's your plan?" Edfrid asked.

"I didn't really have one." Bertly looked ahead toward his statue. They couldn't get there any sooner, and he wanted nothing more than for the conversation to be over. "I thought I could enchant it to do something, or use it somehow."

"You don't have many options. You can sell it for a nice payday, or you can give it back to Lemon so he at least has it for next season. His peppers are most likely dead already. You know what the right thing is." Edfrid looked over at Bertly, with his eyes cast in such a way that Bertly could see his disappointment. "But I'm not going to make you do it. This is your decision," Edfrid added. "I know why you haven't taken it back yet, and it's the same reason I wouldn't have taken it back...if I'm being honest with you."

Bertly and his father approached the statue. The thickness of the crowd became so dense it was hard even for the warden of Stonebank and the Winter Wizard to shove through.

"You wouldn't give it back?" Bertly inquired.

"I am going to answer your question with another," Edfrid replied. "Why haven't *you* given it back?"

Bertly hesitated. "Because I don't want the people of Noskar to know what I did. Everyone is looking to me to bring them...something." His chest loosened and his heartbeat returned to normal. "I feel highly anticipated and overestimated, and all I want is for everyone to like me."

"You've set yourself up for failure if that's your goal." Edfrid snorted. "If you can manage to make a fraction of the people you meet like you, then you've done something right."

Bertly didn't answer, but somehow, he felt like turning around and running all the way back to the Academy.

Edfrid nudged his son. "The reason I'm not mad is because I did the same thing when I was your age."

Bertly's eyelids raised and his lips parted. "You did?"

"Yes, when I was about a year older than you. And I didn't turn it in for the same reasons. My pride wouldn't let me admit to everyone that I'd made such a horrible, irreversible mistake."

"What did you do?" Bertly asked as he and his father squeezed their way past the sculpture of Bertly and toward the castle steps.

"Sold it for a small fortune," Edfrid bluntly stated.

"You what?" Bertly yelled.

Edfrid came to a standstill. "Well, I'll be damned." Spread across the castle stairs were scores of people bowing down and showing their offerings. They held up fresh fruits, vegetables, and buckets of worms. Poised at the top of the staircase was an arrogant gryphon lying on its chest, with its front legs crossed. Its beak was stuck high in the air as humans flocked around and stood on stools just to hand-feed it. Several people surrounded the gryphon's legs, manicuring its sharp talons and grooming its feathers.

One of Bertly's eyebrows raised as his eyes remained half closed. "I see Clia let herself out of the barn."

XIX

Bertly stood next to his father, who sat on his icy throne. The Winter Wizard's arms were crossed across his chest. He glared at Clia's body; she sprawled across the light blue rug that divided the snow-colored room.

Bertly stepped forward. "What happened to staying in the dragon stable?"

Clia turned her head away.

"Guards." Edfrid clapped his hands. "Please fill us in."

"Sir." Amongst the line of guards, one had a symbol of a sword across his chest. "A few moments after you left, the gryphon escorted herself out of the castle."

Edfrid narrowed his eyebrows and lowered his voice. "Did you try to stop her?"

"Yes, sir. But she put up quite a fight," the captain responded. Bertly looked over the group of soldiers. Many had bandages and wore tattered uniforms. "Instead of calling for the archers, we assumed it was best to let her roam the city at will." The lead soldier looked at his men. "I don't think any of us had the intent to harm a gryphon, sir."

"You made the right decision, Captain," Edfrid assured him.

The captain continued, "It only took a couple of hours before word spread across the whole town there was a gryphon in Stonebank." The soldier's voice grew. "Humans have seen a dragon more recently than a gryphon. We took to the streets…" The soldier paused. "The citizens took to the streets and celebrated all night. They assumed it to be a blessing from Cordelia."

"How did word not spread before?" Bertly asked.

"I presume they were too distracted by the return of the Winter Wizard for it to really settle in, sir." The soldier kneeled. "I think only Cordelia herself would have brought more joy for the citizens to see than you, sir."

"Ha." Bertly smirked. "You are too kind." The wizard whipped his cloak behind himself and strolled toward Clia. "So, we leave for five days and you think you run the place?"

Clia let out a drawn-out yawn and rested her head on the ground.

"Well then, I suppose I will just have to leave for the Academy without you." As Bertly walked for the entrance, Clia popped her head back up. That was the most alert Bertly had seen her since he returned.

"You got her attention with that one." Edfrid laughed.

Clia stood up in a rush and paced to the entryway of the throne hall that overlooked Stonebank. Bertly walked out next to her and leaned into her soft-feathered body. Rows of guards were lined up at the bottom of the stairs, holding back masses of humans from rushing the castle. Mixed into the swarms of people were humans waving quilts and holding painted signs. Sprinkled throughout were images of Bertly, Clia, Polly, Edfrid, and Cordelia— most were of the Winter Wizard.

"You haven't been here a full cycle and already they have you painted on wood and sewn into blankets." Bertly nestled his fingers between her feathers. "This is a better home for you, Clia."

She stepped back and let out a gracious chirp.

"You're locked away all day at the Academy, but here…" Bertly closed his eyes and listened to the cheers of the citizens. "Here you will be worshipped." Bertly reached out and rested his hand under her beak. "If you think about it, I won't be all that far away. You're the fastest creature in all of Pangea; you can still visit me anytime you'd like."

Clia pressed her forehead into Bertly's.

"Plus, I think my father will be more than happy to go for nightly rides with you. He needs to get out of the house."

Bertly took his hands and squished them into her cheeks, ruffling her feathers in all sorts of directions. He brought her face closer, making her eye level with him. "I do, however, have one more favor to ask of you." Bertly smiled. "I will still be needing a ride to the Academy."

Clia let out a loud squawk; Bertly assumed she didn't mind at all.

"Wonderful," he replied. "Stay right here. I need to say goodbye to my father." Bertly turned around.

"I get a gryphon, aye." Edfrid was standing with his hands on his hips and his chin up.

"How much of that did you hear?" Bertly lowered his eyebrows.

"Enough to know I get a gryphon." Edfrid clapped and walked in Clia's direction. "We will build the stables just how you like it. I also hear gryphons like high perches."

Clia cocked her head.

"We will get you the tallest perch in the world. I will send some guards to retrieve mammoth hay for you. It's the warmest in all the land."

Clia propped up and rounded her eyes into the shape of plates.

"We have this huge lake just near the south side. We

can fill it with fish in only a few cycles for you."

Clia started to bounce around.

"Father," Bertly interrupted with a smile, "you're rambling. I need to borrow Clia for a day, but she will be back soon. You can get started on all these projects while she is traveling."

Edfrid cleared his throat and adjusted his vest. "Right." His voice dropped several octaves. "Well, I suppose I will be seeing you soon?"

"Yes," Bertly confirmed. "Drizzle Day is less than eighty nights away."

"You'd better not forget, Bertly," Edfrid grumbled.

"Don't worry, I don't think Roderick is going to let me forget." Bertly and his father chuckled. "I haven't had a holiday in nearly seven years, and if I miss this one, I will have to wait another five hundred nights." Bertly shook his head. "I've missed Noskar. Now that I am a master, I will be coming back here more often. I have plans for this country." That rang a bell in Bertly's head. He reached into his travel sack and pulled out the crystals from the Dragon's Crypt. "I almost forgot about these." He extended them to his father. "Keep these safe. I will be needing them."

Edfrid took the crystals from his son. "What did you have in mind?"

"I'm going to leave that as a surprise." Bertly whistled and Clia bent over for him to climb aboard. "I know you hate goodbyes just as much as I do." He climbed aboard the feathered creature. "So let's save it for when we actually mean it."

"Aye," Edfrid agreed. "I will see you in seventy-seven nights."

Clia flapped her wings and whisked away with the Winter Wizard aboard.

***

Clia and Bertly flew through the entrance and scaled down the side of the mountain, beside the tracks of the wooden lift. Bertly could see Polly, Devdan, and Roderick coming into view, all of them resting next to Bear. The wizard's heart skipped a beat; he had forgotten Bear was still down there. Clia made a strange grunt, and Bertly felt her feathers grip him and her body tense up. She burst into a speed he had yet to experience. She landed abruptly and tipped back onto her hind legs.

"Clia, it's okay," Bertly shouted.

Clia flopped onto all fours and growled.

Bertly looked ahead. Standing in front of him was Bear. His friends hid behind her—Polly's dragon was nestled in her arms. Bear snarled her teeth, drool sliding between them. "I did not think about this." Bertly placed his hands on his head. "Clia, this is Bear." He slid off the furry gryphon. "When I was on my trip…I soul-bonded with this bear. Like Alestar did with you."

Clia turned her head toward Polly.

"And that is Polly's new companion," Bertly continued. "She's a dragon. Maybe you two can fly together one day."

Polly jerked her head and stared deeply into Bertly's eyes.

Bertly felt as though he was about to become lunch. "Or not," he added.

Clia crept toward Bear and the others, her body much stiffer than usual. Bear continued to growl as Clia got within breathing distance. However, the gryphon brushed right past Bear. Clia extended her beak and placed her face right next to Polly and her dragon. Bertly could hear Roderick's teeth chattering from a few dozen paces away. Clia poked the dragon and cocked her head back. Polly yelped and Clia trotted back to Bertly.

Bertly spread his arms with his palms facing up. "What just happened?"

Clia chirped and bent over for him to climb aboard.

"I think she likes the dragon, sir," Roderick responded.

"Or she realizes the dragon isn't a threat," Devdan added.

"Either way, I'm glad we still have our ride home." Roderick dashed toward Clia. "This place is too cold."

"I never thought I'd see you so excited to fly, Roderick." Polly chuckled.

As Bertly's traveling partners situated themselves with Clia, he took the opportunity to have a moment with Bear. "I know we haven't had much time together, but I will miss you, big bear." He scratched behind her ear. "I will see you in due time. Don't make it too rough for those guards escorting you." Bear rotated her head and lifted her snout, allowing Bertly to scratch under her chin. Bertly had to reach far above his head just to reach. "No promises, I see. Fair enough." He patted her on the chest. "I really do look forward to seeing you soon. Please come home safe."

***

"Sir?" Roderick placed his pen on the parchment laid out in front of him and walked over to his master. "Sir," Roderick emphasized as he poked him in the chest. Bertly flailed his arms and gasped. "Did you fall asleep, sir? We have a novel to write."

"Of course not, Roderick." Bertly rubbed his eyes and stretched. "I was only resting, *not sleeping*."

"Right, sir," Roderick agreed. "That's why words stopped coming out of your mouth."

"Roderick." Bertly elevated his cheeks to push against his lowering eyelids. "We have a book to write, so I suggest you get back to writing."

Bertly's apprentice sat back in his seat and shook his quill. "Ready whenever you are, sir."

The Winter Wizard began to speak, but the words stumbled out of his mouth. "Which part were we on again? You distracted me."

"The part where we were arriving at the Decomposite," Roderick responded.

"Oh, right." Bertly sat up straight and placed his finger on his chin. "Bertly, along with Polly, the twins, and an incompetent group of failures, made their way through the Remnant Forest."

"I knew you fell asleep!" Roderick shouted. "We were at the part where we were heading back to the Academy."

Bertly's nose crinkled and his face turned red. His fists were so tight that the sound of the leather stretching could be heard. The Winter Wizard clenched his jaw. "Roderick, we do not have time for your tomfooleries. *You-know-who* is almost here, and if we do not finish now, then we may never have the chance." Bertly stood up. "This is not just a story about me, my apprentice. Your legacy is very much intertwined into this tale as well. I suggest you start taking this a bit more seriously."

"Sir, I have written three-fourths of a book, I feel as though I am taking it quite seriously." Roderick shook his head and pressed his quill against the paper. "Ready whenever you are," he groaned.

***

With two days to spare and just before the sun started to shed light, the Winter Wizard and his companions arrived safely at the Academy.

"Remember, you can visit me anytime you'd like." Bertly pulled out Clia's whistle. "And be listening for me, because sometimes *I* may need *you*." Bertly and his gryphon nuzzled foreheads, and in a moment too soon, Clia was in the air and headed back to Stonebank. Bertly would miss seeing her every night, but he knew she had a better life waiting for her, one a gryphon deserved.

"Are you going to be okay, Bertly?" Polly asked.

Bertly turned toward her and shrugged as though he didn't know. "I have Bear now and we are soul-bonded. It wouldn't be fair to her to keep a gryphon around."

"I know why you did it, Bertly." Polly put her arm around his shoulder. "But that doesn't make it easy."

"Sir, I am going inside. I haven't had a good meal in nearly a cycle." Roderick stood with his arms crossed over his stomach. "We elves aren't meant to be starved out like this." Without hesitation Bertly's apprentice took off for the dining hall.

"I'm sorry, ma'am," Devdan added. "I feel the exact same, only I don't complain as much." And just like that, Devdan was out of sight and back in the castle.

"Should we give Master Thel a visit?" Polly asked. "Or did you want to get some rest first?"

Bertly was fatigued and knew he should rest, but he was much too eager to visit Master Thel. He had been flying all night, and unlike Polly and Devdan, he hadn't taken a nap. "Do you think he will be in his classroom this early?"

"He never seems to leave," Polly said. "I think he may live in there."

"Hmm, I don't think I've ever seen him wandering campus." Bertly tapped his finger on his chin. "Come to think of it, he's the only master I haven't seen outside his classroom."

"I rest my case," Polly replied.

Bertly pointed with his finger. "To Master Thel's room it is," he exclaimed.

"Lead the way, Winter Wizard." Polly winked.

Bertly did his best not to blush as he headed into the castle. "Polly?"

"Yes, Bertly?" she answered.

"What's your game plan with the dragon?" he inquired.

"When people ask, I will be honest." Polly's dragon zipped around her head and body like a dwarf bee, yet she didn't seem to mind. "I'll tell everyone I soul-bonded with him and he's my new companion." She rubbed her hand across the dragon's smooth scales. "I presume you'll do the same with Bear?"

"I haven't given it much thought, to tell the truth. I was forced to hide Clia, so naturally, I assumed the same about Bear." The sides of Bertly's mouth pulled backward. "But we don't have to hide our spirit animals." He bit his bottom lip as he smiled. "Everyone else is going to bond with a small bird or lizard. Maybe a koko or dog at best." His eyes rounded out like coins. "But we will have a dragon and a bear." Bertly looked to Polly. "You and I will be the most popular students on campus."

"Oh, Bertly." Polly sighed. "We already are. You don't realize it because you haven't made any new friends since we arrived seven years ago."

"Polly, this isn't the same. That was because of who we are. We are humans with red eyes," Bertly explained. "This time it'll be different. It'll be for something that we actually did."

"Bertly, we already conjured magic before thirteen and were the youngest students to ever get into the Mastery program...I am pretty sure our accomplishments have contributed," Polly countered.

Bertly grunted. "How many friends have you even made anyhow?"

"Dozens, Bertly." Polly stiffened her back and folded her hands. "The Academy is filled with fascinating classmates from all over the world."

As they kept walking, it didn't take long before Polly's dragon started to catch the attention of the always busy Academy. Polly didn't have the chance to continue before hordes of students clogged the halls like a dam.

"Is that a dragon?" one dwarf shouted.

A voice from the crowd resounded, "It's fake! It must be a spell."

Dwarves and elves alike were jumping and prodding at a chance to touch Polly's new friend. The small red dragon flew high toward the ceiling as the students' fingers came just short of touching him.

Bertly and Polly came to a standstill. The halls were more packed than Bertly had ever seen, which was saying something. "How do we get out of here?" the Winter Wizard yelled over the crowd.

Polly gave him a brief look of anxiety before focusing her attention back on her dragon.

Bertly knew she did not appreciate the entire school prodding at her new acquaintance. "I wish Bear were here; she could scare off every student in this place."

A screech came from the back of the crowd, followed by an immediate array of screams. The scores of students looked like the parting seas of the Decomposite that Bertly had always heard about. The indent in the crowd grew closer as the students squealed and ran off. Polly's dragon shrieked and flew into her arms. Emerging from the masses was Slithers, Thel's spirit animal. The long snake circled around Bertly and Polly, forming a barrier between them and the student body.

"Back early, are we?" the young elf interjected.

"Master Thel!" Polly shouted.

"I can see things went satisfactorily." Thel's hair was cut and his face recently shaven. He looked even more youthful than before. Bertly glanced down and saw Master Thel snap his fingers—the school bell echoed throughout the hallways. "Everyone get back to your studies," he instructed. The students mumbled under their breaths and scuffled back to class.

Their spirit quest master looked them both over. "I can see the quest went better for some than others."

Bertly placed his hand over his heart. "Oh, it most certainly did."

Thel's face went blank. "I was referring to Polly."

"Bertly bonded with a spirit animal, too," Polly replied with excitement.

Slithers uncoiled himself, breaking the barrier he had formed, and slid next to his master. "Is that so?" Thel asked as he started to stride down the Academy hallways—Bertly and Polly followed close behind. He did not seem in the mood for conversation.

"Tell me, what have you decided to call this flying lizard of yours?" Bertly asked Polly.

"His name is Dreki." Polly's dragon zipped back and forth down the corridors, spinning and flipping around.

"Dreki?" Bertly questioned.

"Yes." Polly whistled and Dreki came whizzing back. "I think it is rather cute."

Bertly clapped. "Good name, Polly. Will be really fitting when he's big enough to burn down a village."

"Stop it, Bertly." Polly nudged the Winter Wizard and extended her arms. "Dreki isn't burning down anything." The little red dragon swooped down and huddled in her arms.

Master Thel stopped in the hallways and riffled through his pocket. He jingled several sets of keys before finding the one that opened his classroom. Slithers wedged himself through the doorway before his master could finish opening it all the way. The long snake slipped to the corner of the room and spiraled into a ball, tucking his head away. Thel walked to the head of the classroom and filled the chalkboard with notes. "Do you two need something?" he tested. "You don't have class for two more days."

"Well, sir," Bertly responded, "we wanted to stop by early and show you what we accomplished."

Thel stopped writing and turned around. "I can see what Polly has accomplished; however, I am failing to see your successes."

Bertly pursed his lips.

"Assisting someone is *not* accomplishing your spirit quest, young human."

The Winter Wizard clenched his fists as his neck and face turned red.

"I believe both of your missions were to retrieve a scale from the King of all Dragons, no?" Thel looked back and forth between Bertly and Polly. "May I see your retrieved scales?"

Bertly pointed at Dreki. "Sir, we have thousands of scales right here."

"I can see that, young wizard; however, your mission was to retrieve scales from the greatest dragon of all time—you were quite insistent that you could accomplish this." Thel reached out his hand. "May I please see your scales?"

"But, sir." Polly stepped forward. "Certainly, no student has ever come back with a dragon."

"No, you are the first," the quest master acknowledged. "But that was not your mission."

Polly twirled her long blond hair around her finger. "I understand, sir. But you must be able to make an exception. You see—"

Thel raised his voice and emphasized each word with a stern point of the finger. "Did you or did you not retrieve a scale from Cordelia's dragon?"

Polly looked down. "We did not."

"Then why are you in my classroom?" Thel turned back around and continued to jot down notes on the chalkboard.

Bertly's heart started to race; he couldn't hear his own thoughts over the thumping. "Master Thel, you don't understand."

The master's fingertips tightened, breaking the piece of chalk in his hand. "No, I understand." Thel whipped his body around. "I understand that you two have had most things come easy to you. I understand that you thought you could accomplish a mission way beyond your pay grade." The spirit master approached Bertly and Polly. "I understand that despite most advice, you two choose to do whatever you please. I understand that when you arrived in Noskar, you did not find what you were looking for because what you sought *does not exist.*" Thel stood face-to-face with Bertly, looking up slightly; his head came just under the wizard's chin. "Now tell me, is there something I do not *understand?*"

"Master Thel." Bertly's anxiety turned to anger. "You're failing to realize the prestigious accomplishments that Polly and I have just achieved."

"No, Bertly. You are failing to see where you have failed." Thel pressed his finger against Bertly's chest. "If your mission had been to retrieve a dragon, then you would have accomplished that mission. But it wasn't. You cannot fail a task, stumble into a success, and then say you never failed your original mission." Thel placed his hand on Bertly's shoulder. "By the way, congratulations, Bertly, on the success of your supposed spirit animal."

The master held out his arms and examined the empty areas of the room.

"Sir, you are right," Polly interjected.

Thel glanced over to her.

"We bit off more than we could chew. We thought we were an exception to a rule, but we aren't. We still have so much to learn and we realize that." Bertly's anger was dissipating; he didn't know why he hadn't let Polly do all the talking in the first place. "This whole process is new to us—we didn't have brothers and sisters to mess up before us. Or parents to tell us the easiest places to go." She placed her hands out in front of her, palms up. "We have so much to learn, and hopefully, you're still willing to teach us." She sniffled. Bertly had never seen Polly come close to crying before. She was putting on the performance of a lifetime.

Thel sighed. "I presume she speaks for both of you?"

Bertly nodded.

"I suppose I have been rather harsh on you two." The master stepped over to his desk and sat down. "You two are not the only ones to fail your spirit quest this term. Most masters fail their first time trying anyway." Thel riffled through a stack of papers. "There was a group of elves who failed to retrieve a shell from the Leviathan Lake. Unfortunately, this is their second failed attempt, and the next time they come up short, I will unfortunately have to cut them from the program." The spirit master offered Bertly and Polly several pieces of paper. "These are their mission summaries and profiles. I will give you a one-day extension. If you can take this group and return with a shell, then all will be forgiven."

Polly snagged the notes. "Sir, I know these students." She looked up. "I was surprised they were even let into the Mastery program."

"So was I," Thel replied. "Regardless, it is my job to

make sure each student passes this course. I do not plan to make a mockery of this program like the professors before me."

Bertly looked over Polly's shoulder. "Who are they?"

"You wouldn't know them," she retorted.

"I understand I am handing you a full plate with these students, but this mission is more appropriate for a new master's spirit quest." Thel started to scribble on a piece of parchment. "Here is a permission slip to take up to three additional students with you, not including your apprentices."

"Thank you, sir." Bertly snatched the piece of paper from Thel. Retrieving a shell was the last thing he wanted to do. Still, it was better than having to wait until the following year.

"You won't regret this, sir." Polly beamed.

Thel shooed them away. "I have a feeling I might."

As Bertly was exiting the classroom, he froze in the doorway. "Master Thel?"

Thel kept his head down and continued to work. "What is it, Bertly?"

"Is it true that all professors have access to the school's shippers?" Bertly asked.

"I am not shipping you to the lake, if that is what you're asking," his teacher replied.

"No, sir. It isn't for me." Bertly walked back into the classroom. "What if I told you I could show you an Eskosian bear?"

Thel stopped working and placed his hands behind his head. "You have my interest, young human."

"I know Polly bonded with a dragon." Bertly's voice grew and his walk formed into a strut. "But you see, I—"

"You're going to tell me you bonded with an Eskosian bear?" The master raised one eyebrow high. "Those are rare, even in Eskos. How can you know for certain?"

Bertly chuckled. "Hmm…maybe by the fact that she's the size of a mammoth."

Thel stood up. "Show me."

XX

"You see, once Master Thel caught a glimpse of this glorious, magnificent beauty of a creature..." Bertly patted Bear's head and scratched under her chin. "He had no choice but to ship her straight to the Academy."

"We heard it was because he thought she was going to rip his head off," Orin and Orîn hollered.

"Now, Orins." Bertly stood next to Bear just outside the Academy walls. Accompanying him was his apprentice, along with Polly and Devdan. They stood adjacent to the twins—waiting for the students Master Thel had instructed them to travel with. "Does this really look like a creature that would harm poor Master Thel?" Bear rolled over onto her back and wiggled around in the grass. "You see, harmless." As Bertly gestured toward Bear, a drizzle bird flew across his furry companion's face, and without hesitation she snatched the bird out of the air, leaving behind a single blue feather.

Orin snickered. "Very harmless."

"Wouldn't hurt a fly," Orîn added.

Bertly grumbled under his breath. "Polly," he demanded.

"Yes, Bertly?" she responded.

"Where are those useless elves?" Bertly placed his

hand on his hips. "They were supposed to be here half an hour ago."

"Devdan is right here, sir," Bertly's apprentice cracked.

"Shut up, Roderick," Devdan snapped. "You're an elf, too."

"True, but I'm not a useless one." Roderick shrugged.

"Roderick, my chap." Bertly fought back a fit of giggles as his cheeks swelled with pressure, but it was no use. His laughter erupted as he bent over and slapped his knee.

Devdan stood motionless while he looked Roderick up and down. The blond elf pulled back his shoulders and stuck out his chest. Roderick mocked him as though he were Devdan's mirror image, although he barely came up to Devdan's chest. Polly's apprentice lunged toward Roderick, sending him screaming and falling to the ground. Devdan's face changed from a mask of anger to one of amusement.

"Oh, Roderick." Bertly smacked his palm against his forehead. "It seems you're just as useless as the rest of them. Speaking of which…" Bertly tapped his foot. "Where are those good-for-nothing elves?"

"You mean those ones, sir?" Roderick pointed.

"Yes." Bertly frowned. "Where have you been?"

Three elves exited the castle, walking shoulder to shoulder. There were two boys and one girl, who all wore long shiny green cloaks. Their hair was braided and they all look freshly bathed—with no dirt under their nails or knots in their hair. Each had light brown locks and walked at a slow pace.

"Sorry we're late," the female elf replied. "Master Thel never told us where to meet." Her voice was soft and gentle, but still the elf maintained a certain confidence, as though she knew something Bertly did not.

The Winter Wizard's face remained rigid. "It's called

'deductive reasoning.' You should have been able to guess," he snapped.

"Your reputation precedes you, Master Bertly," the woman elf responded. "My name is Faythe. Here to my right is Alwin, and to my left is Sunrel. As you can most likely tell, we are triplets."

"You hear that, boys?" Bertly slapped Orin and Orîn on the backs. "It looks like you have some competition."

"What do you mean?" they asked.

"My apologies." Bertly pinched the bridge of his nose and shook his head. "I forgot to mention why I've invited you here today."

"We thought it was for the bear," the twins replied.

"Believe it or not, that is *not* why I summoned you." Bertly pulled a piece of paper from his inner cloak pocket. "Polly and I have received permission to bring up to three additional patrons on our trip." Bertly pointed with his index and middle finger. "And we have chosen you."

"Splendid!" Orin shouted with joy. "Wonderful, indeed!"

Orîn chimed in, "Who's the third?"

"Three's a crowd," Bertly replied as he smirked at the triplets.

"Bertly, enough teasing." Polly stomped her foot. "Can we please go over the plan? I am not sure if you recall, but we need to go to the Leviathan Lake and back in just three short days."

"Right," Bertly agreed. "We absolutely need to go over the plan." He clapped his hands and overlooked the group. "Plans have changed."

The group talked under their breath. Then Faythe spoke up. "Master Bertly, do you think it wise to deviate from the plans, considering we are in…unfortunate circumstances? I believe we should stick to retrieving a shell." Her brothers remained silent at her sides.

"I still plan to retrieve a shell from the lake if I must. I will not make the same mistake twice. I have learned that having a plan B is not a forgettable option," Bertly explained.

"Sir, if retrieving the shell is plan B, then what is plan A?" Roderick asked.

"Wonderful question, my apprentice." Bertly stood tall and crossed his arms behind his back, which had the effect of puffing out his chest. "We are going to the Decomposite."

Roderick's eyes rolled to the back of his head and he collapsed onto the ground.

"Master Bertly, you can't be serious," Faythe said.

Devdan raised his voice. "Sir, what madness has overcome you?"

"We never agreed to this," the twins blurted.

Arguments broke out between the students. They bantered back and forth with Bertly about sticking to the plan. Until an unexpected voice spoke up. "I am rather up for the adventure," Polly stated.

"Ma'am, you're serious?" Devdan questioned.

The group's banter ceased. "Bertly is right," she explained.

Bertly cocked his head. "I am?"

"Yes, I think we should all consider the legacy we leave behind. Not very many citizens are given the opportunity to become masters, let alone *certified masters.*" Polly frowned and shook her head. "We shouldn't settle on mediocrity. We still haven't even heard Bertly's plan."

Bertly's jaw dropped. "Thank you, Polly." The Winter Wizard riffled through his travel sack, which Bear appeared to be guarding. Bertly whipped out a thick piece of folded parchment. "Gather around." He unfolded the paper, revealing the large map his mother had left behind.

"I've never seen a map this detailed before," Faythe mentioned.

"It was my mother's. She was a traveler and collector. She traveled across all of Pangea looking for every odd or rare trinket she could find. And she found all of them except for one." Bertly ran his hand across the paper, attempting to flatten the crinkles. "My mother placed an X on every place she visited except for…here." Bertly pressed his finger onto the map. "This is the only place she has never been, and she left it for me to find."

Faythe slammed her hand over the map. "I am sorry, Master Bertly, but we are not going on a suicide mission to the Decomposite so you can try to bond with your mother."

Despite his last run-in with Rotters, Bertly still wanted to go to the Decomposite. He rationalized with himself that the last time was only a fluke; plus, it would take years before the Rotters were any real threat. Even if there were Rotters, Bertly would be ready this time. He had soul-bonded with a legendary creature, he was a master, and he had a powerful crew with him—he had achieved his goals. The next mission was to discover whatever he could about the coming Blight, since the Elders refused to take any action. In addition, maybe if more eyes saw the Rotters, the Elders would have to do something immediately.

"Don't touch my map." Bertly slapped Faythe's hand away. "If you don't want to come with me, then don't. But look here." Bertly rested his finger on the map. "The Leviathan Lake is basically touching the border of the Remnant Forest, and just past the entrance of the forest is the area I have marked. We could go to the Decomposite and the lake in the same day." Bertly looked up. Despite how much the Winter Wizard wanted to deny it, he did actually want to discover what he could about his mother, and this was his best lead. "Anyone who is too cowardly to join can stay behind while Bear and I find ourselves that hidden treasure." Bear let out a horrific growl, scaring the nearby drizzle birds out of the trees.

Roderick sat up and rubbed his head. "I'm going wherever Bear is going."

Faythe sighed and was silent as her eyes studied the map. Bertly felt it odd that he had yet to hear a single word from her brothers. "What is it that we are risking our lives for, exactly?" she asked.

Bertly shrugged. "I have no idea. But this is the last thing she left me." The Winter Wizard pulled his spell journal from his pocket and handed it to Faythe. "She wasn't the average human. She created spells that masters at the Academy couldn't figure out. Which I know is odd, considering she never cast one."

Faythe flipped through the pages. "This is unbelievable. I've never heard of most of these spells; some I didn't think were possible."

"Let me take a look at that." Devdan looked over Faythe's shoulder. "Bertly, how come you've never told us about this before? Some of these spells are incredible." Polly's apprentice's eyes moved side to side as he read off the possibilities: "Changing water temperature, increasing movement speed, healing spells…there is even a spell to change one's luck."

"I haven't been able to work that one out quite yet," Bertly said with a mournful sigh.

"Healing spells?" Polly asked, intrigued. The petite blonde human snapped her fingers and shifted the ground beneath everyone's feet, sending the students tumbling to the ground. She picked up the notebook and looked it over.

Bertly stepped over everyone as they were standing up, and pried the notebook out of Polly's hands. "This is why

I know there is something waiting for us in the Decomposite. My mother did not dabble in mundane adventures—she strove for excellence. She wouldn't bother to go there if it wasn't worth taking the risk."

Faythe brushed herself off. "You have convinced me, Master Bertly. However, I think we should grab the shell first, to be sure we complete our quest."

"I considered that as well. But I think we should get it on the way back. It'll take a full day and night to go to the lake and the Decomposite, meaning we will arrive tomorrow morning," Bertly explained. "And I would rather be in the Decomposite during the day than at night."

"I second that," Roderick shrieked.

"Fine, the Decom first it is." The female elf turned her head and marched toward the south, with her brothers by her side.

"The 'Decom'?" Bertly made a puking gesture behind her back. "I guess we are giving the most wretched place in all of Pangea a cutesy nickname now."

***

Roderick flicked his quill across the table and slid his chair back. "How could you?" The young elf stood up with his fists cupped. "You knew what was waiting for us on the other side." Roderick slammed his fists on the table. "You knew and you still took us there." Spit flew from his mouth as his screams pierced Bertly's eardrums.

Bertly put out his hands and slowly approached his apprentice. "Roderick, you don't understand—"

"No, I understand. You cared more about some treasure left behind by your deserting mother than for the well-being of your friends." Roderick stepped away from his master. "You're impulsive, Bertly."

"Why are you just now blowing up about this?" Sweat droplets formed at Bertly's hairline. "If you could let me explain—"

"You always have an excuse. I'm done listening to you explain." Roderick turned around and stomped toward the entrance. He swung the door open. "Write your own damn book."

Bertly jumped back as Roderick slammed the door. He glanced at Bear. "Thanks for helping me out." The fuzzy creature snarled and looked away. She rested her chin on her arm and went back to rest. "I wouldn't be on my side either." Bertly slouched over and fell into the untucked wooden chair that Roderick had left behind. He took a prolonged breath and turned the chair toward the table. The Winter Wizard fixed up the writing station and placed the quill on top of the parchment. Bertly snapped his fingers and the feather stood straight up. "Test. Test." The feather slid along the paper, writing: *Test. Test.*

"There we are. It seems it will be left up to us to finish this tale, my furry friend."

Bear grunted.

The red-eyed human sat up and cracked his neck. "I will check on Roderick soon. There is nothing I can say to ease the loss he's feeling. Plus, he isn't going anywhere. I don't see him climbing down the side of a mountain anytime soon. I'll let him cool off for a bit out on the porch."

Bertly cleared his throat and closed his eyes. "I wasn't looking forward to this part, Bear. But the Blight is here, and besides Cordelia, I'm the only one who knows...everything. If I don't document this, no one will."

The wizard's hairy friend gave no response.

"Ah, then, I suppose it is just the quill and me writing this story."

***

"Sir, are you sure we have to go through there?" Roderick's knees shook. "The lake is just two leagues back."

The group of wizards and witches had paused outside the Remnant Forest. Mist slipped through the gaps between the trees, and scattered howls and screams echoed on the wind. Red sap bled from the cracks of the black trees. The mist was hot, but the air that pushed it was cold. The forest carried a completely different feel than the Decomposite. When Bertly had visited the small town with Alestar, it hadn't felt so distant from the mainland; however, the Remnant Forest held an entirely different impression.

This mist is quite warm, Bertly thought. And he realized that, for the first time in a very long while, his skin was absorbing the wind and the chill beneath it—he could feel it again, and that feeling stirred other emotions within him, which he felt would be best left ignored.

"Do not be a fool, Roderick. 'Tis but a garden." Bertly opened his arms as though there were swinging doors before him, and the fog parted. Red eyes, attached to shadowed and formless bodies, lurked in all directions, just beyond the border of the travelers' vision.

"You've thought this through, Master Bertly?" Faythe asked.

Bertly slapped Bear on the rear. "I promise our fuzzy friend here will be the scariest thing we encounter."

"Then why are all of you wearing armor?" the woman elf asked, twisting her mouth.

"They were gifts from my father." Bertly laughed nervously. "It would be rude not to put the equipment to use." The Winter Wizard motioned forward. "Let's not waste any more time. Onward."

Bertly and his spirit animal led the pack into the eerie forest. Bear slashed through the vines and thick bushes that blocked their path. The ground was covered in small animal bones, and each step that was made left behind a small crunching noise. Ebony-colored dirt covered the ground beneath the white, fractured bones.

"Sir, what are these?" Roderick asked. "They look so cute."

Bertly looked back and saw his apprentice reaching toward a bush full of berries. "Don't touch those!" he screamed as his apprentice poked the tiny fruit.

Roderick screamed. "It *bit* me."

"Yes, Roderick." Bertly tapped his foot. "Those are snapping berries."

"Snapping berries?" Devdan asked.

"Yes—berries that snap." Bertly groaned. "I do not know how else to phrase it."

"These will be useful indeed," the twins cheered. Each of them reached into their travel sacks and pulled out glass jars. They snapped the small fruits at the base of the branches to avoid the sharp bites of the fruit, and stuffed the berries into their containers.

"Are there any other attacking foods we should be aware of, Master Bertly?" Faythe questioned just before leaning toward her brothers to whisper in their ears.

"Bertly," Polly intruded, "you forget not everyone is from Noskar. Most places in Pangea don't have living botany."

Bertly rolled his eyes. "Well, I can show them the elf-eating watermelons when we get back."

"Elf-eating watermelons?" Roderick shrieked. Bertly's apprentice looked at Polly. "Is he being serious?"

"Of course not, Roderick," Polly assured him. "Bertly knows watermelons only grow during the summertime. You'll have to wait until they're in season."

"Shh." Bertly motioned.

"What do you mean wait until they're in—" The Winter Wizard placed his hand over Roderick's mouth.

"I think I hear something," Bertly whispered. "People talking." The voices of others grew louder. Bertly could almost make out their conversation, but due to the thick fog, he couldn't see them anywhere. The group stopped making small talk and crouched low to the ground. Polly's dragon lay at her feet wrapped in a ball. The Winter Wizard remained standing.

"Get down, or you'll get us all seen," Faythe snapped.

Bertly's expression faded and his jaw dropped. "Are you not aware of the mammoth-sized bear next to us?" He tried his best to yell and whisper at the same time. "I am not sure we can do much hiding."

"Well, what do-do-do we have over he-here?" a high-pitched voice asked.

A deeper voice chimed in, "It looks like a few Panheads and their walking rug."

"Look at those ears," a woman's voice said. "Those will fetch us a nice price."

"Let's not be too hasty now," Bertly replied. The wizard's heart knocked at his chest with nearly painful force. His voice trembled just enough for it to be audible, and his mouth was dry. He tried to remain confident. "I am giving you all the opportunity to walk away."

"O-o-o-opportunity?" the high-sounding stutterer screamed. "He-he-he said o-opportunity." Emerging from the fog was a man with X-shaped scars across his eyes. His white pupils matched his hair. Standing beside him was a young-looking girl with tan skin and dark black hair, who looked to the ground as her hands shook. "I-I-I-I don't think you're one-one to be-be making com-com-compromises." His head twitched and flinched like a startled bird. The deranged man clapped his hands. "B-b-boys and g-girls, m-m-meet your new f-friends."

Emerging from the fog were countless men and women in dirty, tattered clothes. Each bore distinguishable scars and boldly displayed trophies of their victims. Some had severed heads tied to their waists, dangling like accessories to their belts, and others had finger, toe, and elf-ear necklaces securely knotted about their necks.

Bear dug her front claws into the ground and lunged forward. She roared with enough force to create a draft of wind. "I think it's time for you to leave," the Winter Wizard demanded.

The group of bandits dove back as the man with white eyes stepped forward and stood in place—unfazed. "You've g-g-got that f-f-fun attitude about you. I-I-I love it." The man licked his lips. "She's g-g-going to m-m-make a wonderful c-c-coat."

The group of barbarians drew their weapons, which were not the swords and axes typical of more industrialized city-dwellers; these men and women held spiked whips, sticks adorned with several dangling knives, and metal torches. Despite the array of sadistic weapons, the one Bertly feared most was what the man with X's for eyes held: nothing.

"Say hello to Cordelia for me." Bertly drew his sword and swiped it to the right, gutting the men standing next to him. The Winter Wizard looked back, and as he feared, the bandits had already wedged between him and his companions.

Devdan leaped to his feet and pounded in a bandit's temple with the knob of his sword. He quickly sidestepped and with two hands slid the tip of his sword through the jugular of the woman lunging toward him. In one swoop, he slipped the blade through the back of her neck and sliced the man behind her.

Polly grabbed Bertly's apprentice by the collar and pulled him in close. She pounded her fists into the ground, causing the bone-strewn dirt to shake. The ground rose and the dirt continued to impact and shape itself until it turned into a stone barrier around Polly and Roderick—Dreki lay at their feet.

Orin and Orîn skated between enemies like fish through water. Orin used an axe while Orîn handled the frozen crossbow he had worked on with his brother and Bertly, back in Alestar's old classroom. Orîn fired off iced arrows, freezing enemies in their place. Orin would instantly swoop in and slash the throat or gut of the frozen thief. It was a ballet that could only be performed by individuals who, while individuals, were inextricably connected to one another.

Bear pounced and landed on top of several soldiers. She crushed the chest cavities of a few of them with her claws and ripped out the jugulars of the rest with her sharp teeth. Bertly shuffled next to Bear while keeping within striking distance of the stuttering man. Bear adjusted her attention to focus on him as well.

"Th-th-think about your n-n-next m-move." The white-haired bandit licked his lips. The man was skinny and stood with bad posture. His hands looked too large for his body because they dangled from such lanky wrists.

"I am assuming you know magic. Because it doesn't look like you could lift a sword," Bertly stated. "I'd best warn you..." The Winter Wizard planted his foot and draped his warblade to the ground with one arm. "I can do both." With his open hand, he made a fist. The vines of nearby trees spun and swirled outward and wrapped themselves around the limbs of the white-eyed man. Bertly turned his wrist, and the vines retracted back into the trees, suspending the man in midair. "You should have taken my offer."

"Oh no, oh-oh no, oh no. We-we-we are just g-g-getting started." The bandit leader laughed hysterically.

Bertly heard screams and armor clashing. He couldn't make out what was happening behind him. Small explosions were set off, and he prayed to Cordelia that the sounds came from the twins. The Winter Wizard grasped his warblade so that every knuckle strained, and he lunged forward. Cordelia's blade extended until it froze just one inch from the man's heart. Bertly tried to push forward, but his arms had frozen. He attempted to step forward, but his body wouldn't budge.

The vines loosened and dropped the man. The moment before he crashed to the ground, he stopped falling and paused, floating in the air. "Th-th-that blade isn't y-y-yours." The man with the X-shaped scars across his eyes gently placed his feet on the soil and glared into Bertly's eyes. "W-w-where did you get that?"

Bertly looked down without moving his head because his neck had been restrained, and he was unable to shift it even the slightest bit. The little girl with black hair stood just in front of him, her pointer finger touching his kneecap. She pushed with her index finger and Bertly collapsed to the ground. He was paralyzed. He couldn't even manage a deep breath because it would require his chest to move. The wizard could only let the smallest amounts of oxygen through his nose, and he felt as though he were suffocating. Bear leaped out and pressed her front paw into the man's body, restraining him against the bone-covered dirt.

"Th-th-think twice, p-p-puppy. M-m-my slave c-c-can snap your little f-friend's n-n-neck with a f-f-f-flick of the wrist." The man blinked over and over. Bear released the white-haired man.

Bertly could no longer hear the sounds of fighting; the swords had come to rest and the voices in the background were gone. He could still hear the bandit leader talking, along with Bear's growls. The little girl released Bertly. As he gasped for air, the wizard heard a crackle followed by an intensifying pressure in his right cheek. A henchman pushed Bertly to the ground and snatched his warblade. The blade retracted. For a man of his size, Bertly thought he would have hit much harder.

The henchman handed the warblade to the white-haired man. "It doesn't seem to work."

"Th-th-this blade only c-calls to C-C-Cordelia." The man waved the sword handle in front of his face. "Wh-why does it a-answer to y-you?" The man's eyes targeted back onto Bertly. "Sh-show me his ears," he yelled.

A man and a woman grabbed Bertly by the arms and pulled his hair back. "He's human," the woman shouted.

"A r-r-red-eyed h-h-human." The white-eyed bandit laughed.

"Zoo!" the henchman screamed.

The barbarians smashed their shields. "Zoo." One after another, they started blaring, "Zoo!" The yells erupted into chants: "Zoo! Zoo! Zoo!"

The leader subtly gestured and the crowd froze over, deathly silent. The man stepped toward Bertly. "M-M-Mother will be m-m-most pleased with her n-n-new p-pet." The group of bandits erupted into chants and cheers.

The Zoo. Bertly remembered where he had heard that word before, from his old master. Alestar's voice rang through his head: *"They will track you down and slaughter you for sport...or worse, they'll sell you to the Zoo...It's a massive colosseum where they force rare species to fight to the death."*

The white-eyed leader waved his hand. A couple of dozen bandits lugged Orin, Orîn, Devdan, and the triplets along the black ground. They pulled them up by their necks and forced them onto their knees and tied their hands behind their backs. A man with fur boots and a shiny chest plate walked next to the bandit forerunner. "The others seem to be locked away inside a rock. It's starting to crack. We will have them out in just a moment."

The man gestured again and the chatter stopped. "L-l-let's t-t-try this again." The bandit placed his hands onto his head. "M-m-my name is F-F-F-F-Felix. B-b-but only with th-three F's."

Bertly thought hard, *FFFelix*. He had never heard this name before. He couldn't help but wonder if the F's stood for something.

"I-i-it's a joke," the man with scars cracked. He looked to his crew. "The P-P-Panheads must n-n-not like jokes." His followers snorted like pigs.

A loud explosion shook the ground behind Bertly. He jerked his head back—rocks and flames filled his vision. Shooting out from the top of the flames was Dreki. The small red dragon shot through the smoke and darted straight toward the Academy. The thieves seized Polly and Roderick.

"Th-there we are. A-a-and l-look. A-a-another elf." Felix gestured for them to come forward. He mentioned nothing of Polly's dragon. They must not have seen Dreki due to the smoke from the explosion or the distraction of it all. The followers hauled Polly and Roderick over and lined them up with the rest of the students. In front of Bertly, every wizard and witch hung their head to the ground, all with fear easily readable on their faces.

"Should we get the fire started?" the henchman asked.

Their leader nodded. "You k-killed half of m-m-my c-crew." The man licked his lips. "S-so now, we are g-g-going to k-kill half of y-yours."

XXI

"I-i-including the c-c-carpet, I-I-I see ten of y-you. So f-f-five h-h-heads is only fair." Felix chuckled.

Bertly knelt on the ground, with his knees digging into the sharp broken bones that covered the forest floor. He listened to the group of bandits argue and debate—they fought over which of his friends to kill first. The fog remained so thick Bertly could've thrown a heavy stone and been unable to see where it landed. The warm mist caused his skin to sweat. Even so, the Winter Wizard couldn't help but shiver.

The stuttering bandit walked behind Faythe. "Wh-why don't y-you choose who d-d-dies first?"

Faythe's breathing grew louder than her speech, and even if she wanted to, Bertly didn't think she could squeeze a word out.

"No-no-no-no answer?" The man shrugged. "Okay." The X-eyed thief pulled a dagger and placed it against her neck. "Are-are-are ya sure y-you d-d-don't have a p-p-preference?"

On each side of Faythe stood one of her brothers, each with their chin against their chest. The boys reached out and both placed a hand on their sister's shoulder.

The scrawny bandit laughed uncontrollably. "Yes-yes-yes." Felix clutched his dagger loosely; his grip didn't seem strong enough to hold it much longer. "Th-this j-just became a-a-a lot more fun." The bandit pointed his blade at each of the male triplets. Two soldiers with black hoods marched forward simultaneously. Latched onto their backs were enormous axes, each with a head larger than the average man's torso. They rested their blades on Alwin's and Sunrel's shoulders, the metal touching their necks just enough to indent the skin.

"Wa-wa-one." The leader waved his dagger and the men pulled their axes back.

The hooded executioners placed their weapons back against the elves' necks. "T-t-t-two," the man shouted. His henchmen again pulled their axes back as though to strike, but placed them right back on the twin's shoulders.

"A-a-and." As the white-eyed man pulled his dagger through the air, at the same time the slayers drew their axes behind their heads. "W-w-wait." The executioners dropped their blades. "I-I-I almost forgot." The man licked his lips. "My-my-my excitement got the b-b-better of m-me." The wretched man made a scissor-cutting gesture.

Squeezing through the crowd was a bumbling and hairy dwarf. Bertly could tell she was talking to herself, but he couldn't make out what she was saying. "I almost thought you forgot about me, my lord," the dwarf projected. "These will fetch us a nice price." The female dwarf went back to talking under her breath. Once she got closer to the kneeling students, she pulled out a contraption. It looked like a helmet, but it had scissors attached to each end. The dwarf approached Alwin. "Now don't move or you'll only make it worse." She placed the helmet onto Alwin, and along with her gesture, a loud *clank!* erupted. The elf started flailing. This was the first reaction of any sort Bertly had seen from the emotionless elf.

The bandit leader giggled. "S-s-s-splendid. A-another, another."

The dwarf removed the helmet from Alwin, and he dropped to the floor as blood gushed from each side of his head, and it was only when he turned his head all the way over that Bertly could see that the elf's ears had been removed.

"It seems I was a little sloppy with this one."

Alwin stopped moving and his body lay motionless.

"You won't get away with this!" Faythe screamed. Tears poured out of her reddened face.

Bertly glanced toward Roderick; he was passed out face-first on the ground. Roderick had elf ears, and he certainly knew the bandits would target him soon. The Winter Wizard would need to find some way to salvage his apprentice.

SHINK. Bertly heard another slice from the helmet— this time it was Sunrel who was the victim. The elf twisted on the ground like a worm dangling from a fishing hook, waiting to be eaten. Blood ran from his head like rainwater down a rooftop. Without a moment of reluctance, an executioner stood over the elf's body and swung down his blade. The elf's head plopped onto the ground and rolled in front of his sister. Faythe leaped to her feet, screaming belligerently. She pulled a blade from her sleeve and cocked her arm back. As she swung forward, the other executioner grabbed her by the wrist and squeezed. With a scream of impotent rage and grief, Faythe's fingers slowly uncurled from the hilt of her blade, and it dropped to the ground amongst the bones of those who were long dead, and the still-warm flesh of the recently deceased.

"A-a-another one with a-a lot of-of s-s-spunk. I l-love it." Felix licked his lips. "Th-th-this one d-deserves something s-special."

"Rotters!" a voice from the crowd yelled.

In a matter of seconds the whole tribe was chanting, "Rotters. Rotters. Rotters."

"B-b-bring out the R-R-Rotters," the frail man shrieked.

Bertly's heart trembled and he could tell his motor skills were turning clumsy. He constantly rationalized with himself that the Rotters were nothing he couldn't handle, but now that he was coming face-to-face once again, the old anxiety he had once felt when he lost his master resurfaced. Bertly was terrified.

The young girl with black hair placed her finger onto Faythe's hip, and the elf stiffened. Faythe's knees buckled and she dropped to the ground—the young girl had paralyzed her. Bertly knew this feeling, as he had endured it moments ago. Until the black-haired girl stopped touching the young elf, she would be rendered motionless.

The two executioners placed their axes onto their backs and walked back into the crowd. Meanwhile, the chants continued. The black-hooded men soon returned with thick metal rods in their hands, and at the ends of those rods were Rotters. The undead elves lashed out in all directions in attempts to maul and attack the nearby bandits.

The dwarf twins fell back and looked at each other as though they had just seen ghosts. They tried to shuffle away, but bandits were right behind them. Polly's coordination was jittery as she scooted closer to Roderick, who remained unconscious. With her hands tied, she nudged him with her hip, attempting to wake him. When Bertly glanced toward Devdan, the blond elf was already staring at him. He appeared more confused than frightened, and it didn't take much thought for Bertly to realize why. The Winter Wizard did his best to appear calm and confident—he couldn't let them know he was afraid.

"Wow-wow-wow. Ya-ya-ya don't know?" Felix walked closer to the lineup of students. "R-Rotters are the n-n-newest residents of the De-De-Decomposite. There m-may be-be-be more of them than us-us."

Faythe's body remained motionless as several executioners loomed around her. The young girl released Faythe and walked back behind her master. The bandit leader pointed down, and in obedience, the executioners pushed the Rotters into a tight circle around the elf's body. She screamed relentlessly as their necrotic flesh closed in on her.

"L-l-lucky for us, R-R-Rotters d-d-don't like elf ears. Th-they'll be-be-be left fully intact." The leader screamingly laughed. The executioners pushed the Rotters down, and the creatures reached out and tore into Faythe's helpless body. Their sharp nails dug through her skin like it was nothing more than sand. Bertly felt sickened by the fact that he only thought about his friends being killed and not the life being taken. He had to come up with a plan, but what could he do that wouldn't simply stall? He tried to connect with Bear, but their bond was too new, he couldn't control her yet. The Winter Wizard contemplated what he cared most about and peered over at Polly; her eyes were shut.

Faythe's screams stopped.

The main henchman leaned toward Felix. "Should we...clean up? The fire is ready."

"Yes-yes-yes. C-c-clean it up." The white-eyed man waved his arm around. The executioners pried the unsatisfied Rotters from the remains of Faythe's body and vanished into the mist. The female dwarf, brandishing a sharpened knife, approached Faythe's nearly untouched head and severed her ears. The black-hooded men quickly returned with shovels. Two of the slayers grabbed Alwin and Sunrel and tossed their bodies into the fire. The others shoveled Faythe's remains and then tossed her innards and head in with her brothers' corpses.

"You promised us two more." The henchmen giggled. "There are three more elves, two dwarves, and the human boy."

"The-the-the h-h-human is for Mother," Felix snarled. "H-how about a-another f-f-female elf?"

"A wonderful choice, sir," the henchman replied.

The executioners drew their axes and slumped in Polly's direction. Their feet dragged on the ground, leaving behind a black trail from where the bones had been pushed away. Polly tried to get up, but bandits pushed down on her shoulders, pinching her knees into the dirt. The smoke from the burning bodies filled the air, making it heavy and smoke-laden. The smell reminded Bertly of the last time he was in the Decomposite. When he and Alestar had to put out a bonfire fueled by the bodies of an entire town.

The executioners lined up before Polly, and one of them stepped forward and placed his axe on the top of her head. The blade extended to her nose, directly between her eyes. Felix snapped; the executioner pulled his arms back.

"Wait!" Bertly yelled. "She's a human."

"S-s-stop," Felix hollered.

"I think Mother would love another human, wouldn't she?" Bertly's voice shook. "She would be most pleased with not one…but two…red-eyed humans?" The wizard gulped.

"H-h-her ears," the scar-eyed man demanded.

The slayer placed down his weapon and pulled back Polly's blond hair. "She's human." The executioner dropped to the ground, a knife sticking out the side of his neck. Devdan charged over and grabbed the axe.

The burning corpses. Bertly had almost forgotten how he'd extinguished the fire with Alestar, but imminent doom seemed to spur his memory—they'd pulled the oxygen from the air. Everyone was distracted, so the Winter Wizard closed his eyes and placed his fingertips on the ground. He had one chance, so he harnessed his energy for one full-scale blow. He felt it conjuring inside him, like a solid mass that could be seen and touched. He pulled his arm back and punched the ground. The bandit army collapsed upon the impact.

Bertly sprang to his feet and charged over to Polly. He grabbed her by the arm and threw Roderick over his shoulder. "Take Roderick and leave. Tell the Academy what has happened here. Tell them Rotters are at the border."

"Bertly, I can't leave you all." Polly's voice trembled so that Bertly could hear a crack in every word.

Bear ran up and growled.

"Polly, we can't talk about this. Roderick will never survive this." Bertly took off his whistle and handed it to Polly. "Blow this from the Academy and Clia will be able to hear you. Tell her I'll be at the Zoo—she'll know where to find me."

Bear grabbed Polly by the straps and threw her onto her back.

Bertly flung his apprentice over his furry friend's shoulder and kissed her on the nose. "Keep them safe."

Bear turned and bolted for the Academy.

As his companions' bodies faded into the mist, Bertly screamed, "Tell them the second Blight is here!"

Devdan, Bertly, and the twins stood in a circle back-to-back as the bandits found their feet. Before the twins could be untied, the boys were already surrounded by bandits. The barbarians drew their weapons and surrounded the young wizards.

Felix pointed toward Northern Pangea. "After them." A group of thieves took off in the same direction as Polly, Bear, and Roderick. "Who d-d-did th-that?" The white-eyed man ground his teeth and flared his nose.

"I did it." Devdan pounded his chest and spit on the ground. "I made all of you weaklings collapse to the ground." The blond elf clinked the executioner's axe against the armor of a dead bandit. "If you were a man, you'd come down here and fight me yourself."

"I-i-it's a-a-a good thing I am-am-am no man." Felix snapped his fingers, a gesture that caused an arrow to shoot into Devdan's arm. "Th-that is f-f-for the elf." He snapped again, and another arrow flew into the elf's leg.

Dev bit down and his face shook. Bertly couldn't imagine the pain he was holding in.

"Th-that is for the c-c-carpet you-you owe me." The white-eyed man snapped, and yet another arrow was launched into Dev's other leg and he slumped to the ground. Felix snapped once more, and another arrow found its home in the elf's other arm. "Th-that is for the h-h-human!" Felix screamed. "H-human!"

Blood poured down each of Dev's limbs. His body seemed like a rag doll, and Bertly couldn't believe he was still upright.

Felix snapped three times. "That's for my th-th-three men." Three arrows plunged into Dev's abdomen, and the blond elf flopped over onto his side. His face dug into the dirt. An executioner placed his foot onto Dev's back; he lunged back, sticking his chin in the air, and then flew forward. Bertly heard the axe sticking into the ground— Devdan's body went limp. "A-a-and that's f-f-for one o- of the h-h-heads you owe me."

Rage was burning within Bertly on Devdan's behalf.

He'd always stood so tall, so straight and proud, and this image of his death was in direct opposition to the dignified man—the selfless man he had been.

"They still owe us one more, Master," Felix's henchman shrieked. Bertly's hands started to sweat, and he caught himself biting his lip hard enough to draw blood. Bertly knew he was being saved for the Zoo.

A woman in long robes approached, appearing nothing like the other bandits. She stood properly and kept her hands folded and shoulders pinned back. "Felix, I think it is best to head back now. The sun is setting, we have lost half of our men, and dealing with the Rotters at night isn't wise."

Felix glared at Bertly and the twins.

"Mother can decide their fate. They still owe us a head."

"Felix!" a bandit hollered. "We have captured one of them." The man with pale skin and dark hair held Roderick up by the back of his collar. His body was lifted off the ground, allowing him to barely touch his toes to the ground.

Oh no, thought Bertly, grinding his teeth together. *Why, Roderick, why?*

"Wh-wh-where is my h-h-human?" The white-eyed bandit fell into the throes of a coughing fit.

"She got away." The pale bandit stepped over and threw Roderick onto the bone-covered soil. "We were on their tails until this one decided to bring down half a dozen trees on us. He fell off the back of their bear as he was attacking us."

At least Polly could still warn the Academy. But Bertly feared she wouldn't get help in time to save all of them.

"I-I-I do not care about this e-e-elf. Wh-where is-is my r-r-red-eyed human?" the barbarian leader snapped.

"Felix, it's getting dark," the woman in robes insisted.

The scrawny, white-haired man's lips quivered. His hands and body shook as though he were shivering, his dagger loosely dangling in his hand. "P-p-put them in the-the c-c-carriage. M-Mother w-w-will decide what to do w-with them." Felix tightened his grip and stabbed his blade into the pale bandit's stomach. The man crumpled to the ground. "M-make sure those ch-children d-d-don't have any more t-t-tricks up their sleeves."

A group of executioners closed in on Bertly and the twins, and they didn't resist. The boys were patted down, their pockets cleaned out, and their travel sacks taken away. The guards grabbed them by the arms and escorted them to a steel-gated carriage a couple of dozen paces away down the road. The group of bandits had several horses, fully supplied, along with multiple carriages in the forms of jail cells. Bertly, Roderick, and the twins were just a few of many prisoners who had been captured.

Felix approached the caged carriage and stuck his nose between the bars. "M-Mother h-h-has been waiting for you, B-Bertly." The leader patted the side of the carriage, and the horse attached lugged the full caravan.

"I killed them."

Bertly peered over to his apprentice, who was sitting next to him. Roderick's face was blank, his cheeks weren't red, nor did sweat drip down his head. "They were catching up to us, so I collapsed the trees behind us and I crushed them all. I didn't even think about it." Roderick's head bobbed with each bump in the road. "I just did it."

Bertly felt callous. He knew he should've been riddled with emotion, but the ones whom he cared for the most were still alive, and keeping them alive was his main priority. He had been here before, with Alestar, and he wasn't going to let it happen again. "You didn't have a choice." Bertly scooted closer to his apprentice. "Polly has to get back to the Academy. They need to know the

Rotters have spread."

"What do you mean 'spread'?" Orin asked.

"Don't you mean 'returned'?" Orîn added.

Bertly cleared his throat. "Yes, of course. Polly needs to warn them that the second Blight has returned."

"No." Roderick sat up and pulled his head back. "That isn't what he meant. He meant 'spread.'" The apprentice scooted away from Bertly. "You already knew about them…didn't you?"

"Don't be ridiculous. We've been through a lot, and I simply misspoke. Roderick, please." Bertly wasn't lying. He had misspoken. He was never supposed to tell anyone what he had seen.

"Where did you go?" Orin asked.

"When?" Bertly replied.

"With Alestar. Where did you go?" Orin demanded.

The Winter Wizard remained silent.

"Where is Alestar?" Orîn questioned.

"I've told you before. He went back to Eskos," Bertly responded. His fingers jittered, and his foot started to tap, seemingly of its own volition.

"No, where is he?" the twins bellowed.

The master took a long exhale and looked away from his companions. "He's dead."

The twins gasped.

"Is that your old master?" Roderick inquired.

Bertly nodded. "He took me on a trip to the Decomposite to retrieve a rare artifact, my warblade…Cordelia's warblade." Bertly untied his hair and picked out the leaves and twigs left behind from their battle. "When we arrived, the city was in ruins. It wasn't long before we were attacked by a massive swarm of Rotters. But it was different. They were in order; they didn't seem so…untamed. They had a leader and they followed orders." Bertly shook his head. "It was nothing like their behavior today. We walked several leagues on foot and never encountered a single one. But these men, they say they're everywhere now."

"They had a leader?" the twins probed.

"Yes, they followed...its orders. They were just as brainless and lifeless, but somehow obedient. These men have no way of controlling them," the Winter Wizard informed them.

"That means something—or someone—specifically controls them," Roderick added. "But who, or what?"

"I am leaning toward someone." Bertly lifted his head. "They worked in perfect unison, as though they were following orders. It wasn't until we had slain their leader that they started acting savage."

The twins shouted, "But who is bringing them back?"

"Only Cordelia knows." Bertly placed his finger over his lips for the boys to lower their voices. "What if Cordelia didn't end the first Blight, but simply put it to rest? She is the only one who discovered the source, and when she did, as the story goes, she sacrificed her life to end it and to save all of Pangea. But what if she didn't kill the source?"

"You're so selfish," Roderick spat through clenched teeth. "You knew all of this and you didn't tell anyone."

Bertly rammed his hand and arm into the steel bars surrounding them. "Of course I told someone. It was the first thing I did." Bertly grabbed his apprentice by the shirt and yanked his face within inches of his own. "I went to the Academy. I told them everything. Of the Rotters. About Alestar. Everything. And you know what they told me?" Bertly pushed Roderick back into the steel bars. "To keep my mouth shut. Not to tell a single soul. I did try to do something, Roderick, and the Academy swept it under the rug. You have to understand if I acted out, they would have expelled me, stopped be from becoming a master. I never would have even had the chance to soul-bond. I would have become nothing."

A terrified scream blasted through Bertly's ears. "Rotters!" a man cried. Chaos had broken loose.

A handful of decayed dark blue elves thrashed their bodies into the carriage, rocking it side to side. Roderick and Bertly jumped to the other side, next to Orin and Orin. The Rotters' arms stretched into the caravan, their hands desperate to grab ahold of living flesh.

Screams from both the living and dead created songs of horror. The mist and trees were gone; the students were out of the Remnant Forest. However, night had fallen, and Bertly's field of vision was limited.

"This carriage has a lock." The twins squeezed past Bertly and hustled to the door of the carriage. "That means we can pick it."

"I'll keep them distracted," Bertly exclaimed. "Lightus." The Winter Wizard snapped his fingers and a small ball of floating light materialized. "Lightus," he repeated several times, creating multiple light sources. The lights floated around the Rotters next to them. Bertly spun his finger in the air in concentric circles, and the lights twirled around the rotting elves. The decayed creatures stopped growling and retracted their arms while their eyes followed the lights around and around.

"It's working, sir!" Roderick cheered. The dead creatures broke their concentration and glared right at Bertly's apprentice. Roderick's eyes widened.

"Roderick, you fool!" Bertly yelled.

"Got it," the twins shouted as they kicked open the door.

Encompassing the surrounding area were hordes of Rotters swarming the group of bandits. Black blood from the decaying creatures was sprayed everywhere, blending into the white bone on the ground and the dark soil. The thieves' numbers were dwindling as scores of undead trampled over their collective.

Bertly led the way. "Hurry, back to the forest!" The boys scurried out of their cage and booked it for the misty trees. They weaved in and out through dead elves and hopped over the dismantled bodies scattered around.

"N-n-not so f-f-fast." Felix stepped in front of the students and held out his hand with his palm facing up. The bandit leader put his half-opened fist next to the Winter Wizard's head and blew. A white cloud of dust struck Bertly in the face. His body froze, and he felt nothing.

XXII

Bertly's head throbbed, and every bump along the road only exaggerated that pain. Lying unconscious beside Bertly was his young apprentice, and just in front of him were the dwarf twins.

The students were locked away in a different steel caravan, but now accompanied by only a few of their kidnappers. The Winter Wizard assumed these beaten-up soldiers were all that remained after the Rotter ambush. Bertly surveyed the remaining savages until the titanic structure down the black dirt pathway stormed into view and diverted his attention.

A magnificent brick-faced colosseum rested atop a two-step platform. The elliptical amphitheater rose seven stories, six of which consisted of arched walkways. Each archway was divided by detailed, engraved columns. The top floor was without arches and had rectangular windows spaced evenly apart. Front and center, at the base of the colosseum, was a grand entrance with statues and shrines displayed on each side of the entryway.

"S-s-say h-hello to your n-new home." The bandit leader walked next to the horse-drawn carriage and ran his dagger across the steel bars—the tinny ring succeeded in waking Roderick and the twins.

"Welcome to the Zoo, where tens of thousands come

each day to watch fighters from all over Pangea."
Strutting along next to the bandit leader was his
consultant, the woman in robes. "This is the main hub of
the Decomposite. Almost all residents of South Pangea
live within a league of the arena," she continued.

"Fighters?" Roderick bit his nails as he spoke. "I
thought zoos had cute animals."

"I think we *are* the animals," the twins replied.
Roderick's face went pale as he slumped over in his seat.

The woman smiled and placed her hands together.
"Every day Mother hand-selects each matchup, providing
her children with nothing short of the greatest
entertainment in the whole world."

"Every day?" Roderick shouted.

Felix smashed the handle of his knife against the metal
bars. "S-s-stop interrupting."

The young elf bit his tongue.

"While there are fights each day, most soldiers do not
fight more than once per cycle. If you are loved by the
crowd, Mother saves you for the full moon." Voices
sounded up ahead, and mingled between the loud banter
were the sounds of children playing. Such mundane
noises emitting from this deadly place caught Bertly by
surprise. The Winter Wizard couldn't imagine a youngling
growing up in the Decomposite.

The poised woman continued, "If you win one
hundred matches, Mother will adopt you and make you
one of her children. Other than being born here, it is the
only way to be granted freedom in this region."

"N-n-no one ever w-wins their f-final match!" Felix
laughed riotously.

"Very few have ever won their final bout." The
woman closed her eyes and smiled. Bertly couldn't tell if
she was happy or humoring her master. "But maybe you
will have better luck. Cordelia was one of those lucky few,

and you two seem to have a bit in common."

The white-haired man spat on the ground. "Wh-why are you g-g-giving them h-hope?" he snarled.

"I am not giving anyone hope, Felix." The woman glanced at Bertly. "I am merely informing them of the Zoo and its history, per Mother's request."

"If a-any of you th-th-think you're g-getting out a-alive, g-guess again." Felix reached through the steel bars, indiscriminately grabbing whoever was nearest to him—squishing Roderick's face against the metal. The bandit leader seemed much stronger than his frail body let on. "S-s-since C-Cordelia, Mother h-hasn't let anyone g-get away."

"Since Cordelia?" Bertly questioned. "That's not possible. That would make Mother—"

"Over three thousand years old, right?" the woman interrupted. "You will come to learn that things in the Decomposite are not always as they seem."

"What does that mean?" With his lips pressed against the bars, Roderick could barely push out his words.

Felix placed his dagger against Roderick's cheek and slowly dragged his blade down Roderick's flesh, slicing a small, thin slit across his face. "I s-s-said no in-interrupting. N-n-next time it's a-an ear." He released his grip, dropping Bertly's apprentice to the floor.

The Winter Wizard lunged forward, but the twins restrained him.

"Oh, B-B-Bertly, you h-have sh-shown your weakness." The man's comments didn't register—*I am already at his mercy—how has he not yet discovered my weakness? Also, how does the man know my name?*

The roar of the crowd carried throughout the village. Vendors with wooden stands were sprinkled around the perimeter of the colosseum. The adults wore colorful and decorated clothing while most of the children wore masks and costumes. The décor was nothing like Bertly had anticipated; despite the ground being black, the wizard couldn't see another dark shade of color anywhere. The arena was littered with visitors who could be seen walking around inside. The arches shined from their gold plating and were clustered with attendees of every race, including giants.

"We're here." The remaining bandits surrounded the carriage with their weapons in hand, awaiting the robed woman's orders. "Please, no one try to be a hero," she said. An executioner unlocked the door and stepped back, fumbling over his feet as he walked away. If Bertly could have guessed, the slayer seemed scared of them. The boys stepped out of the steel wagon. "Bertly, please come with me. Mother would like to greet you personally." Two executioners grabbed him by each arm and another placed his blade against his back. "It's just precautionary," the woman insisted.

"S-s-send the h-h-half-pints to th-the c-cellars. I-I-I will t-take the elf." At those orders, the bandits seized the twins and Roderick.

Orin slapped at the hands of the savages. "Don't touch the merchandise."

"We can walk just fine," Orin shouted.

The bandits stumbled back and drew their swords.

"Fine, but no funny business," a woman retorted.

Bertly's apprentice was dragged by his armor straps and tossed at the feet of Felix. "You're c-c-coming w-with me." The thin bandit latched onto Roderick's hair and marched off.

"Where are you taking him?" Bertly screamed while trying to break free of the executioners' grasp.

"Master Bertly," the robed woman said.

How does she know I am a master? Bertly wondered.

"We understand your abilities far surpass our own, but

please, mind your confidence, and do not make us do something to one of your companions," the woman continued. "Please follow me. I am sure you have many questions for Mother."

"I have a few," Bertly grunted.

"Delightful! Mother loves her pets to be curious."

The Winter Wizard was led around the back side of the colosseum, where there stood a wooden gate guarded by dozens of well-armed soldiers. As soon as the soldiers caught a glimpse of the approaching group, they rushed to open the doors.

"You somehow know my name. Do I have the right to know yours?" Bertly asked.

"Airas." The woman's smile formed wrinkles on her normally smooth face. "Come, up these stairs."

Bertly assumed they were in an area closed to the public since the noise from the guests became muffled and there was almost no foot traffic.

Bertly hiked up a spiral staircase that seemed to ascend forever. The steps were tall, coming up to Bertly's knees. "Has Mother ever invited a dwarf to visit her?" the wizard cracked.

Airas chuckled under her breath. "Only a select few have ever stepped into Mother's quarters. And no, a dwarf has never been inside."

The guards followed close behind Bertly, keeping a blade to his back at all times. "What is she like? Mother?"

Airas looked over her shoulder, her eyebrows cocked at Bertly's incessant curiosity. "Not how you've imagined."

The group rounded the curved stairway until they were cut off by a plain wooden door. The robed woman paused and turned around with her hands folded in front of her. She gave a small wave and the bandit escorts holstered their weapons. "This is where we leave you. Mother is waiting."

"You aren't coming in?" Bertly asked.

"No, and I don't suppose I ever will." Airas knocked on the wooden door. "I look forward to watching you battle on the playground, Master Bertly."

By the time Bertly opened his mouth to ask another question, the robed woman was already rounding the corner and heading back down the stairway. The door creaked, and a woman stood behind it.

"You're shorter than I imagined," she said, peering down at Bertly with her eyes squinted so that her long thick eyelashes obscured the color beyond them. Her figure suggested she was human or elf, but her height fit that of a giant. Bertly was captivated by the way her figure blended together so organically. Her hourglass-shaped body and perfect complexion had the Winter Wizard mesmerized. She blinked in slow motion, her eyelashes as beautiful as butterflies flapping their wings.

"I...um...I'm actually, uh, quite tall for my..." Bertly wiped the sweat off his forehead. "Species. For a human. For a human I am really tall." His mouth wouldn't stop spewing words. "Most people are not as tall as me."

"I remember Cordelia being taller." The woman smirked as she spoke—the slight pull of her lips almost made her look innocent. "Don't you come from a line of mammoth blood?" The woman turned around. "That is quite a rare bloodline, you know."

"I-I know." Bertly stood stiffly in the doorway.

The woman must have detected his tension and sought to relieve it as she waved her hand toward the room. "You can come in."

Bertly tentatively stepped inside, trying to move normally despite the tension in his muscles. The room was elegant and designed in a style Bertly didn't recognize. It was simple with minimal decorations, and every piece of furniture looked as though it had never been used. The furniture was stained white, and the floorboards were a light rustic brown. In the middle of the room was a figure of some sort with a sheet covering it.

Bertly stepped farther into the room, finally feeling somewhat composed. "How do you know so much about me?"

Mother turned around—Bertly lost the composure he'd manage to retrieve because this woman was easily the most beautiful creature he had ever seen. She'd reduced him to near idiocy with a simple glance. A sculptor could not have carved marble with such perfect proportions. "Would you like a drink?"

"I, uh, was waiting until my—" Bertly gulped "—apprentice and I finished our spirit quest."

"How cute." The woman grabbed two glasses and filled them to the brim with red wine. "Please, sit." She gestured toward the chair in front of her with a gentleness that seemed inherent in all her movements, as though she could break a man by pointing too quickly. Bertly wouldn't have been surprised if that were the truth. "To answer your question, I know everything that is important."

"You think I'm important?" Bertly blushed.

"I have eyes everywhere." She tapped on her temple next to her eye. "Nothing in Pangea happens without me knowing about it. Except for your birth. I don't have any eyes in Stonebank; however, I knew the results of your entrance exam testing before you even finished."

"How could you know that so quickly?" Bertly sat in a feathered chair and crossed his ankle over his knee.

"I told you, I have eyes everywhere. I even know that your friend Polly has already arrived at the Academy with your pet bear." Mother took a sip of wine.

"Polly is safe?" Bertly leaned forward. "Wait...where are my friends?"

"Polly is safe." Mother tipped back her glass and finished it off. "Your apprentice will be safe. I have special plans for him; however, I cannot make the same guarantee for the dwarves." Mother smiled. "They are going to make excellent gladiators. Would you like another glass?"

"I haven't finished my first." Bertly didn't know why he so calmly and obediently answered her questions; he should have been infuriated. He felt as though something was influencing his behavior—the woman, the air in the room, the wine—something which had control over him, but over which he had none. "How do you know so many people? Everywhere?"

"I have been around for quite some time. I have had the chance to meet many people in many places." Mother poured another glass of wine.

"I don't understand. How can you be so old?" Bertly's eyebrows furrowed and he looked at the floorboards. "You look so young. How can you know Cordelia?"

The tender woman sat in a throne-like chair and crossed her legs. A large desk rested between her and Bertly. "Tell me, what do you know about the Decomposite—aside from the 'awful species' and 'treacherous lands'?" Mother mocked as she made air quotes.

Bertly looked around. "I don't know, that's about it."

"Nothing else?" she questioned. "Nothing...historic, maybe?"

Bertly shook his head. "No, it's always been like this."

"They really do shelter you north of the forest, don't they?" Mother chuckled, then tipped her glass back, emptying her drink in a single sip. "So you don't know that the final battle of the Blight took place here?"

"No."

"And I suppose you also don't know that prior to that, the Decomposite was no different than the rest of Pangea?" Mother placed her empty glass on the table in front of her.

"No."

"How do you suppose the Blight ended?" She placed her hands under her chin.

"It's lost in history," the wizard replied.

"Lost in history?" the woman shouted. "No, no, no. *Nothing* has been lost in any history. Someone has chosen not to tell you. These are two very different things." Mother reached over and grabbed Bertly's glass. "How do you suppose the war ended? With Cordelia fighting off millions of Rotters on her own?"

Bertly's voice trembled. "Kind of."

The woman took another long, indulgent sip of wine. "Sit back, young human. You have a lot to learn. Would you like a glass of wine?"

"Actually, yes, that sounds good."

***

Bertly stopped writing and looked at his fuzzy friend. "Don't you say a word about my drinking to the elf."

Bear grunted.

***

"The Decomposite used to be like any other part of Pangea. It actually used to be called Little Flower. We had flourishing landscapes and running streams. Until the Blight came. Until *he* came. Why he came...that, only Cordelia ever learned. His Rotter army grew tremendously. They seemed to multiply faster than dwarf flies." Mother tipped the bottom of Bertly's glass for him. The wizard took a sip of the wine; it tasted awful. "And then Cordelia showed up and she had all the answers. She knew who he was—Bishop, but he may as well have been death incarnate himself. She knew where his base was: Little Flower. Once the locations were scouted and her words turned out to be true, we listened to her."

"We?" Bertly asked.

"Yes, me and the rest of the Pangeans who fought in the first Blight. We had no one else to trust. The world was succumbing to Bishop, and we were desperate. She told us she knew how to stop him, but she never told us the cost." Mother finished her glass of wine. "Another?"

"No, thank you." Bertly took a sip of wine and cringed. "What was the cost?"

"Everything. Our lives, our homeland." She opened a new bottle, which looked much larger than the ones in Pangea. "Cordelia did something that day...I don't know how to describe it. I can't even tell you how it made me feel. It's the only thing I have ever experienced like it; nothing in this world can replicate what she did. But the damages can be seen. She destroyed our homeland and let the rest of Pangea use us as a scapegoat. The world closed itself off from Little Flower and started referring to it as the Decomposite. We were devastated by war, our lands were left uninhabitable, and no one wanted us. It made it easy for Pangea—a clear battle of good versus evil. It was easier for everyone to cope if they could blame someone. And eventually, it became a self-fulfilling prophecy."

"That's...that's awful. I'm sorry." Bertly was again distracted, this time by the way her silky brown hair tumbled over her shoulders and chest. "But that still doesn't explain your age."

Mother took yet another sip of wine. "What magic

Cordelia used, no one knows. But it cast some sort of spell over these lands. Time doesn't work the same here as it does elsewhere. In fact, it doesn't work at all."

"Wait." Bertly's mind registered her words as truth. "I actually believe you. That explains something I always wondered about. My old master—"

"Alestar," Mother interrupted. "Yes, he spent a lot of time here. He was not very fond of me, that one."

"Why not?" Bertly asked.

"Because I force dozens of people to fight to the death every day for my amusement." The woman whipped her hair back and batted her eyes.

"Right." Bertly took another sip of wine. The taste was growing on him.

"As I was saying. That's why the leaders of Pangea don't want their residents coming here; once they learn of how the time works, the citizens will never want to live in their home countries again. Despite the scenery." Mother stood and walked back to her liquor cabinet. "Immortality can be quite persuasive."

"Why don't you tell people, then? You can bring glory back to your homeland," the wizard asked.

"Nothing native to these lands can ever leave, and very few couriers are willing to make the journey here. We really don't have much to live for, Bertly. That is why we've found solidarity in the Zoo. This place wasn't constructed for nearly a thousand years after the Blight. We didn't turn into this overnight. Everyone is quite aware of how animalistic it is, but over the years, as our numbers have dwindled, our sympathy for the North has as well."

"From the Rotters?"

"Actually, no," Mother replied.

"Killing each other?" Bertly questioned.

"I'll let you think about it." This time Mother poured a

glass of white wine. "So tell me, Winter Wizard, what else intrigues you?"

Bertly uncrossed his legs and let his hair down. "Why are you telling me all of this?"

"Because none of it matters anymore. The Blight has returned, and you aren't the savior I was hoping for." Mother stood, crossed the room, and opened a dresser drawer. "Rotters roamed these lands for ten years before I heard about you, so when I did, I thought, this is it." The woman closed the drawer and walked back toward Bertly. "This must be the answer. The system of checks and balances is back at work. The Rotters have returned and so have humans with red eyes. But there is one major difference—when Cordelia came, she already knew all of the answers." Mother handed Bertly a brush. "You know nothing."

Bertly grabbed the brush. "Checks and balances? So you think Cordelia was born with the sole purpose of ending the Blight?"

"Yes, and when I heard two red-eyed humans were born, I was terrified because I assumed the Blight would be twice as bad. But now, *now* I don't have any hope, not that I had much before." She walked back around the desk and daintily sat in her throne. "You don't understand the Blight, Bertly. No one but us remembers what we had to live through. I can't put myself through that again. Especially if we don't have a savior."

Bertly stood up. "If I can prove to you that I am, will you let me go?"

"What?" Mother put down her half-full glass of wine. "You can't talk yourself out of this one, Bertly. We know there isn't much time left in this world, so we want to go out with a bang. And a red-eyed human is going out with a bang."

"I can prove it." The Winter Wizard's voice was deep

and confident. "Bring me my sword."

"You must take me for a fool," Mother hissed.

"Have you seen it?" the wizard asked.

"No. Nor do I care what your blade looks like." The woman picked her drink back up and finished it off.

"You may want to take a look." Lines formed around Bertly's mouth and his eyebrows arched. "If you are telling me the truth, then I have something you're going to recognize."

"Guards." Mother stood up. "Guards, hurry."

"Wait." Bertly waved his hands. "If I can't convince you...then I will pledge my life to the Zoo. Even after I win my one hundred fights."

The door burst open. "Get back or your head will be on a platter!" yelled a guard in all black. His frame covered the length of the doorway.

"No need to worry." Mother poured another glass of wine. "Everything is fine. Can you bring me our guest's belongings, please?"

"Yes, ma'am. Right away." The soldier scurried out of the room.

"That soldier there, he is one of the last people with mammoth blood. Maybe a distant relative?" Mother joked.

Bertly took a deep breath and exhaled loudly and slowly. He sank into the feathery seat and sipped the rest of his wine. "Do we have an agreement?"

"You are not in a place to be bargaining, but I have taken a liking to you, little human. You remind me a lot of your old master." Mother smiled and revealed teeth so perfect they couldn't have been replicated by even the most talented painter.

"I thought you two didn't like each other?" The young wizard looked at the bottom of his empty cup.

"Yes, because I broke his heart."

"What?" Bertly cocked his head back.

"Here they are, ma'am." The soldier walked into the room and handed Mother Bertly's travel sack as well as the grip of his warblade.

Mother's eyes widened as she grasped the sword handle.

"Is everything okay?" the man in black asked.

She blinked and looked up. "Yes, everything is fine. Please leave us now." Mother waited for the soldier to close the door. "Where did you get this? Who gave this to you? It was Alestar, wasn't it?"

"Yes."

"I knew it. He knew I had been looking for this for centuries, and he had it right under his nose." Mother glared. "This proves nothing."

"Please just trust me." Bertly reached out. "You have nothing to lose."

Mother passed him the handle.

As the Winter Wizard clutched the warblade, the clear mammoth-ice blade shot out. On his command, the sword retracted, and he placed the grip onto the table between them. "Your original instincts were correct. I am connected to Cordelia."

Mother fell back into her chair. "And Polly. Does it work for her?"

Bertly broke eye contact. "She didn't find out about it until recently."

"Wait a minute." Mother pushed against the arms of the throne and bolted from her seat. She scampered to a nearby wooden dresser and swung the door open. She removed a cape made of gray dragon scales. It had leather straps around the neck and a gray furred hood. "Put this on."

Bertly wrapped the cloak around his body. A sensation of nostalgia overwhelmed him, yet he couldn't connect it to any particular memory.

"I can't believe it." Mother placed her hand over her mouth.

Bertly glanced down to watch as the dragon scales transformed into a vibrant red color. "It matches my eyes." He batted his lashes.

"You don't happen to know where the shield is, do you?" She put her hands together as though she were praying.

"Shield?"

"Blast." Mother bit her bottom lip. "Those were the three items she took to every battle. Her cloak, her warblade, and her shield. You know—" She took a gulp of white wine. "That cloak aided Cordelia in slaying many dragons. It's fireproof. A dragon's scales cannot be burned." The woman ran her well-manicured fingers down the red cape, pressing her hands against Bertly. Goose bumps crawled across his skin, and she dragged her hand from one of his shoulders to the other. "Cordelia really has hand-selected you, hasn't she?"

The wooden door to Mother's chamber shot open, forcing it to slam against the stone walls. "Who dares enter without knocking?" Mother lashed out.

"I am sorry. But this is urgent," the soldier in all black panted.

Mother took her hands off Bertly and squared up with her guard. "Nothing can be—"

"I know you can have my head for interrupting but, ma'am, please," the mammoth-blood warrior asserted. "This is urgent."

The woman's demeanor flipped. "You have only interrupted me like this one other time, Roman." Mother scrambled toward Roman. Bertly could see she tried to maintain her elegance; however, he couldn't help but notice she increased the pace of her strides.

The Winter Wizard did his best to eavesdrop. He could hear their muffled whispers, but he couldn't make out the distinct subject of their conversation. Mother placed her hands over her mouth and turned away from her guard. She sauntered to the middle of the room and pulled the sheet from the covered figure, revealing a white crystal ball that looked as though it were created from the same material as Bertly's warblade.

Mother closed her eyes and ran her fingers over the white orb. The Winter Wizard was expecting it to glow or to emit a magical energy, but he felt and saw nothing change. She opened her eyes—the black pits of her pupils filled her entire eye sockets, giving off a dark and eerie look. The woman's eyes returned to normal after she took a desperate breath, as though she had been suffocating until that moment.

Mother took her hand from the ball and peered at the ebony-dressed soldier. "So, it has begun." She turned toward her liquor cabinet and grabbed a full bottle of wine, ignoring the glass that sat nearby, and took a sip.

"What is it?" Bertly raised his voice. "What's happening?" The wizard slammed his fists on the table. "I demand to know what's going on."

Mother snickered. "Do not forget where you are, young human. You are in no position to be making demands." Mother continued to sip her wine straight from the bottle. "Are you forgetting that your friends are still at my mercy?"

Bertly *had* forgotten. Ever since he had arrived in Mother's quarters, he had forgotten many things, including his feelings. No matter how hard he wanted to be mad, his hostility always subsided.

"Have another drink," the seductive woman insisted.

Bertly looked down at his glass of wine and swirled it around. *It's the wine.* "I think I've had enough for now. I am not used to drinking much." *What is in this wine?*

"I am sorry for Felix's actions," Mother said.

"Pardon?" Bertly challenged.

"He is my brother." Mother lounged back in her seat. "While his methods are...questionable, I cannot kick him to the curb. Not to mention, as long as he has that slave girl by his side, not too many people can actually tell him what to do."

"That's it?" Bertly hissed. "I'm supposed to forgive you?" He glared. "Just like that?"

"Your forgiveness means nothing to me. I always figured it was better to have Felix with us than against us. We don't have room for enemies down here." The woman reached to the side of her desk and grabbed Bertly's travel sack. "Here, take this, as well as the cloak."

Bertly opened his mouth to speak, but Mother gestured for him to keep his mouth shut. "I know you still have a lot of questions for me. But those are for another time."

"Please." Bertly placed his hands together. "Just one last question."

Mother snapped her fingers in a gesture that reminded Bertly too much of Felix for his liking, and her guard left the room. She motioned for the wizard to continue speaking.

"Your body language has changed, and your tone has shifted...what is it that has begun?"

"The second Blight." Mother looked down.

"You didn't need to look into a crystal ball to tell me that." Bertly shook his head. "I already know. And with all the Rotters your soldiers have been dealing with, I'm surprised you didn't know."

Mother inhaled and took her time before replying. "Bishop is marching through the Remnant Forest as we speak. He and his armies will be at Eplium before the next nightfall."

"What does this mean? What do we do?" Bertly tapped his foot and a flush crept over his face. "How many of them?"

"It is hard to estimate," Mother replied. "But it is safe to say the elves are in serious danger, and it is no shock that Bishop would attack Eplium first."

"Because it is closest to the Decomposite?" Bertly guessed.

"No, because Rotters can only come from elves. He is trying to grow his army when his numbers are strongest, and this is his best shot at wiping out the world's largest army while also increasing his." Mother pushed her bottle to the side. "This is how he took over the first time. He must be stopped. Here and now. We have a second chance at this."

The Winter Wizard felt nauseous. He had trained in combat his entire life, yet he had never dreamed of a war. "I thought we were all doomed anyway?"

"That was before you convinced me of who you truly are." Mother pushed Bertly's belongings across the table, inches from his body. "Cordelia's belongings call to you. I can't help but believe that you really are playing a bigger role in all of this."

Bertly hesitated to grab his items. "Why do you care about Pangea now?"

"I don't." The woman grabbed a bottle of wine and slid it inside Bertly's backpack. "But this may be our last chance at ending the Blight once and for all...and returning the Decomposite to what it once was." Mother grabbed the wizard by the arm and urged him in the direction of the exit. "I have sent my guard to retrieve your apprentice. He will be waiting for you downstairs."

"What about my other friends, the dwarves?" Bertly stressed. "I can't leave without them, I've known them almost half of my life."

"You still owe me one hundred fights, Master Bertly." Mother chuckled.

Bertly panicked; he couldn't think of a plan quick enough to convince Mother to change her mind.

"Consider this to be…leverage. To ensure you come back," she continued. "Now, if you take any longer, I will change my mind about the generosity I have shown you."

Bertly threw his knapsack over his shoulder and left her office. He couldn't help but feel wary, as though it were some sort of trap. The wizard paused after his first step out the door. "Wait, how will I get to Eplium on time?"

"Polly and your father are headed here at this very moment," Mother replied.

The Winter Wizard turned around. "They are?"

"Polly and Bear reached the Academy safely. They have told the Elders of what has happened, and the school is acting promptly. The school's teachers and master students are already on their way to Eplium. As for your ride, they are on the back of a gryphon and are nearly here." Mother bit her finger and frowned. The woman grunted and fell back into her throne. "Such a shame. You all really would have made excellent additions to the Zoo."

Bertly opened his mouth, but Mother cut him off before he could get any words out. "You speak too much, young wizard. It will be your downfall one day. Now go!" she shouted. "And don't forget, now that I have met you, I can see you whenever I like."

XXIII

Roman wedged himself between Roderick and Bertly, with a hand on each of their shoulders. They stood just on the outskirts of the village surrounding the colosseum. The Winter Wizard heard the chants of the crowd echo throughout the town.

"I can't stop thinking about Orin and Orîn," Roderick whimpered.

"Me neither," Bertly replied. "But I'm not sure our fate is any better."

"Where is your father?" Roman's deep voice rumbled as he spoke. A thick, overcast sky spread over the Decomposite so that not even the sun could poke through. "I thought gryphons were supposed to be the fastest creatures in Pangea."

Bertly glared in offense. "Gryphons aren't shippers."

"Maybe they should have sent one of those." The tone in the guard's voice didn't change.

Bertly grunted. "I can't tell if you're attempting to have a personality or if you're always this serious." The wizard squinted and could make out a small shadow growing larger in the distance—it crept in their direction.

"Unless it's a dragon, I assume this is your ride," Roman said monotonously.

"Ah, you are trying to be funny." Bertly gave the guard

a soft bump. "You aren't so bad, Roman. Maybe we are distant relatives after all."

Roman released Bertly's shoulder. "Why would you say that?"

"Mother didn't tell you?" Bertly flexed his arms. "Believe it or not, I come from mammoth blood, too."

"You don't say." Roman's voice almost projected in a higher pitch.

"Look." Roderick pointed. "It's them."

Clia pierced the clouds, flapping her wings as though she were being chased by a fleet of dragons. Bertly couldn't see Polly's face behind his father, but he knew she was there from her blond hair blowing in the wind. Clia landed on the ground far from gracefully. Her large talons dragged for several feet, ripping up the ground in her attempt to slow down. Before she came to a full stop, Edfrid leaped off her back and drew his war hammer. He gave a loud battle cry and charged straight for Roman.

"Wait." Bertly jumped in front of his father before he could swing his hammer. "They're letting us go."

"They're what?" Edfrid let the head of his hammer fall to the ground.

"They've released Roderick and me, and they're letting us go with you to Eplium," Bertly responded.

"They captured you, only to let you go?" Edfrid winced and tilted his head back. "How do you know about Eplium?"

Before the Winter Wizard could respond, a large creature tackled him to the ground. "Clia!" Bertly cheered as he spat feathers out of his mouth. "I missed you, girl. Staying out of trouble?"

Clia looked around, distracted and oblivious to the question.

"I'll take that as a no."

"Where are Devdan and the twins?" Polly circled

around Edfrid. Bertly could see that, by the look in his friend's eyes and the worry in her voice, she already knew the answer to her question.

"I'm sorry, Polly. But Devdan…" Although the Winter Wizard wanted to avoid it, he did his best to maintain eye contact. "Shortly after you left, they—"

"I prepared myself for that answer," Polly cut him off. "Part of me was hoping that in some reality, he found a way out. But after everything they did…" Polly's eyes watered, and Bertly saw she was struggling to hold back tears. "I didn't expect anything less. On the whole way home with Bear, I kept picturing over and over what they would do to him once I got away."

Bertly grabbed Polly's hand. "He saved our lives." He held her fist between his palms, fully encompassed but gentle, as though he'd caught a butterfly and was trying to keep it from flying away. "If it weren't for Dev, none of us would be here. Including the twins."

"They're safe?" Bertly heard a sense of joy lift the grief of Polly's tone.

"I am hesitant to use the word *safe*." Bertly gave a pitiful smile. "But they are alive, and we can still save them."

"We don't have much time," Edfrid urged. "We need to get to Eplium. We saw the Rotter army on our way here. They may arrive at the elven kingdom before we do."

"Get me out of here," Roderick cried as he attempted to mount Clia. The gryphon stared at the small elf struggling to climb up. Her feathers slipped between his fingers and his hands could hardly reach more than halfway up her body. "I've had it with this wretched place."

***

The flames from the candles turned to smoke as the last bits of wick became ash. The rising sun pierced the cracks of the cabin, filling it with light. The words continued to flow through Bertly's mind, but they struggled to appear on the paper. Using his quill felt like pushing a hefty stone, so he allowed it to drop to its side.

Bertly stood up and walked toward the front door of the room. "I think I am going to check on our little elf."

Bear grumbled in response, not bothering to move a muscle.

The wizard cracked open the door and peeked his head around the corner with caution. Bertly's apprentice sat on the deck, staring out into the open. "I don't think I could ever get used to this amazing view," Roderick muttered.

"You know, it's much prettier after the morning time." Bertly sat next to Roderick and looked over the thick rolling fog. "Every morning, a fog just like this spools over Stonebank. It's how the town looks so green despite it never raining there. The best part comes afterward, once the fog has cleared; it always smells like a thunderstorm has just passed." Bertly took a deep breath. "Ah, not yet. I was hoping I could take it in one last time before we left. Who knows when we will be back."

"Do you think I will ever return home?" Roderick asked.

"Yes, Roderick, I do." The Winter Wizard put his arm around his young apprentice. "And I will be the one to bring you back home myself because I have to meet the people who raised this ab-so-*lutely* ridiculous excuse for an elf." Bertly put Roderick in a headlock. "Now come back inside and help me finish this story. My hand is killing me."

"We both know there is a better chance of Bear writing that novel than you."

The master's jaw dropped, and his eyebrows narrowed.

Roderick continued, "Cast your writing spell and let's enjoy the view one last time. I actually quite enjoy the fog. We don't have it in Eplium."

Bertly smiled. "Sure."

***

"Let me get this straight," Edfrid asserted. "Cordelia didn't actually end the first Blight? She only...stalled it?" He tugged on his beard. "More or less meaning this is still the first Blight, not the start of the second one?"

"On a very technical level, yes, I suppose so," Bertly replied.

The air was clear and the clouds from the Decomposite were behind them. Bertly, his father, Polly, and Roderick flew on the back of Clia, with their eyes set on Eplium and the Rotter army. The Winter Wizard couldn't tell if she was tired or nervous about what waited for the group at their destination, but he could tell Clia was in no hurry. Her wings flapped and the wind blew against their faces, but Bertly had been on enough flights to know she was holding back.

"And to be clear, the elves, dwarves, and giants may have known this all along?" Edfrid asked.

"Considering the Academy chose to leave out several historical details regarding the Blight, and considering Bablanca, Eplium, and Eskos don't teach any of this, yes."

"What about Noskar?" Roderick followed up.

"We do not have an education system in Noskar, Roderick. It is up to one's parents to teach the children all they need to know." Bertly was amused by his father's and apprentice's questions; however, he couldn't take his eyes off the horizon—in search of Bishop's army.

"How do you know this Mother lady is telling the truth?" Edfrid grumbled. "She could be lying to you."

"It wouldn't make sense for her to let me go if she were lying. Not to mention, she told the truth about some things I already knew to be true." Bertly lost focus on the foreground. "I don't know how, but I knew she was being honest."

"And just so there is no confusion, are you or are you not the reincarnation of Cordelia?" Roderick smiled with apparent optimism.

"Not exactly, I just possess similar powers," Bertly explained. "But based on the stories, she seemed much more powerful than I ever will be."

"What about me?" Polly asked, her voice so quiet, she sounded reluctant to ask.

"Right." Bertly's voice grew louder and his posture perked up. "In fact, Mother even asked about you, Polly. When we are on land, you must try out my warblade and cloak. But wait, I almost forgot to ask you." The wizard twisted his body awkwardly so he could make eye contact with Polly. It hadn't been long, yet Bertly missed being around his blonde companion. "What did the Academy say when you got there?"

Polly looked confused. "It was peculiar, I expected them to be at least...surprised." She hesitated. "They knew exactly what to do, as though they already had a plan in motion. They didn't even care that some of the students died. The Elders dispersed and ran out of the room. Only my master stayed behind." Polly's tone shifted, and her temper built. "When I told Master Dova you were kidnapped, she knew exactly where to find you. So I called your father with Clia's whistle, and we came straight here. We originally had a plan to sneak in and break you out, but you were already waiting for us."

"Did they say what their plan was?" Bertly questioned.

Polly's head pointed down and she raised her eyebrows to look up. "The Elders left the room frantically, but...I snuck around afterward and eavesdropped."

"Attagirl, Polly," Edfrid hollered.

Bertly clapped. "I can see I'm finally rubbing off on you."

Polly giggled, and her cheeks turned red. "They said they were headed to Eplium. But they were worried. The giants never answered their original call, whatever that means, and the dwarves' army won't arrive in time—"

"Dwarves are rather slow travelers," Bertly interrupted.

"It is only going to be the elves and the masters of the Academy fighting this battle. They said Eplium has built a protective wall, except they think it could fall. They have another line of defense, but they didn't say what."

"How many masters does the Academy have? Certainly not many," Edfrid said with a frown.

"My best guess would be about five hundred in total. I doubt they will send all of them, if any at all." While the conversation was serious, Bertly couldn't help but feel happy. He'd missed his flights with Clia, and even more so, he'd missed being with his father. "You must consider, if a substantial number of masters were lost, the Academy could potentially shut down. Ending a generation of magicians."

"Should we be concerned about that?" Roderick shrieked. The small elf's hand wobbled as he pointed to the ground.

Bertly had let his guard down. A gray mass covered the surface of Pangea. With skinless horsemen scattered throughout, a Rotter army spanning the width of a city marched in unison toward Eplium. The Rotters were equipped with armor and bore weapons in hand. The Winter Wizard felt it again, the same agony he'd felt the last time he encountered a skinless horseman. Oddly, his companions didn't seem to experience the same life-extracting force he was.

"Which one do you suppose he is? Bishop?" Edfrid sounded more eager than afraid.

"Maybe that one?" Roderick cried. This time, Roderick pointed parallel to Clia. "How am I the only one noticing any of this?" The elf's voice trembled.

Casting its shadow over a score of Rotters hovered an eerie black dragon. It had holes in its wings and portions of scales missing from its body. Exposed flesh and black dripping blood oozed from the uncovered areas. Its spine poked through its skin, and resting between two vertebrae was its hooded rider. "Bishop." The word slipped from Bertly's lips. "What do you suppose he looks like?" Bertly could hardly tell given the Rotter leader was a few hundred yards away.

"Let's not stick around to find out!" Roderick yelled.

"I actually agree with the little elf this time," Edfrid said. The army spread wide enough that Rotters stood on the ground beneath them.

The creature turned and faced Bertly. Bishop locked onto him as though he'd known the wizard and his companions were flying by the entire time. The hood covered his face, forming nothing but a black shadow where his head would be. Bertly felt Clia's feathers grip him as she tore through the sky—he knew she had been holding back.

"Look, it's Eplium's Lost Tree!" Roderick shouted.

"Lost?" Bertly cracked. "Quite an ironic nickname for the largest tree in Pangea, wouldn't you say?"

Bertly's apprentice rolled his eyes. "It's a long story."

"This isn't good." Edfrid's normally sturdy voice had a

hint of concern behind it. "The Rotters are no more than a few hours from Eplium."

Clia closed in on the elven city. A community of treehouses rested high above a grassy floor. It was intertwined by rope and wooden bridges, along with a canopy formed from tree branches. Protecting the city was a stone wall—built with more focus on its width than height. The gray, calloused wall added a feeling of gloom to the naturally beautiful city. Nestled in the center shined the golden bark of the Lost Tree—a natural topiary with branches that reached for the clouds and spanned wider than a castle.

"You know, they say every leaf can grow into its own tree," Roderick didn't hesitate to share.

Bertly chuckled. For the first time, he actually enjoyed his apprentice's mistimed optimism. "I almost forgot this is your home, Roderick. I really wish we could be visiting on better terms."

"Me too, sir." Bertly's apprentice looked back at the Rotter horde. "Maybe after the battle, we can visit my parents."

Bertly lifted an eyebrow. "To think, there are two elves responsible for this degenerate."

"Roderick, where should I land Clia?" Edfrid asked.

"Uh, the Elders and the king are most likely at the Throne Hall. That is where all the important meetings are held. It's at the top of the City's Tree," Roderick replied.

Openings in the bark exposed the inner workings of the grand tree—and it appeared to be hollow. There were several floors and stories, each with distinct communities, ranging from living quarters and dining areas to elves at card tables and soldiers preparing for battle. Thousands of elves hustled about inside the tree, all seeming to have a task at hand or no worry in the world.

"I don't think the citizens know what's coming," Edfrid stated.

"Neither do I," said Bertly tightly. "Maybe it's best not to cause a citywide panic."

Bertly's father snarled and dismissed his comment. "They could have evacuated somewhere. Kept the citizens safe from all of this."

"There isn't anywhere to go," Roderick answered. "After thousands of years without war, we assumed we wouldn't need the backup castle anymore and turned it into high-end living."

"Is that not the entire point of a backup? For when you need something that you aren't expecting?" Before anyone could answer Bertly's question, Clia tilted back and zoomed vertically into the air, scaling the Lost Tree. The Winter Wizard heard the screams and hollers of the excited elves; he had almost forgotten how rare a gryphon was for most to see.

"How tall is this stupid tree?" Clia soared so high the air felt thinner. "Do they normally use stairs to get to the top?" Bertly yelled.

"No," Roderick answered with his eyes shut and his hands squeezing onto Bertly. "There is a wooden lift inside."

"Like the one at Stonebank?" Edfrid said with a chuckle.

"Yes." Roderick dug his head into Bertly's back, avoiding the sights and sounds around him.

"I thought you would be used to flying by now, Roderick," Bertly joked.

The group hovered near the highest point of the canopy. Up close, the sun could be seen through the gaps in the leaves. At the top of the tree was a large carved-out opening spanning the entire width of the trunk. While there were other windows and spaces throughout the tree, this was the only area completely open. Inside were several tables, chairs, and guards. Centered in the middle and close to the edge was an awe-inspiring wooden throne. The carvings were so small and detailed Bertly couldn't make out what they depicted from afar.

"I don't think we should land in—" As Roderick began to shout, Clia blitzed her way through the tree opening. She took out half a dozen guards as her claws ground deep into the wooden floor. Despite grinding through most of the hall, the gryphon was able to gain control just before blasting through the wooden throne and the lady who sat on it.

A black-haired woman with lightly tanned skin remained in her chair without as much as a flinch. "That's the queen." Roderick's voice cracked.

Surrounding her were several of the Academy's Elders. Nearest to the queen was Master Dova. Accompanying them were several elves whom Bertly did not recognize. Their attire was decorative and appeared to be made of a type of silk material. The Winter Wizard presumed they were consultants to the queen. Surrounding the Elders and queen's consultants stood well-equipped guards. Each had a long bow on his back and a dagger attached to his hip.

"How large is the Rotter army?" the queen asked. "You must have passed the legion on your flight from the forbidden zone."

"The Decomposite," Master Dova added.

Bertly looked around, waiting for someone to make a comment about the shredded-up floor. "Two hundred thousand, give or take. If Bishop wanted, he could be here now; his dragon was the largest I have ever seen."

"About double our numbers…" The queen looked to one of her men and he walked off in a hurry. "You have seen many dragons, I presume?" Bertly couldn't tell if the elven queen was being sarcastic or if she was genuinely interested. "We have heard many greats tales of the Winter Wizard.

"I've seen a couple." Bertly smirked. The mention of dragons brought Dreki to mind, and Bertly wondered where he was. "So, do we have a plan?"

Master Quinric stepped forward. "You are in no place to be asking questions, vile human. It is your fault we are in this mess."

Edfrid leaped off Clia and slapped the head of his hammer into his open hand. "Talk to my boy like that one more time, pointy ears."

The guards went into battle stance and wrapped their fists around the handles of their daggers. The Elders broke into debate at once, and no one voice could be singled out.

"Silence." The queen stood up. "At this time, we do not have any answers as to what has caused this; all we know is there is an immediate threat on our doorstep. This is a discussion for another time." She cleared her throat and patted her chest as she rested back into her throne. "And yes, Master Bertly, we do have a plan."

XXIV

The inside of the tree smelled better than the smoke from a freshly extinguished candle. The wooden surface had a ringed pattern with thousands of lines all along the floor. The Winter Wizard could only assume it was a sign of how far back the Lost Tree dated—if it was anything like the trees back in Noskar.

A handful of guards remained, and those with minor governmental roles cleared the room. The Elders, along with the queen and her few close advisors, were all that remained—they stood circled around Bertly and his companions.

"I forgot to introduce myself." The woman stood up and looked out over her kingdom. "I am Queen Madeline. It is a pleasure to finally make your acquaintance. The Academy has been stowing you away for quite some time."

Bertly kissed the top of her hand and she proceeded to sit back in her throne.

"We thought it was for the best our young master went through schooling the same as any other student," Master Dova chipped in.

"And who might 'we' be?" Bertly mocked with air quotations. "It doesn't appear that even a dozen of you could join us today."

"The important advisors are here," Dova replied. "We cannot risk putting the Academy in jeopardy at this time."

"If we lose this battle, then it isn't going to matter," Bertly snapped. "The next battle could be *at the Academy* for all we know."

Queen Madeline made a dismissive gesture. "I didn't mean for it to become a topic of discussion. We have more urgent matters to examine."

"Before we get started," Bertly said, "I have one quick question."

"Is he serious?" Master Quinric whined.

Dova quickly put her hand across Quinric's chest. The body language of the Elders appeared off. They all seemed as though they had something to say but were too afraid to speak up.

Bertly could see Queen Madeline restrain a grin. He got the impression she might like him. "What is your question, Master Bertly?" the queen asked.

Bertly tightened the straps around his gloves. "Where is my bear?"

Queen Madeline raised her chin. "Pardon?"

Bertly's face was blank. "I have a pet bear the size of a carriage. Where is she?"

The Elders gasped when the human's tone turned sarcastic.

Master Dova took a few steps toward Bertly. "There was an attempt to bring her up here, but there was a slight altercation."

Master Quinric pushed past Master Dova and pointed a finger in Bertly's face. "Your stupid animal put four soldiers in the hospital because she was *too scared* to walk inside the Lost Tree."

"If she didn't want to do it, then why were you trying to force her?" Bertly slapped Quinric's finger out of his face. The Elders gasped.

"Guards." The queen gripped the arms of her throne. "Please show Master Quinric out. He doesn't seem to know his place."

A squadron of guards marched across the hall and grabbed Quinric by the arms. The old master yelled as he was dragged out of the throne hall. His limbs flailed in retaliation, but his resistance had little to no effect on the guards.

Bertly's eyes shot open, and it took everything in his power not to smile.

An advisor approached the queen and whispered into her ear. Madeline spoke: "Your bear, along with your friend's dragon, are both safe and happy, Master Bertly." The advisor leaned over again and continued to speak quietly into the queen's ear. "Speaking of which, we cannot delay any longer; we must discuss the plan. You can both reunite with your pets when our meeting is over."

Bertly and his confidants gestured that they understood.

The queen continued, "In preparation, we have built a wall around the city. Not as glamorous as we would normally construct, but we did not have the luxury of time on our side. We have also built a series of tunnels underneath the battlefield. We have lined the channels with two chemical compounds that will detonate when combined with each other and a source of heat. Any master from the Academy or well-trained wizard could perform the incantation."

"When did you have the time to construct all of this?" Edfrid asked.

Queen Madeline looked first at the Winter Wizard and then his companions. "Well…we have had almost a year to prepare, thanks to Master Bertly and Master Alestar."

Bertly looked back at Polly and his father. Confusion

transformed their faces—they were the only two in the room who didn't know about Bertly and his master's trip to the Decomposite.

"Their sacrifices will be remembered," the queen carried on. "We will hold off the Rotter forces until the majority of the army has marched onto the front line. We will then ignite the chemical compound beneath the battlegrounds, setting the entire Rotter army on fire. The explosion will start in the back and move its way to the wall. This will allow time for our remaining soldiers to retreat. As soon as the flames clear, our soldiers will rally back out and clear the grounds, just to be sure we don't leave any of them alive." Queen Madeline tucked a lock of hair behind her ear and leaned back in her wooden throne.

A whiff of deteriorating flesh traveled through the air. While it was faint, the air that carried the smell was thick.

"They're getting close," an Elder cried.

The queen signaled to one of her advisors.

"Initiate battle preparations!" the advisor shouted. All but a few of the remaining guards and commanders left the room.

A loud horn sounded, sending a vibration rippling throughout the city. Bertly shuffled around and looked out from the Lost Tree. The Rotters were in near-striking distance. They were close enough to notice a clear distinction between each dead elf. A line of Eplium's soldiers, suited in vibrant green armor, marched out onto the battlefield and halted not far beyond the stone wall.

"I support the well-thought-out plan and all." Bertly turned back around and faced Queen Madeline. "But what about Bishop? Surely you have noticed the half-dead lizard floating in the sky."

"Our scouts spotted him as soon as we saw his army. Unfortunately, at this time we do not have a plan for him.

Our goal is to merely win the battle," the queen explained. "We didn't have an answer for him three thousand years ago, and we don't have one today. We are hoping with the destruction of his army, he will retreat, and it can buy us some time."

"A plan running on hope. With our best-case scenario being the enemy decides to cut his losses...That's reassuring." Bertly looked back out over the approaching army. They paraded in a line several times thicker than the army defending Eplium. Dispersed across the entire legion were random drummers, with no tune or rhythm to their drumming—sounds of loud bangs and thuds rebounded from all directions.

"Why are they smacking the drums sporadically like that?" Roderick asked.

"They are trying to break down our communications on the battlefield," the queen replied. "They are creating inconsistent noises loud enough that our soldiers can't shout. They most likely can only talk to those nearest to them."

"This is why all of our soldiers are trained in nonverbal communication," Edfrid cut in.

The queen gave no reply.

As the Rotters encompassed the entire battlefield, their numbers seemed even greater than when Bertly had flown over them earlier. Bishop hovered above his minions from the back line, standing on the saddle of his creature. His dragon's wings flapped only as often as they needed to, and his eyes never broke focus—they were glued to the Lost Tree. The Rotters' skin seemed to be all that was decomposing; the approaching army strutted with strength, stomping every other step, sending vibrations throughout the city. They halted within arm's reach of Eplium's defenders.

It was so silent a leaf could be heard dropping from

within the Lost Tree. Everyone waited for Bishop's next move.

Bertly broke the silence. "So, when exactly are we getting our big explosion?"

Master Dova cleared her throat. "Please mind your attitude, young Master." In the classroom Dova was demanding, but here she was walking on eggshells. "Let the queen handle this. We are not the ones with the army." Bertly's teacher sounded worried to offend him. She leaned in close enough for only him to hear. "You must be mindful of the feelings at stake. Most of the people in this room believe they are losing their life today."

"How do you think they feel?" Bertly never looked to his teacher but focused on the soldiers confronting Bishop's army.

A blown horn expelled an amplified screech and the Rotters' war chant commenced. They thrashed their swords across their steel armor and yelled simultaneously, "*Rah!*" They stomped with their spiked boots and kept screaming, "*Rah!*" Another horn sounded, and the dead in the front line unhinged their personal shields then snapped them all together, forming a solid wall. A third horn sounded, and the back line drew their bows and loaded them with arrows.

"Are you sure there isn't supposed to be an explosion right now?" Bertly blurted.

"He's right." Madeline briskly stood up. "Something's wrong." She rushed to the edge of the tree trunk and looked to the right of the forefront. "The spell should have been initiated by now."

An advisor to the queen handed her a telescope. Madeline pressed her eye near the lens; she let it drop off the ledge and backed up into her throne. "They've overtaken the outpost," she said in a voice that was numb with fear. "They probably took it before they marched out here." She flopped into her seat. "We lost before the battle ever started."

Roderick nudged his master's hip. "Sir, what outpost?"

"Madam, what outpost exactly?" Bertly repeated.

The queen's advisor answered for her. "The one where the explosion was supposed to be ignited."

"Ah, that one," the wizard replied. "That is an important one."

Bishop's dragon slowly moved toward the Lost Tree. A wave of arrows filled the sky, casting a shadow over the whole of Eplium's army. The arrows hit their peak then poured like water over a cliff. The arrowheads pierced the shields and leather armor of the living elves. A substantial number of Eplium's forces were executed on the spot, and the Rotter legion filed forward.

Bertly faced Edfrid, Polly, and Roderick. He locked eyes with his father. The Winter Wizard then glanced at Polly, who was already slipping on her glove.

"Oh no," Roderick screamed. "No, no, no, no, no." Bertly's apprentice shook his head furiously. "No way. No. Stop it." He took a deep breath. "No."

"Two things." Bertly smiled and placed his hand over Queen Madeline's—her hands were not as soft as Bertly would have guessed. "First, I will need a guard to show me to my bear. And second, where exactly is this outpost?"

"Cordelia really has sent you to save us all." The queen wiped a tear and knocked against the side of her wooden throne. A well-fit elf hustled to her side. His hair looked soft and coiled, but also dense enough to hold firmly on its own. "This is Ayce."

"At your service." The elf bowed.

"He is our top archer and knows the kingdom better than I," Madeline carried on. "He will show you to the outpost. I will have another escort your pet to meet with you. Bertly, when you get—"

The wizard cut her off. "Combine the two chemicals; heat them up. I got it."

"Please don't forget what you are up against." Queen Madeline drew in a long breath. "Sometimes being afraid is what keeps you alive."

"I'm the only one here who has already fought these things. I know what I'm up against." Bertly tightened his ponytail and pushed down on the loose hairs that escaped. "Are you all ready?"

"No!" Roderick cried.

"I'm not going with you, Bertly." Polly stood with her feet together and back straight. Her chin was up, and she did her best to maintain eye contact. Bertly noticed she was trying to be firm, but the slight tremble in her lower lip revealed her terror.

Bertly approached his friend. "Polly, I promise, I will never let anything happen to you, or anyone else, ever again."

"I know." Polly placed her hand on Bertly's cheek. "But I don't need your protecting. If anything, I think you might need mine," she teased.

"It's okay, Polly," Roderick interjected. "You can stay here with me. There is no shame in that."

"I'm not staying here, Roderick," Polly clarified. "Bishop is heading here right now, and someone needs to slow him down. If he gets past the wall and into the city, it won't matter what we do to his army."

"I never thought I would say this, but I think I would rather go with my master." Roderick's voice trembled.

Bertly tilted his head. "I don't understand. How do you plan on fighting him?"

Clia squawked. Polly walked to the feathery beast. "I saw a weakness in his dragon. It has exposed openings all throughout his body. On the inside, it looks to be the same as every other living creature." Clia bent over for Polly to mount her. "I don't have time to debate this with you."

"Wait, Polly." Bertly rushed over. "Before you go, take this. It's Cordelia's cloak—hopefully it can help."

Recognition dawned on Polly's face. "It's dragon scales, which means it's fireproof!" Her eyes glistened. "Bertly, are you sure?"

"Yes, please take it." When the Winter Wizard had slipped off his cloak, the red scales lost their coloring and turned back to gray. "You are most likely the strongest witch or wizard in all of Pangea. And we are the only two red-eyed humans since Cordelia. We need to work together on this."

Polly accepted Bertly's offer and slipped the scaled cloak around her shoulders. They waited, yet the cloak remained gray. "Am I doing it wrong?" Polly asked.

"Huh." Bertly scratched behind his ear.

"Son," Edfrid interposed, "try it on again."

Polly handed the cloak to the Winter Wizard and he slung it on once again. It turned red. "Try this." Bertly grabbed the handle of his warblade and handed it over. The blade extended upon his touch, and the elven guards lunged forward. "Oh, calm your leaves," Bertly taunted.

Polly accepted the weapon; however, right when Bertly let go, the blade retracted.

"I don't think Cordelia's belongings call to Polly," Edfrid followed up. "I think they're only meant for you, Bertly."

"But how is that so?" Polly's sounded irritated, an emotion Bertly never heard coming from the soft-spoken human. "We are both humans, both with red eyes. I don't understand the difference."

"Sir, please excuse me. I do not mean to speak out of

line," Ayce intruded. "But we must head to the outpost promptly. The longer we wait, the more enemies will come between us and the outpost."

"I am afraid my soldier is right. This is a matter to be settled another time." Madeline gave a nonverbal cue to one of her guards, and they quickly left the room. "My guard is retrieving Polly a set of light armor. She will be ready to engage Bishop soon, but for now, Bertly, you must go."

"You heard the queen." Edfrid grabbed Roderick by his arms and heaved him over his shoulder. "Let's go make a mess."

Bertly felt a small hand on his shoulder. He turned, and Polly stood close, with her chest nearly pressed against him. "I've spent nearly every day with you for the last seven years, Bertly of Stonebank. I don't know what I would do without you anymore. I think I know you better than myself." Polly brushed her fingers through the Winter Wizard's long and dark hair. "I know you'd never let anything happen to me. That's why I'm not afraid to face Bishop. I know that no matter what happens, you're going to come rushing in to save the day."

Bertly couldn't respond as a rush of emotions flooded his body. He suddenly couldn't fathom the thought of letting Polly face Bishop alone. Feelings of self-doubt ate at him; losing his best friend meant more than losing the war.

"Bertly!" Edfrid shouted. "We need to go."

Bertly's thoughts and actions were out of sync; what he felt and could speak were two different things. "Polly." One word was all he could muster.

"Go," Polly urged. "You need to save the world."

"I know I haven't been the easiest person to get along with, but I'm glad you never gave up on me. You could have been friends with anyone at the Academy, yet you stuck with me. You're better than me in nearly every way, Polly. I'm sorry I was too arrogant to ever see it before." The wizard's legs moved without his mind thinking, and without a chance to see Polly's reaction, he rushed off toward his father. Roderick found his own two feet and followed in pursuit.

***

"There is a secret entrance and exit to the city. We should be able to circle around the Rotters without being detected. As long as they haven't broken past the front line, of course." Ayce's tone and demeanor were confident. His voice never cracked or trembled, and his eyes always made contact. "I suspect the outpost will have at least one surprise for us. Stay on your toes."

Ayce was leading Bertly, Edfrid, and Roderick through a secret passage under the city. The only light source showing inside the passageways was Bertly's lightus spell. The tunnels were foul, cold, and infested with elf mice. Their pointed ears were typically cute enough to make up for their long naked tails, but having them run up his leg every other step made Bertly reconsider his love for them.

"When I thought about visiting Eplium, this isn't what I had in mind," Bertly groaned.

"Have you considered getting some kokos?" Edfrid asked. "I haven't seen a single rat at my house since I adopted Oats."

"They're actually mice," Roderick corrected.

Edfrid rolled his eyes. "Is there a difference?"

"Yes," Ayce and Roderick both quickly reacted.

Bertly put his hands together. "Please tell me that light up there is our exit." For the first time since entering, sunlight peeked through the inside of the stone tunnels.

"Today is your lucky day, Master Bertly," Ayce replied.

Bertly smirked. "I am not sure I would call it that, but I appreciate the optimism."

"Sir, what can we expect to find beyond those walls?" Roderick asked, his face pale and voice shaky.

"Nothing worse than the Decomposite," Bertly reassured him. Though he guessed it probably wasn't all that reassuring.

An outline shaped into a perfect circle was carved into the side of the stone underpasses. If light hadn't been peeping through, Bertly would never have guessed there were any markings on the normally smooth surface. Ayce pushed against the circular door, and the wall shoved outward. The clunk of small rocks hitting the floor echoed throughout the passageways as the stone door and wall ground against one another. When the seal between the entrance and wall broke, noises from the battle cascaded in.

Standing outside the hidden entrance, waiting, was Bertly's furry friend. "Bear!" he shouted.

She let out a loud growl and pranced toward him.

The Winter Wizard leaped, dove straight into the fuzzy animal, and squeezed her tight. "Soul-bonding is something else, Bear. I haven't felt whole since we separated."

She gave a soft snarl in agreement.

"The outpost is just beyond those trees." Ayce had to raise his voice to talk over the metal clanging and soldiers yelling. He seemed indifferent toward Bertly and Bear's reunion. The battle cries and anguished screams overpowered all other sounds. "Bertly, you go first. I will cover the four of you as you cross the field." The strong elf pulled an arrow from his quiver and nocked his bow quicker than most could draw a dagger. "Be ready. They are most likely waiting for our reinforcements to arrive. Surely, they know we are going to try to set off the explosion at all costs. I don't expect there to be many of them. I doubt they want to draw attention to the fact that they overtook the outpost. I do believe that means the soldiers they do have will be much stronger than normal." Ayce drew his bow and stepped back. "I will be right behind you."

Between the group and the next set of trees was an open area with a clear view of the battlefield. Edfrid took charge and sprinted across the field, and Bear followed close behind. Before Roderick had a chance to hesitate, Bertly grabbed him by the back of his belt loop and charged ahead. Roderick bounced up and down, hunched forward as his feet hung just above the ground. Bertly examined the massacre that was taking place as he caught up with his father and Bear, hoping no additional Rotters had caught sight of where they were headed. Out of the corner of his eye, something in the sky grabbed Bertly's attention.

Polly and Clia were closing in on Bishop. Bertly froze. He wished he had taken Clia's whistle back so he could call her to him now. He couldn't help but wonder if he was doing the right thing. Maybe he should have been with Polly; surely his father and Ayce could have escorted another wizard.

Bear stood on the other side of the field and let out a monstrous roar, one that Bertly needed to—but hoped the Rotters did not—hear. Bertly shook his head and ran toward the forest across the way. He looked over his shoulder to see if Ayce needed help crossing the field. To his surprise, the elf was no more than a handful of paces behind them. Ayce moved at a stunning speed. The Winter Wizard dropped his apprentice onto his own feet and drew his sword. Cordelia's blade burst out, appearing more exuberant than ever before. Bertly wondered if perhaps Cordelia's dragon cloak and the warblade working in tandem strengthened the abilities of both items.

"It is right there, in that small cottage," Ayce informed him.

"You built a headquarters inside that garbage?" Bertly smacked his hand against his forehead. Just across from him and his escorts was a small shack. The wooden planks holding it together were filled with cracks and holes—more of the roof was missing than intact.

"We built it underground. The cottage is a diversion," Ayce replied. "I'm surprised there aren't any Rotters outside. Based on Queen Madeline's reaction, it appeared they were swarming the place. Or maybe she noticed none of our guards were left." The elf crouched down and proceeded to approach the cottage. There wasn't a Rotter in sight. The group reached the front door.

"Let me take the lead." The warden of Stonebank held his war hammer above his head and kicked down the wooden door. His powerful thrust took out the door and half of the wall to which it was attached. Inside, the room was nothing but dust, cobwebs, and an old rug laid out in the center of the floor.

Ayce walked over to the rug and pulled the corner, folding it over onto itself. Underneath was a latch, which the elf lifted, exposing a ladder leading into a dark hole. "Humans first." He grinned.

"I don't think you are going to fit down this one, Bear." Bertly nuzzled his companion on the snout. "I hate to leave you behind so soon, but I will be right back."

Bear stood over the hole.

"I swear I will be right back. After this, the battle is far from over. I need you still, but for right now, I need you to wait here." Bertly didn't have time to explain Eplium's plan to his spirit animal, nor would she have understood

him if he did. Fortunately, she did understand his heart
and feelings.

Bear stepped to the side, and the Winter Wizard
climbed down the ladder and into the dark pit. As he
neared the bottom, the pit became brighter and brighter.
The tunnels were well lit and filled with life. Alchemy
stations and workbenches were wedged in every open
corner. Shelving units were filled with elixirs and
ingredients. Books were piled high on the corners of all
the desks and study tables. The Winter Wizard could only
imagine the information held within each one. Buckets on
the ground were filled with colorful runes, crystals Bertly
knew to be rare and valuable.

"Sir, what kind of potions and enchanted items could
we create in here?" Roderick asked. His eyes were wide
with amazement.

"You wizards and your magic," Edfrid mocked.

"Maybe the queen will let you play down here after the
battle," Ayce hollered from down the hall. "Let's go. The
incantation room is at the end of this corridor."

Bertly, his father, and his apprentice followed the elf.
Edfrid walked next to his son and whispered, "Don't you
find it rather suspicious that no one is down here?
Considering the explosion never went off, you'd think
there would be signs of a battle."

The Winter Wizard and his father rounded the corner
and entered the room Ayce was calling them from. "You
mean like those dead bodies." Bertly covered his mouth
and nose. Several bloody corpses were stacked in a pile
and covered in some sort of liquid. Stab wounds and
arrows filled their dismembered bodies. Bertly would
have been surprised if even the deceased's loved ones
could've identified their bodies. The elves were
indistinguishable from one another due to the amount of
skin that had been slashed and cut from them.

Ayce stood in front of the bodies, silent. "Just over there are the chemicals." The confident elf's voice shook. His bow touched the ground and his shoulders drooped. The brave elf looked no more courageous than Roderick.

"Stay here, Roderick, and keep watch at the back door. Make sure we aren't about to get trapped in here," Bertly commanded.

"Understood, sir."

Edfrid and his son paced around the pile of carcasses with caution. They tiptoed with their weapons drawn and ready to strike. At the end of the room was a tall silhouette standing in front of a half pipe filled with liquid. The piping spread in several directions, and Bertly couldn't tell exactly where each pipe headed, as they all eventually disappeared into the walls.

The silhouette moaned and growled. The dark outline had broad shoulders and thick, muscular arms. The creature stood at least two heads taller than the wizard. It stepped into the light. The man had dark, frizzy hair and its jaw was well defined. Its chest and stomach had scars covering the entire surface, some so deep it looked as though full chunks of flesh were missing. The beast took another step forward. Bertly looked deeply into its eyes and gasped aloud.

It was Alestar.

XXV

It might have been Alestar's frame, though Bertly couldn't recognize the soul behind the eyes. A piece of the young wizard felt hollow just looking at his lifeless master. "What have they done to you?" Bertly cried.

"Who is this?" Edfrid probed. Roderick and Ayce remained still as they watched the scene unfold.

"My master, or at least it used to be." A sudden chill swept through Bertly's body. "I saw him die." He felt dizzy, as though he'd stood up too quick.

"Bertly, I need you with me right now." Edfrid stepped in front of his son. "Tell me how to defeat him."

"We can't." Bertly dropped his warblade and pressed his hands into his eyes until all he saw were sparkles and random colors. "I've moved past this. He's supposed to be dead."

Edfrid put up his guard and prepared to strike. "Bertly, if you care about your master, then he needs you right now. You need to end this. Free him."

The Winter Wizard's skin turned clammy, but he knew what he had to do. He tightened his fists and pulled the oxygen from around Alestar. Bertly's master stood uninterrupted. The beast leaned forward and let out a debilitating shriek. This was confirmation—the Rotters were, in fact, more than decomposing, but actually dead, for they did not need air to live.

Alestar reached out, and Bertly felt something grab ahold of him from the inside, though nothing physical touched him. His master waved his arm, and Bertly flew through the air as though he were being pulled by a fishing line. When his master swung up, Bertly flew up. When he swayed to the right, Bertly's body unwillingly hurled to the right. Alestar smashed Bertly's back into the ceiling, then his face and chest into the ground.

An arrow penetrated the dead giant's skull, then another rammed through his heart. Bertly peered over as Ayce loaded another arrow. Alestar roared; the elf's attacks seemed to have made him angrier more than they caused him any harm.

Edfrid charged forward and connected his war hammer to the side of Alestar's head, snapping the giant's neck and spinning his head around. The giant Rotter dropped to the ground, and the crack of his neck echoed through the halls.

The Winter Wizard lay on the ground as blood dripped from a cut above his eyebrow.

"Are you okay?" his father asked.

"Yes, I'm fine." Bertly picked himself up and grabbed his warblade. "I wish he had taught me that one."

Alestar rolled over onto his back and lifted his shoulders off the ground. To Bertly and Edfrid's collective horror, the creature grabbed his own head and twisted his broken neck, snapping it back into place. He stood up.

"I'll just have to knock his head clean off this time." Edfrid charged for Alestar.

"No, wait!" Bertly wailed.

Alestar reached for his side and pulled out a knife. With his free hand, the giant bent his arm and aimed the knife. Edfrid paused. Alestar threw his dagger straight into Edfrid. As the knife drove into his father's sternum, the warden's war hammer fell onto the ground, and Edfrid dropped to his knees.

Every feeling but hatred became foreign to Bertly. An anger consumed him that he had never conceived possible. His soul overflowed with rage. The stones and gravel on the ground levitated. Bertly imagined Alestar's arms and legs snapping in a dozen different places. And they did. He pictured Alestar's head twisting around in circles until it tore off his shoulders. And it happened. The giant's limp body tumbled to the floor, and his head rolled to Bertly's feet.

The Winter Wizard felt as though he had just woken up. His anger had subsided, but delirium was present. He didn't remember *trying* to do anything; it had all simply happened. Bertly and Ayce rushed to Edfrid's aid. Bertly ran in front of his father and crouched next to him. Edfrid's head drooped so that his chin touched his chest.

"Please, I can't lose you yet." Bertly rested his forehead against his father.

Edfrid coughed. "Do you really think one measly eating utensil can take me out?" The mammoth-blooded human rose to his feet. "I am the warden of Stonebank, the protector of Noskar." He ripped the dagger from his chest. "It'll take a lot more than that." He paused and tossed the knife. It clattered as it hit the floor. "Before I stop fighting."

"You aren't going to like this," Bertly said. He then placed his hand against the gash in Edfrid's chest and used his fire spell, cauterizing the wound. Edfrid clenched his jaw. The young wizard wrapped his arms around his father. "Please don't try to be a hero next time."

Edfrid hugged his son. "I can't make any promises."

After the shock of nearly losing his father had faded, the pain of another tragedy settled in. Bertly laid to rest the master he thought he'd lost nearly a year ago. The misery the human thought he had forgotten returned. Alestar had taught Bertly everything he knew. If it were not for him, Bertly might never have lived up to the reputation of the Winter Wizard. Bertly knew Alestar wouldn't want him to be burdened with his loss, but to instead pass along his master's legacy.

Roderick walked next to his master. "Sir, I know I am not one for good timing, but you should probably cast that spell."

Bertly acknowledged that his apprentice was correct. The wizard approached the pipes full of liquid and placed his hands inside the chemicals. He used a magic similar to enchanting in order to combine the elements. The two distinct substances molded into a single color. Bertly placed his hand under the pipe and ignited a fire spell.

A quiet thud followed by a soft tremor filled the room. Every few seconds another thud sounded off, followed by a stronger vibration. Rocks and dirt rained from the ceiling. Soon, the throbs and pulses became like earthquakes. Bertly realized the enchantment had worked and the detonations had commenced. He exhaled in relief.

"We should get out of here before we become rubble," Ayce asserted. The agile elf sprinted out the door and ran in the direction they had come from. No one hesitated to follow. As Bertly ran through the tunnels, the walls started to crack and cave in. The group made it up the ladder and back into the cottage—the passageways had remained intact just long enough.

Waiting inside the wooden shack with a look of angst was the wizard's furry companion. Bear's eyes held a touch of concern, or sadness, as though she knew something dreadful had just occurred.

Feelings of wrath sank and lodged themselves deep

within Bertly's heart once again. What had happened to Alestar was only the start. Bertly was remembering now that they had no clue what Bishop's potential was. Even if they won this one battle, if Bishop survived again, the Blight would not be over. The elves of Eplium would not be the only creatures in danger of his wrath; the whole world would be at risk.

"Clia!" Bertly's body stopped working and his heart stopped beating. "I just killed her."

The group looked puzzled. "Sir?" Roderick voiced.

"I should have known Alestar was still alive. Don't you remember Master Thel's teachings." Bertly was short of breath, he sounded as though he had just come back from a long run. "The fate of the bonder is the same as the bonded. If Master Alestar was actually killed all that time ago, then Clia would have died too."

"But, sir, how could we have known," Roderick replied. "We just learned of Master Alestar's death."

"I should have known. I am going to end this," the Winter Wizard said fiercely, clenching his fists. Without Bertly uttering a word of command, Bear shuffled over and bent down for the wizard to climb aboard. Bertly saddled up, grabbing two handfuls of fur and squeezing tightly with his legs.

"Sir, what are you doing?" Roderick questioned.

Bertly's cloak emitted a slight glow. "What Cordelia couldn't do three thousand years ago."

"We should wait to see if he retreats, sir. Eplium should be sending its second wave of soldiers right now to clear the battlefield," Ayce said in a hurry. "I advise we stick to the plan."

"The plan has changed." With no exchange made, Bear read Bertly's mind and darted for the open field. The Winter Wizard glared into the open field before them, holding on tight.

Bertly could hear Roderick yell to his father as he took off. "Aren't you going to stop him?"

"How?" Edfrid responded. "He could take all three of us."

Bear dashed across the open field, ripping apart the grass with every step she took. She leaped with every jolt, digging her front paws into the ground and propelling herself forward. Bear could have given a Bablancan cheetah a run for its money.

They joined the heaps of Eplium soldiers spilling through the few openings of the stone wall. The fighters rushed, headstrong, into the devastation—weapons in hand.

Smoke billows rose from the ground and cast a black cloud over the city. The dark haze made it dim outside, although it was the time just before sunset, when there was light enough to see by, but it was dark enough to head in for the night. The air smelled foul from the burning Rotters. Limbs and innards squished and cracked beneath Bear's hefty paws. The dusk made it difficult to assess the full damage of the situation. The chants and drums of the Rotters were silenced. Bertly couldn't see a moving, rotting elf anywhere. Some were still intact, but most were motionless and dismembered.

Bertly searched that murky sky for Clia and Polly. Despite the distorted atmosphere, the wizard managed to spot his companions skirmishing overhead. His friends were on the defensive, barrel rolling and dodging the fiery breath of Bishop's dragon. The firestorms that roared from the dragon's jaws were almost the size of its body— if one were to catch Bertly's friends, they would be done for. Clia appeared sluggish, she was slowly falling closer to the ground, and her feathers were shedding as though she was losing her winter coat. She didn't have much time left.

Bear advanced through the dismembered pieces of soldiers and Rotters.

"I'm down here!" the Winter Wizard blared at Bishop. "I'm right here. Come and get me!" The Rotter leader couldn't—or chose not to—hear him.

Bertly knew no spell that could dispatch anything into the air. But a long-pondered idea returned to him, and there was no better time than the present to test it. Bertly pulled back his elbow, the tip of his warblade pointed at Bishop, and, gripping the hilt so he wouldn't drop the weapon, he thrust the blade upward with all his strength. Cordelia's warblade jutted out and ripped through the air. With Bear charging and Bertly's sword extending, the pair closed in on their main threat. Cordelia's warblade was as long as fifty swords and it still grew, though the weight of it never shifted.

The dragon momentarily stopped breathing fire, and Bishop turned toward the Winter Wizard. The dragon discharged a sphere of fire that slid down Cordelia's blade. The dragon followed it in pursuit of Bertly. The young human had no time to act; the flame charged until it hit Bertly and it exploded on impact. The blast sent the wizard flying off Bear and tumbling into the cratered ground. Bertly's head throbbed in addition to the already-present pain from when Alestar bashed him into the ceiling.

Bertly got to his feet and watched as Bishop's dragon swiftly landed. The crash from the massive weight of the dragon rattled the demolished ground. Bertly was confused; the creature had moved so slowly while in flight. The dragon extended its long neck and came so close Bertly could feel its breath on his face. The beast opened its mouth and lunged forward. Bear wedged herself between Bertly and the creature. She ran her claws through the inside of its cheek, tearing a hole straight through. Bertly could see its teeth even with its mouth closed.

Bear's head was smaller, but her body was muscular and much heavier than the head and neck of the dragon. Bear leaped on top of the creature's skull and pressed it into the ground. She bit into the back of its neck and tore at it ravenously.

Bertly seized the distraction. His warblade was retracted, so he leaped forward again. Bishop was within striking distance—a distance he had managed to close before with Alestar in the Decomposite. The blade slashed through the chest of the Rotter king. Thoughts of the Winter Wizard finally ending the Blight once and for all flooded Bertly's mind as he twisted and turned the blade inside Bishop.

The dragon whipped its head back, shaking off Bear. Bertly turned his attention from Bishop. The furred beast rolled and tumbled onto her side. The dragon reared its head back again, a flame roiling in the back of its throat as it started to open its mouth. Bear quickly found her footing and pounced on the dragon's cranium, closing its jaw just as the flames were about to discharge. Fire shot out from the hole of the dragon's missing cheek.

Bertly regained his focus. Bishop had slid all the way down his warblade, with the mammoth ice still through his chest when his feet touched the ground. Even up close, Bertly could not see the details of Bishop's face through the shadow cast by his hood. The being stood nearly as tall as a giant and smelled like rust.

Bishop grabbed Bertly by the neck and squeezed until his airways were blocked. Cordelia's warblade retracted. Death's grip tightened, and Bertly felt fingernails pierce his skin.

Bertly's eyes lost focus. Everything surrounding Bishop blurred. The wizard tensed his body; a final adrenaline rush forced him to twist and jerk about, trying to jar himself loose from the grasp of the creature. Bertly's limbs grew tired of flailing as the wind left his lungs. His lids grew weighted, and the urge to close them overwhelmed him.

The nails scratched and dragged across his neck as Bertly's throat was suddenly freed from Bishop's grip. Bertly fell to the ground, gasping for breath in the horrid air. When his vision returned, he saw that Bear had tackled Bishop to the ground. Bear had Bishop's body clamped between her jaws, and she whipped him around like a chew toy. Clasped between her teeth, the overlord grabbed her nose and bottom teeth and pried them apart. He slipped her grip and punched her in the temple. Bertly wanted to charge them, to save his friend, but he still couldn't breathe. He was locked to the spot he'd been dropped in. Bishop repeatedly bashed the side of Bear's face until she hit the ground.

"Please." Bertly pushed the word out with the little breath he had. "Stop."

I'll stop when she gives me what I want. A raspy and deep voice infiltrated the Winter Wizard's head; its register was the lowest he'd ever heard.

Bishop raised his arm. The Rotter horde's armor shuffled, and objects on the ground shifted. The overlord walked to the young wizard and grabbed him by the top of his head. He lifted him off the ground and turned him around, forcing him to overlook the cataclysm. He looked on as the ground shook, though he wasn't aware of another explosion and couldn't fathom the cause. Pushing themselves off the ground were the intact Rotters. Across the entire combat zone, heads of dead elves sprang up like weeds.

The city horn sounded, and the soldiers again retreated from the battlefield. A substantial number of Rotters were defeated, but enough still stood to kill a majority of the remaining soldiers. The dead elves ignored the city guards and surrounded their master.

Bishop loosened his grip and let Bertly drop to the ground. Bertly scurried away on his hands and knees, his heart throbbing and bones shaking. He scuttled to his feet and faced the demon once again.

Rotters filled the space between him and Bishop. There weren't many yet, and he understood this was his brief opening before their numbers multiplied. Bertly grabbed a shield off the ground.

The Winter Wizard was going to fight to the death. He had already lost his master; he wasn't going to lose Polly.

He charged forward.

Shields collided with flesh as the crack of bone and wood echoed through the field. Bertly held steady as he absorbed the shock of a Rotter crashing into his wooden shield. The enemy fell as the impact of the blow sent sharp pain through Bertly's shoulder. There was an opening to the right, and Bertly gripped the hilt of his sword. With the point of the sword, he stabbed and connected with the rib cage of a Rotter, and the impact sprayed a mist of blood through the air. With his vision impaired, Bertly ripped the sword free, releasing a second gush of blood from the Rotter. The Rotter fell to the ground and dematerialized into dust. The wind washed away the powdered corpse.

It was the first time since the Eternal Cave that Bertly could feel the air move.

Bertly cleared his way through the dead elves and smiled; a moment of hope had presented itself. Talons latched onto the shoulders of Bishop and took him high into the air. Polly leaped off Clia. Bertly tried to run toward the gryphon, but she rocketed upward like a firework, carrying the Rotter king into the heavens. Her

wings flapped clunkily and her eyes were bloodshot red.
The coloring in her beak was turning gray, and her body
showed signs of cramping. As she flew into the sky, a trail
of feathers flew off and trailed behind her. Polly raced
and jumped on top of Bear while the ground rose and
encompassed them in a stonelike barrier.

Bishop was in the air, but there was still a dragon.
Bertly was terrified, but he understood he had to be
brave. The young wizard remembered that Alestar had
forced him to memorize the chemicals of the human
body. The wizard dug his feet into the ground as the
dragon flapped its wings and took flight. Bertly extracted
magnesium from the millions of exposed body parts and
countless pounds of innards. The Winter Wizard
obtained a larger amount than expected—the Rotters
must have contained higher levels than humans. Bertly
arranged the magnesium around Bishop, and he spread it
out enough that he could not see it. This was his chance
to also wipe out a number of Rotters.

Bishop squirmed and slashed at Clia as she carried him
high into the air. She could barely flap her wings, yet she
waved them relentlessly. Bertly squinted and saw the
demon conjuring some sort of white energy in one of his
hands. The white light extended and formed into the
shape of a spear.

The gryphon looked down, but Bishop was midstride
and had plunged the spear through her chest. Clia's body
plummeted from the skies, but she managed to keep her
grip around the demon overlord.

Bertly wanted to rush to Clia's aid, but Bishop's
dragon was building up a flame burst once more, and it
was aimed straight for the Winter Wizard. The moment
the dragon opened its mouth, the wizard frantically
forced the magnesium powder down the creature's throat,
and in an attempt to shield himself from the chemical

explosion, he wrapped Cordelia's cloak around his body. He could feel the force of the detonation but not the heat. Chunks of dragon intestines hurled in all directions, and scales fluttered down like snowflakes.

Bertly uncovered himself, eager to check on Bear. But looking him dead in the eyes, with nothing but the hunger of revenge, was Bishop's dragon. It was mostly skeletal, with some meat still left on the bones, but it appeared alive as ever. The Winter Wizard glanced at his furry counterpart. She was covered; Polly's stone shell appeared to have protected them from the blast.

Bishop walked back to the fight, seemingly untouched from his drop. As Bishop approached the Winter Wizard, Bertly could see strands of gray hair peeking out from under his hood. Surely no mortal could survive such a fall. Bertly panicked. How could he kill something that could bring the dead back to life?

The boney animal nose-dived and took a snap at Bertly. The wizard rolled to the side, but the dragon grabbed hold of his cloak. It tossed him into the air and snatched him like a seal catching a fish. Bertly's lower half was midway down the dragon's esophagus. He stabbed and sliced the dragon continuously, yet his warblade didn't leave a scratch on the dragon's bones. Its teeth dug into him, and Bertly could felt them sink beneath his skin. He imagined a dozen knives being rammed through his back and stomach.

The wizard felt the warmth of rivulets of his own blood as they ran down his body. Cordelia's warblade felt heavy, much too heavy to hold. Bertly dropped it on the ground. He was tired and ready to sleep. The Winter Wizard had never felt so alone and whole at the same time. He imagined his life was fading, although it wasn't how he had imagined it would feel. His physical body was dying, but his soul felt stronger and his mind healthier. A piece of him he never knew was missing had returned. *Maybe death isn't so bad*, he thought.

A beam of light broke through the black skies and shined down on the Winter Wizard. The warmth from the sun was comforting. A bolt of lightning tore downward through the air and impaled Bishop's dragon—snapping its neck in half. The skeleton's head detached from the monster's body and the wizard was freed from its grip. The creature tumbled to the ground. Regardless of being released, Bertly was much too weak to move.

A glowing figure stood between Bertly and Bishop. The Rotter king screeched, and his minions surrounded him. The glowing figure raised its arm to the sky, and hundreds of lightning strikes pierced the heads of the Rotter army. Bishop screeched once more, and the dead elves encompassed him. Bertly could not believe it, but the backs of the Rotters were to him—they were retreating.

The glowing faded. The figure turned and looked at Bertly. It was a woman with umber brown skin and braided black hair. She bent down in front of the young wizard and picked up his weapon. "I see you have found my warblade."

XXVI

Bertly was looking at the soul of the world. It was her. Before him stood Cordelia herself. He could hardly fathom how she could be alive and before him. Her energy radiated from her body, giving off a presence that Bertly could almost touch and feel. The young wizard had slayed and seen the undead before, but this, this was incomprehensible.

"B-but you d-died," Bertly stuttered. "Three thousand years ago." So many questions rushed through his mind he didn't know which to ask first.

Cordelia ignored Bertly's comment and placed her hand over his wounds and looked him over as he lay lifelessly on the ground. Her eyes were gentle but telling. The woman's frame was that of an experienced warrior. She was tall with a layer of muscle. Bertly assumed she was not only strong but could also move with great speed.

The wizard's cuts felt strange, as though a spider were stringing its web between the gashes in his body. Before long, his energy returned.

Cordelia helped Bertly to his feet and brushed the dirt off his shoulders. "Bertly, I do not mean to be rude, but I'd like my items back now." She reached out her hand and raised her eyebrows.

Bertly choked on his own spit. "Pardon?"

She slipped her warblade into its sheath. "My cloak?" Cordelia tightened the lapels on her armor and adjusted her boots. She seemed more interested in suiting up than conversing with Bertly.

The Winter Wizard's jaw dropped. Without a word he removed his cloak and handed it over. Cordelia shrugged into the cloak, and it shined much more radiantly on Cordelia than it ever had when he'd worn it. Bertly had never imagined meeting Pangea's savior in the flesh, and if he had pictured it, he certainly hadn't thought it would play out like this—even in his dreams.

Cordelia tied the cloak around herself and held the fur hood up to her nose and took a big whiff. She closed her eyes and looked up to the sky—Bertly could tell a rush of memories was coming back to her. "And my shield?" she asked abruptly.

"Shield?" The only shield Bertly had was the one he had picked off a Rotter.

Cordelia punched Bertly in the shoulder. "Yes, surely you must have my shield."

She thinks I'm joking, Bertly thought. He shook his head.

"That's impossible." Cordelia's tone quickly changed from playful to skeptical and slightly annoyed. "I wouldn't be here if you didn't have my shield." She stood tall and rested her hand on the hilt of her warblade. Her body language was much closer to that of a soldier than a sorcerer.

"You're really going to have to catch me up here." Bertly had typically dozed off in his history classes, but surely he would have remembered learning about this, and would be even more certain if he possessed the shield.

"Three thousand years ago I made it my obligation to

defeat Bishop. But I could never do it." Cordelia was straightforward. It was a refreshing change from most of the folks in Pangea. "It was not from a lack of effort. For years I tried; however, I was never able to beat him, so I took a desperate measure. Since he is technically a creature, I soul-bonded with him. As I presume you know, the fate of the bonder is the fate of the bonded. Meaning if I died, he died. I wasn't strong enough to kill him, so I had to let him kill me."

"Incredible. But I still don't understand." Bertly pinched the bridge of his nose. "Then how are you here now?"

Cordelia walked toward Bishop's dragon. "I thought I could cheat death by merging parts of my spirit into my warblade, shield, and cloak. In the hopes that one day, a powerful wizard would come along and reawaken me using the items I left behind." She grabbed one of the boney beast's teeth, broke it off from its jaw, and quickly examined it. "This will make a fine dagger."

"But if I don't have your shield, then who does?" the Winter Wizard asked. "And why has Bishop returned?"

"You aren't very quick, are you?" Cordelia broke off another tooth and tossed it to Bertly. "Bishop and I are soul-bonded; the only reason he died is because I died."

"Which means, since you came back, he came back." It was starting to click together. "Which also means either we need to kill him ourselves…or you need to sacrifice yourself again."

"That's correct," Cordelia replied. "As for my shield, I do not know for certain. But I would not be here unless all three of my items were activated."

"Any idea where it could be?" Bertly inquired.

Cordelia broke off a few more of the dragon's teeth and shoved them into her pockets. "Not for certain, but I have a guess as to where we can start looking."

"And where would that be?" Bertly was perplexed. She did not act as though she had been locked away for so long.

"Bablanca, home of the dwarves," Cordelia responded. "Whenever something eludes me, I always start there. Dwarves always seem to be involved in these types of situations."

"A situation is one word for it," Bertly cracked. "What makes this time any different? Why would you want to come back if you knew Bishop would also return?"

"Because this time I have you," she replied.

The hardened dome surrounding Polly and Bear cracked. The shield formed from the ground turned into dirt and collapsed around them. Bear stood on all fours with drool dripping from her mouth and blood running down her front shoulder—Polly was sitting on top of Bear, tightening her glove.

"Bertly, you're okay!" Polly cried. "Once the noises stopped…we assumed the worst." She slid down the side of Bear and ran into Bertly's arms, nuzzling her face into his chest—the top of her head didn't even come up to his chin.

Bertly was overjoyed to see Polly. He felt the sting of tears play behind his eyes, and a sigh of relief escaped his lips. She was safe. A warmth flowed through him as she buried her face in his chest and gripped him with such strength that he wouldn't have expected even from Bear. Oddly, he wanted to forget the world and continue to embrace his friend, but Polly broke from him the moment she spotted the woman standing with Bertly.

She stepped back and looked at the tall, strong woman. "Who is this?" Polly asked.

"Hello, I'm Cordelia." Cordelia reached out her hand and kept a straight face. "It is nice to meet you, Polly.

Although I have to say, I was not expecting you to be here."

"Um, hello." Bertly watched as Polly examined Cordelia's cloak. "So it really is you. But…how?"

While Polly stared in awe, the wizard took a moment to think before directing his attention to Cordelia again. "Wait a minute, what do you mean, you weren't expecting her to be here?"

"I just never imagined you and the daughter of Bishop to be working together," Cordelia commented. She didn't sound concerned at all with the remark she made.

"What?" Bertly blinked.

"That's a lie," Polly cried. Bertly wrapped his arm around her. But why would Cordelia tell them anything but the truth?

"When one of my items, which I now assume is my shield, was activated eighteen years ago, it brought my consciousness back to life, along with Bishop's. Not physically, but in a spiritual form. Even though we did not yet have our bodies back, that did not stop Bishop from making the first move." Cordelia pulled out her warblade, the blade only extended a few inches, and she used it to sharpen the dragon's teeth she had collected. "He passed along his abilities to a pregnant human woman, more specifically, the child she bore. Since humans no longer had the ability to possess magic and were mostly closed off from the rest of Pangea, it was the perfect place for her to go unnoticed."

"That's why none of your items work for Polly." Bertly needed to sit. He was growing overwhelmed.

Polly remained silent.

"So I countered," Cordelia continued. "I sent along my abilities to a human as well."

"But why me?" Bertly asked.

"I needed to make an immediate decision. I didn't

have time to think it through, or else Bishop would have had a leg up on me." Cordelia's almond-shaped brown eyes looked at Bertly. "I went with the safest decision and chose my newest-born relative. Shortly after passing along my abilities, I once again lost my consciousness."

"Relative?" Bertly asked, the oxygen sucked from his lungs.

"Surely you must be aware that we descend from the same lineage?" Cordelia broke eye contact and continued to sharpen the rest of the dragon teeth. "Unless something has changed, there are not many humans who come from mammoth blood. We are typically quite easy to spot, considering giants are the only race larger than us." She looked him up and down. "You aren't very big for a male. You haven't gone through the ceremony yet, I presume."

"Not yet, my father is still the warden of Stonebank," Bertly replied. Bear rested her head in his lap.

"Interesting, when I was your age, every boy drank mammoth blood, not just the warden. I am, however, glad some things have remained the same." Cordelia tucked the sharpened dragon teeth into her utility belt. "We are still the protectors of Stonebank, you say?"

"Of course." Bertly raised his voice proudly. "My...our family has defended those lands since the day you left."

Cordelia walked back over to Bertly and rested next to Bear. She gave Bear one pat and focused her attention back on the conversation. "Good. It makes me happy to know we still run the rightful capital of Pangea."

Bertly gasped. "Say what now?"

Cordelia sighed. "A lot has changed in three thousand years. It's sad to know Noskar fell so much after I left. Maybe after all of this is done, we can return the human country to its former glory." Cordelia's voice grew a little higher, letting a slight hint of happiness show. It was revitalizing for Bertly to see a human side to her seemingly callous personality. "But first, we need to track down my shield. We don't want it to slip into the wrong hands, and if it has, we are going to need to get it back."

"Wow, Bishop is a lot prettier than I had imagined." Bertly heard the irritating voice of his young apprentice accompanied by yet another ill-timed comment. He could only assume his apprentice was referring to Cordelia.

The Winter Wizard looked back and saw his father standing, posed for battle, with Ayce by his side, his bow drawn. Roderick was wedged between them, holding up a wooden shield. Bertly assumed he'd grabbed it off a Rotter on their way over to him.

"I can't say I disagree, Roderick." Edfrid smacked the head of his war hammer into his palm. "But I'm the warden of Stonebank, and I will rip the head off anyone who touches my gryphon."

"There is no need for that." Cordelia waved her hand vertically. Edfrid's and Ayce's weapons were stripped from their hands and pinned to the ground. "I am the furthest thing from Bishop. I am Cordelia."

"Clia," Bertly muttered, suddenly remembering.

"Bertly, how could we have forgotten?" Polly stressed, pain and guilt straining her voice.

Edfrid, Ayce, and Roderick stood idly in awe of Cordelia's presence. They appeared more petrified than if they had seen a ghost. To Bertly's amazement, his apprentice was still conscious.

"The same way they have been distracted now. By bestowing their eyes on the savior herself." The Winter Wizard tapped Cordelia on the shoulder. "We need your help. Our friend is in critical danger. Can you please heal her?"

Cordelia didn't hesitate. "Take me to her."

Bear plowed through the wreckage on the battlefield, clearing a path for everyone to follow behind. Bertly could not spot Clia amongst all the debris—he relied on Bear's nose to sniff her out.

"Sir, do you think she is going to be okay?" Roderick asked, a quiver in his voice.

"Yes, Roderick." Bertly did not want to consider the alternative.

Bear pressed her claws into the dirt and dragged her back legs across the ground, coming to an abrupt stop. Bertly sprinted past his spirit animal.

He stopped when he saw Clia lying motionless across a heap of dead Rotters. Her eyes were shut and her body ceased to rise and fall with the breaths she took, if she took any at all. He examined the puncture wound in her chest. The hole was too deep to see where it stopped.

"Clia!" Edfrid cried. The warden threw his war hammer to the side, rushed to the gryphon, and placed her head in his lap. Tears ran down his cheeks as he softly brushed her beak and whispered to her, "You're going to be fine, girl."

Ayce watched from a distance as Roderick and Polly surrounded their friend. Polly draped her arms around Clia's neck and burrowed her face within the gryphon's feathers.

Cordelia sighed and fumbled with her hands, looking at them as though they were useless tools. "I am so sorry." Cordelia knelt down next to Bertly and looked at him, her eyes compassionate, yet stern. "But my magic only works on humans. I didn't know…"

A silence enveloped the group. A thick silence filled with grief and rage, memories and their own failures. Edfrid let out a low groan. "No, no, no. No. She's my best…no." Edfrid gulped, petting the gryphon. He looked back up at Cordelia. "You're *Cordelia*. If anyone can help her, *you* can," Edfrid asked, but in such a way that it sounded more like a demand.

Cordelia opened her mouth, but nothing came out. She shook her head as though she didn't want to speak. "It won't work. I-I'm so sorry." She placed a hand on the gryphon, waited a moment, and shook her head once more.

"I thought you were supposed to be the savior. The strongest magician in history." Edfrid's cheeks reddened, and veins popped from his forehead.

"I'm still only a human," Cordelia replied. "I wish I were more, but I am not. I see what she means to you, and if I could—"

"Fine. I'll do it." Roderick stood and placed his hands on Clia's lifeless torso. "Teach me how to soul-bond."

"You will only suffer the same fate if you try to..." Cordelia hesitated before finishing her reply. "If you try to bond with a dying soul."

"Just tell me how to do it!" Roderick shouted.

Bertly bit his bottom lip as his eyes welled up. He couldn't look at his father and see the loss in his eyes. He felt it sharply himself as he petted Clia; her feathers still had a slight grip to them, just as they had when they'd flown together. "Roderick, stop!" Once the first tear fell, the rest poured out like a stream. Torment filled Bertly's soul. It wasn't anger or sadness, but the sharp ache of truly losing something. He had loved this animal more than almost any living being. He felt suffocated from how far he buried his face into her body—her feathers had lost the grip that had once held him in place, kept him safe and protected. They were simple feathers now, and the wind blew through them, giving them a slight illusion of life. An involuntary hiccup slipped through his lips, and he tasted the salt from the tears that covered his face.

She was the last tether Bertly had to his master. Alestar

was dead, dead and gone, but at least his master had lived on, in a small way, through Clia. There was something missing from Bertly already. Each loss created a hole somewhere deep within. How could humans, or others, walk with so much loss each day with their souls still intact? He'd learned long ago that those wounds of loss heal, but never fully. They open again and again all through life.

Cordelia approached Clia and plucked a feather from her body. The gryphon's feathers then faded from their bright white to gray and finally to black. Her textured body felt like loose soil. Clia slowly turned into a frail, ashen frame, and with the first gust of wind, she drifted away.

Cordelia placed Clia's last feather in Bertly's hand.

Polly sat next to Bertly and wrapped Clia's whistle around his neck. Bertly rose up and wiped the tears from his cheeks. "How do we kill him?" Bertly asked. Bear growled in agreement.

"First, we need to get my shield," Cordelia replied. "I cannot reach my full strength until I have it."

"Son, wait. Don't act on anger," Edfrid urged, his own voice still cracking, his eyes damp.

"I'm not acting out of anger. Bishop isn't going to run off into hiding. He is going to rebuild and come back stronger. That means we need to be stronger as well." Bertly picked a sword up off the ground. He waved it around to feel its weight. "This will take some getting used to." He slid the blade into the sheath that Cordelia's warblade used to occupy. "Cordelia, you mentioned Bablanca?"

"Bablanca?" Roderick shouted.

"Yes, I did." Cordelia crossed her arms. "But the dwarves and I didn't end on very good terms. I doubt they are going to let me into their mountainside kingdom."

"What happened?" Roderick probed.

"I don't want to talk about it," Cordelia snapped.

"Well, can't you just...I don't know...let yourself in?" Roderick continued to prod. "Is anyone really powerful enough to stop you?"

Edfrid's laugh sounded raspy. "I am assuming none of you have ever been to Bablanca." He stood up, carefully avoiding any of Clia's last remaining ashes. "There is not a single soul who can break through the gates of Bablanca. The barrier protecting the mountain they live in must be made of the strongest magic in all of Pangea."

"The warden is correct," Cordelia added. "Not even I can break through the barriers of Bablanca. No one has ever entered Bablanca if they were not allowed inside."

"Unfortunately, they are also not very welcoming to outsiders," Edfrid said.

"Sorry if I am speaking out of turn, but what about the Blight?" Ayce stepped into the group circle. "Maybe if we explain to them the severity of the situation, they will be willing to help."

"Highly unlikely. The dwarves are perfectly happy staying locked away in their mountain until the end of time." Cordelia grunted. "As a people, they will never take an unnecessary risk."

"Well..." Bertly looked at Roderick and Polly. "We actually have a couple of friends who may be able to help us out."

"Is that so?" Cordelia squinted, appearing skeptical.

"Yes," Polly said. "A set of dwarf twins, in fact."

Cordelia put out her arms. "Well, where are they?"

"Right." Bertly's voice was still sore from crying. "They're in a slight predicament right now."

"Predicament?" Cordelia sounded unamused.

"Mother has them held hostage at the Zoo."
Roderick's voice cracked.

"They're at the Zoo?" Cordelia's eyes widened and her
voice rose. "I was hoping never to return there."

"It didn't seem so bad when I went there." Edfrid
walked over and picked his war hammer off the ground.

"What kind of deal have you made with Mother?"
Cordelia glared at Bertly. "No one ever makes it out of
the Zoo."

"Well, I guess you could say I have a running tab."
Bertly scratched the back of his head. "The twins are
being held as leverage to ensure that I return...and finish
the one hundred fights I owe her."

Cordelia crossed her arms. "That sounds more like it."
She sighed.

"A hundred what?" Edfrid hollered.

Bertly shrugged. "Mother has a way with words."

"And enchantments. She makes everyone fall for her
little games," Cordelia grumbled. "Well, it looks like we
are headed to the Zoo."

"Aren't we going to tell the queen?" Ayce stressed.
"And the Elders?"

"Yes, sure." Cordelia shooed him away. "Do as you
please. But I do not answer to any elf queen or the
Elders. Not after they expelled me. I answer only to the
ruler of Noskar." She glanced over to Edfrid. "Which, I
suppose, is you."

Edfrid pointed at himself in shock.

"Wait a minute, back it up," Bertly interjected. "You
were expelled?"

"Yes, but that is a story for another time. We have
much more urgent matters to attend to." Cordelia looked
to the sky and pointed at the sun. She turned to the east.
"I will need to retrieve Levy before we embark. It will
take me at least a fortnight to track him down. Where

should I meet you?"

"Levy?" Roderick asked.

"Yes. My dragon," Cordelia responded. "I left him swimming the depths of the ocean all those years ago. Now that I am alive again, so is he...I can sense it."

"I suppose we would all like to return home before embarking on...whatever it is we are getting ourselves into." Bertly observed Polly and Edfrid, who both seemed to be in agreement.

"Roderick, sadly you don't have a choice." Bertly gave him a playful bump, despite the emptiness he felt at losing another friend. He was lucky to still have his friends and his father with him. Together, they would ensure that Clia's death would not be in vain. "You're still my apprentice. You have to follow me."

Roderick bowed his head and didn't bother arguing.

"It sounds like a plan. Your Eskosian bear should have no trouble getting you to Stonebank in a few days' time." Cordelia tightened her bootstraps and the lapels on her armor. Bertly was impressed by the fact that she didn't wear any gloves. Her hands must have been tougher than leather. "Once I reunite with my spirit animal, I will pick you all up from Stonebank, and we will head for the Zoo to retrieve your friends. Hopefully by rescuing a couple of dwarves from the Decomposite, we can gain our entry."

"What about Bear?" Bertly questioned. "I certainly do not want to leave her behind."

"Are you serious?" Cordelia paused for a moment. "You're serious...okay. Let's just say my dragon has lifted much bigger things."

"Well, sweet Cordelia!" Bertly shouted. "I can't wait to set my eyes on this beauty."

"Pardon?" Cordelia glared out of confusion.

"Sorry, it's a...it's a common phrase." Bertly pursed his lips, embarrassed at his awkward outburst.

"Right." Cordelia clapped her hands and started walking away. "I will see you all very soon. Safe travels."

"And just like that, she's gone." Bertly was in awe. A small part of him felt as though Cordelia filled a void he didn't know was there. Bear walked up to Bertly and bent down for him to climb aboard. "I suggest we don't waste any more time. I would like to get some rest before we go on another adventure." Bertly pondered a moment while his father, Roderick, and Polly hopped on. "Maybe I will start documenting all of this; it is starting to become too much to keep track of. Not to mention, I don't want things being lost in history again."

"That sounds like a lot of work, sir," Roderick commented.

"You're right, my apprentice," Bertly replied. "That is why you are going to help me with it."

"Wonderful. I have a few small apartments we can stay in while we wait," Edfrid pointed out. "Just at the top ridge of Stonebank, on the outskirts of town. No one will notice us up there. We can spend our last few days resting, in peace, and I suppose, writing your version of history."

"Are we really going to leave the queen and the Elders in the dark?" For the first time since their meeting, Ayce seemed agitated. He had been nothing but respectful and much too timid to speak out until this point. "You're just going to leave everyone to die?"

"Listen, Ayce," Bertly said firmly. "The elves did nothing today. If it weren't for Cordelia, Bishop would have overrun the entire city. Not only that, his plan was to convert your dead ones into more Rotters." The wizard tightened his grip and held onto Bear. "We're going to be on the winning side of history. Cordelia ended the Blight once, and she is going to do it again. Pangea as a whole isn't ready for something like this, so we have to follow those who are." Bertly peered ahead, and Bear dashed for Stonebank.

"Wait," a faint voice cried out.

Bertly looked back, Ayce had his bow on his back and was sprinting at full force. "Wait for me," the elf pleaded.

Bear came to a stop.

"Please, you're right." Ayce was bent over, panting. "I don't want to wait around to see what happens. Please, let me come with you."

Bertly smiled and reached out his arm. He locked hands with Ayce and pulled him on top of Bear. "Hold on tight."

***

"Is that her?" Roderick stood up and leaned out over the ledge.

"I believe it is, and just in time, too." Bertly gathered the pieces of parchment and tied a string around them. He opened his travel sack. A quiet hum slipped through the bag as Bertly put the bundled pieces of paper away—it was the golden pepper. "I have big plans for you, little one," Bertly whispered to the sleeping pepper.

"Should I go grab the others?" Roderick asked.

"Roderick, why don't you make yourself useful and grab Polly and my father?" Bertly said, pretending not to have heard his apprentice. "Hurry along. In the meantime, I will open the sliders for Bear."

"Of course, sir. I will be right back and make myself useful." Roderick rolled his eyes. "It's not like I haven't slept since we started writing your book or anything."

Bertly stood alone on the balcony, overlooking Stonebank one last time. The silhouette of Cordelia's dragon progressed quickly—it nearly doubled in size within moments. The young wizard turned and faced the entrance of the wooden cabin he and Roderick had been staying in. He walked over to the far left side and unbuckled a hinge connecting the back-patio wall to the rest of the house. He then grabbed the unfastened hinge and slid the wall open. The wooden panels glided completely over, as though the whole wall were removed.

The entire inside of the cabin was exposed to the outside. A gust of wind blew past Bertly, filling the small wooden room and blowing out the fire next to Bear. Across from Bear, on the other side of the room, was a door leading to the outside. Roderick had left it cracked open from when he'd exited to retrieve the others. The door led to flat ground, where the cabin could be entered without having to scale the entire cliffside of Stonebank.

The fire going out awakened Bertly's fuzzy friend. Bear stretched out her front paws and unleashed a big yawn. The furry beast shook her head and strolled over to her human companion. Bertly scratched behind her ear as she sat next to him and watched Cordelia's dragon approach.

"So just how big is this giant lizard?" Edfrid mocked as he walked through the door.

"See for yourself," Bertly replied.

"Well, I'll be." Edfrid paused in the middle of the room with Polly, Roderick, and Ayce standing just behind him. "Polly, is Dreki going to get that big?" the warden cracked.

"I hope." Polly gave a depressed smile. Her normally bubbly attitude had all but faded. Bertly could only assume it was from the news of her real family. He didn't think much of it because he knew her to be the kindest woman he knew; however, she didn't even seem like her mind was even in the same room as him. The Winter Wizard was stressed for his friend's well-being. For him nothing had changed, but for her, everything was different. Polly's small red dragon zoomed around her head and fluttered about like a feather caught in the wind. It had already grown tremendously in size, starting out the size of a koko and already reaching the mass of a large dog.

Cordelia's blue dragon hovered outside, only an arm's reach from the balcony. It had ferocious red eyes that rested inside an angular, rigid skull. Several horns sat atop its narrow head like a crown. A golden hook was chained between its rounded nostrils. The ornate nose ring was lined with diamonds, almost distracting from the large fangs that poked out of its mouth. The gust from its wings flapping in place was enough to almost blow Bertly over.

The dragon grabbed the balcony with its claw and extended its flattened wing out so that it could act like a bridge. "Well, come on then. There is no time to waste," Cordelia urged.

The group of unlikely accomplices climbed aboard Cordelia's ancient dragon, and together, they flew over the endless horizon.

About the Author

Nick McNeil is the author of The Dubious Tale of the Winter Wizard, the first novel of a fantasy series that he finished writing while still in college.

Nick is now a physical education teacher. In the meantime, he is a financial advisor and youth sports coach.

Mr. McNeil currently resides in San Francisco with his cat. You can reach out to him online at: facebook.com/nick.mcneil.author

40260493R00241

Made in the USA
San Bernardino, CA
25 June 2019